Beneath the Depths

By Bruce Robert Coffin

BENEATH THE DEPTHS
AMONG THE SHADOWS

Beneath the Depths

A Detective Byron Mystery

BRUCE ROBERT COFFIN

WITNESS
IMPULSE
An Imprint of HarperCollinsPublishers

Digital Edition AUGUST 2017 ISBN: 978-0-06-256949-3

Print Edition ISBN: 978-0-06-256950-9

Cover design by Guido Caroti
Cover photographs © Shutterstock

FIRST EDITION

HB 06.19.2023

For Karen.

Don't let history cloud your judgment.

—MICHAEL STANTON

Beneath the Depths

Chapter One

Tuesday, 11:05 P.M., April 26, 2016

ATTORNEY PAUL RAMSEY was having a bad run, capped off by one of the worst days of his professional life. He had been preparing for a change of fortune, awaiting the news that he'd finally been made a full senior partner at Newman, Branch & DeWitt, the law firm where he'd worked for the past fifteen years. He knew he deserved, and fully expected to see, his name following the ampersand on every sign, television commercial, and business card. Even on the billboards down in Massachusetts, along the Route 1 corridor, just outside of Boston. He'd also been planning to celebrate an eight-figure win, but that wasn't what happened.

He was a litigator. A good one. One of the best in Maine. And yet, as he was well aware, many people saw him as an asshole. But he knew he was the asshole they wanted in their corner inside any courtroom. As a trial lawyer he had been hugely successful even before the offer to join N, B & D, having gotten acquittals for his clients in a handful of prominent murder cases. One of

the defendants, accused of strangling his fiancée, who had ben-
efited from his talents was the son of a prominent state senator.
That victory, along with the ensuing press coverage, led to his
being hired by Portland's most successful and most expensive
law firm.

It was after eleven Tuesday night and Ramsey had been planted
firmly on a bar stool at the Red Fox pub for the past several hours.
He'd been trying to engage the barkeep in conversation, while
drowning his sorrows, but Tony was obviously more interested
in the broadcast on the flat-screen television mounted above the
Johnny Walker mirror behind the bar, where Boston's Celtics
were struggling to keep pace with Atlanta's Hawks.

"Can I help it if the judge was too damn stubborn to listen to
my argument?" Ramsey said, knocking on the highly polished bar
top with the bottom of his empty glass. "He should've properly
instructed the jury on the meaning of gross negligence. That's his
job, for chrissakes."

The touch of silver creeping around the sides of Tony's jet-black
hair had always reminded Ramsey of Jimmy Conway, Robert
De Niro's character in *Goodfellas*. Tony's shirtsleeves were rolled
up, revealing the muscular forearms of someone who either had a
day job as a manual laborer or lived at the gym. Ramsey had never
cared enough to ask. Tony strolled over and silently prepared a
fresh glass of bourbon and rocks, the bartender's eyes shifting
only briefly from the television.

"You know they're only considering her for partnership 'cause
she's got a nice rack, right?" Ramsey continued.

"Uh-huh," Tony said absently.

"Told me a strong female presence might be good for the firm's
image." He made air quotations with his fingers to accentuate the

point, vaguely aware that his speech was tinged with a faint slur, and not caring. "How about some fucking talent?"

"Uh-huh," Tony repeated.

"I mean, if I had those legs and tits I could sleep my way to the top too. It's just not fair. Okay, so I just lost a major case. It's not like I control what goes on in the mind of the judge, or for that matter, the goddamned jury. Losing one fucking trial shouldn't be a deal breaker. Am I right?"

"Sure, Paul," Tony said.

"There'll be other cases. Can't win 'em all. Right?" Ramsey looked around the room for agreement, catching the eye of a young leggy blonde sitting at the far end of the bar. He leered at her like a dog in heat. "I've made those pricks so much money it's *my* turn."

Tony placed Ramsey's glass on a white paper napkin, both of which were embossed with the outline of a red fox, and slid them across the bar toward Ramsey. "Uh-huh," Tony said again before returning his attention to the game. The Atlanta crowd cheered wildly as Kyle Korver sunk a three and drew the foul.

The ice clinked as Ramsey tipped his glass back and took a sizable swallow. He held the tumbler in his hand, studying it. "I've got five years on that bitch," he continued. "She hasn't earned it."

"Ya know, the only bitch I see is you," a gruff male voice said from the other end of the bar.

Ramsey turned on his stool and delivered his most menacing smile, the one normally reserved for prosecutors, to a heavily tattooed young man in a yellow wife-beater. He was sitting beside the blonde.

"How's that, friend?" Ramsey asked.

"I ain't your friend, slick. All you've done since you came in here is bitch and whine about some skirt who got your promotion. Maybe you should either shut the fuck up or leave. Nobody wants to hear your shit."

"Cool it, Donny," Tony said.

"No, that's okay, Tony," Ramsey said. "It's a free country." He looked back at Wife-beater. "Donny, is it? Allow me to enlighten you. It's a partnership not a promotion. Big difference. Partnerships are something that happen to intelligent, hardworking, lawyerly types. Although I wouldn't expect you to know about that." Ramsey flashed his most condescending smile. "Tell me, did you enjoy your five years of high school, Hemingway? Or did you just opt for the GED?"

Donny stood, noisily scraping the bar stool backward over the wooden floor. His fists were clenched. "Whatcha call me?"

The barfly with the blond dye job sitting beside Donny put her hand on his arm to try and calm him. He shook it off.

"I called you Hemingway," Ramsey said, continuing to smirk at the young man.

"What the fuck's a Hemingway?" Donny asked as his cheeks began to flush.

"Who, not what."

"Paul, that's enough," Tony said, removing Ramsey's glass from the bar. "I think you'd better go."

Ramsey turned his attention back toward the bartender. "What the hell? Come on, Tony. I'm not the one who started this." He cocked his thumb in the direction of Donny. "It was Hemingway."

"That's it," Donny said, stepping toward Ramsey. "You and me, outside, right now."

"Sit down, Donny," Tony said in a commanding tone Ramsey had never heard from the normally reserved barkeep.

"It's you and *I*, Donny," Ramsey said, goading him.

"Get out, Paul," Tony said. "Now, or I call the cops. Go home and sleep it off."

"I haven't paid for the drinks," Ramsey said as he stood and fumbled for his wallet. "I always pay my debts."

"You can square up with me later. Just go."

"Alright. I'm leaving." Ramsey looked back at Donny. "Lovely conversing with you and your lady friend." He looked her up and down. "I'll bet she's just as refined as she appears too."

"Fuck you," Donny said.

"Ah, now I see how you won the Nobel. It's your true gift for understatement."

"I mean it, Paul," Tony said as he picked up the house phone. "Go. Last time I'm askin'."

Ramsey held up his hands in surrender. "Okay, okay."

He staggered out the front door and onto the brick sidewalk of Portland's Commercial Street. The nearly deserted waterfront thoroughfare was shrouded in mist. The sodium arc lights, refracting off suspended water droplets, reminded him of Van Gogh's *Starry Night*.

Ramsey paused on the sidewalk, inhaling deeply the salty tang of the Atlantic. In spite of his calm outward appearance, his heart was racing. He'd let that punk get the better of him. Not a banner day for Paul Ramsey, Esquire, he thought. He paused, closing his bloodshot eyes, and allowed the cool night air to soothe his frayed nerves.

What he needed were the two things that would set him right. A little blow and a whole lotta Candy would surely do that. They always had, without fail. After regaining his composure, he opened his eyes and fished around in his pocket for his phone. He pulled it out and hit the speed dial.

"Hello?" a sultry-sounding female voice said from the other end of the line.

"Do you have any idea what hearing your voice does to me?"

"I've got a pretty good idea," she said.

"Can we meet at tu casa?" he said, exaggerating the accent.

"Not here. I've got my daughter for a few days. How about your favorite spot?"

"Mmm. That sounds delightful. I need something gift-wrapped too."

"I've got just the thing. Give me a few minutes to freshen up."

"Don't keep me waiting."

Ramsey reached back into his pocket, switching the phone for his keys. Wearing a big grin on his face he turned the corner, heading unsteadily up the cobblestone side street toward his SUV.

"Hey, friend." A voice came from directly behind him.

Ramsey turned just as the first punch landed.

Chapter Two

Thursday, 4:30 A.M., April 28, 2016

SUNRISE WAS STILL an hour away. Portland's Casco Bay was heavily fogged in, a condition the locals referred to as "in the soup." The winter had been unseasonably mild and although the air temperature had continued to warm gradually, the Atlantic Ocean, a chilly forty-nine degrees, had not.

Earl Nesbit, Maine native and Peaks Islander, was checking his traps without his stern-man, Billy, for the second time in the past four weeks. Billy liked to drink, and when he drank he liked to fight. The lobsterman's only companion on this morning was his chocolate Lab, Otis.

Nesbit's boat, the *Dorian Grey*, was a blue and white fiberglass Duffy lobster conversion with a small sleeper berth in the bow, where his AWOL stern-man often slept. At forty-eight feet in length, the *Grey* was hard enough to navigate through the rocky shallows of Hussey Sound when Billy was with him. Nesbit was grateful for calm seas as he steered the rumbling hulk through the mist. Otis stood on his hind legs, resting his front paws up on the side rail, while monitoring the passing buoys with great interest.

Nesbit had spent considerable time in the Sound, traveling between the two islands abutting it: Peaks to the south and the aptly named Long Island to the north. With nearly forty years of fishing the waters of Casco Bay under his belt, Nesbit had developed an uncanny knack for knowing precisely where the lobstering was best. When he made the decision to move his traps, many among the elder crustacean hunters were savvy enough to follow his lead.

This morning he was working near Whaleback, named for the distinctive shape of its shoreline, in Josiah's Cove. He pulled the *Grey* alongside one of his buoys with the precision of a driving instructor demonstrating parallel parking. Each lobsterman's buoys were easily identifiable by a unique color scheme, registered with the state of Maine. Nesbit's were painted brown with a double yellow band. He hooked it and pulled it into the boat. Threading the nylon rope into an electric pulley, he raised the pot from the bottom, some twenty feet below. The trap broke the ocean's surface, revealing three ensnared blackish-green creatures. He measured each, tossing the two undersized lobsters back into the water, while the keeper went into the live well. He replaced the bait with a fresh piece, then to the delight of several dozen screaming gulls, tossed the rotting carrion over the side. After restoring the trap and buoy to their former locations, he returned to the helm, spun the wheel, and throttled up the *Grey's* engine. He steered toward the next buoy, one of three hundred he would check today.

By six o'clock Nesbit had already pulled and replaced more than three dozen traps. The *Grey* was idling just off the point between Spar and Wharf coves. The fog was beginning to burn off. Nesbit was hoisting another when the winch snagged.

"Son of a bitch."

Nesbit quickly shut down the electric motor before it burned out. He removed the rope from the pulley and leaned over the side, muscling the trap up by hand.

Otis barked. With his front paws up on the starboard rail, he looked over the side into the water. His tail wagged excitedly.

"Whatcha think, boy?"

Otis barked again.

"Jay-sus," Nesbit said, straining against the weight of it. "Either I've just caught Maine's biggest lobstah or a fuckin' log." Otis vocalized his agreement.

The burly old mariner continued to struggle with the rope, pulling hand over hand, one foot at a time, until something large began to materialize. He squinted into the murky depths. Caught facedown on top of his trap, wrapped in seaweed, was the clothed body of a man.

"What kinda Christly mess is this?"

He continued tugging until the body was just below the surface. Hoping to keep the gulls at bay, he left it there, and tied the rope off to one of the Grey's rusty cleats. Standing upright, he tipped his cap back and scratched his bald head.

"Jay-sus, Mary, and Joseph, whatdaya know 'bout that, Oat? Shit. Guess we won't be gettin' done early today after all."

Chapter Three

PORTLAND POLICE DETECTIVE Sergeant John Byron's brain was buzzing. It had only been twenty minutes since the dispatcher's call woke him but he'd already set a number of things in motion, making a half dozen calls of his own. One of those was to request the fireboat be readied to transport his team of investigators to the back of Peaks Island.

He slid the unmarked Malibu into one of the spaces on Commercial Street reserved for emergency vehicles, parking in the looming shadow of the black and white evidence van. Already waiting at the ramp were Detective Diane Joyner and Evidence Technician Gabriel Pelligrosso. Byron had also contacted police dive team supervisor Sergeant Jamie Huntress to request assistance. Huntress and two of his divers were already with the Coast Guard en route to Peaks.

The Portland fireboat, or the *City of Portland IV* as she's known in maritime circles, was constructed in 2009 on the Meteghan River in Nova Scotia. The Ranger-class, aluminum-hulled vessel was built to replace the aging iron workhorse *COP III*. With a price tag of more than three million dollars, the sixty-five-foot, thirty-eight-ton, red and white beauty was the crown jewel of the Portland Fire Department's expansive fleet of equipment. Manned by a crew of three and housed at the Maine State Pier, the *COP IV* was a formidable firefighting weapon, complete with five water cannons, or turrets, each capable of pumping seven hundred gallons of water per minute, or foam if need be. Additionally, the boat was a fully functioning ambulance, ready to respond to any maritime medical emergency occurring within the waters of Casco Bay.

None of the impressive capabilities of the *COP IV* would be needed today, as the person responsible for this massive mobilization was neither on fire nor in medical distress; he was dead.

The engine was already idling and warm. The crew was waiting with two uniformed beat cops as the detectives boarded.

"Ahoy, mates," Captain Thomas said cheerfully. "Understand you need a ride out to Floater Alley."

"Morning, Cap," Byron said. "That'd be great. Never knew you guys had a special name for the back side of Peaks."

"Hang on a sec, Sarge," Thomas said as he grabbed the radio mic. "Marine One."

Static crackled over the radio speaker as the dispatcher acknowledged, "Marine One, go ahead."

"Marine One, ten-eight, en route to Peaks with four."

"Ten-four, Marine One."

Like their police counterparts, firefighters announce their movements by radio. All emergency professions share this common philosophy: if the dispatcher doesn't know where you are, and what you're doing, no one else will either. That unseen voice is often the only lifeline.

Thomas banged the mic back into its cradle just to the right of the gleaming ship's wheel. "Sorry about that, Sarge. You were saying?"

Byron raised his voice in order to be heard above the rumbling diesel engine. "I said I didn't realize you had a name for that area."

"Oh yeah. 'Cause of the funky way the tides move between the islands, Hussey Sound is prime real estate for floaters. If we don't recover them right away, they tend to come through here eventually."

Like every other city, Portland had its share of dead bodies, and some of them ended up in the surf. Many having only themselves to blame, drunkenly wandering the working wharfs before stumbling into the ocean, while others intentionally took the sixty-five-foot plunge from the Casco Bay Bridge. Then there was the third type, the ones that mattered most to Byron and his detectives: those bodies that ended up in the Atlantic at the hands of another.

The fog had retreated from the coastline to a point slightly beyond the larger islands of the bay. It hung there like something from a Stephen King novel about secret government programs gone awry, always threatening to return and blind Casco Bay's many pleasure boaters and day sailors. Sunshine sparkled on the water's surface like diamonds.

The *COP IV* cut effortlessly through the water, her cabin filled with the heady aromas of coffee, salt air, and diesel fuel. Byron stepped out onto the bow for a moment of privacy, nodding to veteran officer Sean Haggerty as he went. Haggerty was aboard with his charge, a still wet behind the ears sandy-haired rookie named Cody.

The wind whipped Byron's hair and clothing. His tie danced about his head absurdly, like one of those tall thin cartoon balloon people that auto dealers are so fond of. He moved to the rear of the boat, out of the wind, and removed his cell from the breast pocket of his suit coat and punched in the number for Dr. Ellis, the state of Maine's chief pathologist. Following their brief conversation, the decision was made to transport whatever remains Byron found straight to the medical examiner's office in Augusta, where a thorough autopsy would be performed.

Byron looked down at the recent text messages on his phone. He still hadn't responded to Katie's message. Katie Whitehill, his niece, was the youngest of three children of Janice and Thurston Whitehill, his well-to-do ex-in-laws from Cape Elizabeth. Janice was the sister of Byron's ex-wife, Kay. He knew it wasn't proper to admit to loving one relative more than another but Katie had always been Byron's favorite, and not just because the other two couldn't be bothered to stay in touch. She'd been like the daughter he never had.

Katie's text read, "U R coming to my party, right, Uncle John? It won't be the same without U." Her parents were throwing a big shindig on Sunday to celebrate her high school graduation. A bright young girl, she'd been accepted to Colby.

He began to type. "Katie, I don't know if I'll be able to make it but I promise I'll try. I'm very proud of U. Luv U, kiddo." His thumb hovered over the send button on his cell. *Don't be an asshole. You need to be there for her.* It wasn't her fault her parents were dicks.

Thurston, a pompous, materialistic, well-known Portland surgeon, had never attempted to hide his disdain for Byron or his chosen profession. As if law enforcement was an undignified career path. Janice, only slightly less judgmental, had remained cordial with him, at least until her sister and John had divorced. Byron wanted to be there for his niece but he knew full well what kind of a shit show her party would likely be. He thumbed the backspace button until the entire message was deleted, then shoved the phone back into his pocket.

Byron steered his mind back to the floater. What would it be this time: young, old, male, female? As long as it was an adult. He despised working the deaths of children. Victims in his cases often played an active role in their own demise. Befriended, stole from, or just pissed off the wrong person. With kids it was damn hard to lay any blame at their feet. More often than not, if a child ended up on the wrong side of the grass, it was due to a lack of supervision, or worse.

It took twenty minutes to reach Wharf Cove. As the COP IV rounded the bend, Byron saw the Dorian Grey and the U.S. Coast Guard vessel Shackle floating next to each other, about two hundred yards from shore. A large flock of gulls soared above the boats; haloed by the sun's rays they resembled angelic vultures.

The Shackle, a sixty-five-foot tug, housed at the South Portland Coast Guard Station, was responsible for maritime security and all search and rescue operations throughout Portland Harbor and outlying areas of Casco Bay. Captain Thomas carefully maneuvered the fireboat alongside the Shackle while the crews worked quickly to lash the two vessels together.

Sergeant Huntress greeted them with a wave from the deck of the Shackle. Already dressed in his maroon dive suit, he was assisting one of the other officers with his. "Nice day for a swim," he hollered. "Wanna join us?"

"All set, thanks," Byron hollered back.

"What's the plan, Lord Byron?" Huntress asked.

"Strictly recovery. The M.E. isn't coming, so let's extract as much as we can."

"All right. We'll bag it up before the gulls can make breakfast out of it."

The detectives stood on the deck looking over the side at the submerged corpse. The dark-haired male body was dressed in a light-colored suit and tie. The right foot was encased in a brown wing tip; the other shoe was missing.

"Can't really see much from up here," Officer Cody said excitedly. "I've never seen a floater before. You guys must see a lot of these, hey, Sarge?"

Byron nodded and looked to Haggerty for help.

"Cody, why don't we get a statement from the lobsterman?" Haggerty said. "While they oversee the recovery."

"Yes, sir," he said with obvious disappointment.

Haggerty winked at Byron as he and Cody trotted off to find the witness who'd found the body.

Most of what Byron knew about the young towheaded officer he'd gleaned from reading his reports. Cody was a bright kid with a promising career in law enforcement, if only he could get past his impetuousness. Byron had seen his kind before. Officers so anxious to save the world from itself they tended to miss the little things, things like a concisely written report. If anyone could turn him around it would be Haggerty.

During the half hour that followed, Byron and Diane looked on while Huntress and the other divers worked carefully to recover the remains. The body was photographed from two different perspectives. Pelligrosso captured the surface shots while Huntress took care of everything below.

Huntress surfaced, removed his mouthpiece and mask, and used his hand to wipe the water from his face.

"Well?" Byron asked.

"The fisherman's rope is just barely holding him up," Huntress said.

"How's he look?" Byron asked. "Anything obvious?"

"Not that I can see."

"Okay, let's bag him and get him on deck before we lose him."

Pelligrosso lowered a bright yellow vinyl body bag down to the divers and they carefully worked John Doe into it.

With the help of the fireboat crew, the divers were able to hoist the bag containing the remains onto the deck of the *COP IV*. Byron requested that they take the trap and check the ocean floor beneath for any evidence.

"John, this bay is a murky fucking mess," Huntress said. "The sun doesn't penetrate more than a few feet below the surface. Pretty hard to see anything down there."

"Humor me."

"Your ball game."

The divers resumed their search while Byron and Diane helped Pelligrosso open the body bag. Pelligrosso needed to perform a visual inspection and to photograph the face and clothing. The remainder of the fireboat crew had gathered on deck to watch the proceedings. As the bag was opened, several dozen crabs, varying in size, skittered from various parts of the body and onto the deck. Two of the firefighters jumped back, trying to avoid the scavengers as they made their way to the edge of the deck and back into the ocean.

Byron suppressed a smile as he observed the frightened reaction of grown men. Portland's bravest.

Carefully, Byron and Diane helped Pelligrosso reposition the body, rolling it face up.

"How long do you think he's been in, Gabe?" Byron asked.

"Tough to say, but if I had to guess, no more than a day or so. Any more than that, the sea creatures would have done a lot more damage."

And the face was damaged, eyelids and lips were missing, forever altering the man's expression.

"There's not much in the way of decomp either."

"What's that mark?" Diane asked, pointing to the corpse's forehead. "Looks like an entry wound."

Pelligrosso leaned in for a closer look. "It is."

"Where's the exit wound?" Byron asked.

"I don't see one," Pelligrosso said.

"Done," Officer Cody said, walking up and interrupting them. "We finished with the lobsterman. Hey, cool."

Byron looked at Haggerty, who just rolled his eyes. "Anything?" Byron asked the rookie.

"Not really, Sarge. Said he knew the trap was caught on something big, but he just figured it was a log."

"How did he seem?" Byron asked.

"Seem?"

"Yeah. Normal, crazy, drunk?"

Haggerty stepped in. "I got this, Junior. He seemed sober, Sarge. Nothing weird about the guy so far as I could tell. Name's

Earl Nesbit," Haggerty said, referring to his notebook. "He's a Peaks Islander. Lived here his whole life. I had Dispatch run him. Nothing in-house and nothing in NCIC."

"Thanks, Hags," Byron said.

Pelligrosso put his camera down for a moment and turned to look at Byron.

"You're never going to believe who this guy is."

"Who?" Byron asked.

"See for yourself," the evidence tech said, passing him a water-logged leather wallet.

Byron, who had donned rubber gloves, opened the wallet and looked through the fogged plastic at a state of Maine driver's license. He recognized the picture on the license immediately.

"Well," Diane said. "Who is it?"

"Take a look," Byron said, handing her the wallet.

"*Paul Ramsey,*" she said. "Holy shit."

"Who's that?" Cody said.

Fire Captain Thomas, watching the proceedings, chimed in. "Big-shot attorney. He's on the front page of today's *Portland Herald.*"

"You know what Bill Shakespeare would have called this?" Pelligrosso asked with a grin.

"Yeah," Byron said. "A good start." He turned to face Diane. "This is gonna be a shit storm."

"Yup," she said, nodding her agreement.

"Let's get the body to shore," Byron said, addressing Thomas.

"You got it, Sarge."

Byron turned his attention to Pelligrosso. "Gabe, I want you to follow the funeral home transport to Augusta. Diane and I will meet you there. I'll tell Ellis we're coming."

"Sarge, would it be okay if Cody went up with you guys?" Haggerty asked. "He's never attended a post."

Byron looked at Cody. "You in?"

"I'm going to an autopsy?" Cody asked excitedly.

Byron pulled out his cell and dialed the CID commander, Lieutenant Martin LeRoyer. "Unless that's a problem?" Byron said as he waited for LeRoyer to pick up.

"No, sir. Sweet."

Chapter Four

Thursday, 10:30 A.M., April 28, 2016

BYRON AND DIANE stopped in Falmouth for a quick coffee and a paper before jumping onto the interstate for the sixty-mile ride north. As they neared Yarmouth, he pulled out his cell, hit the speaker button, and dialed the number for Detective Dustin Tran.

"Detective Tran speaking."

"Dustin, it's Byron."

"Hey, Striped Dude. Heard you had a floater. Whatcha got for me?"

Tran was anything but the stereotypical detective. Opinionated, and much too informal when addressing superiors, but he was good. When it came to computer forensics, there was none better. For that reason alone, Byron, who was results-oriented, allowed his unorthodox detective more leeway than he allowed the others.

"Diane and I are headed up to the post. I need you to dig up everything you can on Paul Ramsey while we're gone."

"The attorney?"

"Yes."

"He's dead? Wowza. You know he's on the front page of today's *Herald*?"

Byron looked over at Diane, who was already reading the article about Ramsey's big loss. She didn't appear to be listening.

"So I've heard," Byron said. "Just get me all you can, okay? I'll reach out to you after the autopsy."

"You got it, Boss Man."

Byron ended the call and slid the phone back into the pocket of his suit coat. "How did that kid ever make it through the academy without being murdered by his cadre?"

"Uh-huh," Diane said absently.

Byron and Diane had been seeing each other casually for months. Their attraction was mutual but Diane had been the one to make the first move. To her credit, she'd waited until Byron had been served with divorce papers from his ex-wife, Kay. While their relationship had been a good thing, at least in his opinion, it carried with it the additional baggage of their being coworkers in a stressful occupation. Actually, he thought, not even coworkers. He was her sergeant, a no-no by any professional standard and the reason they'd been forced to keep their relationship a secret. He suspected that her moodiness might be a sign that she wanted more from their time together. A commitment on his part. Although going in she'd clearly stated that she wasn't looking for anything long term, he knew all too well that changing one's mind was a woman's prerogative. Hell, it was probably genetic.

"You okay?" Byron asked. "You seem a little off today."

"Fine. Why?" she said, sounding defensive, and making his point.

"No reason. You just seem a little distant."

"I'm fine."

"I do something to piss you off?" he asked.

Still holding the *Herald*, she dropped her hands to her lap, crinkling the paper. "It's not always about you, John."

"Okay," he said, holding up his hand in mock surrender. He tried changing the subject. "Anything useful in the story?"

"I don't know. I haven't been able to finish it yet." She picked up the paper and resumed reading.

Byron shook his head and sighed. He wondered why it always had to be this way. All of the women in his life, at least the ones he'd cared about, had a knack for not saying what was on their minds. He knew she'd eventually share whatever was bothering her, but not until she was ready.

He glanced over at her again as she flipped the newspaper to the last page of the section, where he assumed the article continued. She maintained her silence, sipped her coffee, and read. His eyes returned to the road, his thoughts to the floater. Why would Ramsey be in the bay? Suicide? Maybe. Murder? More likely. Byron knew from firsthand experience that the photogenic attorney was a son of a bitch with plenty of enemies. With any luck, Dr. Ellis, as he had so many times before, would point them in the right direction.

AUGUSTA, SIXTY MILES to the north of Portland, houses the office of Maine's chief medical examiner, a small nondescript brick building tucked behind state police headquarters, in a lower lot, almost as an afterthought. Byron had always found the building's placement odd. In the grand scheme of homicide investigation, cause of death was just as essential as proving *who* had caused it.

Byron slid the charcoal gray Malibu into the vacant space next to the PD's black and white evidence van. Pelligrosso and Cody were already inside.

Diane had hardly uttered two words during the forty-five-minute drive, and apparently had no desire to break precedent. They walked toward the service entrance in silence.

Byron pressed the delivery buzzer. After several minutes the heavy steel door swung open exposing a pale, diminutive young man.

Nicky, Dr. Ellis's lab assistant, gave a silent nod upon recognizing the detectives.

"Hey, Nicky," Byron said. "We're here for the Ramsey autopsy."

The skinny lab tech, dressed in light green scrubs and booties, looked at each of them and mumbled something that may or may not have been a greeting. He nodded at Byron. "Follow me."

Byron had never been able to figure out what made Nicky tick, and wasn't sure he wanted to. Nicky was to Dr. Ellis what Igor had been to Dr. Frankenstein. Nicky hardly spoke unless spoken to, and given Diane's current mood Byron thought they'd make a great pair. Dark circles under his eyes made him look ghoulish. Byron wondered if Nicky had an actual residence or if Ellis just locked him in a cage at the end of each day.

They followed him down a long stark corridor into the viewing room, a glass-walled area that overlooked the examination area.

"Greetings and salutations, Detectives," Ellis said in his usual theatrical manner. "Welcome to the humble abode of the good Dr. E."

"Morning, Doc," they said simultaneously.

Ellis might have sounded like a stage actor but he looked more like an aging rock star. Dressed in medical scrubs, the top of which barely hid his ample belly, he looked somewhere between

Neil Young and Elvis: shoulder-length black hair, combed straight back, with sideburns.

"Who is it today, Doc?" Byron asked, referring to the vintage rock concert tees Ellis always wore. "AC/DC, or maybe Lynyrd Skynyrd?"

Ellis shook his head. "I went online and purchased some new ones." He lifted his smock and smiled proudly. "Foghat."

Byron nodded his approval. "Classic."

Pelligrosso and Cody stood on the opposite side of the cavernous room near one of the stainless steel exam tables. Cody was pacing like an expectant father. On top of the table lay the bright yellow body bag containing the remains of their floater. Byron looked at Cody's face, noting with amusement that the flushed excitement previously occupying the rookie's cheeks, while they'd been aboard the boat, had been replaced by a sickly green pallor, similar in hue to Ellis's scrubs.

The examination room was spotless. The twelve-foot-high concrete block walls were painted entirely in white, with the exception of the bottom four feet, which were covered in subway tile. Scores of white metal cabinets and rows of shelving had been affixed to the walls, each containing various supplies and implements of deconstruction, or destruction, depending on one's point of view. A half dozen gleaming stainless steel exam tables were scattered throughout the room, each with its own digital hanging scale for weighing organs. The harsh fluorescent lighting made everyone in the room look clinical and cold, even the living.

In the world of police investigations, postmortem examinations were considered a rite of passage, albeit a morbid one. With the exception of Cody, they'd each attended countless autopsies.

And although they were all focused on the matter at hand, Byron could see from the expressions on everyone's faces, including Ellis's, that they were all secretly looking forward to the rookie's reaction. Even Diane's mood seemed to have improved as she eyed the young officer.

Ellis began the exam by gloving up and donning an apron. Carefully, he unzipped the bag containing Ramsey's remains, releasing the foul fishy odor of decomposition. Rivulets of water ran onto the table, forming reflective pools. A pair of silver dollar-sized black crabs skittered from the bag to the table then dropped down onto the concrete floor. The unlikely stowaways had evidently secreted themselves somewhere inside the remains, continuing to feed during transport to Augusta.

Byron glanced over at Cody, whose face was now as white as a sheet. Pelligrosso, having taken up a position behind the officer, caught him easily before he could collapse onto the floor. Byron and the others carried Cody into a nearby office and laid him on a sofa, while Ellis waited with a satisfied grin on his face. Byron returned to the exam room, making a mental note to avoid seafood for the foreseeable future.

Ellis began by describing in detail everything he observed into a digital recorder. Each item of clothing was carefully removed from Ramsey's body. Pelligrosso took custody and bagged every item of wet clothing, all of which would be taken back to 109 Middle Street, Portland police headquarters, and air-dried in the lab. Ellis next performed a slow methodical examination of Ramsey's body, checking for signs of rigor and taking note of any visible injuries or abnormal marks.

Ellis turned to Byron. "When was Mr. Ramsey last seen alive?"

"We haven't established a timeline yet," Byron said. "We know he was in court early Tuesday afternoon. But we haven't had time to talk with anyone."

Ellis lifted one of Ramsey's arms and tried to bend it. "Still a bit of stiffness present," he said, referring to rigor mortis. "Cold water would slow the process somewhat." Ellis addressed Pelligrosso. "I assume you checked the ocean temp, my boy?"

"Forty-nine."

Ellis nodded.

"Any idea, Doc?" Byron asked.

Ellis shook his head. "Best guess? And that's all it would be. Probably sometime Tuesday night or early Wednesday morning. Too many variables on this one to count on rigor. I'm basing most of my guess on the damage from ocean feeders."

Byron scribbled another quick note.

"Shall we begin?" Ellis said as he picked up his scalpel and made the first incision.

DURING THE HOUR that followed, the detectives watched closely as Ellis cut and removed, weighed and examined, every square inch of Paul Ramsey's remains. Each time he found anything of significance he invited Byron and Diane over to have a look. The detectives jotted in their notebooks while Evidence Tech Pelligrosso snapped digital photos. As usual, Nicky silently and efficiently provided whatever Ellis required.

Byron noticed that Cody had rejoined them in the lab, but the young rookie wisely sat on the opposite side of the room, away from the autopsy, behind the glass viewing partition.

"Take a look at this," Ellis said, holding up the top of Ramsey's skull like a ceramic bowl.

Byron and Diane both moved closer.

"See these marks?" Ellis said, pointing inside.

Pelligrosso snapped another photo.

"What are those?" Byron asked.

"Impact points," Ellis said. "The bullet appears to have entered through the forehead and for whatever reason didn't penetrate through. Why you didn't see an exit wound. It just sorta bounced around in there, scrambling his brains."

"If the bullet didn't come through, where is it?" Diane asked.

"Most likely still trapped inside the brain tissue."

Ellis went to work with the scalpel, carefully removing Ramsey's brain and carrying it over to a metal tray. He methodically sliced until he located the bullet. "Here you are," he said, pushing the round to the center of the tray and rinsing it off with a small squeeze bottle of distilled water.

"Jacketed round," Pelligrosso said. "About the size of a .380 or maybe a 9 mm."

"That's a pretty big round," Diane said. "Any idea why it didn't penetrate?"

"Guy had a hard head," Ellis said.

"Could have been old ammo," Pelligrosso said.

Byron knew that when it came to knowledge of firearms, Pelligrosso was a veritable *Encyclopedia Britannica*. The flat-topped ex-soldier had received training on every weapon imaginable.

Pelligrosso continued. "The powder may have been fouled. Or perhaps the killer reloaded their own ammo and didn't use enough powder. Even a bullet this size wouldn't go all the way through the head if it's underpowered. It will act more like a smaller round, more like a .22 or a .25 caliber."

"Think there's enough detail left for a ballistic comparison?" Byron asked his evidence tech.

Pelligrosso bent down to examine the deformed round more closely. "It's pretty dinged-up but it looks like there might still be enough."

"You can package it up and take it with you when I'm finished here," Ellis said.

"How much of what we're looking at for facial trauma is postmortem, Doc?" Byron asked.

Ellis pulled Ramsey's forehead back onto the skull. "Some. The eyelids and lips sustained cuts and bruising prior to death, probably what attracted the crabs so soon. You can see where they were feeding."

"So he took a few knocks to the face before he was shot?" Byron asked.

"Either that or he fell down, landing on his face."

"Could he have been in a fight?"

"Doubtful. No damage to his knuckles. The body is pretty well developed. A regular at a gym, no doubt. You don't get to look like this hanging out in a courtroom. More likely he'd have my svelte physique," Ellis said, grinning. "Unless the tox shows that he was blistered, he should've been able to fight back."

Byron made a note to check.

"So what are you thinking, Doc?" Diane asked.

"I think he may have been struck from behind, knocking him down."

Ellis produced a stainless steel tray containing several tiny black specks. "I removed these from the skin in the back of his head. They were imbedded within the hairline."

"What are they?" Pelligrosso asked.

"Broken pieces of some type of polymer," Ellis said.

"Plastic?" Diane asked. "I don't get it."

Byron nodded his understanding. "He was struck in the back of the head, and the plastic was left behind."

"What would be hard enough to knock someone his size down that was made of plastic?" Diane asked.

"Plastic shielding a metallic frame. The grips on a handgun," Pelligrosso said.

"Bingo," Ellis said, pointing a bloody gloved finger at the evidence tech.

"So he was pistol whipped?" Diane said.

Ellis set the tray down. "That'd be my guess. The attacker whacks him from behind with a gun. Victim falls forward, landing face-first on the ground."

"Or a boat," Pelligrosso said.

Byron looked at Ellis. "Don't suppose you can magically analyze those bits of plastic and tell us where this all happened?"

"Sorry," Ellis said. "Dr. E.'s supernatural powers do have limits. Although, if it helps, the stomach contents indicate Ramsey's last meal consisted of french fries, clams, and shrimp. Ironic considering that the crabs were recently dining on him."

"Doesn't help much that every establishment in the Old Port probably serves those," Pelligrosso said.

"Anything else?" Byron asked.

Ellis showed them several oddly shaped bruises on the outer skin at the right side of Ramsey's rib cage.

"Any idea what those marks are?" Byron asked.

"Business end of a gun, maybe," Ellis said. "Someone may have pressed the gun against his ribs to get him to cooperate. No detail, I'm afraid, because it was pressed through clothing."

Pelligrosso snapped several more photos.

Ellis continued. "On the self-inflicted front, his liver was in bad shape from chronic ethanol abuse."

Byron and Diane scribbled notes as Ellis spoke.

"Also, the good Mr. Ramsey liked his blow."

"How's that?" Diane asked, looking up from her notebook.

"Cocaine," Ellis said.

"How can you tell?" Byron asked.

"Ramsey's preferred method was snorting," Ellis said, holding his hand under his nose and pantomiming the act. "The cartilage between his nostrils was nearly worn away. There's actually a small hole in the septum." Ellis pushed a long stainless steel rod with a hook at one end through the opening. "See. Right here. This guy was a regular vacuum cleaner."

Byron had heard the rumors about Ramsey's propensity for illegal drugs. He had also heard rumors about Ramsey's firm having diverse financial interests. He wondered if there might have been some truth to those rumors after all. Had Ramsey's addiction led to his demise? Or was someone sending a message to his employer?

Pelligrosso snapped another picture.

Ellis, still holding the rod in Ramsey's nose, turned to the camera and smiled.

"Glad I never picked up that habit," Diane said with a grimace.

"You don't make enough money to afford such a habit, Detective," Ellis said, giving her a wink.

"What's the bottom line, Doc?" Byron asked. "Was he still alive when he went into the water?"

"No. Nothing I've found indicates he was still breathing when he went into the water."

"Any chance the bullet wound was self-inflicted?" Diane said.

"The entry wound is non-contact. The barrel of the gun wasn't close enough to leave either flash or powder burns. Unless he had a magic selfie stick designed to fire a handgun, someone else shot him in the head."

"Then dumped his body in the ocean," Byron said, trying it on.

Ellis eyed Ramsey's body. "Did I hear you right? He was a Portland attorney?"

"High-priced trial lawyer," Diane said.

"High-priced asshole," Pelligrosso added.

"Looks like somebody shares your opinion, my boy," Ellis said.

Chapter Five

Thursday, 2:00 P.M., April 28, 2016

BYRON AND DIANE drove back to Greater Portland in search of Mrs. Ramsey, while Pelligrosso and an embarrassed Officer Cody returned to 109 Middle Street, or what the cops simply dubbed 109. On the way, Byron called Detective Tran and obtained the Ramseys' Yarmouth address.

Mast Landing wasn't a landing at all but a quaint little cul-de-sac consisting of four colonial-style homes, each positioned to allow for an ocean view.

Diane whistled through her teeth. "What do you think these babies go for?"

Byron, pleased to see she was in a better mood, said, "Dunno, but I wouldn't want to be responsible for the property tax."

"That looks like the one," she said, pointing to a white three-story structure with maroon shutters and an attached three-bay garage.

"The biggest one on the street, of course," he said, turning the unmarked into the driveway, constructed from landscape stones laid out in a herringbone pattern.

"God, I hate these," Diane said.

Byron, knowing that she was referring to death notifications, agreed. No cop wanted to be the bearer of such grim news. But it was part of the job, especially important in murder cases. How people reacted to news of a loved one's death was often telling. Seasoned investigators always paid attention. You never knew when you might be addressing the killer.

"How do you want to do it?" Diane asked as they approached the granite front steps.

"You up for this?" he asked, raising a brow.

"I'm fine, John. I was just a little out of sorts earlier. Really."

Byron stepped to the side. "Have at it."

She reached out and pressed the doorbell.

"Mrs. Ramsey?" Diane asked as the front door opened.

"I'm Julia Ramsey," she said, her eyes shifting back and forth between them. "May I help you?"

Julia Ramsey was dressed in white slacks, sandals, and a light blue short-sleeved blouse. According to the Maine Bureau of Motor Vehicles, she was sixty-one, five years Ramsey's senior. Byron wasn't sure what he'd expected her to look like but she certainly didn't look old enough to be on the other side of sixty. Ramsey's widow was attractive, tan, and fit. Byron imagined she had a private gym membership or, more likely, a personal trainer.

Well-rehearsed and nearly synchronized, the detectives each displayed their credentials.

"Mrs. Ramsey, my name is Detective Joyner and this is Detective Sergeant Byron."

Ramsey nodded, gave each ID a cursory glance, and acknowledged Byron with a weak smile.

Diane continued. "May we come in?"

Ramsey looked directly at Diane. She appeared to be studying the younger woman's face. "You've come to deliver bad news, haven't you?" she said finally.

"I'm afraid we have," Diane said.

"It's Paul, isn't it?"

"I'm very sorry to have to tell you this, Mrs. Ramsey. Your husband is dead."

Ramsey's gaze shifted toward Byron. Her eyes welled up with tears. "Won't you please come in," she said, suddenly looking much older.

THE DETECTIVES FOLLOWED Mrs. Ramsey through the foyer and into the living room.

"Would either of you care for something to drink?" she asked. "Coffee, perhaps, or tea?"

"We don't want to put you to any trouble, Mrs. Ramsey," Diane said.

"Please," Ramsey said. "It's no trouble. And it will give me something else to focus on."

"I'd love some tea," Diane said.

Byron wasn't in the mood for either, but experience had taught him that everyone handles grief differently. Mrs. Ramsey appeared to be in shock at the news of her husband's death and if being on hostess autopilot was working for her, he certainly didn't want to break the flow. Besides, he had already given Diane the lead on this interview. "Coffee would be great," he said.

"Why don't I give you a hand," Diane said.

Byron remained behind as the two women disappeared into the kitchen and, like any good investigator, he used the time to look around.

The living room was large and richly appointed, the furniture plush, everything tastefully decorated. It was obvious that Mrs. Ramsey either had a keen eye for design or had hired a professional. Byron wondered how someone so refined had ever ended up married to such a pompous prick. He walked past a large picture window toward the fireplace. Standing atop a gleaming white ornamental mantelpiece was a row of silver-framed black and white photographs. He picked one up and looked at it. Seated on the home's front steps were three women and a half-dozen children. The Ramseys' grown children and grandchildren sans spouses, he guessed. Paul Ramsey hadn't seemed the fatherly type, at least not the one Byron had known. He looked more closely. Each of the women bore a striking resemblance to Mrs. Ramsey. He wondered if Paul might not be the father. Perhaps he had been a second husband and these were his stepdaughters and stepgrandkids.

He was replacing the picture upon the mantel when the women returned from the kitchen. Diane carried a silver-colored serving tray upon which sat a large carafe and three ceramic mugs.

"How do you take your coffee, Sergeant Byron?" Mrs. Ramsey asked.

"Cream only, thank you," he said, making eye contact with Diane and mouthing the word *Well?*

Diane gave an almost imperceptible shake of her head as she sat down next to Ramsey on the sofa.

Byron walked over to the center of the room, taking a seat in one of two plaid overstuffed chairs on the opposite side of the coffee table.

"Here you are, Sergeant," Ramsey said, passing a mug across the table to him.

"Thank you."

"So, Detective Joyner," Ramsey said after they were all settled. "What can you tell me about my husband's death?"

"Well, we're still awaiting the medical examiner's findings, Mrs. Ramsey."

"Where was he found?"

Diane looked to Byron for help.

"We recovered his body from the ocean," Byron said. "He was found by a commercial fisherman near Peaks Island."

Ramsey's hand was visibly shaking as she sipped from her mug.

Diane reached out and took Ramsey's left hand in her own.

"Did my Paul drown?" Ramsey asked.

"No," Diane said.

Ramsey looked at Byron. "Was he murdered?"

"We are treating your husband's death as suspicious," Byron said.

Ramsey leaned over and with a trembling hand set her mug on the coffee table, very nearly spilling it in the process. She waited a beat, cleared her throat, then looked up at Byron. "How *did* he die, Sergeant?"

He knew she deserved the truth, but he also knew that preserving as much detail as possible about the cause of death was key to solving any case. Details given to family members oftentimes got leaked to the media, making it much harder to avoid dealing with crackpots. Those folks who will confess to something they didn't do for the sake of attention.

"He was shot, Mrs. Ramsey," Byron said, taking a chance.

She covered her mouth with her right hand and closed her eyes tightly. The detectives waited a few moments, allowing her time to deal with the shock.

Diane reached over and gently rubbed the widow's back.

Finally, after composing herself, Ramsey lowered her hand to her lap and opened her eyes. "I'm sorry. Please proceed."

"Mrs. Ramsey, it's very important that you don't share any of the details we've given you about your husband's death. Even with your family," Byron said. "Having information get out prematurely could hurt our investigation. Make it much harder to catch the person responsible. Do you understand?"

Ramsey nodded. "I understand."

"Sergeant Byron and I were hoping to get some background information about your husband if you're up to it," Diane said.

Ramsey nodded then picked up the cup and took another sip.

Byron pulled out a notepad and flipped it open.

"When did you last see him?" Diane asked.

"Tuesday morning. He left for work about seven-thirty."

"Is that a normal time for him?"

"There was nothing routine about the hours he kept. Paul is . . ." Ramsey paused, obviously trying to keep her emotions in check. "Paul *was* an accomplished trial lawyer. The law firm had him working ridiculous hours."

Byron scribbled in silence, watching Ramsey carefully.

"Did he drive himself to work?" Diane asked.

"Yes, he drove his black Lincoln. Did you find it?"

Diane glanced at Byron. "We didn't realize it was missing," she said.

"Is his Lincoln an SUV, Mrs. Ramsey?" Byron asked, remembering having recently seen Ramsey park a black MKX near the Cumberland County Courthouse.

"Yes, but I don't know what it was called. The model. But it had a vanity plate, 'I Win.'"

"I'll call it in," Byron said as he rose and excused himself.

He stepped outside and hit the speed dial on his cell for the dispatch center.

"Police Dispatch, Mary speaking."

"Mary, it's John."

"Well, if it isn't my favorite detective sergeant," she said. "How are you? Sexy as always, I imagine."

"I do my best," Byron said.

"If only I were twenty years younger," she said in a husky voice.

Mary O'Connell had worked as a dispatcher for the Portland Police Department since before Byron had joined the force. Back when Byron's father, Reece, was still on the job. She had always treated Byron like family. During the past four decades O'Connell had seen it all, yet somehow she'd kept her humor.

Dispatchers and emergency operators tended to be under-appreciated. Neither one, Byron thought, seemed to garner the credit they deserved. Perhaps because they were unseen, only voices on the other end of the phone or radio. The people they dealt with were always in crisis, either witnesses to crimes or the victims themselves. Getting anything useful for information out of a crazed 911 caller was at times impossible. Likewise the stress of sending officers into harm's way and then feeling helpless as they waited for news that the crisis had been averted and the officers were safe. Only voices. But as Byron and every other cop worth a damn would tell you, when you were outnumbered or outgunned those voices were the lifeline providing the officers hope. Hope that they might survive the encounter and return home safely to their families. Hope that they'd live to fight another day. Byron had learned many times over the years the value of those unseen allies. The voice of Mary O'Connell.

"So, what can I do for you, Sergeant?"

"I need you to have the area car swing by Jacob's Wharf and see if they can locate a black MKX, Maine registration 'I Win.'"

"Certainly. And if it isn't there?"

"Put out a regional ATL," he said, referring to an attempt to locate. "It's registered to Paul Ramsey. If it's found, I want it secured for processing."

"I'll take care of it."

Byron reentered the Ramsey home and returned to the living room where Mrs. Ramsey and Diane were still conversing.

"Paul was under a great deal of stress at work recently," Ramsey said.

"How so?" Diane asked.

"You saw this morning's *Herald*?" Ramsey asked.

"You're talking about the civil trial?" Diane said.

"Yes. Losing that case was devastating to Paul."

"Did you speak with him after the verdict?"

"No, but I know. He had a great deal riding on it, including his position at the firm."

"His position?" Byron asked.

"A full partnership," Ramsey said. "You'd have to talk with Devon Branch about that."

"Do either of you own a gun?" Byron asked.

She paused before answering. "What are you implying, Sergeant? Do you think Paul took his own life?"

"I'm not implying anything, Mrs. Ramsey. But we have to look at every possibility."

"I understand," she said. "Paul didn't own a gun and neither do I. There have never been any guns in this house."

"Was it unusual for him to stay out all night?" Diane asked.

Ramsey set her mug down on the table and removed her hand from Diane's grasp. "Not particularly." Ramsey clasped her hands together on her lap. "Paul had a dark side, Detectives. He had unusual ways of dealing with stress."

"Like?" Diane asked.

"If it's all the same, I'd rather not discuss it."

"Was your husband seeing someone else, Mrs. Ramsey?" Diane asked.

Ramsey turned to face Diane. "Are you married, Detective?"

"No."

"My husband loved me. But he loved his work more. It's just a fact. Be careful you don't fall for a man like that."

Byron shared an awkward glance with Diane.

"Did Paul mention receiving any threats or seeing anyone suspicious recently?" Byron asked, quickly changing the subject.

Ramsey's eyes widened. "Oh my gosh, I'd completely forgotten about that. Yes, he'd been receiving emails at work from a man threatening him. Emails and maybe voicemails."

"Do you know who the man was?" Byron asked.

She shook her head. "No, Paul never told me his name. It had something to do with a case he won. Years ago. That's all I know. The firm would probably know. Do you think that man killed my Paul?"

"It's too soon to say, Mrs. Ramsey," Byron said. "We will follow up with his employer."

"Did this man ever phone or send threatening emails to the house?" Diane asked.

"I don't believe so."

"Do you remember having seen anyone strange following you recently or maybe coming by the house?" Byron asked.

"No."

Ramsey turned her attention back to Diane. "Will my husband's death be on the news?"

"It's very likely," Diane said.

Ramsey stood. "If you'll please excuse me now, I must contact my children. I don't want them finding out about their stepfather's death on television."

"Of course," Diane said. "Here is my card, Mrs. Ramsey. I've written my cell on the back. We may need to contact you further as the investigation proceeds. Is that okay?"

"Certainly, Detective. Anything I can do."

They followed Ramsey back down the hallway to the front foyer.

The detectives stepped out onto the porch and Byron turned to face Ramsey. "We're very sorry for your loss, Mrs. Ramsey."

Ramsey's face hardened, once again showing her age. "Sergeant Byron."

"Yes, ma'am."

"I know that you had a history with my husband. I'm aware that he didn't have many police friends, but you and Paul particularly didn't get along."

"We just saw things differently," Byron said, forcing a smile.

"Regardless, I want you to make me a promise."

"If I can."

"Promise me that whoever killed my Paul will answer for their crime."

Byron hesitated a moment. He knew the cost of making such

a promise. Many homicides are never solved. Often, even in cases where there's little doubt as to the doer, the evidence may be insufficient to risk taking the case to trial. Double jeopardy only allows one bite at the apple.

"I'll do my best," he said.

It was nearly three-thirty by the time Byron and Diane arrived at PD headquarters. Byron walked in on LeRoyer, who stood in front of the locker room mirror practicing his statement to the press regarding the recovered floater.

". . . and that's all we are prepared to say at this time. Are there any questions?"

"Yeah, I've got one," Byron said, startling the lieutenant. "How'd you get that spot on your tie?"

"Dammit, John, you scared the shit out of me." LeRoyer frowned and looked down. "Do I really have something on my tie?"

Byron took a second look. "Let me guess, lunch at Geno's."

"How in hell can you tell that by looking at my tie?"

"Looks like barbecue sauce."

LeRoyer lifted the tie, examining it closely. "Shit."

Byron walked up to the urinal and unzipped. "Eloquent as always, boss. You should try and work that word into your press conference."

"You missed CompStat, *again*, Sergeant. Conveniently."

"Hey, what can I say? Death investigations take precedence over bullshit stat meetings. Besides, if it had been held yesterday, like normal, I'd have been there with bells on."

"Uh-huh. Seems like you've always got an excuse."

"If it makes you feel any better, you can tell Chief Stanton

I'm working on a plan to cut down on the number of dead attorneys in the bay. Should have something for him by next Wednesday."

"We're sure it's Ramsey?" LeRoyer asked, wetting a paper towel and dabbing at the orange-colored spot on his tie. "I heard the fish were already at him."

"Yeah," Byron said as he flushed the urinal and moved to the sink. "In addition to having Ramsey's wallet, Pelligrosso matched up the prints."

"And the preliminary cause of death is drowning?"

"Not according to Ellis."

"What, then?"

"Someone shot him in the face."

"You're shitting me?"

"Nope. I'd never shit you, Lieutenant. He may have been assaulted beforehand. Somebody executed him. One round to the head," Byron said, pointing at his own forehead.

"Stanton expects me to give a press conference shortly, for the evening news. Now what the hell am I supposed to say?"

"I don't care what you tell the chief. As for the media, say what we always say. The matter is under investigation. We aren't prepared to release the cause of death yet. Tell them we're waiting on the medical examiner's official report."

"When will we have that?"

"Ellis agreed to wait until the tox screen is done before releasing anything."

"How long did he think that would be?"

"I asked for at least a couple of days so we can get a head start on the interviews."

"You think I enjoy this shit, John? I'd like to see you try going up in front of those vultures and saying absolutely nothing."

"Sorry, Marty," Byron said, tossing the wet paper towels into the overflowing trash bin. "Not my thing. Besides, that's why you make the big bucks."

Byron pulled the door open and walked out of the locker room, leaving the lieutenant to clean up the press statement, and his tie.

He was just passing through the doorway to his office when his cell rang.

"Byron," he answered on the second ring.

"Sarge, it's Hags."

"Hey, Sean. What's up?"

"Think I found what you're looking for."

Chapter Six

Thursday, 4:00 P.M., April 28, 2016

BYRON PARKED ON Veranda Street's paved sidewalk, short of the Martin's Point Bridge. Haggerty was waiting for him. Pelligrosso had yet to arrive. As Byron exited the car he saw the top of the black MKX parked halfway down the gravel incline, exactly as Haggerty had described.

"How'd you happen to find it?" Byron asked, looking around as he approached on foot.

"Figured since we found him in the water, I'd start a coastline search," Haggerty said.

"Nice work."

Officer Sean Haggerty was what Byron fondly referred to as an old-school beat cop. He knew his area of the city inside and out, and did things by the book each and every time. Byron had seen plenty of uniformed officers fuck up crime scenes simply by being stupid. Hags was a breath of fresh air.

Haggerty had already circled the wooded area widely, stringing bright yellow crime scene tape from nearby trees. Ramsey's SUV was parked facing the water. The access road, normally used by day fishermen who'd park on the road then walk up to the bridge to fish for stripers and blues, was hidden from the view of passing traffic. The surrounding underbrush was littered with beer cans and broken glass bottles. Byron noticed a discarded prophylactic wrapper lying nearby, suggesting that fishing wasn't the only recreation taking place here.

"I assume I don't need to ask," Byron said.

"Didn't lay so much as a finger on it, Sarge," Hags said. "Heard the kid didn't make out so well at the autopsy?"

Byron grinned. "He didn't see half of it. Where is Officer Cody?"

"I left him at 109 to write up his reports."

They both turned to the sound of the approaching diesel engine of the evidence van.

Pelligrosso pulled up onto the sidewalk behind Byron's Malibu and got out.

"Ramsey's Lincoln?" Pelligrosso asked as he walked toward them toting the oversized lab camera and his black evidence collection kit.

"Yes," Byron said. "I figured you could start with photos until I get the okay from Diane."

"The okay?"

"She's on her way to get consent from Ramsey's widow."

The evidence tech nodded and got to work.

"I'll get out of your way and start on the paperwork, Sarge," Haggerty said, retreating to his car.

"I DIDN'T EXPECT to see you so soon, Detective," Mrs. Ramsey said to Diane.

The two women were seated at Ramsey's kitchen table. Diane noted the pad of paper next to the box of tissues. She could see that Ramsey had compiled a list of people she needed to contact regarding her husband's death.

"I'm sorry to interrupt you," Diane said, pointing to Ramsey's list.

"It's alright. I've done this before."

Diane tilted her head, indicating her lack of comprehension.

"My first husband, Peter, died of pancreatic cancer twenty years ago."

"I'm sorry."

"He was about ten years older than me. When Paul and I married almost sixteen years ago, I thought, since he was younger, that I wouldn't have to go through this again. Guess I was wrong." Ramsey's tears began to flow again. Diane waited while she composed herself.

"Anyway, what can I do for you?"

"As I mentioned, we've located your husband's SUV, Mrs. Ramsey. We will need to process it for evidence."

"Julia, please," Ramsey said. "Do you need me to sign some kind of consent?"

"Yes, Julia, so we can search the Lincoln. The vehicle is registered to both of you."

"Well, I purchased it for him, but it was his vehicle."

"That's why we do this. If we locate evidence, we don't want it to become inadmissible later on."

"I understand."

Diane slid the form across the table to Ramsey and handed her a pen.

"Do you need me to explain it?" Diane asked.

Ramsey shook her head. "No. I've probably seen enough legal paperwork during my marriage to Paul that I could practice law."

Diane smiled. "I'm sure you have."

Ramsey pushed the signed consent to search form back across the table. "Can I ask where you found it?"

"Near the Martin's Point Bridge," Diane said. "The Portland side. Can you think of any reason your husband may have had for going there?"

"I don't know. Is that near the medical building on Veranda Street?"

"Martin's Point Health Care, yes. Did Paul have some connection to them?"

"Not that I know of."

Ramsey's cell began to vibrate on the table. "I'm sorry, I have to take this. It's my daughter."

"I'll go now. Give you your privacy."

Ramsey reached out and put a hand on Diane's arm. "No. Please wait. I need to tell you some things about Paul. Things you should know."

BYRON WAS WATCHING Pelligrosso and thinking about his next move when his cell rang. He checked the ID. Assistant Attorney General Jim Ferguson.

"Counselor," Byron answered.

"Well now, you've had a busy day, Sergeant," Ferguson said.

"And it isn't over yet."

"I heard Paul Ramsey is no longer with us."

"You heard right. Fished him out of the ocean this morning."

"I'll forgive the pun. What's it look like?"

"Looks like somebody punched his ticket then tossed him in the water. One to the head."

"Ouch. Robbery?"

"Doesn't look like it. He still had his watch and wallet."

"Any leads?"

"We just located his vehicle, abandoned near the Portland-Falmouth line. Parked near the water."

"What can I do to help?"

"We're playing catch-up at the moment, but I will need a subpoena for his cell records."

"Do you have the phone?"

"No. It wasn't on his person. It may be in the SUV—we haven't gotten inside yet. If it isn't, we'll need access to the carrier's digital records of his account history."

"How about a warrant for the truck?"

"I don't think we'll need it. Diane Joyner is with Ramsey's wife as we speak, getting a consent form signed."

"Okay. Give me the cell number and I'll draft up what you'll need and fax a copy to your office."

After filling Ferguson in, Byron ended the call, then checked his cell for texts. Still nothing from Diane. He punched in the nonemergency number for police dispatch.

"Police Communications, Operator Gostkowski speaking."

"Dale, it's Byron. Can you transfer me over to Parking Control, at city hall?"

"Sure thing, Sarge."

Byron waited as the phone rang at the other end of the line.

"Parking Control," a bored-sounding male answered following a half dozen rings.

"This is Byron over at the PD."

"Oh, hello, Sergeant Byron. It's Al Greene." His voice dripped with condescension. "You calling to find out your balance?"

Greene was the biggest parking Nazi the city had. He'd personally written at least a dozen of the tags currently stuffed in Byron's glove box. Byron was sure Greene intentionally sought out his unmarked when he was on the street tagging. "Got you inside today, huh, Al? That's too bad."

"Not to worry, Sarge. Be pounding the pavement tomorrow. Got a new box of pens."

Byron could hear the glee in Greene's voice.

"Need you to run a scoff check for me," Byron said.

"Yours?"

"No. Maine vanity—'I Win.'"

"Gimme a sec."

Byron listened to the clicks of a keyboard as Greene typed the request.

"Twelve outstanding tickets," Greene said.

"Where?"

"Looks like they're all in and around the Old Port. One on Spring Street, two on Union, three on State, one on Jacob's Wharf, and five on Commercial."

Byron knew the first three were next to Ramsey's office. He didn't have a clue about State Street but was fairly sure the Commercial Street and Jacob's Wharf tags were all from visits to the Red Fox pub, a bar that Ramsey was known to frequent. "Would you email that list to me?"

"Of course. Serving you is why I'm here, Sergeant Byron."

It took every ounce of restraint he had not to threaten the beady-eyed parking control officer with bodily harm. But he needed the list and pretending to be cordial seemed the most expedient way to get it. "Thanks."

"See you soon, Sarge."

Byron pressed the red button on his cell, mercifully ending the call, just as his phone chimed with an incoming text from Diane. It was the one he'd been waiting for.

"All signed."

Byron hollered over to Pelligrosso, who was busy snapping pictures of the Lincoln from every angle. "Good to go on the search, Gabe."

Pelligrosso gave him the thumbs-up and went back to work.

Byron instructed Haggerty to remain with Pelligrosso until Ramsey's SUV was secured in the basement garage at 109. Then he headed off. Greene's information had given him a clue about where Ramsey may have spent his last night among the living.

HAVING GROWN UP in Portland, Byron had witnessed the Old Port change dramatically over the last five decades. No longer the rough-and-tumble streets of his youth. Gone were most of the dilapidated wooden piers, replaced by concrete and steel. Vanished, too, were the train tracks and cobblestone of Commercial Street, long since removed and paved over. The broken-down fishing shacks and storefronts that he and his childhood friends once explored had given way to upscale condos and bars. Buildings which once served the needs of a booming fishing industry now thrived on tourism. The Port City's waterfront gentrification was in full swing.

It was nearly five, the workday over for most folks. Many were headed home to be with their families. But for others it was playtime, and their playground was the Old Port. Byron couldn't locate an empty space near the Red Fox on Commercial Street and opted instead for a No Parking zone, half hoping that Greene and his ticket book would find him.

The Fox was a bit rougher around its edges than most of the Old Port establishments, reminding Byron of his formative rookie years when he'd broken up more fights than he could count in bars exactly like the Fox. No yuppie college kids would have been caught dead there. The clientele tended toward the thirtysomething to sixtysomething range, many of whom had criminal records. A foursome of nicotine addicts stood sentry on the sidewalk in front of the Fox. Byron walked past them, giving a nod, and entered the bar.

Inside, two flat-screen televisions were competing for the attention of a dozen or so patrons. One was blaring the Boston Red Sox pregame show, the other a local news broadcast. Byron still hoped to catch the story on Ramsey, knowing no real news would be shown until six. The local affiliate's early editions were normally filled with nothing but commercials, teasers, and multiple looks at the weather.

Most of the tables were empty. Byron grabbed one in a corner farthest from the door, where he could sit with his back to the wall. He noticed the bartender signaling the leggy, bleached-blonde cocktail waitress. He watched as she made her way over to his table.

"What can I getcha, hon?" Blondie asked.

"I'll take a diet soda and some information," he said, fixing her with his most charming smile.

"On the wagon or working?"

He was immediately impressed with her powers of deduction. "Both actually."

"You a cop?" she asked, placing a hand on one hip and raising a brow.

"Busted."

"One diet coming right up. And I'll bring a menu."

"I'm not really hungry."

"Handsome, I work for tips. You want information, you'll order something from the menu."

"A menu would be great, thank you."

Byron enjoyed his drink, which was predominantly ice, while pretending to read the menu. He watched Blondie flit about the room in her short skirt and fishnets catering to other patrons. He also caught the occasional glance from the bartender. Byron figured she'd either outed him as a cop, or the barkeep and Blondie were an item.

Byron had only a hunch to go on, but knowing Ramsey and how much he hated to lose, Byron guessed it was likely he'd come to the Fox to drown his sorrows following the jury's finding. It was exactly what Byron would have done.

He'd narrowed his choice to the foxy burger with curly fries, or a fresh catch fish sandwich with chips and a pickle, when Blondie reappeared.

"Well?" she asked.

"Thought you guys all wore name tags?"

"You know how many times I get hit on in a night? Last thing I wanna advertise is my name."

"I'm trying to find out if someone might have come in here the past couple of nights."

"Food first," she said.

He chose the foxy burger, well done, and a refill on the soda then handed her the menu.

"Okay, who?" she asked, tucking the menu under one arm.

"Paul Ramsey."

"The lawyer?"

Byron nodded.

"They just mentioned him on the news. He in some kind of trouble?"

Byron couldn't imagine much bigger trouble than Ramsey was in. "You could say that. He's dead."

Blondie appeared to be trying to decide if he was serious or not. "I'll put your order in and be back."

Byron's phone vibrated with a text from Diane. "Headin' back from Yarmouth. Where R U?"

"Meet U at 109 by 6," he texted back as the bartender approached.

"Lexi says you asked about Ramsey?"

Of course it's Lexi, Byron thought. *Or Candy or Dixie. Take your pick. The Huey, Dewey, and Louie of cocktail waitresses.*

"You're a cop, right?" the bartender asked.

"Detective sergeant actually," he said without getting up. "And you are?"

"Tony the bartender," he said, puffing out his chest.

Byron grinned at the lame attempt to intimidate. "Well, Tony. I must say that's an unusual middle name."

Tony's face registered his confusion. "What?"

"Never mind. I'm investigating the death of Paul Ramsey. I understand he was a regular here."

"Yeah, I knew Paul. Didn't know he was dead, though. Not until I saw his picture on the news."

"Has he been in here the last couple of nights?"

"Yeah, he was."

Byron waited for more. "Both nights?"

"Nah, just Tuesday night."

"And?"

"And what? That's it."

Byron grinned again, the grin he reserved for assholes and Tony had just made the list. "See, Tony the bartender, this is why we police officers get such a bad rap. I came in here looking to find out if a guy, whose death I'm investigating, might have spent his last few hours in here, and if anything happened that might possibly point me in the right direction. I just had a nice little chat with Lexi the waitress. Hey, you guys have the same middle name."

Tony's confusion continued.

"Anyway, I ordered a nice meal, which should be here any moment, and I'm trying to politely get some information, or what we in the cop business call clues. Now, you've gone and ruined my appetite. Being all rude and trying to act like some hard case when clearly you're not."

Byron could see Tony was becoming antsy, shifting from one foot to the other and looking around at the other patrons.

Byron continued. "Now the way I see it, you have two options."

Tony crossed his arms and glared at Byron. "And what might those be, *Detective Sergeant*?"

"Either sit down and tell me what I want to know, like a gentleman."

"Or?"

"Or I'll drag you out of here for questioning as a material witness to a homicide. Then I'll make a phone call to another detective sergeant, the one who supervises all drug investigations in Cumberland County, and tell him about your lack of manners. By the time his guys are finished with this bar, your customers will have moved on to greener pastures, assuming they aren't all in jail for distribution or possession, and you'll be out of a job."

Tony dropped the tough-guy façade, pulled out a chair, and sat down. "Okay, okay. What do you want to know?"

Lexi brought Byron's order, then scurried off to tend bar.

Byron ate while Tony, whose last name turned out to be Regali, regaled him with tales from Tuesday evening.

"Who's Donny?" Byron asked.

"Donny McVail," Tony said. "He's just a local yokel. Harmless. Likes to run his mouth a bit."

"What happened?"

"Ramsey was complaining about getting passed over for some promotion or something and Donny called him a bitch."

"What'd Ramsey do?" Byron asked, almost sorry he'd missed the interaction.

"I think he called him a name."

"Like what?"

"I don't know. He was kinda talking down to the kid. Making fun of him, I guess. Asked if Donny had a GED."

"Then what happened?"

"Donny got up, like he was gonna fight him."

"Did they fight?"

"No, I stopped it. I threatened to call the co—you guys, if Ramsey didn't leave."

"Did he?"

"Yeah. He said a couple more things to Donny and then he left."

"And? What did Donny do?"

"Nothing. He sat back down and ordered another drink. He and the girl he was with left about an hour later."

Chapter Seven

Thursday, 6:55 P.M., April 28, 2016

IT WAS NEARLY 7:00 P.M. by the time Byron made it back to 109.
The local news had long since ended. He found Diane in the CID
conference room populating the whiteboard, which hung on one
of the rectangular room's long walls. She had affixed photos of
Ramsey and his Lincoln at the center of the board and was filling
in a timeline on the left. The television was on but muted.

"Hey," Diane said.

"You get a chance to catch LeRoyer's statement to the press?"
he asked.

"I caught 13's and the end of Channel 8's broadcast. It was lead
on all three of the local networks."

"How'd it go?"

"Perfect. He said Ramsey's body was recovered in the ocean
and that we're waiting on findings from the medical examiner."

"No mention of an assault or shooting?"

"None."

"Any speculation by the reporters?"

"The WGME reporter said it might be related to the loss of the civil trial."

"Suicide?"

"She didn't come right out and say that but it was implied. How about you? Anything from the bar?"

"Ramsey was at the Fox Tuesday night, left around eleven. Got into an argument with a local shithead named McVail. Donald McVail."

"What happened?"

"According to the bartender, Tony Regali, it was just verbal. Ramsey was goading McVail. McVail wanted to fight."

"Did they?"

"Regali said he made Ramsey leave. Said he threatened to call the police."

"McVail follow him?"

"Not according to Regali. Said he sat down and ordered another drink. Left with some girl about midnight."

"Think he's being straight with you?" Diane asked, grinning.

"Add McVail to the board. I wanna talk to him and the girl to confirm."

"Ask me about my conversation with Julia," Diane said as she carefully added the new name to the whiteboard.

"First name basis now?"

"Yup. See? You remove one over-dominant male detective sergeant from the room and the widow opens right up."

"You're saying I'm not good with the ladies?"

"Oh, you're good with one lady."

"What'd she tell you?"

"Apparently, our victim liked to chase skirt, to include a local stripper and maybe even someone at the firm."

Byron raised an eyebrow. "She say who?"

"Said she wasn't sure, but the infidelity thing had been going on for quite a while. She also knew about the cocaine."

"She know where he got it?"

"Not a clue. But she made him keep it out of the house. As far as she knows, he did."

"She let you look around?"

"A little. I didn't want to push."

Diane finished filling him in on the way to 109's basement garage, where Pelligrosso was busy searching the SUV.

"How's it going, Gabe?" Byron asked.

Pelligrosso backed awkwardly out of the front passenger's side doorway. "Slow."

"Anything yet?" Diane asked.

The evidence tech peeled off his rubber gloves and took a swig from his water bottle. "Yeah, fucking heat stroke. Why is it that they can't keep the heater working down here in the winter but can't shut it down when it's nearly May?"

"Seriously," Byron said. "Have you found anything?"

"Well, so far I've checked for prints on all the door handles, inside and out, the rearview mirror, the steering wheel, and the shift lever."

"And?"

"Got a ton of prints. The guy was kind of a slob. Nice ride but he didn't keep it very good."

"Don't suppose you found a gun or a shell casing?" Byron said.

Pelligrosso shook his head.

"Or a phone?" Diane said.

"Nope."

"Anything else?" Byron asked.

"Yeah, I recovered two long blond hairs, one from the left front seat and one from the right. No idea who any of it belongs to but I'll go out on a limb and say they weren't Ramsey's."

"Any blood?" Diane asked.

"Possibly. Found a smudge on the inside of the left front door glass and another on the steering wheel."

"Any chance the shooting occurred inside the SUV?" Byron asked.

"Won't be able to tell for sure until I light the inside of this thing up with Luminol, but I'd bet against it."

"Anything else?" Byron asked.

"Yeah, I found three pharmaceutical folds between the driver's seat and the center console."

"Residue?" Diane asked.

"A white powdery substance," Pelligrosso said.

"Field-test it?" Byron asked.

"Not like I had anything else to do."

Byron frowned.

Pelligrosso backed down. "Sorry, Sarge. Guess the heat's making me cranky. It's coke."

Byron wasn't the least bit surprised. Even before Ellis's findings during the autopsy, and Mrs. Ramsey's admission to Diane, there had been rumors of Ramsey having a bad cocaine habit. He'd never been charged, but attorneys are slippery creatures. Hard to catch.

"You need any help on this?" Byron asked. "Mel's still working with Nuge on last week's bank robbery but I'll drag her in if you want. Or I can get one of the new guys if you think they're up for it?"

Pelligrosso considered it for a moment. "Nah, I'm good. It's only one vehicle. Better for continuity if it's just me anyway."

Byron knew he was right. Murder trials were a bear. So many things could go wrong. The last thing they needed was to unnecessarily lengthen the chain of custody.

"I'm gonna talk with Huntress about getting his team back in the water," Byron said. "I want to be sure the gun didn't get tossed near the bridge."

"That reminds me, I plan on going back to recheck the wooded area more thoroughly tomorrow. Okay to call in some help for that?"

"Whatever you need, Gabe."

"I'll let you guys know if I can match any of this stuff to someone."

BYRON AND DIANE grabbed a couple of drive-through burgers at the Burger King on Forest Avenue. They sat in the car eating and discussing their next move.

"We need to fill in the rest of Ramsey's timeline for Tuesday," Byron said. "And maybe part of Wednesday morning."

"Well, we know he was in court until early afternoon on Tuesday. I'll try and find out from the clerks or the news reporters what time he left the courthouse."

"And we know he was at the Fox until eleven or so."

"The bartender say what time he got there?"

"He wasn't sure but he thought it was around seven."

Byron's cell rang. LeRoyer.

He stuck it in the dash-mounted charger and pushed the speaker button. "Byron."

"John, just checking in. Making any headway?"

Diane rolled her eyes.

"Actually, we are," Byron said. "Diane is sitting here with me. She's about halfway through her fries and I just finished a Whopper."

"Great. I'll be sure and let the chief know. He'll be so happy. Where are we at?"

"We were just discussing that. Gabe's still processing Ramsey's SUV. And we were about to try and find one of Ramsey's girl-friends."

"Thought he was married."

Byron looked at Diane and rolled his eyes. "Yeah, Marty, he was."

"Have you checked in with Ramsey's employer yet?"

"Been a little busy today. Why?"

"Devon Branch has been calling the chief looking to talk to the lead investigator."

"Well, Devon Branch will just have to take a number. Don't worry, Lieu. I plan to visit the law firm of Dewey, Fuckum & Howe in the morning. We're still trying to establish a timeline for Tuesday."

"Any idea where Ramsey was Tuesday night?"

"Looks like he was at the Red Fox until eleven. After that we still don't know."

"Okay. Let me know if something breaks."

"You'll be the first."

Byron ended the call and noisily finished his soda. He turned to Diane. "What do you say we pay a visit to the Unicorn."

"You read my mind."

POLICE BEAT REPORTER Davis Billingslea sat alone in his cubicle on the second floor of the *Portland Herald* building. Most of his coworkers had gone for the day, leaving him to slurp hot and sour soup and munch on wontons from the China Dragon on Exchange Street while staring at the blinking cursor on his desktop monitor. The young reporter had been covering the civil trial against Maine Medical Center in the weeks leading up to yesterday's decision by the jury. Ramsey, who'd been plenty forthcoming with information when it looked like his clients, the Elwells, might actually win the ten-million-dollar suit, told Billingslea to "Fuck off" as he left the courthouse on Tuesday. Much as he would have loved to put that quote out to the general public, he knew it would never pass muster with his editor, or any editor for that matter. His attempts to get statements from either the aggrieved family or Ramsey's firm had met similar resistance. But now that Ramsey had literally washed up, Billingslea had a whole new angle to pursue. Did the trial lawyer become despondent and take his own life? Did someone in the family seek retribution? Were the Elwells upset enough about the loss to go after their attorney? After all, winning that trial meant that someone would have finally paid for taking their son's life. Or could it have been any number of victims' families still suffering after Ramsey had successfully gotten a murderer off? Paul Ramsey was a wrecking ball. Losing this eight-figure case was the biggest blow the young reporter had ever seen Ramsey take. Actually, it was the only blow.

Lieutenant LeRoyer hadn't provided him with anything following the news conference and Billingslea knew better than to approach Byron. Once again he'd been shut out. He picked up his cell and scanned through the contact list until he found the name he was looking for. Amy Brennan. Amy worked as a paralegal in the law offices of Newman, Branch & DeWitt. She was single, *very* attractive, and late twenties, about his age. But most importantly, she'd despised Paul Ramsey.

Billingslea sat up in his chair and cleared his throat like a DJ about to go on the air. He pressed in Amy's number and waited.

"Hello?" a feminine voice answered.

"Amy, it's Davis. Davis Billingslea."

BYRON AND DIANE stood waiting in the lobby, exchanging awkward glances with the hostess and a very large barrel-chested guy sporting a gray suit and tie, with a neck the size of his waist. The music in the next room was barely discernible over the booming bass notes.

They'd been waiting several minutes when a side door to the lobby swung open and out walked an olive-skinned man wearing a black Armani suit, white shirt, and maroon power tie.

Armani approached them wearing a predatory smile. "Detectives," he said. "Sorry to keep you both waiting. I am Vincenzo Kakalegian. How may I help you?"

After making the introductions, Byron asked if there was somewhere private they could talk. Kakalegian led them back through the side door and up a flight of stairs to the second level.

"Can I interest either of you in an adult beverage?" Kakalegian asked.

"No thank you," Byron said, noticing that Kakalegian's eyes were roving over Diane. "We're actually here on official business."

"In that case, please have a seat," Kakalegian said, gesturing toward several plush low-backs near the two-way mirror that overlooked the club floor below.

"This place is classier than I remember," Byron said.

Kakalegian raised a brow. "Oh, you've been a frequent guest?"

"Not frequent, but I was here last year. When the previous owner was still here."

"Ah, Mr. Beaudreau. Well, Orsolini Holdings is an upscale entertainment corporation. We only go top class."

"Nothing classier than the exploitation of women, Mr. Kakalegian," Diane said.

Kakalegian's smile faded a bit. "Miss, I can—"

"Detective."

"I beg pardon. Detective. While I realize that dancing isn't everyone's cup of tea, I assure you that our girls are highly paid and treated well. We run a respectable business here."

"Actually, we're here to discuss another matter," Byron said, giving Diane the hairy eyeball. "We understand that one of your dancers may have had a relationship with the victim of a case we're working."

"Oh? Who's the victim?"

"Paul Ramsey. He was somewhat of a local celebrity."

"Is that the man who was in the news this morning? Attorney? Lost some big civil case, right?"

"That would be him," Diane said. "Did you know him?"

"Can't say as I did. You say he was seeing one of *our* girls?"

"That's our understanding," Byron said.

"Well, I don't know anything about that, but you're welcome to accompany me downstairs to the dressing room. You can ask them yourselves."

"RAMSEY? No, I don't think so," a statuesque brunette dancer said.

Byron was having a hard time concentrating as he spoke with the scantily clad curvy woman. She couldn't have been much older than twenty-five. He was also having a hard time taking her seriously due to the ostrich feathers being used to conceal her most intimate parts.

"Got a picture?" the dancer asked.

Diane pulled the newspaper clipping with Ramsey's photo out of her suit-coat pocket and handed it over.

"Nope. Don't recognize him. You sure he was dating one of us?"

They showed several other women, but each claimed not to know Ramsey.

Byron left Kakalegian with a business card. Kakalegian promised to check with the other dancers.

As they walked across the lot to Byron's Chevy, he caught Diane staring at him.

"What?" he said, trying hard to sound innocent and hide a grin.

"Don't what me. You were loving that, weren't you?"

He gave up trying to contain the grin and let out a full-blown smile. "Oh, okay. Like you never went to a male strip club when you were down in New York."

"That was different. It was my duty as a bridesmaid."

He raised his brows in disbelief.

"All six times," she said.

"That's what I thought."

"And gotta tell ya, I've never seen such tight abs and buns."

"Okay, I get it. Don't need the gory details."

"You started it."

They were getting into the car when Diane noticed a small white slip of paper stuck under the right-hand wiper blade. She snatched it up.

"What is it?" Byron asked.

"A note. 'Talk to Joe.'"

"Joe who?"

"Don't know. That's all it says. Mean anything to you?"

He shook his head. "No number?"

"Just the name." She showed him the note.

"Maybe somebody knows more than they told us."

"Perhaps they weren't comfortable talking to us in front of Mr. High Class."

"Maybe not," he agreed as he started the car.

IT WAS AFTER eleven by the time Diane and Byron arrived at his place. Diane stretched out on the sofa, a glass of merlot in her hand, her stockinged feet in Byron's lap.

Byron stared absently at the television while massaging the soles of her feet. He was exhausted but he knew his mind wasn't about to let him fall asleep easily. It never did, not while he was working a homicide.

"You have any idea how good that feels?" she cooed. "Think you missed your calling."

A month prior he'd moved out of the shitty little one-bedroom apartment on Danforth Street and into the recently renovated Forest Avenue condo. New flooring and new paint made the place feel as if it was recently constructed. It even smelled new. Quite a step up from his last. Following the divorce, Kay, his ex, refinanced what had been their home, then gave him a check for half of the equity. The money wasn't enough to purchase a house, not on a detective sergeant's salary, but it did allow him to make a healthy down payment on the condo, healthy enough to keep his monthly expenses manageable.

"You know, John," Diane said, scanning the room, "you really should unpack."

"Uh-huh," he said absently.

"Earth to John."

"Sorry. Just thinking about Ramsey."

"Oh, I see. So a dead attorney is more important than me?"

Byron leaned over and kissed her on the neck. "Hardly."

She reached down, caressing him through his slacks. "I'll say."

He kissed her deeply, exploring the softness of her mouth, tasting the sweetness of the wine. After a moment, he came up for air.

"Hey, have we made it in your spare bedroom yet?" she asked.

"I don't think so," he said. "There's no furniture in there."

"So?" she said as she got up from the sofa, gulped the remainder of the merlot, and began to unbutton her blouse. "What do those dancers have that I don't have?"

"Don't know. I haven't seen you dance," Byron said, getting up and following her as she danced seductively back toward the stairs.

"They say it's good luck to christen every room in a new house."

"Is that what they say?"

"You wouldn't want to have bad luck, now would you?"

"This coming from a black cat," he said as he reached for her.

"Ah, excuse me? A sexy black cat." She laughed then turned and took the stairs two at a time up to the second floor.

Byron was hot on her heels.

BILLINGSLEA WAS ALREADY seated at a table, nursing a beer, when Brennan walked in. He waved her over.

"Hey, Amy," he said. "Wasn't sure you'd come on such short notice."

"Oh yeah, me being such a social butterfly and all."

She was dressed to the nines, wearing high heels, a knee-length pleated brown skirt, and a light colored low-cut sweater, revealing just enough cleavage to make him strain to keep his eyes fixed on hers. Billingslea felt his heart skip a beat as she smiled and sat down. He reminded himself that this was work and not a date.

"Surprised to hear from me?" Billingslea asked.

"Pleased is more like it." She smiled again.

"Get you something to drink?"

"That'd be great. How about an Appletini?"

"What brand of vodka?"

"Absolut."

"Be right back," he said. Billingslea stood and strolled to the bar, trying hard to hide his nervousness.

While waiting for the bartender to mix the drink he glanced back at Brennan. She waved at him. His heart fluttered again.

Billingslea returned to the table, walking gingerly so as not to spill her drink.

"Thank you so much, Davis," she said, taking the glass from him. "You didn't need to do that. I could have ordered it myself."

"I thought it was the least I could do after the way you helped me during the trial."

She sipped the emerald liquid. "Mmm."

He took long swig of beer while thinking of something to say that wouldn't betray his purpose in meeting her. "Do you get out to the Old Port much?"

She took another sip then shook her head. Her dark curls danced at the side of her face. "Not as often as I'd like. Ms. Davies keeps me pretty busy."

"I'll bet. What's it like to work at such an important firm?"

She laughed. "Probably not much different than working at a newspaper, I imagine. There's always a deadline and more work than time to do it."

"Is Lorraine Davies good to you?"

"She's very good to me. Not sure where I'd be without her."

"Tell me about Paul Ramsey."

"Why, Mr. Billingslea, did you lure me out here under false pretenses?" she said, giving him a wink.

He could feel the blood rush to his cheeks. "No, I . . . I—"

"Relax," she said, sliding her hand over his. "I'm only teasing. I know you've got a job to do."

Billingslea let out a sigh of relief. "You're not mad?"

"Of course not, silly." She gave him a mischievous grin as she took another sip. "What would you like to know?"

A HALF HOUR later, Byron and Diane both lay spent in the dark, on the soft Saxony carpet in the spare room, arms and legs entwined.

"Mmm," Diane said.

"Think I'll have good luck now?" Byron asked.

"If you don't, it won't be my fault."

They remained that way for several minutes, listening to each other breathing.

Diane rolled to one side, resting her head on his chest. "What did Mrs. Ramsey mean today when she said, 'I know you didn't get along with my husband'?"

Byron sighed. "I don't wanna talk about it."

"Is it because he was better looking?" she teased.

"It's a long story."

"John, I'm not even sure which floor my pants are on. We've got plenty of time. Did something happen between you and Ramsey?"

He'd known this subject might come up as soon as he realized who the floater was. He'd expected that she might bring it up before. "Yeah, it was a long time ago. Before you left New York City to come to Portland. I was still a young detective."

"Before you became a dashingly handsome detective sergeant?"

"Way before. I was still working with Ray Humphrey at the time. He mentored me in the bureau."

"What happened?"

"Ray and I caught a case. Home invasion. An elderly couple lived out in Deering. The Simpsons, Betty and Gene. One night a meth-head with a gun broke into their house looking for drugs. He was tweaked out of his mind. Turns out he had the right street but the wrong house. The dealer lived three doors down but the asshole didn't know that. He duct taped both of them to chairs in the kitchen and beat Gene senseless. Broke his arm and gave him a concussion. The asshole turned the house upside down, stole some money and jewelry, then fled, leaving them tied up."

"Did you catch him?"

"Eventually. The lab guys recovered prints and we were able to ID him. Local shit bag named Dwayne Travers with priors for trafficking and armed robbery. I got one of my snitches to tell me where I could find the guy. I should've waited for Ray, but I didn't. I found him alone in his apartment and he resisted. Anyway, I got him to confess, recovered the gun and some of the jewelry."

"Let me guess, Ramsey defended him."

"Ramsey argued that I beat a confession out of him, making everything I obtained after inadmissible."

Diane nodded her understanding. "Fruit of the poisonous tree."

"Yeah. And the judge agreed with him. Turned Travers loose."

"I'm sorry, John."

"Doesn't matter much now."

"What happened to the victims?"

"The husband died a few months later from a blood clot. Complications from his injuries. Betty Simpson moved down to Florida."

"What about Travers?" she asked.

"Son of a bitch died six months later. Drug overdose."

"I can see why Mrs. Ramsey would be worried."

"You don't really think I'd put less effort into investigating his murder because Paul Ramsey was an asshole?"

Diane lifted her head and faced him. "Of course not."

"In this city we'd have a tough time ever investigating a murder if that were true."

"I know that, John."

"It's our job to speak for the dead." But he wondered, in Ramsey's case, if that were *really* true.

"I'm sorry I said it. Okay?" She leaned in and kissed him on the lips. "We good?"

"Yeah," he said, kissing her back. "We're good."

Diane ran her fingers through his salt-and-pepper hair.

"You really think Ramsey was better looking?" Byron asked, pretending to pout.

"Hardly," she said. She kissed him again.

"You're kidding," Billingslea said.

"Not at all," Brennan said.

Billingslea watched as she picked up her drink and took another sip, leaving a trace of her lipstick on the rim of the glass. "So then why go through with the trial? I would think a settlement of one million dollars would have been more than enough for the Elwells."

Brennan shrugged her shoulders. "I don't know. Maybe they wanted the hospital to pay more. The suit was for ten million. Maybe they didn't think one was enough."

He mulled that over for a bit. "Tell me more about Ramsey."

"What about him?"

"Well, I know he cut his teeth doing mostly court-appointed work. He became famous, at least around Southern Maine. Then he began charging an arm and a leg to defend people in criminal court. How did he end up working for Newman, Branch & DeWitt?"

She laughed. "I don't know. That was way before I began working there. He's a really gifted trial lawyer. I assume that's why they brought him on."

Billingslea considered what she'd said. It made sense but he realized that just about anything she said made sense at this point. He was smitten.

"I don't understand why they'd have him try a civil case when his background was criminal defense," he said.

"Most of the prep work for these cases is done by people like me. Compile the information, organize it, type the briefs, file the motions, do the research, all of it. The firm's senior partners conduct strategy sessions about how to handle a case, then, once they decide something is going to trial, they'll pick the litigator who gives them the best shot at winning. Paul's background didn't really matter. He knew courtroom procedure. He knew how to play to a jury and handle witnesses. Paul Ramsey was simply their best hope to win."

"Still, a million bucks is a million bucks," Billingslea said, lifting his glass and finishing the last swig of beer.

"Yeah," she said. "But it isn't ten."

Chapter Eight

Friday, 6:45 A.M., April 29, 2016

AT 6:45 THE next morning, Byron sat impatiently behind the wheel of his unmarked at the St. John Street Dunkin' Donuts drive-through. Waiting like some well-dressed addict to score an extra-large cup of America's last legal stimulant. He had his cell pressed to his ear waiting for Sergeant Huntress to pick up.

"Don't tell me you've got another floater, John?" Huntress said, skipping right past the usual pleasantries.

"Thought you guys lived for this stuff," Byron said.

"Well, I do have a life, ya know, unlike you psychos in CID. Besides, half my shit is still wet from yesterday."

"We recovered Ramsey's vehicle late yesterday afternoon."

"I heard. Martin's Point Bridge, right?"

"Below it. The old access road, where Veranda ends."

"I know right where that is. The anglers use it. So what are we looking for today?"

"Hang on a sec." Byron pulled up to the window and handed the clerk three ones. He took his coffee and change then pulled away from the window.

"Sorry about that."

"Where are you?"

"Java stop."

"Good for you. So you were about to tell me what you hoped to find."

"The gun used to kill Ramsey."

Huntress agreed to assemble his team for a ten o'clock dive. Byron had just ended the call when his cell rang. The caller ID showed a blocked number.

"Byron," he answered.

"Top o' the morn', Sergeant."

Ellis.

"Hey, Doc. You're up bright and early."

"Maine's most brilliant pathologist is on his way to the gym."

"Seriously?"

"Don't sound so surprised. My GP says I gotta drop a few if I don't wanna end up on my own table."

Byron laughed, picturing the portly throwback sweating atop an elliptical. "Damn doctors, huh? Think they know it all."

Ellis chuckled. "Actually, that's why I'm calling. I know what Ramsey had in his system."

"That was fast. Do tell."

"Counselor Ramsey had himself quite a little party before meeting his demise. BAC was .16 and his blood also contained a very high level of what we in the doctorin' biz call cocaine metabolites."

"How high?"

"Over five hundred nanograms per milliliter of blood. Pretty typical for a chronic user."

"So, no surprises."

"Not so fast. There was a third substance on board. Fentanyl."

"Fentanyl? Thought you said he was a coke addict?"

"He's got all of the usual indicators. Doesn't mean the late Counselor Ramsey didn't occasionally partake of the other white drug."

Fentanyl, a powerful narcotic analgesic, didn't match what Byron knew about Ramsey. But Ellis was right, the deceased might have experimented with other drugs. They'd need to track down Ramsey's supplier.

"Where would he get his hands on something like that?" Byron asked.

"Hey, you're the detective, Sergeant. Ha! Get it."

"Yeah, I got it. How long can you keep the cause of death under wraps, before you start getting grief?"

"How long do you need?" Ellis asked.

"A week?"

"I'll give you till Monday."

BYRON TOTED HIS extra-large coffee into CID. He grabbed a medium-sized stack of overnight crime reports off the printer, then walked to his office. First order of business, check voicemail. According to the automated female voice on his desk phone, he had sixteen new messages. Typical during the first few days of a murder investigation. Three of the calls were from the ever persistent Davis Billingslea, and one each from the newsrooms of Channels 6, 8, and 13. He deleted them one at a time until finally getting to one that actually mattered.

"Sarge, Gabe. It's eleven-thirty and I'm going home before I fall down. I categorized and entered the fingerprints from the door handle into AFIS, no matches on file. Also, I checked the weight on the bullet, figured I'd give you a head start. It's a .380. Same diameter as a 9 mm but weighs a bit less. Haven't gotten to the ballistics yet but I will in the morning. I'm planning to be in by eight-thirty. Later."

"Hey there, good lookin'," Diane said as she walked in carrying a large coffee of her own and commandeered one of the chairs across from Byron.

"Really?" he said, looking past her to the doorway.

"Relax, lover. Nobody's even here yet."

Their physical relationship had begun last fall, immediately after he'd been served with divorce papers by his ex. It bothered him how nonchalant Diane had become about their relationship. He wondered, and not for the first time, how badly things were likely to go if they were found out. Which one of them would LeRoyer kick out of the bureau? Or would Stanton see to it that they were both booted back to the street? Department regulations were very clear regarding fraternization between members of the same unit. They needed to be more careful.

"Didn't hear you take off last night," Byron said.

"I left about one. You were out cold. Must have been my little sleeping pill," she said with a wink. "Any word on the tox?"

"Ellis just called. Alcohol, coke, and fentanyl."

"Fentanyl? Thought our boy was just a blowhard."

"That's what I said. Doc said it's not unheard of for a user to experiment."

"Normal levels?"

"Who knows what was normal for Ramsey? Ellis said his BAC was .16 and the level of coke was typical."

"Anything from Gabe?"

"He left a message. No match on the print. The round is a .380."

"Ballistics?"

"He hasn't done that yet."

"Where do you want to start?"

"We've got a lot to do. I want to pay a visit to Ramsey's bosses at the firm, find out what they know and get some background on this guy who was threatening him. Also, we need a list of phone numbers and contact info from all of the firm's employees." He held up the subpoena. "We need to get this served on Ramsey's cell carrier and put Tran on the research. I want to know everyone Ramsey was in contact with leading up to his death. We need to find the asshole from the bar—"

"McVail?"

"Yeah, and the girl McVail was with. I may put Nuge and Mel on that. Anything else you can think of?"

"We should try and find out who Ramsey's supplier was. Ramsey may have been in arrears on his dope payments. I'll check with Crosby's guys and see if they've got a line on who's dealing at the Fox."

"Good. I'll reach out to the firm and put Dustin to work."

"Don't forget about the note from the Unicorn," she said.

"That's right. Talk to Joe?"

"Want me to check on that, too?"

"Nah. I'll give that to Dustin as well."

After Diane departed, Byron finished giving a cursory listen to the rest of his voicemail messages before heading down to see Tran in the computer lab. The only other noteworthy message was left by attorney Devon Branch, from the law firm of Newman, Branch & DeWitt, looking to have a sit-down. Byron wasn't surprised by the call. He figured Ramsey's former employer would look to minimize any exposure that might damage their reputation. And, as it so happened, Byron needed to find out a few things from them as well.

Detective Dustin Tran's office was located on the third floor of 109, next to the Regional Crime Lab. While technically the Computer Crimes Unit, it was only one room with one detective, Tran.

Tran was on the phone when Byron walked in. He held up a finger, signaling that he was almost finished.

"Yeah, that's what I thought as well," Tran said into the phone. "But after checking further into the subfiles on the C drive, I think there might be more."

The bulk of Tran's workload was searching the computers of predators for child pornography. Byron didn't care to think about what other files might be contained in whatever C drive subfiles Tran was checking. He perused the shelves stacked with computer towers and hard drives, all waiting to be analyzed. The heat generated by the electronics made the small room uncomfortably warm and gave it an oily mechanical smell. He wondered, and not for the first time, why if fighting cybercrime really was the inevitable future of law enforcement the city hadn't funded more than a single detective stuck in a closet. It felt more like the usual window dressing thinly applied to the issue of the day. Something he'd seen far too often in his twenty plus years.

"Okay," Tran said. "I'll let you know. Later, alligator." He hung up, turning his attention to Byron. "Morning, Striped One."

A typical greeting from his highly unorthodox detective. Tran was one part police officer and at least two parts computer geek. He wouldn't have lasted a day in the military, Byron thought, not with their rigid chain of command structure. But Tran was good at his job. He could sniff out information in his sleep and password cracking was one of his specialties. Every visit to the computer virtuoso was another reminder for Byron to change his own passwords.

"I've got some work for you," Byron said.

"Ramsey?" Tran asked excitedly.

"Ramsey," Byron said, nodding. "You got time?"

"For you, sire, I'll make time."

Byron handed him the subpoena that Ferguson had faxed overnight, then filled Tran in on everything he knew about Attorney Ramsey, his wife, Donald McVail, the law firm, and the name Joe. Tran promised to fill in the blanks ASAP.

Byron was exiting the fourth-floor stairwell when he bumped into Lieutenant LeRoyer.

"John, glad I caught you," LeRoyer said, falling into step with his sergeant.

"What's up?"

"Any progress?"

"No. Ramsey's still dead and we haven't made an arrest yet."

"Do you have to work at being such a prick or does it just come naturally?"

"It's early. Wait till I get warmed up."

"Stanton has commanded an audience," LeRoyer said.

"Give him my best."

LeRoyer scowled. "With both of us, sunshine."

"Great. Let me find Diane."

"Ah, she's gonna be busy for a bit."

"Doing?"

"I sent her to take care of something."

Byron stopped walking. "Might be nice if I knew what it was. She does work for me, Lieu."

"Yup, she does," LeRoyer said as he continued toward his office. "And last time I checked you work for me." He held up his arm and pointed to his watch. "Stanton's office, ten minutes."

ONE OF THE things Byron disliked most about Chief of Police Michael Stanton was his fondness for describing murder as nothing more than an aggravated assault that the victim never walked away from. Byron hated the dismissive implication in that statement. More than once he'd been forced to restrain himself from telling the chief exactly where he could stick that notion. Investigating and, more importantly, solving a murder requires commitment, even if Stanton couldn't comprehend it. Commitment to the deceased and a never-ending commitment to the victim's loved ones. Byron had always thought of murder as the theft of life, and unlike most thefts, there was no way to make restitution.

Stanton's office occupied most of the northeast corner of the fourth floor at 109 Middle Street. With the exception of the floor-to-ceiling window wall, every vertical surface in the spacious room was decorated in twenty-first-century egocentric, or what Byron sarcastically referred to as "walls of me." Pictures of Stanton posing with various celebrities and dignitaries adorned each wall from chair rail to ceiling. Byron counted at least three presidents, two major sports stars, and a foreign dignitary. Any space devoid of a photo was occupied by some award or plaque that had been presented to Stanton: Lawman of the Year, Elks Club Man of the Year, Parade Magazine Cop of the Year, et cetera. Stanton was a textbook narcissist. Byron wondered if any of the rooms at Casa Stanton were adorned in similar fashion and what shortcoming Stanton might be trying to overcome.

Byron and LeRoyer waited in awkward silence as Stanton finished up his business in his private washroom. Evidently, having your own washroom was another perk that came with being the head of Maine's largest municipal policy agency, Byron thought.

Stanton exited the bathroom drying his hands on a towel. "Gentlemen," he said. "Thank you both for coming on such short notice."

"Not a problem, Chief," LeRoyer said cheerfully.

Didn't realize I had a choice, Byron thought but did not say.

"How was your vacation?" LeRoyer asked.

"Oh, we had a great time down there, Marty. Either of you ever been to Tampa?"

Byron shook his head.

"The wife and I went once," LeRoyer said. "Left the kids with her parents. Got to see the Sox play at the Trop. Did you catch a game, Chief?"

"Nope, strictly the beach for me and the missus," Stanton said as he began knotting his tie into a Windsor.

"I was going to mention your tan," LeRoyer said.

It was all Byron could do not to roll his eyes.

"Gonna be a bitch keeping it up here," Stanton said as he plopped down in the chair behind his large wooden desk. He turned his attention to Byron. "I understand you're investigating a new homicide. How's it going?"

"Going okay. Still early."

"What can you tell me about the case?"

As little as humanly possible. "Not much to tell, really," he said. "Yesterday morning, we pulled Attorney Paul Ramsey out of the ocean behind Peaks."

"Drowning?" Stanton asked.

Byron could tell by Stanton's expression that the chief already knew better, but if he wanted to play twenty questions, Byron was more than willing to play along. "No."

"Do we have an official cause yet?"

"We're still waiting for the official report from the medical examiner, Chief," LeRoyer nervously interjected.

"So we don't know *anything* yet?" Stanton asked, raising a brow.

"Not until we have Dr. Ellis's findings," Byron said.

Stanton gave Byron a knowing glance before moving on. "We have any idea how he ended up in the ocean?"

Byron wondered what number question they were currently on. "Not yet."

"I know I don't have to tell you how sensitive this case is," Stanton said. "Ramsey was a lawyer with Newman, Branch & DeWitt, one of the city's largest firms."

"The biggest," LeRoyer chimed in, as if it somehow mattered to the case. It didn't.

Byron listened to Stanton pontificate, waiting for him to get to the point and wondering which of the three wise men had already reached out to the chief.

"I got a call last night from Devon Branch," Stanton said.

And we have a winner, Byron thought.

"Devon is a personal friend of mine and a major benefactor to this department. His firm has donated nearly all of the money for our K-9 program."

Byron figured the chief was likely personal friends with anyone willing to make him look good. Every chief wants a pet project to take credit for. Stanton's had been to update and expand Portland's K-9 unit, adding bomb detection, more training and equipment, including Kevlar for the dogs. Stanton had funded this effort with donations from Newman, Branch & DeWitt in the form of several rather large checks each delivered with plenty of fanfare in front of news cameras.

Stanton continued. "Devon expressed concern about details of the case coming out. Details which might reflect poorly on the firm."

"Details, Chief?" Byron said, aware LeRoyer was squirming uncomfortably in the chair beside him. It might even have been fun if Stanton wasn't once again trying to insert himself into one of Byron's cases. "What details are those? Does Branch have information pertinent to Ramsey's death?"

Stanton stared back at Byron, his displeasure obvious. "That's something you'll have to take up with him, *Sergeant*. My point is that I don't want us to be playing fast and loose with any aspect of this case." Stanton shifted his gaze toward LeRoyer. "And I don't want to read anything inflammatory in the papers."

Ironic, Byron thought, as it was often Stanton behind the media leaks.

"I'm aware that you and Ramsey had a history, Sergeant," Stanton said. "Don't let that history cloud your judgment."

"It won't," Byron said flatly.

After several more minutes of pointless chatter, Stanton dismissed Byron but told LeRoyer to stay behind. The after party where a real conversation would be had.

Byron left the office wondering why Devon Branch was working so quickly to circle the wagons. *What was it that the firm was so worried might come out? What was Ramsey involved in?* Time to pay a visit to Chief Stanton's benefactor.

"Marty, I want to discuss something else with you," Stanton said, following Byron's departure.

"Oh?" LeRoyer said, his curiosity piqued.

"Have you given any thought to the assistant chief's position?" Stanton asked.

"Hadn't really thought about it," LeRoyer lied. In fact, the department's number two seat was all he had thought about, ever since the death of its previous occupant, Reginald Cross, nearly eight months prior. LeRoyer, feeling his excitement building, was trying hard to remain outwardly calm.

"City Hall finally agreed to allow me to fill the slot," Stanton said. "Those tight-assed pricks on the finance committee made me wait so they could save a little money."

"Well, you've got some great people to choose from, Chief. I think either one of your captains would do a fine job."

Stanton looked thoughtfully across his desk at his CID lieutenant. "You think so?"

"Absolutely."

"What would you say if I told you that I've been considering you for that role?"

LeRoyer was momentarily speechless. "I—I'm not sure. You're serious?"

"Very much so," Stanton said with a grin. "Marty, I've given this a great deal of thought. I want you to be my right hand. I need a good man to help me steer this ship, keep her on course. I need someone I can trust to handle things, even when I'm not around."

"Don't you have to go through a process to fill that spot, testing or interviews or something?" LeRoyer asked as he wiped his sweaty palms on the legs of his slacks.

"Not this time. I got the city's blessing to go ahead and pick whomever I felt would do the best job."

"I don't know what to say, Chief."

Stanton's brow creased. "If you need time to think about it—"

"No, sir, I don't," LeRoyer said quickly, not wanting to show any indecisiveness. "I'd be honored to be your assistant, Chief."

"Good," Stanton said as he stood and came around from behind his desk to give his lieutenant a firm handshake. "Keep this between us for the time being, okay? I plan on making it official next month. After the start of the fiscal year."

"You won't be sorry, Chief."

"Now, about the Ramsey case. I want you to keep Byron on a short leash on this one. Understand?"

"I'll stay right on him."

"There are some powerful people connected to this case, Marty. And I don't want John stepping on their toes."

"Not to worry," LeRoyer said.

Stanton clapped him on the back. "I knew I picked the right man."

Chapter Nine

DIANE KNOCKED TENTATIVELY on the open door to the city manager's office. She saw City Manager Clayton Perkins conversing with Councilor Sheila Cornwell.

"Detective Joyner," Perkins said, rising from his chair and gesturing with his hand. "Please, come in."

Cornwell turned her head and smiled but remained seated.

The large room was excessively ornate, suggesting the power held by its occupant. All of the doors and windows were trimmed in dark richly grained hardwood. Matching crown molding bordered the fifteen-foot plaster ceiling.

Diane walked to the center of the office where she was met by Perkins's outstretched hand and a firm, enthusiastic shake.

Cornwell stood, slowly and deliberately smoothing her skirt before joining them in the center of the room.

"Councilor Cornwell and I were just discussing you."

"Diane," Cornwell said, dropping the formality of rank and extending a hand.

"Councilor," Diane said, tightly gripping Cornwell's hand. The chairwoman of the Public Safety Committee had either never learned the meaning of a firm grip or she was far less enthusiastic about Diane's presence. Diane guessed it was the latter.

Perkins gestured again to the decorative wood captain's chairs surrounding the expansive greeting area of the office. "Come, have a seat, Detective."

Diane struggled to maintain her friendly smile, although she was certain it looked as painted on as it felt. Perkins's smile appeared genuine but with career politicians you could never tell.

"How are things in the world of detectives?" he asked.

"Fine."

"Any interesting cases?"

"Well, we're working on the Ramsey homicide."

"Ah, Attorney Ramsey," Cornwell said.

"And how's it going?" Perkins asked.

"We're following leads," Diane said, still wondering why she'd been summoned.

"I suppose you're curious about why I asked you here?" Perkins said.

"A little. Am I in some kind of trouble?"

Perkins laughed. "Goodness, no, Detective."

Diane looked over at Cornwell. The councilor was wearing a grin on her face that was anything but genuine.

"It's about the sergeant's list," Cornwell said.

"That's right, Detective," Perkins said. "We understand that you've made the top of the list."

"Not exactly," Diane said. "I'm number five, so you'd never even get to me."

"Don't be so sure," Cornwell said.

"Afraid I'm not following," Diane said. "There is only one vacancy in the department, right? Don't you still take the top three names?"

"Correct," Perkins said. "If there were only *one* opening." He glanced at Cornwell.

"We've decided to create another sergeant's position within the department," Cornwell said.

"We want you for the new position," Perkins said.

"There are still four good officers ahead of me on the list," Diane said, not liking where things seemed to be headed. "I haven't even interviewed yet."

Perkins looked over at Cornwell and nodded.

"Diane, you're the only female in the top five," Cornwell said.

Don't you mean, black female? she thought.

"This department needs to be brought in line with the current century," Cornwell continued. "In the history of the Portland police, no woman has ever attained the rank of detective sergeant."

"I wouldn't be eligible for that job, even if there were an opening," Diane said. "If I accepted a promotion, I'd be probationary for the first six months. Probationary supervisors aren't eligible for specialty positions."

"Unless the chief of police deems it necessary for the betterment of the department," Perkins said, quoting the civil service language. "Detective, we've decided to create a new sergeant's position that would handle all press releases. A media relations sergeant, if you will."

"You would handle all of the inquiries from the press," Cornwell said. "And you'd be the liaison between Chief Stanton's office and the media."

"That's not exactly a detective sergeant's position," Diane said.

"You're right," Cornwell said. "It isn't. But in six months your probationary period would be up."

"And you'd be the new face of the department," Perkins added.

Diane thought it over in silence. She hadn't known why she'd been summoned to City Hall, but she certainly couldn't have imagined this. She'd only taken the test to keep her options open. She hadn't even told Byron. Things were happening much too quickly. "I'm not even sure I want a promotion," she said. "I took the sergeant's exam on a whim. I still enjoy working as a detective."

"And you're a good one," Perkins said.

"Just think how good a detective sergeant you could be," Cornwell said.

"What does Chief Stanton have to say about all of this?" Diane asked, looking from one to the other.

"Actually, it was his idea," Perkins said.

Cornwell nodded in agreement, giving another weak smile.

"So, what do you say, Sergeant Joyner?" Perkins asked.

BYRON RODE THE empty elevator to the tenth floor, the top of the Emerson Building. He stepped out into a brightly lit main lobby. The name of the firm was spelled out along the wall directly across from the elevator in garish chrome letters. Each of the letters was mounted away from the wall surface, far enough to cast a shadow beneath, creating the appearance that they were floating. Cream-colored Berber carpeting covered the floor and soft piano music drifted through the lobby from unseen speakers. A large window to his right overlooked Casco Bay, providing an impressive view of the harbor and islands beyond. He turned to his left where an attractive twentysomething brunette wearing a Bluetooth headset sat behind an ornate wooden counter bookended by two large potted ficus.

"May I help you?" Bluetooth asked, bestowing a warm and practiced smile.

"I hope so, Linda," he said after glancing at the name plate atop the counter. "I'm here to see Devon Branch."

"Actually, it's Amy. Our receptionist is off today." She glanced down at what he imagined was a day planner. "Is Attorney Branch expecting you?"

"He left a message requesting to speak with me. My name is John Byron," he said, displaying his badge and police identification.

"Detective Sergeant Byron," she said, reading from the ID. "If you'd care to take a seat, I'll see if he's in."

"Thank you."

Byron turned away from the desk and strolled over to one of four burgundy leather armchairs surrounding a chrome and glass coffee table. Briefly he perused an assortment of legal periodicals stacked upon the table before settling back empty-handed into a wingback to wait.

"Detective Sergeant," Amy said as she came out from behind the counter. "Attorney Branch will see you now. If you'll just follow me."

Interesting, he thought. *Demonstrating his importance by not coming out to greet me.*

Byron followed her down a long zigzagging hallway. Amy was easily a foot shorter than Byron, even with the heels she was wearing. He couldn't help but notice the tanned shapely legs protruding below her skirt. They passed at least a dozen other offices before finally stopping in front of a set of heavy-looking wooden double doors behind which, according to the brass plaque adorning the wall, sat the office of Devon Branch, Esquire.

She knocked before opening the right-hand door.

"Ah, Sergeant Byron," Branch said as he stood and approached them. "Thank you, Amy."

Branch looked to be midfifties, average height, slender build, receding sandy blond hair with a slight wave. The attorney's features had an almost feminine quality and his voice was rather meek, not at all what Byron had conjured up for one of the managing partners of Portland's most powerful law firm. He'd pictured someone more like Ramsey. Someone who exuded power. Byron wondered how many times during Branch's formative years he'd had his ass kicked and his lunch money stolen.

"Attorney Branch," Byron said, giving his hand a quick firm shake.

"Thank you for responding to my message so promptly," Branch said.

Byron's eyes shifted to the other man who also stood and walked toward them.

"This is Gerry DeWitt, one of the other principal partners in this firm. I invited him to join us."

DeWitt stuck out his hand. "A pleasure to meet you, Sergeant."

"Likewise," Byron said.

"Here," Branch said, gesturing toward a chair. "Have a seat, Sergeant Byron."

DeWitt, the taller and more handsome of the two men, returned to his chair in front of Branch's desk and Byron sat across from him.

Branch's corner office had a view even more spectacular than the one in the lobby, featuring two adjacent window walls that looked out across Portland's harbor and Casco Bay beyond. Byron noticed that unlike Chief Stanton's self-serving shrines of accomplishment, not a single plaque or award appeared on either of the remaining walls; displayed instead were nautical maps and several black and white poster-sized prints of a large sailboat being put through her paces on the open sea.

"Can I offer you anything to drink, Sergeant?" Branch said after the three men were seated.

"Probably too early for scotch," DeWitt said, addressing Byron.

"I'm fine, thank you. My condolences on the loss of your friend, gentlemen."

"Thank you, Sergeant," DeWitt said, giving a nod.

Branch fixed Byron with a perplexed look as if he hadn't understood Byron's gesture of goodwill. "Paul and I weren't friends, Sergeant Byron. We were merely associates in the same law firm."

"All the same."

"I appreciate your attempt at civility. However, I'm all too familiar with Paul's reputation within law enforcement circles. And I suspect you weren't a fan."

Byron got the feeling he was being tested. "I wasn't. But, personal feelings aside, I still have a case to solve."

"Ah, the case. Precisely why I contacted you," Branch said, leaning back in his chair as if waiting for Byron to enlighten him. "What can you tell us so far?"

"Nothing."

Branch lowered his brows disapprovingly. A gesture Byron took as an attempt to seem intimidating. It wasn't.

"How did Paul die?" Branch asked.

"Mr. Branch, this is an active investigation. My detectives and I aren't in the habit of giving out information. I'm here to gather information, from you. Specifically, I want to know if Ramsey had any enemies, if there had been any threats directed at him or the firm."

"Only one person I'm aware of. He'd left threatening messages on Paul's voicemail and occasionally on his email. But as you acknowledged, you weren't a fan and I suspect there were many who felt similarly."

"Tell me about the messages," Byron said.

Branch lay his hands across his stomach, interlocking his fingers. "Several years before Paul joined our firm he made a name for himself defending people on trial for murder. He was very successful getting defendants off either completely or convicted on a reduced charge like manslaughter."

"I assume that's why you hired him," Byron said, watching as the two attorneys exchanged a quick glance.

"Good litigators are hard to come by, Sergeant," Branch said. "Not only did Paul know how to pick a jury, he also knew how to manipulate its members. A skill which has paid great dividends to this firm."

"If he was so important to the firm, why wasn't he being considered for full partnership?" Byron asked in an attempt to verify Mrs. Ramsey's story.

"Actually, he was," DeWitt piped up.

"As I said, Paul had a pretty impressive track record at successfully defending murder suspects," Branch continued. "One of those cases was a twenty-three-year-old man accused of vehicular manslaughter in the death of his fiancée. Paul convinced the jury there was a possibility the victim was driving instead of the very intoxicated defendant."

"Reasonable doubt," Byron said.

"It's one of the ways we keep the lights on," DeWitt said.

"I remember reading about it. Is that case related to the threats against Ramsey?"

"It is," Branch said. "The victim's father, a man by the name of Matthew Childress, has struggled greatly in coping with her death. He has also taken umbrage with Ramsey's convincing the jury that Childress's daughter may have caused the accident."

"Why blame Ramsey?" Byron asked. "Why not the defendant that Childress's daughter was engaged to?"

"The defendant's family whisked him away from here," Branch said. "Rumor has it they got him out of the country. Childress probably doesn't know how to locate them."

"What about the threats from Childress?" Byron asked. "Did Ramsey take them seriously?"

"Not really," DeWitt said. "Mr. Childress gets liquored up every so often and starts leaving messages and emails. It's understandable."

Byron could relate. Alcohol and grief had caused sufficient damage to his own life. "Even so, I'll need his name and contact info. We'll need to speak with him."

"I'll make sure you have them before you leave," Branch said.

"Also, I'll need a list of all the firm's employees and contact info, including phone numbers."

"Why would you need that?" DeWitt asked.

"We've subpoenaed Ramsey's cell records. We want to know who he was in communication with before he died."

"You think he knew the killer?" Branch asked.

"It's always something we look at. More often than not,

murderers tend to exist within the victim's circle of acquaintances. Will you provide me with a list?"

"I'll have a PDF printed for you before you leave."

"I'd also like a look at his email communications."

Branch shook his head. "I'm afraid that's not possible. Too much sensitive information. Besides, unlike his cellphone, Ramsey's email and computer belong to this firm. They're protected."

"What about personal emails?" Byron asked. "They wouldn't fall under that umbrella. There may well be something helpful contained in them."

Branch looked over at DeWitt and nodded.

"We'd have to scour his account to see if there were any such emails," DeWitt said. "That will take some time."

"I'll need you to do that as soon as possible," Byron said. "In cases like this, time is of the essence."

"I'll assign one of the paralegals to go through his electronic files today," Branch said. "Okay?"

Byron nodded. It wasn't the best scenario but he figured it was as much as he could hope for. "What about the civil trial your firm just lost?"

Branch frowned again and turned to DeWitt.

"You think there could be a link between our wrongful death suit and Ramsey's death?" DeWitt asked.

"According to yesterday's paper, the family you were representing, the Elwells, just lost ten million dollars, and Ramsey was the lawyer of record. I'd say it might be a motive."

"I'm afraid the details of that suit are also privileged information," Branch said.

"But not for the plaintiffs. I want to speak with the family."

"I can get you their contact information, Sergeant, but there's no guarantee they'll want to speak with you, nor are they obligated to."

"I'll worry about that," Byron said.

The door to Branch's office opened. "Devon, I just finished looking over the—Oh, I'm sorry. I didn't know you were in a meeting."

"It's okay," Branch said. "Gerry and I were just speaking with Detective Sergeant Byron about Paul Ramsey. Sergeant, this is my wife, Lorraine."

Dressed in a formfitting gray skirt and cream-colored blouse, neither of which left much to the imagination, she was strikingly beautiful.

Byron stood and extended a hand. "Pleased to meet you, Mrs. Branch."

"Actually, it's Davies," she said, giving him a firm and prolonged handshake and a smile of perfectly aligned teeth. Her steel blue eyes sparkled and her long blond hair framed an unblemished face.

"My wife doesn't believe in that taking the husband's last name thing," Branch said.

"It's a bit too old-fashioned for my liking, Sergeant. Stifling, really. I'm more of a progressive." Davies released his hand. "Well, I don't want to intrude. I'll leave you gentlemen to it. We can go over this later, darling," she said, waving a stack of papers at Branch. She turned her attention back to Byron. "A pleasure to meet you, Sergeant Byron."

"Likewise."

Byron watched Davies walk back toward the door, in heels that were almost too long to be professional, before closing it softly behind her.

"She's smart, too," Branch said, obviously having caught Byron's wandering eye.

"How's that?" Byron said, seating himself back in the chair, trying to pretend he wasn't checking her out.

"I don't blame you for looking but there's more to her than meets the eye. Top of her class at Harvard. She's only been here for six years and she's already being considered for senior partner status. Isn't that right, Gerry?"

"It's true," DeWitt agreed.

Probably didn't hurt that she married a principal partner, Byron thought. He wondered how someone like Devon Branch had managed to end up with someone as beautiful and smart as Davies. If she was as bright as Branch indicated, she should have held out for a better husband. One that didn't talk about her like she was some trophy he'd won.

"Back to the matter at hand," Branch said. "I must say, I am pleased to find you unwilling to give out information on this case. Are we to assume you'll maintain the same discretion in dealing with the media? While I confess I'm not the least bit concerned with Paul Ramsey's reputation, I am with this firm's. And I'd prefer not having anything Paul may have done or been involved in sully the good name of Newman, Branch & DeWitt."

"Especially the Branch name, I imagine," Byron said.

Branch frowned again. "My father started this practice, Sergeant."

Byron studied the faces of both attorneys. "What exactly was Ramsey into that has you so worried?"

BYRON HAD LEARNED long ago not to get caught up in the panic and maniacal behavior exhibited by some of the police command staff as they scurried about like ants after sugar, seeking immediate results. Slow and methodical was the only way to construct a solid murder case. As he often pointed out to the new detectives, investigating crimes after the fact is a far cry from responding to them as they're actually occurring. And investigating homicides is an altogether different animal. There's never a good reason to rush any aspect of an investigation; the victim is already dead. Rushing only leads to mistakes and mistakes lead to cases falling apart during the years of scrutiny that inevitably follow. Motions to exclude evidence, motions to overturn decisions, motions for new trials—so many things were out of Byron's hands after he turned a case over to the courts. An airtight case was built one piece of evidence at a time until a formidable mountain had been constructed, impervious to judicial erosion. Byron's motto had always been: Be as thorough as possible while you still have control.

Byron left Branch's office with more questions than answers, but he had obtained the information necessary to follow up on two different leads: Childress, the building contractor who'd made repeated threats against Ramsey, and Justin and Paula Elwell, plaintiffs in the recently lost civil trial. Both had lost a child and although Ramsey wasn't responsible for either he had played a hand in how both cases were resolved. And neither party was happy with the resolution.

According to the article Byron had read in the *Portland Herald*, written by Davis Billingslea, the Elwells had brought suit against Maine Medical Center, charging that their son was misdiagnosed by one of the hospital's specialists. That surgeon elected to remove their son's spleen. What the Elwells deemed an unnecessary surgery resulted in complications which caused their seventeen-year-old son, Robbie, to lapse into a coma. Following a three-week stint in intensive care, with intravenous feeding, Robbie died. Ramsey filed the malpractice suit on behalf of the Elwells, seeking ten million in damages.

Had the Elwells' loss driven them over the edge? Byron wondered. Had someone in the family felt wronged enough to kill? If so, was the surgeon now in danger?

He clicked the remote, unlocking the doors to the Malibu, and was climbing inside when he noticed a parking citation pinned beneath the windshield wiper.

Fuckin' Greene, he thought as he snatched up the ticket. Sure enough, the parking control Nazi's badge number, 121, was penned in next to an expired meter violation.

"It wasn't expired, dumb-ass," Byron said. "Can't be expired if I never paid."

He reached across the console and crammed it into the glove box along with the others. As he inserted the key into the ignition, his cell rang. Detective Mike Nugent.

"Hey, Nuge."

"Calling to see if you could use a little help with Ramsey."

"Indeed, I could. Where are you?"

"Mel and I are just leaving 109. Wanna meet up?"

Byron checked his watch. It was only ten-thirty but his stomach was already grumbling over the lack of breakfast. "How about Becky's Diner?"

"See you there, Sarge."

Chapter Ten

DICKENS'S SCROOGE HAD been warned by Marley that the spirit within every man was required to go out and walk far and wide in support of his fellow men, and if not in life they would be condemned to do so after death. As Byron sat at the Commercial Street diner, sipping hot coffee from a chipped white and blue ceramic mug, he couldn't help wondering what Ramsey's condemnation might look like.

He'd commandeered an empty booth at the rear allowing him to sit with his back to the wall. The habit of positioning oneself for a tactical advantage was second nature to any veteran cop, an automatic reflex like breathing or blinking. He never consciously thought about it until someone said something. Kay, his ex, had always teased him for it and would often intentionally grab the seat she knew he'd want when they went out. Taking him out of his comfort zone, she'd called it.

Why the hell are you thinking about Kay? He didn't know, but she'd been occupying his thoughts a lot of late. Perhaps it was some psychobabble ex-spouse PTSD, he thought. Whatever the reason, he didn't need Kay taking up space in his head. He had enough going on up there as it was.

"Hey, Sarge," Detective Melissa Stevens said as she and Nugent slid into the booth across from Byron.

Stevens and Nugent had been an unlikely pairing as partners. Stevens was single, gay, and paid homage to her no-nonsense attitude by wearing her blond hair short and spiky. Nugent, on the other hand, was follicularly challenged, married, with two kids, and had a truckload of inappropriate vaudevillian humor always at the ready, the likes of which would have made Henny Young-man proud. The two detectives had asked to be assigned together following the retirement of Detective Ray Humphrey, Byron's one-time mentor and friend. They say opposites attract, but at the time Byron had merely considered it an experiment. He'd never imagined it would actually take, and yet somehow it had.

"So Paul Ramsey finally got his, huh?" Stevens said.

"Saints be praised," Nugent said, speaking in an improvised Irish brogue. "Couldn't have happened to a nicer guy."

"How'd he buy it?" Stevens asked with a twinkle in her eye.

Byron pointed at his own forehead making an *L* with his index finger and thumb. "Handgun. Close range."

"Yowch, that leaves a mark," Nugent said. "Where's Diane?"

"Ah, I don't know," Byron said, momentarily dropping his guard and allowing his frustration to show. "The lieutenant's got her doing some secret errand or something."

He saw Stevens and Nugent exchange a quick glance, but neither commented.

A no-nonsense waitress with curly black hair strolled up to the table with a fresh carafe of caffeine. She wordlessly held it up and both detectives nodded. "Either of you eating?" she asked.

Both responded in the negative.

After flipping their mugs upright and pouring, she topped off Byron's then departed.

"So, what's the latest?" Stevens asked.

Between cups of coffee and a heaping plate of corned beef hash, scrambled eggs, and home fries, Byron brought both detectives up to speed, recapping the previous day's recovery dive, right through his meetings with Stanton and Branch.

"Nice to see the chief didn't waste any time sticking his nose in," Stevens said.

Byron couldn't have agreed more, but resisted the urge to comment, burying his thoughts under a forkful of hash.

"So, what's the plan?" Nugent asked.

"As soon as Diane's finished doing whatever it is she's doing, we're gonna head down to Kennebunkport," Byron said.

"What's in Kennebunkport?" Stevens asked.

"Matt Childress."

"Who's he?" both detectives asked at once.

"Some big-time York County commercial building contractor."

"Never heard of him," Nugent said.

"Lost his daughter in a drunk driving accident," Byron said. "Sounds like her fiancé was probably driving but Ramsey got him off at trial."

"There's a shocker," Nugent said. "Hey, how many jurors does it take to screw in a lightbulb?"

Stevens rolled her eyes at her partner's inappropriateness.

"Anyway," Byron continued unabated. "According to Branch,

Childress has been threatening Ramsey. Blames him for getting the fiancé off."

"I blame the educational system," Nugent said as he reached over and stole one of Byron's home fries.

"Where would you like Nuge and me to start, Sarge?" Stevens asked, ignoring him.

"Why don't you see if you can find the asshole from the Red Fox, Donny McVail."

BYRON WAS STILL pissed that Diane wouldn't divulge the secret errand she'd been sent on as they drove into the town of Kennebunkport, but he was trying hard not to show it.

"This looks like the place," Diane said.

Byron looked up at the large black and white Childress Construction banner hanging on the side of the unfinished building. He turned left off Route 9 onto the packed gravel drive, which, at least according to the sign, would eventually be the corporate headquarters of Down East Credit Union. "I'd say Mr. Childress is a little more than some guy who occasionally gets drunk and leaves threatening messages."

"Think Branch underestimated him?" she asked.

"A bit. How much do you figure this project is worth?"

"Millions."

Byron slowed to let a large flatbed delivery truck cross in front of them before continuing on. He guided the unmarked Chevy toward the center of the dusty lot and a group of long white trailers. The trailers were the kind used by contractors as mobile offices. He parked between two oversized green pickups, each possessing dual rear wheels and bearing the Childress company logo on their doors. The registration plates bore commercial variants of CCC—Childress Construction Company—followed by a number. One of the plates read "CCC-1." Byron guessed it was Childress's truck. Mounted to the windshield of the truck was a blue E-ZPass device. Byron despised the blue ones as they tended to make every vehicle look like an undercover police vehicle. The truck was also tricked out with extra chrome not affixed to any of the others.

The two detectives climbed the mud-caked steps to a makeshift plywood platform. Byron banged on the dented aluminum trailer door.

"Come!" a brusque male voice said from inside.

They stepped into the cramped and cluttered trailer. A burly unshaven male with a sunburned face was stooped over a metal bench, looking at blueprints. He wore brown Carhartt pants, tan work boots, and a tight-fitting green T-shirt emblazoned with the Childress logo.

Fuck, I hope this isn't him, Byron thought as he studied the veins on his bulging biceps.

"Help ya?" the man said, standing upright as he turned to face them.

They both produced their department IDs and badges.

"We're looking for Matthew Childress," Byron said.

"You found him," Childress said.

The driver license info they'd obtained from Maine's Bureau of Motor Vehicles obviously hadn't been updated. Childress was taller than Byron by several inches, making him at least six foot seven. Byron guessed his weight to be in the neighborhood of 275, none of which appeared flabby. Byron wished they'd brought the entire detective division, maybe even a couple of uniformed backups.

Childress's eyes moved from Byron to Diane, where they lingered before returning to Byron. "What'd he do now?"

"Who?" Diane said as she pocketed her credentials.

"Mattie Junior. Figure if you're from Portland, he's done something stupid again. Fuckin' Old Port is the bane of my goddamned existence."

Byron exchanged looks with Diane then quickly scanned the room for weapons. The closest thing he could find was a nylon tool belt with a hammer, lying on a table about five feet away from the big man.

Childress leaned back against the bench and folded his arms across his expansive chest. "The wife and I don't pay all that tuition to the University of Send Me Money so he can major in fuckin' barhopping. So, what's he done?"

"Mr. Childress, my name is Detective Sergeant Byron and this is Detective Joyner. We're not here about your son."

Childress raised an eyebrow. "Oh?"

"We came to speak with you," Byron said.

"Me?"

Byron kept an eye on Childress's hands. He knew if there was a point at which this interview was likely to go to shit, they'd reached it.

"We're investigating the death of Paul Ramsey," Diane said.

Childress's mouth spread into a grin that Byron wasn't sure how to take.

"Heard they found that piece of shit dead," Childress said matter-of-factly. "Can't say that breaks my fucking heart."

"Where did you hear that?" Byron asked.

"On the radio this morning. How'd he die?"

"We don't know yet," Diane said.

"We fished him out of Casco Bay yesterday," Byron said.

"And now you're here because you think I killed him, right?" Childress said.

"We don't think anything, Mr. Childress," Byron said. "But we do know you have a history with the deceased."

"A history? Is that what I have?" Childress looked toward the floor and rubbed his right hand over his beard stubble.

Byron was on guard, waiting for any sudden move on Childress's part. He knew from Diane's body language that she was ready too.

"Mr. Childress, where were you Tuesday night?" Byron asked.

MELISSA STEVENS WAS scanning the visitor's computer monitor in the Records Division on the second floor of 109, while Nugent played with one of the Lektrievers occupying the middle of the room. The giant storage unit's resemblance to supermarket rotisserie ovens ended with the thousands of police file folders crammed inside, that and the absence of the aroma of roast chicken.

"Wish I'd invented this stupid thing," Nugent said as he continued to play with the rocker switch, periodically reversing the direction the shelves rotated. "I'd be rich."

"Okay, I got something," Stevens said.

"Give me a number," Nugent said.

"Fifteen dash thirteen one eighty-five. Looks like his latest arrest. Disorderly and possession."

Nugent brought the Lektriever to a stop on one of the shelves containing the 2015 case files. He scanned the folders until he located the corresponding numbers then pulled the file.

"Find it?" Stevens asked.

"I think so. Yup, here it is. Donald McVail, arrested for disorderly and possession of a controlled substance. Says here he's on probation."

"Good. What about a work or home address?"

"Uh-huh, both. Gotcha, douchebag."

A HALF HOUR later Byron and Diane sat at a red light in the left-turn lane of Route 1 in Biddeford, waiting to jump on the turnpike toward Portland.

"You believe him?" Diane asked.

"He didn't seem all that surprised to see us," Byron said.

"No, he didn't."

Diane punched redial on her cell and put the phone to her ear. "It's still going to voicemail."

"So, either Childress's alibi has his phone off or he's on the phone right now, getting his story straight. Either way, it won't be worth much." Byron pulled out his cell and dialed Nugent. "Nuge, it's Byron. Any luck locating McVail?"

"Not yet. We found his apartment but he wasn't answering. Mel's talking with a friend of his who may know where he works."

"Didn't we have a work address from his last arrest?"

"We did, but he got canned from that job right after the arrest. He's on probation but his PO hasn't called back yet."

"Give Tran a buzz. He's like a hound dog."

"Will do. How'd you guys make out with Childress?"

"He denies any involvement. Says he was at his brother-in-law's Tuesday night, watching the Celtics game."

"Tough game. You happen to catch it, Sarge?"

"Missed that one."

"What did he say about Ramsey being dead?"

Byron looked over at Diane. "I think it made his day."

"Ha! I'll bet."

"Listen, Nuge, we're on our way back. Let me know as soon as you find him." Byron hung up just as Diane reached Childress's brother-in-law.

"Hello, Everett?" Diane said, putting the phone on speaker. "Everett Mead?"

"Yeah. You the detective who called?"

"This is Detective Joyner. I'm from the Portland Police Department."

There was a brief pause at the other end of the line. "What can I help you with, Detective?"

"Everett, I'm investigating a case and I need to know if you're free to meet up with me so we can talk."

"Well, I'm kinda busy at work right now. How about I call you back later?"

"Actually, it's kind of important that I see you now. Are you still employed by Milford Chevrolet in Saco?"

"Ah, yeah. But like I said, I'm working."

Byron could hear the wavering in Mead's voice as he struggled to avoid meeting Diane.

"That's okay, Everett. It'll only take a second. I'm right around the corner."

"Well, I, ah—"

"See you in a minute," Diane said as she disconnected the call. "Think he's pissin' his pants right now?"

"Or worse," Byron said, grinning as he signaled and coasted off the pike onto the Saco connector.

They managed to hit every single one of the half dozen red lights between the off-ramp and the dealership.

"So much for element of surprise," Diane said as Byron swung into the lot of Milford Chevrolet. "Watch out!" she yelled as a large white F-250 cut directly in front of them without stopping.

"What the fuck!" Byron stood on the brakes, making the antilock mechanism kick in. The front of the Malibu missed striking the side of the truck by inches.

The male driver of the pickup never slowed as he continued north on Route 1. The sound of acceleration roared from the tuned exhaust.

"You okay?" Byron asked.

"Fine," she said as she bent to retrieve several folders and an empty Styrofoam coffee cup from the floor beneath the dash. "What the fuck is wrong with people?"

"Wonder how many times they've had a vehicle totaled during a test drive?" he asked.

"I don't care if he totals it, just as long as he doesn't kill us."

Byron drove to the far end of the lot, parking the car near the rear of the building beside two large open bay doors. Hanging on the wall between the doors was a sign identifying the building as the Parts and Service Division.

The sharp sputtering of air wrenches and revving engines was earsplitting as he and Diane strolled through the cavernous garage bay. A dozen vehicles of various makes and models were hoisted up on hydraulic lifts. He wondered how many of the mechanics would need hearing aids by the time they were his age, if not sooner.

The counter was manned by two service technicians dressed in white smocks. Standing in their spotless outfits, they bore a closer resemblance to physicians than auto dealership employees. The detectives approached the younger of the techs who was bent over the counter scribbling out information on a form while his partner, the more seasoned of the two, was busy arguing with an unhappy balding male customer over the cost of a repair.

"We're looking for Everett," Diane said, intentionally keeping her ID hidden.

"He expecting you?" the dark-haired young man inquired as he looked up from his paperwork.

"Yes," she said. "We just spoke on the phone. He told me to come right in and ask for him."

"I don't care what your bill says," the customer barked angrily to the other tech. "You guys never called me to tell me it was gonna be more. I never authorized this repair."

The young tech glanced at Byron, rolled his eyes, then pointed to an office on the second level. "His office is upstairs. Go on up."

They climbed the metal grate steps to the upper level and entered through a heavy glass door. The administrative offices were much quieter. Byron guessed the glass windows overlooking the garage were thicker than normal, providing soundproofing.

A middle-aged woman with horn-rimmed glasses sat behind a desk surrounded by metal file cabinets. She was just hanging up the phone as they entered. "Can I help you?" she said.

"We're here to see Everett," Diane said. "Everett Mead."

"And you are?"

They both produced their IDs for her examination.

"Well, Detectives, he just stepped out for a moment. Not sure if he's in the building. I'll try paging him."

"Thank you," Diane said.

Byron walked over to the far wall where pictures and various awards were hung. He couldn't help but be reminded of Chief Stanton's office back at 109. The common denominator in each of the photos was a short, pudgy, heavily freckled man, glad-handing various NASCAR drivers and dignitaries. Byron guessed this was Mead.

"Everett Mead, please report to the service office." They could hear the secretary's voice both within the confined space of the office and simultaneously reverberating throughout the building over a PA system.

As they waited, Byron approached the windows that overlooked the entire garage bay. He was scanning the room below as Diane walked up and stood beside him.

"Right there," Byron said, pointing to an open bay door where a heavyset male in a gray suit was talking animatedly on a cellphone while looking up at them.

"Mead?" she whispered.

Byron shook his head then answered in his own quiet voice. "No." He cocked his thumb toward the wall. "Mead's the guy in those pictures. But I'll bet a week's pay that guy down there is talking to him. Probably reporting on what we're doing."

The phone on the secretary's desk rang, and she answered.

"Milford Chevrolet, Parts and Service. Vicky speaking."

Both Byron and Diane turned to look.

"Oh, Everett, yeah, there's a couple of Portland detectives here to speak with you. Uh-huh."

Byron made eye contact with Mead's secretary, trying to get a read. Her expression wasn't giving away a thing.

"Okay. Alright, then. I'll tell them." She returned the receiver to its cradle. "I'm sorry, Detectives. Mr. Mead's been called away on an emergency."

Byron studied the faint roses blooming on Vicky's face. There was no doubt she was covering for her boss. She was telling the same little white lie Byron himself had asked his own secretary, Shirley Grant, to tell countless times. It was a perfect way to avoid speaking with anyone he didn't wish to.

"Thanks," Diane said. The word tinged with obvious sarcasm.

Byron turned back to look at the suit on the phone, but the suit had vanished.

"Mr. Mead said if you wanted to leave me your number he'll get in touch with you later," Vicky said, completing the fib.

"Here," Diane said, handing her a business card. "But don't have him go to any trouble. We've already got *his* number."

They turned to leave but, as he was prone to doing, Byron stopped, hand on the doorknob, and turned back toward Vicky the secretary.

"Just out of curiosity, does your boss drive a dealership car?"

"Certainly," she said. Her annoyed tone suggesting that Byron's question was ludicrous. As if a man of Everett Mead's stature would drive anything less. "All the management staff at Milford drive dealership cars."

"Let me guess," Byron said. "He probably gets a flashy red Camaro?"

Mead's secretary laughed, momentarily dropping her guard. "Not since last summer. No, he drives a full-sized pickup now."

"A black one?" he asked, already knowing the answer.

"No, white. Why do you ask?"

Byron and Diane exchanged glances.

"Thanks again," Diane said. "And tell Mario Andretti we'll be in touch."

"INTERESTING," DIANE SAID, holding her phone to her ear as they walked back to the car.

"What?" Byron asked.

"Mead's not answering his cell. Straight to voicemail."

"Go figure."

"Childress's alibi already ducking us. Damn near killed us actually."

"Maybe Childress picked the wrong guy to give him an alibi."

"You wouldn't have picked your brother-in-law?" she said smugly.

"No, but mine was kind of an asshole anyway, so I'm probably not the best person to ask."

They climbed into the car and Byron backed out of the parking spot.

"Shit," she said, looking down at her phone.

"What?"

"I missed a text from LeRoyer. He needs to see me ASAP."

"What the fuck? Not like we're working a homicide or anything."

"We're heading back to Portland anyway, right?"

"Let me guess, another secret meeting?"

Diane glared at him. "I don't know yet, do I?"

He stopped at the edge of the lot, where it met the roadway, waiting for a break in traffic.

"How we doing your way?" he asked Diane.

"Clear if you go right now."

He accelerated out onto Route 1, merging into the passing lane back toward Portland.

"So," Diane said. "Assuming Childress's and Mead's wives actually were in Boston shopping, what do think has Mr. Parts and Service so spooked?"

Before Byron could answer, his cell rang. Tran.

"Hey, Dustin."

"Striped One, think I located McVail."

Chapter Eleven

Friday, 12:45 P.M., April 29, 2016

BYRON DROPPED DIANE at 109 for her meeting with LeRoyer. He then met up with Nugent and Stevens. After a brief strategy session, the three detectives drove directly to Union Wharf, just off Commercial Street. McVail worked at Mercer Seafood, whose fish processing facility was housed in a large orange two-story warehouse that ran the length of the wharf. Byron knew the business well, having served many arrest warrants there. Publicly, Mercer Seafood touted themselves as hirers of Portland's most diverse workforce, making them golden in the eyes of the city council. In reality, they habitually employed less than savory characters who, due to criminal records, weren't likely to find employment elsewhere. The only thing more diverse than Mercer's workforce were the crimes they'd committed.

Byron parked his car off to the left side of the corrugated steel building; Stevens and Nugent pulled in beside him.

He stepped out of the Malibu directly into an oil-slicked fishy-smelling puddle. "Fuck," he said as the cold water entered his shoe, saturating his sock.

"Puddle?" Nugent asked, taking a page out of LeRoyer's book, stating the obvious.

"How'd you guess," Byron growled. "Dammit. Right in it." He glanced at them and saw both detectives attempting to hide their amusement. As Byron leaned against his car and removed the shoe, he hoped the puddle wasn't an omen.

Tran had described Donald McVail as a two-bit punk with priors for aggravated assault, criminal threatening, and carrying a concealed weapon. He was also currently on probation and had a reputation for fleeing whenever the police showed up. Armed with this information, Byron figured they'd use McVail's reputation against him.

The three detectives sidestepped the front office, not wanting to take a chance on McVail being tipped to their presence until they were ready, opting instead for the open loading dock doors along the building's east side.

They climbed rusty grated metal steps onto a cement platform where a beefy-looking guy, wearing a filthy white Mercer Seafood smock and matching hard hat, was busy moving stacks of opaque plastic tubs onto a box truck, which had been backed up to the loading dock.

"Excuse me," Byron said, pulling out his ID. "We're—"

"Cops, right?"

"Right," Byron said, glancing at the other two detectives and returning the unopened ID case to his jacket pocket.

"Suits gave you away." He removed a glove and wiped the sweat from his brow with the back of his hand. "Who you lookin' for today?"

"Donald McVail," Stevens said.

"Donny, huh? Figures." Beefy pointed inside the warehouse, toward the back of the loading area. "Through those double doors. He's down back, on the processing line."

Byron looked wordlessly at Nugent.

"We'll take the back," Nugent said as he and Stevens walked back down the stairs toward the far end wharf.

Byron paused a moment, giving his detectives time to get into position.

"Expecting trouble?" Beefy asked.

"Always," Byron said.

DIANE PLODDED DOWN 109's back stairwell to the plaza. Her mind swirled like river whitewater. LeRoyer hadn't pressured her, but he had added his two cents to the mix. She knew Ramsey's murder was supposed to be occupying most of her gray matter but the possibility of promotion had now wedged its way in, along with her guilt at not telling John about the sergeant's exam.

She'd told herself that she was taking the test to keep her options open, options she'd need if her relationship with John were ever found out. Forced transfer from CID for one or both of them would be the likely punishment. Besides, what was her relationship with John, anyway? An occasional dinner out, under the guise of friendship, followed by the occasional romp in the proverbial hay, under the guise of lovers. If taking the test had only been a way to keep her options open, why then did it feel as if those options were quickly evaporating? And what the hell was up with City Manager Perkins and that bitch Cornwell? What did they think they were doing, dangling the first female detective sergeant carrot in front of her? Were they expecting her to just jump at the chance to be, what? The department's token spokesmodel? Neither of them said it, but they hadn't needed to. Her being black would be a double coup for the city. An African-American woman promoted to the rank of detective sergeant. That's what this was really all about, she thought. The city was dealing her the race card from the bottom of the deck, expecting her to play it. *Fuck that. I've never even been to Africa. I'd be the token American Black Woman.* She'd never considered herself to be anyone's token anything. And, dammit, she wasn't about to start now.

BYRON QUICKLY SCANNED the processing lines in the noisy production room. Dozens of men and women cutting, filleting, and packing various varieties of seafood. He stepped back to allow a forklift carrying a full pallet to pass. He spotted Donny McVail gutting fish in the last row just as the young man looked up.

McVail lowered his hands slightly while maintaining eye contact with Byron. He paused for only a moment, then spun to his right and bolted toward the back end of the warehouse.

"He's rabbiting," Byron yelled into the portable radio as he gave chase. "Dispatch copy?"

"Ten-four, 720," the dispatcher said. "One-oh-one copy?"

"One-oh-one, negative!"

"Respond to Union Wharf. 720 is in foot pursuit."

"En route!"

DIANE PUNCHED THE remote entry button on her key, unlocking the door to her unmarked, and slid inside. She sat in solitude, keys in hand, letting her thoughts wander. *Where would the CID opening come from?* Six months, Perkins had said. None of the CID sergeants had tested for lieutenant, at least as far as she knew. *Did they mean John?* Perkins said it was the chief's idea. LeRoyer implied the same thing. *Was Stanton planning to force John out?*

This was becoming absurd. Her emotions threatened to overtake her. She could feel the hot sting of tears. How could she have allowed herself to be manipulated like this? Why had she taken that damned test in the first place? Or gotten involved with John? *Where had that thought come from?*

She closed her eyes, drew a deep breath. After composing herself, she inserted the key into the ignition and turned it forward.

The base crackled with distorted radio traffic. People were frantically covering each others' transmissions. Something was going on.

"One-oh-one, negative!"

"Respond to Union Wharf. 720 is in foot pursuit."

"En route!"

McVail. Diane slammed the shift lever into Drive, activated the blues and siren, and tromped on the accelerator, tires screeching as she maneuvered out of the garage toward the waterfront.

BYRON WAS DOING his best to keep up, but the smooth soles of his dress shoes provided little in the way of traction on the damp concrete as he dodged pallets of seafood. He briefly lost sight of McVail as the young man passed through a heavy plastic thermal curtain into the back of the warehouse. Byron slowed and pulled his sidearm. He hadn't seen whether or not McVail tossed the knife but it didn't matter. Best to assume he was armed. Whoever murdered Ramsey had shot him, and Byron had no intention of being the next victim. Cautiously, but quickly, Byron parted the curtain, leading with the barrel of his Glock 9 mm. He caught a flash of movement to his left, turning to look just as McVail hit the metal crash bar on an exterior door. One moment McVail was silhouetted in the open doorway, the next he was gone. The door slammed shut.

Fuck. Byron sprinted toward the door while keying the portable mic. "He made it out the back."

DIANE SLOWED FOR the red light at Union and Commercial, her siren still blaring, just as a black-and-white came screeching into the intersection from her left, turning onto the wharf. She eased the Ford out onto Commercial Street, eyes darting left, right, and left again, trying to avoid being T-boned by one of her own or some civilian with their head up their ass. All clear. She mashed the accelerator pedal and shot through the intersection.

Diane tailed the cruiser onto the wharf, racing down the left side of the building until neither vehicle could go any farther. She stood on the brakes, popped her seat belt, jammed the transmission into Park. She was out of the car before it had ceased moving.

BYRON BURST THROUGH the gray steel door onto the rear steps. Brilliant sunshine assaulted his eyes. He squinted as he scanned the area, waiting for them to adjust.

Nugent and Stevens were standing in the alley, thirty feet away, next to a stack of wooden pallets. McVail lay on the ground at their feet, moaning.

Byron holstered his sidearm just as Diane and a uniformed officer came sprinting around the corner of the building. "What happened?" Byron asked.

Nugent grinned. "Mel was just giving young Mr. McVail a lesson in physics. A body in motion tends to stay in motion unless acted upon by an equal or greater force." Nugent looked on as the uniformed cop helped Stevens search and handcuff McVail. "End of the lesson, punk."

Stevens stood up and looked at Nugent. "Who are you supposed be, Clint Eastwood?"

"Dirty Nugent," he said in a deeper than normal voice.

Byron keyed the portable radio mic. "Suspect in custody."

"Ten-four, 720."

Byron turned to Diane.

"Where the hell have you been?"

BYRON WAS SITTING on a bench in the CID locker room, changing out of his wet socks and dress shoes, when Lieutenant LeRoyer walked in.

"Heard you guys had a foot chase," LeRoyer said. "What happened?"

"Not much of a chase, I'm afraid," Byron said without looking up. "It was over when McVail met up with Mel's elbow."

"So he's not here voluntarily?"

"Did you really think he would be?" Byron raised his head. "Any chance you're done playing secret squirrel with my detective?"

"Ah, she's still *my* detective, Sergeant. And, in answer to your question, yes. I'm done. For the time being."

"Great," he growled. "When is someone going to tell me what the hell is going on?"

"That's up to Diane." LeRoyer directed his gaze toward Byron's replacement footwear. "Nice sneakers. Very stylish. Business casual?"

"Very funny. They're the only thing I have that doesn't smell like fish."

LeRoyer approached the sink, and checked himself in the mirror. "Think he'll talk?"

"We'll know soon enough," Byron said.

"Can we hold him?"

"For a while. He's on probation. I just spoke to the PO. He's on his way over."

"What about evidence?"

"He's got cuts on his hands. I'll have Gabe photograph those and take his boots and the ring he's wearing."

LeRoyer crinkled his brow. "Ring?"

Byron stood up and closed his locker door. "With any luck we'll find some of Ramsey's DNA embedded in it."

DIANE ENTERED THE interview room where McVail sat handcuffed. An odiferous combination of fish and body odor permeated the air. She acknowledged the uniformed officer standing in the corner. "Thanks, I'll be okay," Diane said.

The uniformed cop shot McVail a menacing glance then looked back at Diane. "I'll be right outside the door."

Diane nodded, sat down opposite McVail, established eye contact, and waited for the door to close before speaking.

"Donny, my name is Detective Joyner."

McVail looked her up and down. "So, what, they send a good-looking lady dick in here and think I'll just give up the goods?"

"Something like that," she said, ignoring his lame attempt to sound like a Hollywood badass. "Can I get you anything?"

He extended his arms out across the table. "Ya. How about getting these cuffs off?"

"'Fraid I can't. Regulations. Anything else?"

McVail shook his head. "Nah, I'm good. Had to try, right?"

"You know why you're here?"

"I guess. Cop brought me in said you wanted to question me about some assault or something."

"That's right, but that isn't the only reason."

McVail lowered his gaze to the tabletop. "What else?"

"I'll explain everything but first I have to read you your rights. Are you familiar with the Miranda warning?"

McVail nodded. "Yeah, yeah. I got the right to remain silent, and if I don't you'll use it against me, right?"

"That's pretty good, Donny. But my bosses expect me to read it verbatim. Okay?"

"Whatever."

Diane read each line from a printed page and recorded McVail's verbal response next to each. After finishing, she pushed the paper toward him, along with a pen. "I need you to sign at the bottom, acknowledging that you understand your rights."

McVail reached up with his hands still cuffed in front, signed the document, then slid both items back. "What do you want to know?"

BYRON SAT BOOKENDED by Mike Nugent and Melissa Stevens in the CID conference room. He scribbled notes onto a legal pad as they monitored Diane's interview on the large wall-mounted flat screen. He'd have preferred sitting right in there with her, grilling McVail about his Tuesday night activities, but given the recent pursuit and McVail's high opinion of himself as a ladies' man, Diane was clearly their best hope at keeping the young punk from lawyering up.

Evidence Technician Gabriel Pelligrosso appeared in the conference room doorway. "Sarge, you wanted to see me?"

Byron turned in his chair. "Gabe, I need you to gather some evidence off an asshole."

Pelligrosso looked up at the monitor. "Would that asshole's name happen to be Donny McVail?"

"Yeah," Stevens said. "You know him?"

"Arrested him a few times when I was still patrolling a beat. Likes to run."

"MAYBE I *WAS* at the Fox the other night," McVail said. "I go there a lot. Can't remember."

"Well, let me refresh your memory," Diane said. "You got into a beef with an older gentleman at the bar."

"The asshole in the suit?"

Describing Ramsey to a tee was definitely an admission, Diane thought. "So you do remember?"

"Yeah. It was Tuesday night. I was in there with Debbie, my girlfriend. We was watching the basketball game 'cause I had some money on the Cs. This asshole at the bar just keeps bitchin' and whining about some broad. He won't shut up. Finally, I say something to him like, 'Shut the fuck up.'"

How original. "How did he respond?"

"He started talkin' down to me, like that suit made him somebody. He made fun of my GED, called me a hummingbird or something."

"A hummingbird?"

"I don't really know what he was talking about but I know when someone's fucking with me." He stabbed the tabletop with an index finger, accentuating his point.

"What happened next?"

"I challenged him to a fight but Tony told us both to knock it off or he'd call the cops."

"Tony?"

"Yeah, he's the night bartender at the Fox."

"And then?"

"Asshole keeps running his yap but Tony made him leave."

"What did you do?"

"Nothing. I sat down and finished my drink, with Debbie."

Diane looked up. McVail trailed off as he said the name, almost as if he'd tried to pull it back. "What's Debbie's last name?"

He squirmed in his chair. "Why do you need that?"

"We're gonna need to talk to her, Donny. To verify your story."

"HEY, GUYS," PO McNamara said as he strolled into the CID conference room, sporting a thick auburn-colored handlebar mustache which would have been more at home on a firefighter.

"Kevin," Byron said extending a hand. "Thanks for coming so quickly."

"We got yo' boy," Nugent said, giving McNamara a mock salute. "He's in a heap o' trouble, is that lad."

"What's my little lost lamb done this time?" McNamara said as he pulled out a chair and sat down at the table.

Byron gave him a thumbnail sketch of the incident at the Red Fox.

"So, you think he killed Ramsey?" McNamara asked.

"Honestly? I don't think he even knows Ramsey's dead," Byron said.

"He certainly doesn't act like he knows," Stevens added.

"Yeah," McNamara said, looking up at the monitor. "Donny's not one for keeping abreast of current events."

"Huh? You mean he doesn't have the *Herald* delivered to his door?" Nugent asked, grinning.

"So, what do you need from me?" McNamara asked.

"He's reluctant to give us anything further without talking to an attorney," Byron said.

"Lawyered up, did he? Shocker."

"I assume you'll authorize a hold?" Byron asked.

"Sure, but I can only stall his release for a week without a probation violation hearing."

"Maybe you could have a chat with him. Explain how much trouble he's in for running from us, failing to tell us that he was on probation, possession of a dangerous weapon, resisting arrest."

"Wasn't the knife part of his employment?"

"I'll still charge it," Byron said.

"Pretty thin, Sarge," McNamara said, shaking his head and twirling the ends of his mustache as he thought it over.

"He's invoked his Miranda rights, Kev," Byron said. "We can't entice him to talk with us now, not unless he changes his mind. Maybe if you went in, on your own, not because I asked you, and explained how much time he's facing. Maybe he'll feel differently. Tell him if he cooperates you'll talk to us about dropping the new charges."

"Will you?"

"If he comes clean about the fight with Ramsey."

"What if he really did kill Ramsey?"

Byron looked up at the monitor. "Well, if he did, nothing you say is gonna mean much anyway, is it?"

FOLLOWING A BRIEF back-and-forth between McNamara and McVail, Byron and Joyner stepped into the interview room. McVail was pouting.

"My PO says if I tell you what happened the other night you'll drop some of the charges against me," McVail said.

"We can't promise anything," Byron said. "Not until we hear what you've got to say."

"What did the asshole in the suit tell you?" McVail asked, referring to Ramsey.

"We wanna hear your side of it, Donny," Diane said. "Are you waiving your Miranda rights?"

"Yeah, yeah. I'll talk to you."

McVail recounted the entire night, including following Ramsey out of the bar and sucker punching him.

"Tony the bartender said you didn't follow him out," Byron said.

McVail shrugged. "Yeah, well."

"How many times did you punch him?" Byron asked.

"I don't know. A couple."

"Looking at your eye I'd say he got one good one in," Diane said.

McVail nodded. "Lucky."

"What happened next?" Byron asked.

"Nothing. I told him to watch who he made fun of, then I left."

"What was the other guy doing when you left?" Byron asked.

"Bleeding."

"Was he conscious?" Diane asked.

"Yeah. He told me to fuck myself."

"Did you know the guy?" Byron asked.

"Not personally. I'd seen him at the Fox before. Think he's some big-shot attorney. So what, is he pressing charges?"

"No," Byron said. "He isn't. He's dead."

THE TWO DETECTIVES stepped out of the interview room and retreated to the CID conference room, giving McVail time to contemplate his future.

"What do you think?" Diane asked Byron. "I thought his eyes were gonna pop out when you told him Ramsey was dead."

Byron looked at McNamara. "Ever known him to carry a gun?"

The probation officer shook his head. "Nah. Donny's stupid but he's not *that* stupid."

Diane raised a brow. "Coulda fooled me."

"He likes to sling a little dope, fight, and get drunk, but that's about it."

"We still only have his word about what happened," Stevens said.

"Mel's right," Byron said, addressing McNamara. "Can you authorize holding him for a few more days so we can work this case? I don't want to release him, then find out later that he's the shooter."

McNamara continued to toy with the ends of his mustache. "What about the concealed weapon and resisting charges?"

"Give me a few days. If nothing else points to McVail as the shooter, I'll have the DA drop those charges."

"Assuming he makes bail on your current charges, most I can give you is five days. After that he gets a hearing or goes free."

LeRoyer stuck his head in the door to the conference room, looking directly at Byron. "John, I need to see you and Diane in my office."

"Give us a second, Lieu. We're almost f—"

"Now!" LeRoyer barked.

Chapter Twelve

Friday, 1:35 P.M., April 29, 2016

"HOW THE FUCK did Billingslea get this information?" LeRoyer said, pointing at the computer monitor on his desk where a *Portland Herald* article filled the screen.

Byron and Diane leaned over his desk trying to read the article. The headline read Prominent Local Attorney Murdered After Losing Case.

"I'll save you two the trouble of reading the whole thing," LeRoyer said. "Somebody leaked information about the manner of Ramsey's death."

Byron could feel himself getting hot. "It wasn't any of my people."

"No?" LeRoyer said. "Because he also writes about Ramsey turning down the hospital's offer of a seven-figure settlement a week before the trial started. How many people knew about that?"

"*We* didn't even know about that," Byron said.

"Branch is wild. Stanton is wild. And frankly, I'm a little pissed off myself, John."

"Branch might want to check himself," Byron said. "If that little shit Billingslea got inside information about a settlement, it came from the firm."

Diane attempted to weigh in. "Lieutenant, I can assure you that—"

LeRoyer held up his hand, signaling her to stop. "Can it, Detective. Don't want your assurances. What I want is an end to these goddamned leaks." He turned his attention back to Byron. "This story makes the plaintiffs in the lawsuit against Maine Med look like the prime suspects in this murder and you guys are up here fucking around with some street punk. Has anyone even talked to the people who brought the suit?"

"The Elwells. Not yet. We've been running down Ramsey's last evening and a building contractor who's been threatening him first." Byron pointed his thumb back toward LeRoyer's closed office door. "By the way, that street punk you're talking about just confessed to following Ramsey out of the bar and assaulting him, Tuesday night. That may have been the last time anyone saw Ramsey alive."

"Did he confess to shooting him?" LeRoyer asked.

"No, he didn't."

"Then you still don't have anyone we can charge with the murder. And Davis-fucking-Billingslea looks like he's doing our job better than we are," LeRoyer said, pointing toward the monitor. "I want the Elwells interviewed by the end of the day. And if that leak *is* coming from here, I want it plugged. We understand each other?"

Diane nodded in silence.

Byron, resisting the urge to get in LeRoyer's face, or worse, joined her. "Got it."

BYRON ASSIGNED DETECTIVE Nugent to get a written statement from McVail before transporting him to the county jail for booking. He tasked Diane with making contact with the Elwells to try and set up a meeting for early afternoon. Byron retreated to his office and closed the door. He picked up the receiver on his desk phone and punched in the number for the *Portland Herald*.

The young reporter answered on the second ring. "Newsroom, Billingslea."

Byron clenched his jaw. "It's John Byron."

There was a brief pause. "Good morning, Sergeant."

He heard the faintest crack of nervousness in Billingslea's voice. "Why are you fucking with my case?"

"I'm not fucking with anything. I came by some solid information and I ran with it. Don't we both do the same thing?"

"No, Davis, we don't. I'm trying to solve a murder and you're grandstanding. Maybe you've forgotten how badly you nearly screwed up my last case. Where the hell are you getting your information?"

"I'm not gonna share that with you. You know as well as I, unless they tell me otherwise, my sources are protected."

"My bosses think you're getting your intel from inside the PD. And I'd better not find out that's the fucking case."

Another pause. "Maybe if you and I were to share information it could be mutually beneficial," Billingslea said.

"Share this," Byron said, slamming the receiver back onto its cradle.

There was a knock on Byron's office door.

"What?" he snapped.

The door opened and Stevens stuck her head in. "Hey, Sarge. Don't mean to bug you. Did you want me to drive down to County with Nuge?"

"No," he said, composing himself. "I've got another job for you. Grab Dustin and head down to the Old Port. I want the entire area between the Red Fox and where McVail said he fought with Ramsey canvassed for outside security cameras. The Fox doesn't have any working surveillance but I know some of the nearby businesses do. See if you can find anything."

"You got it."

Byron's cell began to vibrate on the desk. He picked it up and checked the caller ID. Huntress. "Hey, Jamie. Any progress?"

"Not yet. We just got on scene. One of my guys had to testify in Grand Jury and the other had a sick babysitter. We're getting ready to dive now."

"Okay. I'm heading outta town for an interview shortly. If you need anything, Nuge and Mel are both running around down here."

"Roger that. We're gonna do a grid search from the end of the road directly out toward Falmouth. We'll go back and forth between the bridge and a point about a hundred feet to the east."

Byron was visualizing the coverage area in his mind from the previous day's visit. "What if they tossed it off the bridge while fleeing toward Falmouth?"

"If they did, you're pretty much fucked, John. Martin's Point Bridge is a quarter mile long with strong tidal currents underneath it. Christ, as it is we'll have to tether our divers to keep them on line. Our best shot is that they tossed it from the shore near where you recovered Ramsey's SUV."

"All right," Byron said.

"Aside from the gun is there anything else we should be looking for?"

"A .380 shell casing would be nice. And anything else you can find that doesn't belong."

"You've obviously never been at the bottom of Casco Bay. You wouldn't believe the shit we find down here. You remember that stolen Honda we found at the end of Holyoke Wharf?"

"Best you can do, Jamie."

"I'll keep you posted."

TWENTY MINUTES LATER Byron and Diane were on Interstate 295 headed north toward Bowdoinham.

"You cooled off any?" Diane asked.

Cool wasn't exactly the word he would've used to describe how he was feeling. "Not much."

"Penny for your thoughts?"

"I'm thinking Branch is holding out, but I don't know why. Ramsey's wife is talking about her dead husband's extracurricular activities but she probably doesn't know the half of it. Someone is leaking intel to Billingslea and I don't know who. And you want to know the worst part?"

"What's that?"

"That fucking news story is directly impacting this case."

"Because Billingslea is making us look bad?" she asked.

"No, because his story is controlling the way we have to investigate it. You know as well as I, we solve these cases methodically, patiently, piece by piece, until we've built a mountain that can't be eroded by a defense attorney, at least not entirely. That's how it's supposed to work. But not on this case. Right now, the only reason you and I are headed to see the Elwells is because Billingslea is steering this ship. And that's bullshit."

It was nearly three as Byron turned onto the cracked asphalt drive of the run-down Cape Cod owned by the Elwells. There was more vegetation growing in the driveway than on the desolate patch of ground that passed as a lawn. A rusted silver Camry sat in front of an unattached two-story garage. Parked off to one side, in among the weeds, was a black primed four-by-four with flat tires. Byron looked over at Diane, who was already jotting notes, a trait she'd possessed since the day he'd first met her at the scene of an unattended death.

"Mrs. Elwell?" Diane asked the bathrobe-clad woman standing in the open doorway. "We spoke earlier on the phone. I'm Detective Joyner and this is Detective Sergeant Byron."

Elwell looked briefly at both IDs. "Please, come in."

She looked significantly older than the forty-one years indicated by the records at the Bureau of Motor Vehicles. Byron guessed stress from the trial and her lack of makeup probably had something to do with it. They followed her into the kitchen.

The table was buried beneath a pile of mail and file folders. A quick glance and Byron could see that most of it was legal correspondence bearing the letterhead of Newman, Branch & DeWitt. Atop the opened envelopes and letters were several framed pictures of a good-looking young man, and a mountain of used tissues.

Diane followed Elwell's lead and sat opposite her. Byron cautiously settled into a rickety wooden chair at the end of the table, wondering whether or not it would support his large frame. The wood groaned in protest.

Elwell lit a cigarette, inhaled deeply, and held her breath for a tick before exhaling a plume of bluish smoke. Even had the tissues not been present, the red eyes and puffy cheeks made it obvious she'd been crying.

Byron broke the awkward silence. "Thank you for agreeing to speak with us, Mrs. Elwell."

Elwell fixed him with her hollow eyes. "Paula, please."

"We are very sorry for your loss, Paula," Diane said.

Byron nodded at the sentiment. "Our condolences."

"Thank you both. That's very nice." Elwell's eyes widened and seemed to clear as if she had just come out of a trance. "Where are my manners?" She stood up, bumping the table, knocking over a stack of papers. "Can I get either of you something to drink? Coffee? Soda?"

"Please, don't go to any trouble on our account," Byron said, holding up his hand.

"It's no trouble, really. I was going to make some more coffee for myself anyway."

"Okay," Byron said.

"Can I help you?" Diane asked.

"I'm fine, thank you, Detective," she said with a weak smile.

Byron picked up one of the framed photographs from the table and studied it. He recognized the boy's picture, having seen the same one in the newspaper. A handsome young man wearing a blue and white Mount Ararat High School football uniform. "Is this your son, Paula?".

Elwell turned away from the sink where she was busy filling a glass carafe with water. Her expression softened. "That's my Robbie's senior class picture."

Byron couldn't help but notice how much the young man in the picture resembled his mother, with the same hazel eyes and deep dimples when he smiled.

"He was a good-looking boy," Diane said as Byron passed her the picture.

"My friends think he looks like me, but I've always thought he got his looks from his father."

"What position did he play?" Diane asked.

"Safety. He set the Eagles' single season record for interceptions. I still remember how proud he was the day he made the team. We were all so proud of him."

She finished setting up the coffeemaker and returned to the table carrying three empty mugs and a small glass pitcher of cream. "He didn't get sick until after graduation," she said, her voice cracking.

"Can you tell us about the lawsuit?" Byron asked.

Elwell lit a fresh cigarette. "It started when Robbie got sick. He began having nosebleeds and getting rashes on his shins. They said that it was bleeding into the skin. He was diagnosed with ITP, immune thrombocytopenia. I still can't pronounce it right. The doctor said that his body was producing too many antibodies. They said the antibodies were attacking his blood platelets so his blood wouldn't clot. So, they performed a splenectomy. His doctor removed his spleen. A month later Robbie was dead."

Byron and Diane sat in silence as Elwell continued to explain.

"We found out afterward that he'd been misdiagnosed. They could have treated Robbie with medications first. Apparently, taking out the spleen is a last resort. We didn't know. We figured that Robbie's doctor knew what he was doing. You know, it's almost a relief that it's over."

"A relief?" Diane asked.

"Our lives have been consumed by this, Detectives. For the past three years."

"So you filed a wrongful death suit against the hospital?" Diane asked.

"Attorney Ramsey assured Justin, my husband, and me that we had a good case. His firm filed a wrongful death suit against the hospital on our behalf."

"How did you happen to choose Paul Ramsey?" Byron asked.

"His firm approached us. Mr. DeWitt actually."

Like sharks, attorneys always pick up on the scent of blood, Byron thought.

"We understand there was some kind of settlement offer," Diane said.

Elwell nodded and flicked the ash off her cigarette into an empty mug. "They offered to settle just before the trial started. Paul advised us to turn it down, said we'd prevail at trial." She paused and picked up a picture of her son. "He said we'd definitely get justice for Robbie."

Byron felt the anger rising in him again as he watched the fresh tears streaming down Elwell's cheeks. He could hear the pompous attorney saying those exact words to the bereaved family. He knew from personal experience that justice was the last thing Ramsey gave a shit about.

"Where is Justin?" Diane asked.

"Back to work. He's a long haul trucker. He had to take the last three weeks off on account of the trial. We didn't have any money coming in." She scanned the cluttered tabletop. "The bills have been piling up."

"How is he handling all of this?" Byron asked, trying hard to remember that the Elwells were still possible suspects in Ramsey's murder.

He saw the fog return to Elwell's eyes as she thought about her husband.

"He handles these things much better than I do. Justin's strong like that. He's torn up about this same as me, but he doesn't show it." She dabbed the corners of her eyes with a fresh tissue. "Losing this lawsuit was like losing our Robbie all over again. Justin will hide in his work. That's how he'll get through it."

"What about you, Paula?" Diane asked. "How will you get through it?"

"I'm not sure. One day at a time, I guess."

The coffeemaker gave a shrill beep, signaling that it was done. Elwell got up and returned with the pot, filling each of their mugs with an unsteady hand. "How do you take it?"

"Black is fine," Byron said.

Elwell shifted her attention to Diane. "Half-and-half okay?"

"That'd be great, thank you."

Elwell finished pouring the creamer into the remaining mugs then returned to her chair and sat down.

"You mentioned a settlement offer," Byron began. "Can you tell us about that?"

Elwell set her mug on the table and began absently scratching at the back of her left hand. "Paul came to Justin and me about a week before the trial started. I remember it was just before they were going to pick a jury. He came to the house and showed us a letter he'd received from the hospital's insurance company."

"What did it say?" Diane asked.

"They were offering us one million dollars if we'd agree to settle the matter out of court. They wanted us to drop the suit and release them from any further liability. And they wanted one more thing, something about not discussing the amount." She closed her eyes, pressing her fingers against her forehead. "I can't remember the exact term."

"A nondisclosure agreement?" Byron asked.

Her eyes flew open. "Yes. That was it. They wanted us to sign that too."

"You obviously didn't accept their offer," Diane said.

Elwell shook her head. "No, I told you Paul advised us not to. He said it meant that the insurance company was getting nervous. Told us it was insulting and that we should go for the whole thing. Said it was the only way to get justice for Robbie." Elwell's voice cracked again as she said her son's name. Her eyes leaked fresh tears.

Byron exchanged glances with Diane. He wondered how Ramsey could so easily screw this poor couple over, when they so clearly had nothing. The money wouldn't have brought their son back but it might have provided some closure, some measure of justice, real or imagined, for Robbie. If nothing else, it would have provided for the Elwells during their remaining years.

Elwell recomposed herself and lit another cigarette. "When we spoke on the phone, Detective, you said that you wanted to talk to me about a case that you're investigating."

"Did you know that your attorney, Paul Ramsey, died?" Diane asked.

"Yes. I saw it on TV."

"Have you seen today's paper, Mrs. Elwell?" Byron asked.

"No. I'd planned to go out shopping for groceries but as you can see I haven't left the house."

"Paul Ramsey was murdered," Byron said.

"How?"

"Someone shot him in the head then dumped his body in the ocean," Byron said, intentionally being blunt, watching closely for her reaction.

Elwell remained stoic as she digested what she'd been told.

He caught Diane glaring at him.

"Where were you and Justin Tuesday night?" Byron asked, ignoring his partner's obvious displeasure with the tactic.

"Do you think we killed Mr. Ramsey, Sergeant Byron?"

"Doesn't matter what I think, Mrs. Elwell. We have to explore every possibility. And a million dollars is more than enough motive for some."

"Tuesday evening Justin was on his way to Kansas City. I spent the night at my sister's in Brewer."

"We'll need to confirm that information, Paula," Diane said.

"Of course. I understand."

"Uh-oh," Nugent said, looking over at McVail, who was seated on a prisoner bench in Intake.

McVail looked up but said nothing.

"You've been a bad boy, Donny," he said, holding up one of McVail's steel-toed black leather boots. The heel had detached and was lying in Nugent's other hand. "What have we got here? Who do you think you are, 007?"

"Those aren't my boots," McVail said.

Nugent looked at one of the intake deputies who was leaning across the counter grinning. "Betcha never heard that one before?"

"Nope. First for me," the jail guard said.

Nugent turned his attention back to McVail. "I guess this isn't yours either?" He removed a small clear baggie of white powder from a hollowed-out cavity within the rubber heel.

"Never seen it before," McVail said.

BYRON AND DIANE drove back toward the interstate in silence. She hadn't spoken a word since they left the Elwell home.

"What's eating you?" he asked.

She turned and faced him. "Did you have to be so hard on that poor woman? Don't you think she's been through enough?"

"What are you talking about?" he asked, surprised by her reaction. "I was questioning a possible murder suspect."

"Did you really have to be so direct with her?"

"Direct? Don't you mean uncaring?"

"You said it."

"Yeah, I guess I did. Sometimes this job requires a direct approach."

"You used her, John. A woman already fragile from all she's been through, and you used her to get what you needed."

"Don't you mean *we*? What *we* needed? We need to either rule her and her husband out or put them under a microscope. I'm trying to put a murderer away. I did what I had to. Period."

"You sound like Ramsey."

"What the hell is your problem? We catch killers, Diane. That's what we do. I don't know how you did it in New York, but up here we like to pull out all the stops to see that justice is served."

"Really?"

"Yeah, really."

"So, where is Paula Elwell's justice?"

He opened his mouth to respond then stopped. Diane was one of the best detectives he'd ever encountered, tough with suspects but gentle with witnesses, when it was called for. She could be equally tough with witnesses when it wasn't. Whatever it was that had taken Diane off of her game, it certainly wasn't the Elwells, nor was it his handling of a possible suspect. No, something else was going on with her and arguing about it was an exercise in futility.

Byron's cell rang. He checked the ID. Nugent.

"Hey, Nuge."

"You guys still out of town?" Nugent asked.

Byron glanced over at Diane, who was busy ignoring him, again.

"On our way back. What's up?"

Chapter Thirteen

Friday, 4:30 P.M., April 29, 2016

BYRON DROPPED DIANE off at 109, after she'd curtly agreed
to follow up with Levesque Trucking and confirm Justin Elwell's whereabouts on Tuesday night. She had maintained her
coolness toward him for the remainder of their trip back to
Portland and he had figured it might be best for all parties if
they did some sleuthing separately. He jumped back onto the
interstate and drove toward the dive site. Nugent was waiting
on him at the county jail but Byron wanted to check in with
Sergeant Huntress first. He was forced to park in the lower
paved lot of 331 Veranda Street as the access road and sidewalk
were jammed with marked police units and several personally owned vehicles belonging to members of the dive team.
A number of gawkers had gathered on the bridge to watch the
proceedings. Byron couldn't help but notice Davis Billingslea
standing among them.

He walked down toward the shoreline, passing a bearded

cameraman and what looked to be a teenaged female reporter from one of the local news affiliates.

"Sergeant Byron," the reporter shouted excitedly upon recognizing him. "Can I get a few words?"

"No," Byron said. "You want a statement, call Lieutenant LeRoyer."

"Is this dive related to the death of Attorney Ramsey?" she continued, undeterred by Byron's brush-off.

"Gee, I don't know. What do you think?" He hated investigating outdoor scenes during the daytime. News reporters were as plentiful as seagulls, and just as annoying. Fighting for any scraps the police might toss their way. Byron was more than happy to leave the scrap tossing to someone else. Ignoring her next question, he stepped under the bright yellow crime scene tape and winked at the uniformed officer standing post to keep the onlookers away. "Regular circus, huh?"

The officer nodded, grinning as he crossed his arms. "They won't get by me, Sarge."

Byron spotted Huntress at the water's edge. He was standing beside a man with curly gray hair and a pot belly. Byron recognized the second man as one of the local dive instructors. They were monitoring the two divers still in the water. Off to the right were two others seated on the open tailgate of a pickup, half in and half out of their wetsuits, taking a break and hydrating. Byron knew they were only allowed thirty minutes in the water at a time.

"Hey, John," Huntress greeted.

"Jamie."

"You know Phil Goodall, right?" Huntress asked. "He's our volunteer dive master."

"Sure, we've met before," Goodall said as he shook hands with Byron.

"Thanks for helping us out with this, Phil," Byron said. "Any luck?"

"We found a gun," Huntress said.

"Really?" Byron asked hopefully.

"Yeah. Pretty sure it's not your murder weapon, though," Huntress said as he produced a rust-colored hunk of steel that was at least the approximate shape of the gun.

"Pretty sure you're right," Byron said, handing it back and looking for something to wipe his hand on.

"Told you you wouldn't believe what we find down there."

"Any luck with a shell casing?" Byron asked, knowing full well that if they couldn't locate the gun, the casing would be nothing more than a pine needle in the proverbial forest.

Huntress shook his head. "Nope. Pelligrosso was by earlier. Had a couple of guys out here with metal detectors checking the surrounding bushes and shoreline but I don't think they found too much. Trash mostly."

Byron sighed as he scanned the area.

"You positive Ramsey was killed out here?" Huntress asked.

"On this case? I'm not positive of anything."

DIANE MADE A quick left onto Franklin Street from Congress, skillfully guiding the unmarked through the rush hour traffic.

"Have you told the sarge about the promotional exam yet?" Stevens asked.

Diane glanced over at her then back to the road. "No."

"You do care about him, don't you?"

"Very much."

"Then you need to tell him, Di. Before he finds out some other way."

Diane took a deep breath then exhaled loudly. "I know, you're right, Mel. It's just—"

"What?"

"My relationship with John. It's complicated."

"News flash, all relationships are complicated. How complicated can yours be?"

Diane slowed then stopped for the red light at Marginal Way. "You know what I mean. I'm not even sure it's really going anywhere. We never go out, not like on a real date. This trying to hide it thing sucks. I want everyone to know we're together."

"Have you told him that?" Stevens asked.

"Not in so many words."

"You need to be honest with him, Di. He deserves that from you. He's not only your sergeant, he's your lover."

Diane liked the sound of that. She and John were lovers, and it had been good between them. But something was still missing.

"You owe him the truth," Stevens said.

"I know. And I feel like such a hypocrite. This dishonesty bullshit is exactly why I left New York."

"Your husband?"

"Yup."

"You've never really talked about him. He was on the job, right?"

"Yeah. You think I'd learn, wouldn't you? First few years were great, but then he became a controlling asshole. Men, right?" Diane said, looking at Stevens and rolling her eyes.

"News flash, men haven't cornered the market on that. I've been with a few of the fairer sex who were just as bad. One was worse."

"After that he started lying to me," Diane said.

"Kinda like you're lying to John?"

She realized she had no comeback for that. Mel was right. "I'm just worried how he's going to take it."

A car horn blared loudly from directly behind them.

Stevens whipped her head around toward the backseat and flipped the driver of a silver Nissan off through the rear window. "Relax, dickhead."

"Jesus, Mel," Diane said, laughing as she proceeded through the intersection and up onto 295. "This is a city car, ya know."

"Screw him. Your problems are more important than that macho asshole's."

Diane smiled as she activated the left blinker, and merged into the interstate's southbound traffic.

The Pathfinder roared past them in the next lane; the driver returned Stevens's one-fingered salute while laying on the horn.

"So, you gonna take the media job?" Stevens asked.

"I don't know. Guess I'm still conflicted."

Stevens shook her head. "Sounds to me like you're not sure about much of anything. If you really want to be with John, why not take the job they offered you? End the conflict."

"Because I've got serious reservations about accepting the position," Diane said.

"Like?"

"The city's motives."

"Let me guess, you think they're only making this offer because you're black?"

"They all but said it, Mel. Waved the first female detective sergeant thing right in my face. But what they really meant was that I'd be the first *black* female detective sergeant."

"So?"

Diane hadn't expected that response. "How would you feel? What if they were making the same offer to you because you're gay?"

"Does it really matter how you get it? I mean, you're totally qualified. Who cares if they're just trying to capitalize on your lineage?"

"My lineage? Did you really just say that?"

Both of them broke up laughing for a moment.

"Shut up," Stevens said, still laughing. "You know what I'm saying. You'd make an awesome detective sergeant, Di."

"You really think so?"

"Hell ya!" Stevens said, giving her a playful smack on the arm. "You go, girl!"

Diane fixed her with an appreciative smile. "Thanks, Mel."

BYRON HAD DEPARTED from Veranda Street and was headed for the jail when his cell vibrated. It was Pelligrosso.

"Sarge, it's Gabe."

"What's up?"

"We finished recanvassing the area where Ramsey's SUV was recovered. Thought you'd want to know."

"Yeah, Huntress said you'd been by. Anything?"

"Not really. Oh, there was one thing. We found a makeshift homeless camp in the bushes nearby. Abandoned."

"Anything left behind?" Byron asked.

"Just some random trash. A ripped plastic tarp, empty soup cans, and an As' cap."

Byron caught an image in his head. Portland had more than its share of homeless folks. They arrived by any means necessary to what some thought of as the land of milk and honey, collecting bottles and cans or standing on street corners with cardboard signs in all manner of dress. But the As' cap could only mean one man: Erwin Glantz. Or Winn, as Byron affectionately referred to him. A combat veteran of the first Gulf War who hailed from sunny California. And like so many before Winn, serving his country had left him damaged, both physically and psychologically. After earning two Purple Hearts and an honorable discharge, Winn returned to the States, quickly finding himself on the wrong side of the law and on the outs with his family. He had spent several agonizing years trying to assimilate out west, before pulling up stakes and dragging himself as far from his family as possible, settling in Portland. Byron had crossed paths with Winn soon after. Winn had been casing the RSVP liquor store on Forest Avenue about to commit a burglary, and Byron knew it. Instead of busting Winn, Byron drove him to an all-night diner and fixed him up with some food and drink. Winn, who had never forgotten Byron's kindness, had been a great source of information when Byron had needed it. What goes around comes around.

"Did you seize any of those items?" Byron asked.

"I did," Pelligrosso said. "Didn't think any of it was connected but you never know, right? I grabbed the hat and a couple of miscellaneous items."

"Anything you can print?"

"The soup cans, maybe. I can try."

"Let me know."

Byron disconnected the call, pausing a moment before returning the phone to his pocket. It could have been any one of several hundred homeless people camped out in those bushes. But he'd be willing to bet a paycheck it was Winn. Had he seen something that caused him to abandon camp? Or was it only a coincidence that Ramsey's vehicle had been dumped there? If it was Winn, leaving his prized ball cap suggested he'd left in a hurry. Byron needed to find him.

BYRON STOOD WAITING beside a uniformed jail guard. He stole a sideways glance at the acne-covered face of the deputy. Byron knew he couldn't have been much older than twenty-one. The guard looked up at the security camera, a signal to the tower guard that they were in position. There was a loud buzz followed by an equally loud metallic clank as the electronic lock was disengaged. The hinges protested loudly as the guard pushed the heavy iron door inward. Byron followed him down a small corridor, which led to three different visitor rooms, each with a rectangular metal table and four chairs. The walls were nothing more than painted concrete block. No doors, no frills, and no privacy. The first two rooms they passed were empty. Byron, who couldn't help but be reminded of Stockton's story *The Lady or the Tiger*, turned the corner and entered the third where Detective Nugent and McVail were already waiting.

"All set?" the deputy asked Byron.

"We'll be fine."

"Okay, I'll be right down at the other end of the hall. Holler if you need anything."

"Thanks," Byron said, turning his attention to McVail and taking a seat next to Nugent. "I guess this just isn't your day, huh, Donny?"

Nugent chuckled. "He claims that neither the boots he was wearing, nor the coke hidden inside them, were his."

"Tough luck, huh?" Byron said.

"I got nothing to say," McVail said.

"That's too bad," Byron said. "I just got off the phone with your

PO. He's considering having you serve every single day of your remaining sentence."

McVail fixed him with a smug grin. "That's bullshit. No way they'll make me do eighteen months. Wouldn't be fair."

"Nothing to do with fair, Donny. You got caught holding again. You beat up a guy who's now dead and you resisted arrest." Byron turned to Nugent. "I forget anything?"

"Don't forget about the knife."

"Oh yeah, that's right. And one more thing, it's not just possession on the drug charge."

"What do you mean?" McVail asked.

"You brought coke into a jail, Donny. The courts frown on that sort of thing. What's the legal term for that, Nuge?"

"Legally? I'd say he's fucked, but I believe they still call it trafficking in prison contraband."

McVail scoffed. "Whatever. That's just a misdemeanor."

"Wrong again, Donny ol' boy," Byron said. "Class C felony."

McVail's eyes widened. "Fuck that! There was only a half a . . ."

"Half a what, Donny?" Nugent asked. "Thought it wasn't yours."

"Whatever. You guys are just bullshittin' me."

"I don't bullshit," Byron said.

"Of course, if you had a prescription for the coke you'd be okay," Nugent teased. "How 'bout it, sport? You got a doctor's note for blow?"

"They have that?" McVail asked hopefully. "Same as weed?"

"No, Donny, they don't," Byron said. "And if you thought eighteen months was bad, imagine what five years will feel like."

"And you wouldn't be doing it here in the county lockup either," Nugent added. "Nope, right to the big house in Warren.

They're gonna love you. Literally. Just try to imagine what that's gonna feel like."

McVail hung his head. His arrogance was gone. "What do you want from me?"

Byron put his forearms on the table and leaned over close to McVail. "The name of Paul Ramsey's supplier."

BYRON DEPARTED THE jail mulling over the information McVail had provided. He was also contemplating the next move. Downtown traffic was crawling as he drove east on Congress Street scanning the numerous vacant storefronts interspersed among Portland's more prosperous and longstanding establishments. On display in some of the empty commercial properties were signs of promise, along with the high hopes of new lessees, The Future Site of, and Opening Soon. Starstruck entrepreneurs with a vision to restore vitality to Maine's struggling economy.

Years earlier, as a young detective, when he hadn't been immersed in the middle of a major case, Byron and his old mentor, Ray Humphrey, would intentionally drive the Congress Street route back to 109. Humphrey had been fond of calling it the "Congo run," mainly because the human interaction along Portland's main downtown thoroughfare was both primal and fascinating. More like a jungle than an urban landscape. There were aggressive panhandlers, scared business folk hurrying to or from meetings, street corner musicians and preachers, the mentally deranged talking aloud to themselves, and more scared business folk. Summertime saw the addition of tourists, mindlessly snapping selfies amid the throngs. Portland had it all. The good, the bad, and the unmedicated.

He stopped at the red traffic light where High Street intersected Congress. A young man stood in the median holding a cardboard sign: Out of Work Vet. Anything Helps. God Bless. Byron wondered exactly which war the teenager was claiming to be a veteran of. He also wondered how it was that he could be begging for money while wearing two-hundred-and-fifty-dollar cross-trainers, talking on his cell, and smoking cigarettes. Hell, Byron couldn't afford to take up smoking.

He recalled having seen an early twentieth century sepia tone photograph of Civil War General Joshua Chamberlain riding proudly on horseback down this same thoroughfare during a parade. As Byron watched the "well-to-do indigent" taking hard-earned money from passing motorists, he wondered what General Chamberlain would have thought of his beloved city's transformation. He wondered, too, what Chamberlain might have thought of Paul Ramsey.

Reaching into his coat pocket, he removed his cell. McVail had given them a solid lead and, as much as Byron hated the idea, it was time to reach out to Sergeant Crosby for help.

"HELP YA?" THE balding man with the beer belly said from behind the open sliding glass counter window.

"I hope so," Diane said. She and Mel both flashed him their IDs.

"Lady cops, huh? You here to bust me?" he asked, raising his arms for effect.

"Not unless we have to," Stevens said, deadpan.

Lines of confusion appeared on Beer Belly's forehead. A white oval name tag bearing the name Skip was sewn onto the breast of his faded chambray shirt.

"She's kidding," Diane said. "We're looking for information about one of your long haul truckers."

"Which one?"

"Justin Elwell. He works here, right?"

"Justin's a sub."

"Sub?" Diane asked.

"Subcontractor. Owns his own rig. We just hire him to transport our trailers."

"Where would he normally take them?" Stevens asked.

"Wherever. Depends on the shipping schedule. And believe you me, there's nothing normal or routine about that. Why you askin' about Justin anyway? He in some kind of trouble?"

"We don't think so, but we need to verify his whereabouts for the past week," Diane said.

Skip grabbed a grungy olive-colored three-ring binder off the desk and brought it to the window. He slipped a pair of black-rimmed reading glasses out of his shirt pocket and up over his greasy nose. "Let's see," he said, licking a finger and flipping pages. "He was off last week."

"He didn't make any deliveries?" Diane asked.

"Not for me."

"What does that mean?" Stevens asked.

Skip looked up from the notebook, grinning. There was a dark-colored gob of food stuck between his front teeth. "Means the guys who have their own rigs work for whoever they want. Good money in moonlighting. Actually, he's been off for a few weeks. Some legal thing."

Diane wondered if Skip had any idea how much had been at stake regarding Elwell's "legal thing." She doubted he'd even care. "Do you know when he came back to work?" she asked.

"Yup. Right here," he said, pointing to an entry and spinning the binder toward the detectives.

Elwell's name was written in the margin several times at the start of the week. "This shows him working Monday and Tuesday," Diane said.

"Why are the entries different?" Stevens asked.

"'Cause Monday was a short hop," Skip said.

"What's that?" Diane asked.

"What we call a one-day run. A down-and-back. Usually New England states. Can only log so many hours driving in a day. Any more than allowed and the Staties get their panties in a bunch." Skip's face turned a blotchy shade of crimson as he realized what he'd said. "Sorry about that. You know what I mean."

"Do I ever," Stevens said, exaggerating the act of adjusting her belt with both hands.

Diane worked hard to maintain her poker face. "So what's with Tuesday's entry? That wasn't a short hop?"

"No, ma'am. We sent him to Kansas City to pick up a load of tires."

"When did he leave?"

Skip spun the book back around, so it faced him. "Signed out a trailer at three-thirty Tuesday afternoon."

"When did he return?"

"He hasn't."

"He hasn't returned?" Diane said, surprised.

"Not yet. Probably won't be back till tomorrow."

"Aren't you worried that something may have happened?"

"Not really. It's not like I'm paying him by the hour. Driving long haul can be a pain in the ass. All kinds of shit can go wrong. Accidents. Weather. Exceeding your driving time per day."

"I could drive out there in less than a day," Stevens said.

"Yup, if you didn't stop, you sure could," Skip said. "Problem is, the truckers only get eleven hours of driving time per day. That's the max. As I said, them Staties don't have much of a sense of humor."

"Can you at least call and see if he ever made it to the pickup?" Diane asked.

Skip checked the clock on the wall. "I could, 'cept the warehouse is closed now."

"So he just drove an empty trailer all the way to Kansas City to pick up some tires and bring them back?" Stevens asked.

Skip grinned. "We'd never make any money operating like that. No, he picked up a load of flat-screen TVs in Portland for delivery to Ann Arbor. The tires were the return trip." He turned his attention back to Diane. "You sure he's not in some kind of trouble?"

"I want you to contact us as soon as he returns," Diane said, handing him a business card.

A NEATLY STACKED pile of pink phone message slips sat in the middle of Byron's appointment calendar. A not so subtle reminder from Shirley Grant, the CID secretary, that he hadn't been keeping up with his office work. Sliding them to one side, he flipped open his notebook and picked up the phone. He dialed the number Paula Elwell had provided for her sister-in-law, Meagan Metcalf.

"Lincoln County Sheriff's Department," a young-sounding male voice answered. "How may I direct your call?"

He'd been unprepared for such a greeting. "I'd like to speak with Meagan Metcalf, please."

"Can I tell Lieutenant Metcalf who's calling?"

Lieutenant? Something else Elwell had failed to mention. "Detective Sergeant John Byron, Portland PD."

"Certainly, Sergeant. I'll check and see if she's in."

"WELL?" LeROYER SAID from the office doorway. "Tell me about the Elwells."

"Mrs. Elwell has an alibi," Byron said, sitting back in his chair, rubbing his eyes, and wondering why the lieutenant was hovering so close on this one. "She was with her sister-in-law in Wiscasset Tuesday night."

"How do we know the sister-in-law's not just covering for her?"

There was nothing Byron enjoyed more than being second-guessed by his superiors. "She could be, I suppose, but it doesn't seem likely."

"Why?"

"Because her alibi happens to be a lieutenant for the Lincoln County Sheriff's Office," he said, trying hard to hide his irritation. Byron pretended to reach for the phone. "You want me to call her back, Marty? See if she'll admit to lying? Maybe I can ask her to submit to a polygraph?"

"What about the husband?" LeRoyer asked, ignoring the sarcasm.

"According to Diane and Mel, Justin Elwell was probably halfway to Michigan about the time Ramsey left the bar."

"Michigan?"

"He's a long haul trucker."

"Have they spoken with him?"

"Isn't back yet. Don't worry. We'll track him down."

LeRoyer stepped into Byron's office and closed the door. "John, about earlier. I just wanna say—"

Byron interrupted him. "Save it. You already know how I feel about the press. I told you, that leak didn't come from here."

"Yeah, I know how *you* feel, but that doesn't mean one of the detectives wouldn't throw it out there, just to give one last jab to Ramsey. He wasn't thought of very highly around here, ya know."

He wasn't thought of highly anywhere, Byron thought. "The only people they'd be jabbing are the Ramsey family. And my people wouldn't risk fucking up a case. Besides, leaks are Stanton's thing, not mine."

"So, now what?" LeRoyer asked, seemingly satisfied.

"We look harder at the Fox."

"You really think McVail is responsible for Ramsey's murder?"

Byron thought about it for a moment before answering. "I don't know if he is or he isn't, but he's into a lot more shit than we thought."

"I'm not following."

"I just got back from County. They found coke hidden inside McVail's shoe."

"McVail sold to Ramsey?" LeRoyer asked.

"Not according to him. Said Ramsey got his stuff from some dealer named 'D.'"

"'D'? What the hell kinda name is 'D'?"

"The kind of name Crosby would be familiar with."

BYRON WAS ON the phone waiting for Kenny Crosby to pick up when he received a text from Tran in regards to the subpoena. After leaving a voicemail for the drug sergeant, Byron headed downstairs to the computer lab.

Byron found Tran under his desk doing something related to the maze of wires running back and forth among multiple computers. "Got your text, Dustin. How'd you make out?"

Tran stood up and brushed his hands against the legs of his trousers. "Hey, Striped One. Think I've got a few things you'll find interesting."

"Like?"

Tran plopped down in his chair, slid a printout over to the edge of his desk, and woke his desktop computer. "Like, how late do attorneys typically work at Newman, Branch & DeWitt?"

Byron shrugged. "No idea. I'm sure they work late sometimes. Why?"

"Well, I found some interesting late-night calls from Ramsey's cell to one of the other attorneys."

"How late?"

"Anywhere from ten until midnight, two to three times a week."

"Whose phone was he calling?"

"Branch's wife, Lorraine Davies." Tran tapped the printout. "It's listed as her condo number."

"Let me see that," Byron said, taking the printout from Tran. He compared the numbers on the screen to the numbers supplied by the firm. "How do we know whose condo it is? He may have been calling Branch."

"Maybe. But the printout doesn't say anything about it being Branch's number."

"Do we have an address?"

"Forty-five Eastern Prom. The Portland House. The last after-hours call Ramsey made to her was during the final week of April, and it was the only call he made to her during that week."

"Nothing since?" Byron asked.

"Nope. Little late to be chatting up a married woman, Sarge. Looks like a booty call to me."

"A booty call?"

"Yeah, you know. Hookin' up."

"Could be they were just working a case together," Byron said, trying out the idea. "Maybe they were just spitballing some ideas after work."

"Maybe," Tran said, grinning. "Only one problem with that theory, Sarge."

"What's that?"

"The average length of the calls is about thirty seconds. Sounds more like ballin' than spitballin', Boss Man."

He knew Tran might be right. Either way it necessitated a visit to the condo.

"What's this number?" Byron asked, pointing to the last number dialed.

"That's the very last number Ramsey ever called. Made it at 11:15 Tuesday night."

"Do we know who it belongs to?"

"No. Doesn't match any of the numbers listed for the firm employees. It is a number he's called before and it's a cell but that's all I can tell you."

Byron considered the time and duration of the call. A late-night outbound call only twenty-six seconds long, and Ramsey's last. Another late-night hookup? His dealer? Either one was possible. And it was also possible that he'd been murdered as a result of that call. "We'll need another subpoena."

"Yup."

Byron looked up from the printout. "Any luck with the name Joe? Maybe connected to the Unicorn?"

"I checked every call and follow-up we've had there. No Joes, no Josephs, nothing."

Chapter Fourteen

Friday, 7:05 P.M., April 29, 2016

BYRON STOOD INSIDE the vestibule between the glass entry doors
of the Portland House, waiting for the security guard in the navy
blue blazer to buzz him inside.

"Help you?" the guard said as Byron pulled the door open and
stepped into the lobby.

"I'm here to see Lorraine Davies."

"Your name?"

"Detective Sergeant Byron." He held out his credentials, waiting as the olive-skinned man copied down his name.

"She expecting you?"

"No."

Byron waited as the guard dialed her number.

After a very brief conversation, the guard said, "Sergeant
Byron, you're all set. Head down this hallway and take the elevator to the top floor. Ms. Davies is in apartment D."

Of course it's the top floor, he thought. Nothing but the best for Branch's princess.

"Thanks," Byron said as he started toward the far end of the hall.

Several minutes later, Byron stepped out of the elevator onto the carpeted hallway of the fourteenth floor. To his right the hall angled out of sight. To his left it ran the length of the building to a dead end several hundred feet from where he stood. Absent windows, the space was illuminated by recessed lighting and fancy bronze sconces, reminding him of the Caribbean cruise he and Kay had taken when they were first married. The door to Davies's apartment, located at the far end of the hall, was the last door on the left. Byron stopped next to her entryway where a large ornamental mirror hung directly above an antique side table. He checked his appearance then knocked on the door.

He was about to knock again when he heard the faint sound of heels clicking across an uncarpeted floor.

Davies opened the door. "Sergeant Byron," she said, greeting him with a warm smile.

"Ms. Davies."

She was even more radiant than he'd remembered from their brief encounter in Branch's office. Dressed in a painted-on pair of faded designer jeans, a white cashmere pullover, and bloodred high heels. Byron, unsure of himself, felt more like a nervous schoolboy come to collect his date than a detective sergeant following up on a lead.

But Davies didn't appear the least bit nervous. Standing behind her was the receptionist from the law office, holding a stack of file folders. "I believe you've already met my assistant, Amy Brennan."

"Yes," Byron said. "We met this morning."

"Nice to see you again, Sergeant," Amy said.

"I hope I'm not interrupting anything," Byron said.

"Not at all. Amy was just leaving."

"Night, Ms. Davies," Amy said as she brushed by Byron. "Good night, Sergeant."

"Won't you come in?" Davies said, stepping back slightly so he could enter.

"Thank you," he said.

She closed the door behind him then led him through the marbled tile foyer and into the main living space.

"Have a seat, Sergeant," Davies said, gesturing toward a large, expensive-looking leather sectional. "Can I interest you in something to drink? I have wine, whiskey, even beer if you'd prefer."

"No thanks. I don't drink."

"Ever?"

"It's complicated."

"Well, I think I'll just freshen mine." She picked up a pair of drinking glasses from the coffee table then paused a second. "If you don't mind."

"Not at all," Byron said with a wave of his hand.

"Make yourself at home," Davies said, before flitting off toward the kitchen.

The open concept apartment had a large sunken living room, decorated with lots of dark hardwood and brass, giving it a nautical feel. Floor-to-ceiling windows overlooked the choppy waters of the Atlantic. An open sliding glass door led out to a metal balcony. Byron stepped outside and gazed to the horizon. He imagined being able to see Nova Scotia from this height as he stared down at the bird's-eye view of Fort Gorges and the islands of Casco Bay.

Byron turned and reentered the condo. He crossed the room

toward the leather couch as he heard Davies's footfalls returning from the kitchen.

"Like what you see?" she asked, heading over toward the bar.

"Very much. How long have you and Mr. Branch lived here?" he asked, putting Tran's theory to the test.

Davies laughed as she returned with a fresh drink. She kicked off her shoes and took a seat beside him on the couch. "Devon doesn't live here. Guess you'd call this my home away from home. I have no interest in driving to Topsham every night."

"Topsham?"

"That's where our family home is. I spend most weeknights here."

"Weekends too, I guess."

"Sometimes." She gestured with her free hand toward the room like Vanna White. "Cozy, don't you think?"

Byron agreed, but he wondered how cozy her marriage to Branch was if they never spent any time together. Perhaps Tran was right.

Davies stared seductively at Byron as she dipped a finger in her glass and stirred the liquid. She removed her finger from the drink, placed it between her lips, then slowly withdrew it.

"So, Sergeant Byron," she said. "What can I do for you?"

In spite of her obvious attempt to rattle him, Byron maintained his composure. "We've been going over Ramsey's cellphone records."

"And?"

"Several of the numbers he frequently called matched the contact numbers your firm provided."

She smiled coyly. "Oh? Anyone I might know?"

"Specifically? He called you, Ms. Davies."

"Well, as you said, Paul and I work—excuse me—worked for the same law firm."

"Were you and Ramsey working on a case together recently?"

"Not that I can recall, but we often run scenarios by each other. You know, for a second opinion."

Byron was picturing several possible scenarios, and none of them concerned the law. "So it wouldn't be unusual for you to telephone one another after hours?"

"Not at all."

"Do you remember getting any specific calls from him? Say, within the last couple of months."

"I remember him calling occasionally, but I don't recall the subject matter," she said.

"But it definitely would have been case-related advice, right?"

"Most definitely."

"Huh. See, that's interesting, because the phone records show he made several dozen calls to your cell and your apartment during the months leading up to April. None of the calls lasted longer than about a minute. I can't imagine Ramsey running much by you in such a short amount of time. You must have met up to have these discussions."

"Sometimes we did."

"I'm curious. Where would the two of you meet? Especially given the time of night these calls were made. Did you ever meet here?"

Byron caught a faint flicker of something on her face as she reacted to his question. Then it was gone.

"Of course. I frequently work here at night."

"With Ramsey?"

"Occasionally. And as you've already seen, my assistant and I work here as well. What exactly are you implying, Sergeant?"

"Were you and Ramsey having an affair?"

BYRON DROVE BACK to 109, happy to be out of Davies's condo/ love pad or whatever it was she was keeping. She hadn't admitted to anything other than meeting with Ramsey occasionally to discuss cases. Byron didn't care how she chose to live her life, as long as those choices hadn't led to Ramsey's demise. Were she and Ramsey having an affair? She'd denied it, of course. But if they had been having an affair, had Branch found out? Branch hadn't been the least bit bashful in telling Byron that he and Ramsey weren't friends. Certainly Branch must have been suspicious about his young wife needing a separate place to spend time away from him. Byron would have had concerns had he been in Branch's shoes. Not wanting to make the thirty-mile drive to Topsham every night sounded like a pretty hollow excuse. And why did the frequent phone calls between Davies and Ramsey cease so abruptly? Davies said the cases she and Ramsey were discussing had been resolved. Were they really discussing cases? Or was it possible she *was* telling the truth? Maybe they'd worked so closely on a case, things just went too far. A common scenario in the workplace. Certainly he and Diane were a testament to how something like that could happen.

He slowed as he approached 109 then turned right onto the ramp that led down to the police department's basement garage.

He reached out and keyed the radio mic. "Seven-twenty. Raise the door, please."

"Ten-four, 720," the dispatcher responded.

He waited on the ramp as the huge steel door trundled slowly up on its tracks, squeaking and groaning in protest. Byron wondered how many times that door had been raised and lowered over the course of 109's forty-five-year existence. Back in the 1970s, when his father had worked here, the basement of Portland's police headquarters had been equipped with a half dozen prisoner cells. One officer was assigned to monitor the inmates around the clock. The cells were only meant to house short-term weekend offenders, mostly for minor violations like drunken driving and disorderly conduct. Men who'd gotten drunk and started a bar fight, or assaulted an officer, or even a spouse. They'd be transported to 109 and held until Monday morning when they would be marched over to court to face a magistrate. Some would be released, sentenced to time served; others might earn their release by paying a fine. But the more serious offenders would be shipped off to the Cumberland County Jail to await trial or until they could make bail. Byron wondered how many thousands of men had spent time in 109's now defunct Gray Bar Hotel.

He drove the rest of the way down the steep concrete ramp and into the well-lit basement, taking care not to bottom out the Chevy where the exaggerated angle of the ramp met the metal grill of the water drain and the basement floor. He swung the car to the left, into one of the diagonal command staff parking spaces. Attached to the wall above each space was a small blue and white metal sign designating which member of the department it belonged to. Byron parked in the only unmarked spot. A pale rectangle of discolored concrete was the only reminder that a sign once marked the parking spot for Assistant Chief Cross. Reginald Cross, the Ass Chief. The man who'd caused more grief for two generations of Byrons than could be measured. And not just the Byrons but countless other Portland officers as well. Byron, who took a certain satisfaction in occupying this particular space, climbed out of the car and began to whistle. He strolled over to the support column where the garage door controls were mounted and pressed the down button.

IT WAS AFTER eight o'clock by the time everyone had gathered in the CID conference room. LeRoyer had sprung for pizza out of petty cash.

"So where are we at?" LeRoyer asked, wiping cheese and marinara from his chin.

"We've got more suspects than you can shake a stick at," Nugent said as he poured himself a cup of soda.

"We're still trying to catch up with Childress's alibi," Byron said.

"That the car dealer guy?" LeRoyer asked. "Relative or something, right?"

"Brother-in-law," Diane said. "We'll pay an unannounced visit on him tomorrow."

"What else?" LeRoyer said.

"We're still looking for the stripper Ramsey may have been seeing," Byron said. "We were hoping she danced at the Unicorn."

"Have we even ID'd her yet?" LeRoyer asked.

"Not yet," Byron said. "Diane and I were out there last night. We got the distinct impression that the owners frown on any police cooperation from their staff."

"Figure if we can ID her, we'll have better luck talking to her away from the club," Diane said. "Mel and I will swing out there again tomorrow."

"Maybe I should have a talk with those girls," Nugent said. "Ya know, work my charm."

"Yeah, your wife would love that," Stevens said.

Nugent pretended to pout.

"What about the name Joe?" LeRoyer asked.

"Nothing yet, Boss Man," Tran said. "No Joes work at the Unicorn."

"What about the dive? Did we turn up anything there?" LeRoyer asked.

"Nothing," Byron said.

The conversation continued until the pizza had been reduced to gobs of mozzarella and rust-colored smudges on the cardboard. They were preparing to call it a night when Sergeant Crosby strolled into the room.

"Hey, guys," Crosby said. He turned and addressed LeRoyer. "You wanted to see me, Lieu?"

BYRON AND CROSBY sat side by side in LeRoyer's office discussing the next move. Byron wasn't a fan of Crosby's. Too much had passed between them. He'd asked LeRoyer to set up the meeting hoping Crosby could help, but he knew how guarded the muscled-up drug sergeant was about giving up any inside information. In addition to their mutual history, Byron also didn't care for Crosby's arrogance, which wafted off him like cheap aftershave.

"The Fox is well-known for drug activity," Crosby said in response to a question from Byron. "But we don't spend much time on it."

"Why the hell not?" LeRoyer asked.

Crosby shrugged indifferently as he checked the text messages on his cellphone. "It's an older crowd in there. They tend to police themselves."

"Didn't know we got to pick and choose which drug dealers we went after," Byron said, intentionally trying to provoke a reaction.

Crosby looked up from his phone, glaring at Byron. "Hey, I only have five agents, John. How the fuck am I supposed to take care of Cumberland County with five agents? I prioritize. Like you could do any better."

"Knock it off, you two," LeRoyer said. "Let's just focus on this case, okay? Tell me about the Fox."

"We know a couple of guys who deal out of there regular," Crosby said.

"We grabbed a little coke off Donny McVail. Is he one of them?" Byron asked, already knowing he wasn't, but wanting to see what Crosby would give up in the way of intel.

"Nah, he's strictly small-time. Mostly just a user. One of the dealers is Alonzo Gutierrez. He slings a little weed, a little rock, mostly to the aging hippy crowd."

"Who's the other?" LeRoyer asked.

"Guy by the name of Darius Tomlinson. Goes by 'D.'"

"What's his specialty?" Byron asked.

"Coke, H, pills."

"Sounds like your guy, John," LeRoyer said.

"Would he have mixed with Ramsey?" Byron asked.

"D? Probably. He's a player. Dresses sharp, drives a BMW, wears a lot of bling. D likes to make a statement."

Byron wondered if Crosby realized that he'd just described himself.

"Sounds like they were made for each other," LeRoyer said, looking at Byron.

"Brothers from another mother," Crosby agreed.

"How soon can you get something on Tomlinson?" Byron asked Crosby.

"How's tomorrow sound?"

BYRON BEGRUDGINGLY DRAGGED himself to his own office. They'd been going nonstop for nearly two days and it seemed like all they'd managed to do was expand the list of possible suspects in the Ramsey murder. He couldn't wait to see what tomorrow would bring. He picked up the desk phone receiver and punched in Diane's cell as he sorted through the tower of pink phone message slips left on his desk by Shirley.

"Hey," she answered. Diane's tone was a clear indicator of whether or not she was still pissed at him from earlier. She was.

"Where are you?" he asked as softly as he could, not wishing to escalate the tension.

"On my way home to get some sleep. Thought we were done for the day."

"We are. I was just . . . hoping to catch up with you before you'd left."

"John, I don't want to do this right now."

"Do what?"

"I just don't agree with how you handled questioning Mrs. Elwell. Okay?"

"Really? That's what's eating you?"

"That's it."

"You sure it isn't about your secret meetings and errands for LeRoyer?"

"I'm not doing this now."

"What the hell, Diane?" he said, raising his voice. "Think I deserve a friggin' explanation."

"I'll see you tomorrow."

Byron heard the click as she disconnected the call. He removed the receiver from his ear, staring at it in disbelief. He was about to slam the phone down when LeRoyer stuck his head through the door.

"G'night, John."

He looked up, trying to hide his frustration. "Yeah."

"Everything okay?"

"Yeah. Just tired, I guess."

"Go home. Get some sleep."

Byron forced a weak smile. "Night, Lieu."

Following LeRoyer's departure, Byron reached for the redial button on the desk phone. He paused, his finger hovering above it. *Don't do something you'll regret*, his inner voice cautioned. He hated that voice, but for once it was right. He pulled his hand away.

This is why you don't get involved with a subordinate, John.

Byron slammed the receiver down.

"Fuck you," he said to the voice.

Chapter Fifteen

Saturday, 6:05 A.M., April 30, 2016

SATURDAY MORNING DAWNED gloomy and gray, in perfect harmony with Byron's mood. He'd spent the night tossing and turning and was still at a loss to comprehend what had Diane so worked up. She wasn't normally given to brooding. He walked down to the end of his driveway where someone's trash bin was lying on its side. He dragged it over to the curb next to an empty recycling bin. Since moving into the condo he had only met two of his neighbors: a pretty young divorcée who, even in their brief encounters, had already shared far more information about her ex than Byron was comfortable knowing, and a paunchy middle-aged cop groupie who always wanted to know what Byron "had on." As if he were some television supersleuth who only required an hour to solve a murder, less if you counted commercials. Not only did Byron not care to know about the personal lives of his neighbors, he also had no interest in sharing his, especially given the sensitive nature of his relationship with Diane. After establishing his neighbors' schedules, Byron worked hard at avoiding them. He was genuinely surprised to hear his name being called from behind.

"Good morning, Officer Byron," said a male voice with a heavy Middle Eastern accent. The odd pacing of the words, betraying that English was not his first language, gave a Christopher Walken–esque quality to the man's delivery.

Byron turned, observing a tall, slim, dark-skinned man walking toward him with purpose. The man's hand was extended and he wore a smile on his face. "Morning," Byron said, wondering which of his neighbors had been gossiping about him to the others.

"How are you doing today, Officer Byron?"

"I'm well," Byron said, giving the man a firm handshake.

"I am Khalid Muhammad. I live two doors down with my family. I have wanted to say hello since you moved in, but I never see you."

"I keep crazy hours."

"So, you are the policeman?"

He wondered if that meant that Muhammad had already met the construction worker, the cowboy, and the rest of the Village People. "That's the rumor." Byron's joke only generated a perplexed look from Muhammad. Evidently, Muhammad had never danced to "YMCA." "Yes, I'm a detective sergeant with Portland PD."

"Ah, yes. An investigator. I am most pleased to be making your acquaintance," he said, giving a slight bow of his head.

"And what do you do for work, Mr. Muhammad?" Byron asked, trying hard to project that it mattered.

"Please, call me Khalid. I'm an accountant."

"One of the local firms?"

"No, no. How do you say, employed for myself?"

"Self-employed."

"Yes, yes. That is it." Muhammad beamed with pride. "Self-employed. Many people of the Somali community come to me for help with their finances."

"Good for you." Byron checked his watch. "Well, I gotta get to work."

"Yes, I know you are a busy man. It is good to be making your acquaintance, *Detective Sergeant* Byron."

"Likewise, Khalid. I'm sure I'll see you around."

With a nod of his head, Muhammad was gone. Byron watched him stroll across the lawn toward his own condo, pleasantly surprised that his new immigrant neighbor seemed to grasp the concept of boundaries far better than the homegrown had. *Perhaps Khalid won't be someone I'll have to avoid*, he thought.

JOHN BYRON'S FOURTH-FLOOR office was situated at the end of a back hallway, at the opposite end from LeRoyer's. The hall ran the length of the northeast side of the building, perpendicular to the main corridor, connecting the offices of CID's command and supervisory staff. The walls of Byron's modest work space were devoid of the awards and recognition found in other supervisors' offices. Their absence wasn't because he hadn't earned them; he had. They were missing because he didn't believe in "walls of me." A simple metal desk, with a navy blue laminate top, three chairs, two filing cabinets, and a desktop computer were all he needed. The eggshell-colored walls were spare: a large round black framed clock, a lithograph of a police funeral painted by a cop, and a black and white photo of Byron and his late father, Reece, taken when John was just a boy. The fourth wall held a floor-to-ceiling window that looked out on Franklin Arterial and Casco Bay beyond.

Byron was deeply engrossed in the details of Evidence Technician Pelligrosso's supplement on the Ramsey murder when his desk phone rang.

"CID, Byron," he said, grabbing it on the second ring.

"Hello, John," a familiar female voice said. "It's Kay."

His throat tightened at the sound of her voice. He remembered the smell of her skin, the fiery look of her auburn hair in the morning sun. He hadn't spoken to his ex in nearly eight months. The same amount of time, coincidentally, that his relationship with Diane had been gestating. He'd been attempting to move on with his life. He thought the new condo might help. A change of venue from his shabby little Danforth Street flat and the months he'd wasted there lying to himself about the temporary nature of their separation. It all came flooding back in an instant. Like he'd been injected by some mind-altering, time-traveling hypodermic.

"How are you?" she asked, breaking the silence.

"I'm good," he croaked after realizing he hadn't spoken.

"Nice to hear your voice."

Was it? Or was she simply being polite? "Good to hear yours as well," he said.

"I wondered if you might be available to meet me this afternoon? For lunch? Say around noon?"

Byron hated that their marriage had ended so badly. Several times he'd considered reaching out, hoping for a more amicable relationship with the woman he'd shared a home, a bed, a life with, for nearly two decades, but he hadn't. Now, here she was affording him the opportunity to reconnect and he was neck-deep in a murder investigation. Again. The job, having played such a large part in eroding their marriage, was standing in the way once more.

"I'm in the middle of a homicide, Kay. Hard for me right now."

She paused a moment without speaking. Byron was beginning to think she hadn't heard him, when at last she spoke up.

"Is it the attorney?" she asked. "The one found in the ocean?"

"Yeah. Paul Ramsey."

Kay paused again. "That's why I need to see you."

DIANE CHECKED THE clock on the wall. It was 9:15. She was growing impatient, having played this same game with Mead only the day before. Melissa Stevens had her face buried in a dog-eared fitness magazine, featuring a shirtless ripped-ab Matthew McConaughey on its cover, from the outdated stack on the table between them.

"Excuse me," Diane said to Mead's dutiful secretary. "Any idea how much longer he'll be?"

The secretary glanced at her desk phone then fixed Diane with a polite smile. "He's still on the phone, *Detective*. I'm sure it won't be much longer though." Her mouth was smiling but her eyes were not. Her eyes said, *Bitch*.

Five minutes later, the door to the back office opened and out strolled Mead.

"Sorry to keep y'all waiting," Mead said, extending a meaty paw toward Diane. "I'm Everett Mead."

After the obligatory introductions, Mead led them down a short corridor into his office.

"Have a seat, ladies. Getcha some java?"

"No thanks," Diane said for both of them.

"Okay," Mead said. "You said on the phone yesterday that you wanted to speak with me about something. I'm all ears."

Actually, you're all belly, Diane thought.

"Who were you just talking with on the phone, Mr. Mead?" Diane asked, trying to catch him off guard.

She studied Mead as he looked at her. The pause was barely noticeable but long enough to give Mead time to come up with a lie. The truth wouldn't have required such a pause.

"Oh, th-that was one of our parts suppliers," Mead said, stammering slightly.

"Everything okay?" Stevens said, playing along.

"Yeah, they been giving us a bit of trouble, but I sorted 'em out."

"I'm glad to hear it," Stevens said.

"Mr. Mead, do you remember where you were Tuesday night?" Diane asked without any warning.

"Sure. I was at home watching the Celtics game with my brother-in-law, Matt."

"Matt Childress?"

"Yes, ma'am."

"Just the two of you?" she asked.

"Yup, couple of bachelors," Mead said. "The little women snuck off down to Boston to do some shopping."

"Little women?" Stevens asked, her disapproval obvious.

Mead flushed.

"Your wives?" Diane asked.

"Yup. They spent the night in Beantown, so Matt and I stayed in and had some beers and watched the game." Mead turned his attention toward Stevens. "Either of you happen to catch it?"

"Missed that one," Stevens said.

"Well, I never miss the Celtics when they're in the playoffs."

"You remember what time Mr. Childress left your house?" Diane asked.

"Can't say for sure. I know he was there for the tip-off at

eight-thirty. We had a couple more beers and shot some pool after the game. Musta been about midnight when Matt headed home."

Diane jotted something in her notebook. She caught Mead craning his neck to try and see what she'd written.

"Y'all mind if I ask what this is about?" Mead said, sitting back and folding his hands over his belly.

"Not at all," Diane said. "Detective Stevens and I are investigating a suspicious death that occurred Tuesday night. We're checking on Mr. Childress's alibi for that night."

"Well, he was with me," Mead said, beaming his most insincere smile.

"So you said," Diane continued. "We'll need contact information for you and your wife, Mr. Mead."

"Of course," he said. He pulled a pen from his shirt pocket and began to jot names and numbers on company letterhead.

"When was the last time you spoke with your brother-in-law, Mr. Mead?" Stevens asked.

Diane watched Mead exaggerate the act of squinting as if he were actually struggling to recollect their last conversation. "Guess that woulda been Tuesday night, or Wednesday morning if it was after midnight when he left."

Diane made another note. "So you haven't spoken to him by phone since Tuesday?"

"Nope," Mead said, passing her the information.

"You're sure?"

"Positive."

Diane flipped her notebook closed and looked at Stevens. "Well, looks like we're finished here."

"Thank you for your time, Mr. Mead," Stevens said.

"Pleasure meetin' you both," Mead said, standing and extending his hand again. "Hope this helped you out."

Neither detective spoke until they were outside of the building, not that the noise inside the garage would have let them.

"What do you think?" Diane said, already knowing the answer, as they reached the car. "Think Mead was lying?"

"Lying his ass off," Stevens said. "He services cars and his lips were moving. Couldn't wait to tell you who he was with Tuesday night. Think he would've volunteered Childress's name if he hadn't been coached?"

"No, I don't."

Diane unlocked the doors and they both got in. "Especially when the only question I asked is where *he* was Tuesday night."

"Exactly."

BYRON SAT STARING through his office window at the jam of weekend commuters on Franklin Arterial. Both southbound lanes were backed up halfway to Congress Street with a sparkling assortment of brightly colored metal boxes. His eyes were on the cars but his thoughts were occupied by other things. Ramsey, Diane, Kay, and another large coffee, although not particularly in that order. He was also thinking about Childress and his alibi. Watching the Celtics with his brother-in-law, he'd said. *Must be nice.* Byron's crazy life didn't allow for such leisurely pursuits. In fact, he hadn't watched or even listened to a game since the late Johnny Most was still calling the shots in his signature raspy tone. He grinned, fondly remembering how Johnny would often lose his voice as the excitement built to a crescendo when Bird or maybe Ainge drained a three late in a close game.

"Thomas," Childress had said. "Helluva night." Byron was

familiar with the name from the *Portland Herald* sports page, usually left in the stall in the CID locker room, jammed between the dual toilet paper dispenser and the wall.

He tapped the keyboard, bringing his computer back to life, and searched for the Boston Celtics webpage. Finding it, he clicked on the link recapping Tuesday's playoff game against the Hawks.

"Good morning, Sergeant," Shirley said from the doorway, pulling Byron out of his investigative trance.

"Shirley," he said with a nod. "Thanks for coming in on a Saturday."

"Of course. Those statements won't type themselves. Wondering if Kay managed to get ahold of you?"

"Kay?"

She shot him a disapproving scowl. "Your ex-wife. I left you a message yesterday. You didn't even look at them, did you?"

The stack of pink slips. He hadn't taken the time to look through all of them. "Yes. She did. We're meeting for—" He stopped himself. *Why had he started to tell her about his lunch date?* If Shirley knew, everyone else would too. She couldn't help it. "I got it. Thanks."

Shirley opened her mouth to say something but the ringing of Byron's desk phone interrupted her. He glanced at the caller ID. Tran.

Saved by the bell.

"You ready for this, Obi-Wan?" Tran asked as Byron entered the cramped office of the Computer Crimes Unit.

Frustrated and looking for anything resembling progress, Byron hid his annoyance with his detective's usual unprofessional greeting. "What've you got?"

"You were right about the building contractor's alibi being bogus. What did Childress tell you he did Tuesday night?" Tran asked, dragging out his big reveal.

"Said he spent the evening at his brother-in-law's, watching basketball."

"In York County, right?"

"Correct."

Tran passed a digital printout to Byron.

It was a chart of dates and times. "What's this?"

"That is a printout from the E-ZPass account of Mr. 'Bob the Builder' Childress, showing a vehicle registered to him getting on the turnpike in Saco on Tuesday night at 8:05 P.M."

"Childress owns a big construction company," Byron countered, disappointed that Tran's excitement had been for naught. "He has access to a fleet of vehicles. How do we know this was Childress and not one of his employees?"

Tran was beaming as he handed Byron yet another piece of paper, this one an inkjet photo. "Because, Striped Dude, here he is behind the wheel in black and white. This vehicle is registered to him *personally*. Maine vanity 'Chill 1.'"

Byron studied the picture. It had been blown up to fit the page and was somewhat pixelated, but there was no doubt it was Matthew Childress. Alone and crammed in behind the wheel of the late model Dodge Challenger, he looked just as massive as he had inside the construction trailer.

"That photo matches up perfectly to the time and date stamp on Childress's E-ZPass account," Tran continued.

"Still doesn't put him in Portland," Byron said. "He could've driven north or south from there. How would we know where he exited?"

"We wouldn't," Tran said. "But we do know what time he got back onto the pike—6:44 Wednesday morning."

"Where?" Byron asked.

Tran grinned and tapped his index finger on top of his desk. "Exit 48. Right here in Portland."

Chapter Sixteen

Saturday, 11:30 A.M., April 30, 2016

BYRON WALKED INTO interview room one with folder in hand, closed the door, and sat across the table from the burly contractor. Maintaining a painted-on smile, Byron dispensed the usual pleasantries before navigating Childress along the thorny path of Miranda.

Byron had always found the concept of Miranda ludicrous. It was like telling a heavyweight boxer to fight with both arms tied behind his back, as if he might talk his way to victory. He understood the importance of safeguarding people's rights, even the scumbags that they routinely had to deal with. But he didn't understand why his superiors, and ultimately the general public, were surprised whenever police detectives failed to obtain a confession. Miranda basically states that if you've broken the law and you agree to speak with the cops, they not only have the right to jam it up your ass sideways and break it off, they will. Luckily, not all criminals are as smart as they think they are. Some just can't help themselves. *God bless the stupid ones.*

After obtaining a waiver, Byron opened the folder, carefully placing the signed document atop the growing pile of paperwork.

"You lied to me, Mr. Childress," Byron said. "I'd like to know why."

"What are you talking about?"

"Isaiah Thomas didn't play worth a damn Tuesday night. In fact, he only scored seven points."

"Maybe I got the games mixed up," Childress said. "I watch so many of them."

"Possibly," Byron said. "But then there's still the issue with the Maine Turnpike Authority."

The skin between Childress's eyes crinkled into a tight knot as he scowled. "What issue?"

Byron reached into the file folder and tossed a photograph on the table.

Childress looked down at the photo without touching it, as if it might bite. Deep creases formed upon his ruddy forehead. "What's this?"

"That is a picture taken at the tollbooth on the Maine Turnpike in Saco, shortly after eight o'clock Tuesday night. Same time you told me you were at your brother-in-law's house watching the Celtics."

Childress shrugged. "So, maybe I was late getting there."

"That would certainly explain it," Byron said. "I mean, going through the tollbooth doesn't mean anything, right?"

Childress gave him a smug look and tilted the chair back on its rear legs. "That's right, it doesn't."

"Sure," Byron said. "I mean, all this proves is you passed through the tolls. Doesn't mean you came to Portland, right? You could've gone southbound to your brother-in-law's just like you said."

Childress eyed Byron warily without answering. The chair groaned in protest.

"Only trouble is, the toll cameras caught you getting back onto the pike." Byron threw a second photo on the table. "Bright and early the following morning. Exit 48 in Portland."

Childress picked this one up and studied it.

"Check the date and time on the bottom," Byron said. "Why did you lie to me?"

Childress returned the photo to the tabletop, setting it beside the other one. He looked up at Byron. "Think I'd like to speak with my lawyer now."

DAVIS BILLINGSLEA SAT on a wooden bench in Tommy's Park checking his Twitter feed as he waited. On the phone, Crosby had made it sound as if he'd be right over to pick him up, but that was twenty minutes ago. He was wondering if he'd been stood up when he heard the throaty sound of a high-performance engine. He looked over toward Exchange Street where a charcoal-colored Charger was parked at an odd angle next to the curb. Crosby, who was behind the wheel, revved the V-8 engine again.

"Come on, come on, let's go. I can't be seen talking to you," Crosby said as Billingslea opened the door and climbed in.

Billingslea wisely clicked on his seat belt as Crosby chirped the tires rounding the corner from Exchange onto Middle, causing the rear of the Dodge to fishtail wildly.

"So, what's this big scoop?" Billingslea asked. "You got something new on Ramsey?"

"Not directly. Hell, I already gave you stuff on that."

Yeah, Billingslea thought, that he'd been murdered. Big deal. He would have gotten that sooner or later. "What, then?"

"Well, it is related to Ramsey. A juicy little byline for you, after we make a quick stop."

"Where are we going?"

"Lunch. I'm starving and you're buying."

Once again Billingslea was reminded of why he hated dealing with this egocentric bully. A bully who reminded him a bit too much of Danny Simonelli, the too-big-for-his-age kid who had tormented him throughout grade school. But he had to admit, Crosby's information was always solid.

Billingslea pressed his feet against the floor, pushing himself back into the plush leather seat, and held on as the crazy drug detective wound his way through the streets of downtown Portland.

BYRON EXITED THE interview room, closing the door behind him. He addressed the uniform who was seated just outside. "Stay with him, okay? He's still in custody."

The officer nodded.

Byron checked his watch then headed to the conference room where Diane was monitoring the interview.

"So, now what?" Diane asked as he entered the room.

"We let him make a call to his attorney. Maybe he'll want to talk with us after."

"And if he doesn't?"

"I'll run it by Ferguson. Can you do me a favor and keep an eye on him?"

"Why? Where are you going?"

"I've got a twelve o'clock meeting with someone who might actually have information on this case."

Diane frowned. "So why am I stuck babysitting this asshole? We are partners on this, right?"

Byron carefully considered his response. The conversation wasn't going at all as he'd planned. It was his fault. He should have told her right up front about Kay. But he hadn't and now that she was worked up about it, he couldn't. A half-truth would have to suffice.

"Of course we are," he said. "It's just that the person I'm meeting with doesn't want anyone to know where the information came from. It's kinda sensitive."

"Well, you could've told me that," she said.

"You're right," he said. "I'm sorry."

"I mean, you don't have to get all secretive about it. Jeez. 'Sorry, Diane,'" she said, making her voice deeper to sound like him. "'I have to meet a CI. You can't come.'"

"Sorry, Di, but I've gotta meet a CI. You can't come."

"Don't be an asshole."

DiMillo's on the Water was located on Long Wharf at the center of Portland's waterfront. In the 1940s, before being converted into a restaurant, the boat had gone by the name *New York*, and was operated as a car ferry between her namesake and New Jersey. It was bought and sold by several other states before the DiMillo family purchased the vessel in 1982, opening the only floating restaurant on the Upper East Coast.

Byron hurried down the long ramp connecting the pier to the restaurant. Running ten minutes late of the noontime meeting time she had requested, he entered the foyer and headed down the corridor to the right of the reception desk, away from the bar lounge, toward the restaurant side of the boat.

"May I help you?" the young female maître d' asked as he mounted the steps.

"I'm meeting someone," he said, peering over her shoulder into the dining area.

"A lady?"

"Yes. She may already be here."

"A very pretty lady?" the maître d' asked, giving him a sly grin.

Realizing that she was toying with him, Byron returned the smile. "Yes. A very pretty lady."

"She's waiting for you, seated at a table on the far left."

He thanked her and entered the dining room, where Dr. Kay Byron was seated by a window overlooking Portland Harbor. As Byron approached her table, she rose and greeted him with a warm smile. Tall and trim, with piercing hazel eyes, she wore a navy blue pantsuit and a white blouse open at the collar. Her long auburn hair was pulled back neatly into a ponytail.

"It's good to see you, John," she said.

Byron hugged her. It was the kind of awkward embrace two people, once very intimate, give to each other when they're no longer sure what they are.

"I'm glad you called," he said. It was all he could think to say.

They settled into chairs across from each other as the waiter appeared at their table carrying a silver pitcher and charged Byron's water glass.

"Good afternoon," he said. "My name is Nunzio and I'll be taking care of you today. Can I interest either of you in something from the bar?"

"I'll have a glass of merlot," Kay said.

"Coffee, please," Byron said.

Nunzio smiled and nodded, then he was gone, leaving the two of them alone.

Kay raised a brow. "Coffee? Are you—?"

He nodded. "Six months."

"Really?" she asked.

"Self-imposed exile, I guess you'd call it."

"I'm impressed. Any reason?"

He considered her question. "Guess I needed my control back."

She smiled and took a sip of her water.

She didn't ask how it was going; for that he was grateful. He wondered what she was thinking. Being married to a psychotherapist had always left him feeling exposed. It was a feeling he didn't like. "You look great," he said, trying hard to make conversation but itching to know more about why she had called.

"Surprised to hear from me?"

"A little. It has been a while."

"I know and for that I am sorry," she said. "Guess I needed some distance and a little perspective."

They continued to make small talk as Nunzio brought their drinks and took their orders.

"So, as I mentioned on the phone, I need to talk to you about the case you're working," she said.

"The Ramsey case."

"Yes. How exactly was he murdered, John?"

"You know I can't discuss an ongoing investigation," he said, carefully taking another sip from the hot mug.

"They said on the news he was found in the ocean."

Byron nodded. "He was."

"He didn't drown, did he?"

DIANE SAT AT the conference room table going over her case notes. The monitor was still on but was muted. She had stopped the recording as soon as Childress's attorney entered the interview room. Everything discussed between the two men was privileged communication. Diane stood up to stretch her back when her cell rang.

"Detective Joyner."

"Detective, this is Justin Elwell calling. I got a message saying you wanted to talk to me."

"Thank you for responding so quickly, Justin. Yes, we need to talk. Where are you?"

"I'm on my way to Bangor at the moment but I'll be in Portland tomorrow afternoon. I'm bringing my truck down for service. Portland Transport, out on Warren Avenue."

Diane copied down the address from Elwell and agreed to meet him there the following afternoon. She was just hanging up as Shirley Grant walked by and deposited several mustard-colored interoffice envelopes on the table in front of her.

"Thanks," Diane said. She resumed checking her notes without bothering to look at the mail.

"Got anything that needs to be entered or transcribed?" Grant asked.

"Yeah, I've still gotta download the audio file of my last interview. I'll email it to you shortly."

"Oh, okay."

Diane, sensing that Grant was still standing there waiting for something, stopped what she was doing and turned to face her. She'd known Grant long enough to know the middle-aged office assistant was bursting with some news she desperately needed to share. Some dirty little secret that needed telling.

"What?" Diane asked.

Grant looked around as if making sure no one was listening. Diane didn't understand the point of her gesture as she'd soon be telling everyone her newfound secret.

"Well?" Diane asked.

"It's about Sergeant Byron," she said, her voice an excited whisper.

Diane felt a dark cloud materializing above her head. *Had John learned about the promotion? Shit.* Mel had warned her. She should've told him before now.

"I think he and Kay are getting back together," Grant said, nearly breathless.

BYRON COCKED HIS head to one side. "What makes you say that?"

Kay glanced over at the table directly across from theirs, where two young women were seated and deeply engrossed in their respective love lives. Satisfied that no one was listening in on their conversation, she continued. "My work puts me in contact with a great many troubled people."

"Well, there's something we still have in common," he said, regretting the words as soon as they were out of his mouth.

She looked at him as if wounded. She turned to look through the window at a passing watercraft.

"I'm sorry," he said. "Pay no attention to the asshole seated across the table. He's new at this."

She turned back to face him. Her smile reappeared. "As am I."

"Please. Continue."

"I've been treating a man for the past six months, a number of different problems. Yesterday he came to see me without an appointment. He's never done that before. I could see something had really upset him."

Byron took another drink of coffee, waiting for her to get to the point.

"My patient has an abusive boyfriend. It's one of the reasons I'm treating him."

Byron nodded but remained silent. The thought occurred to him that he and Kay might still have been married had he been this good at listening when she wasn't providing information on a case.

"My patient thinks his boyfriend may have killed Paul Ramsey."

Byron hadn't known what information Kay was planning to share, but he certainly wasn't prepared for this revelation. The lengthening list of suspects was making him wonder whether they'd ever apprehend Ramsey's killer. "What's your client's name?"

She gave him a disapproving scowl. "You know it doesn't work that way, John. I have to maintain confidentiality."

"Then why tell me any of this?"

"I need to know how Ramsey died. If it was the way my patient thinks, he would be willing to meet with you."

"How did he tell you it happened?" Byron asked.

The waiter returned with their meals, momentarily interrupting the conversation.

"Do either of you need anything else?" the waiter asked.

"We're fine, thank you," Byron said.

Following Nunzio's departure, Kay continued. "My patient told me that his boyfriend got into an altercation with Ramsey. That it got physical."

"Did he tell you where this happened or why?"

"I think the boyfriend and Ramsey knew each other from the gym where the boyfriend works. Was there any evidence Ramsey had been in a fight?"

Byron nodded. "There was."

"Was he shot?"

Byron debated sharing sensitive case information with Kay. He knew he could trust her but keeping case information close to the vest was instinctive. Expanding the list of people who knew the facts was always a dicey proposition. "Yes. He was."

Kay sat back, dropping her hands in her lap, and sighed. "I was afraid of that."

"Did your patient witness the murder?" Byron asked.

"I don't think so. He said his boyfriend told him about it. Even showed him the gun."

"What else did he tell you?"

"I think you'd better ask him."

As they ate, Kay attempted to steer their conversation in other directions. Byron, wanting to stay on topic, kept bringing it back to her patient. Talking about the case was safe.

Byron's cell rang. Haggerty's name was displayed on the ID. Byron had previously left a message saying that he needed to speak with him. The call signaled the end of their lunch date and, ironically enough, was precisely the kind of thing that had eroded their marriage. Kay hadn't been willing to share her husband's every waking moment with the City of Portland and its police force. And, if he was being honest with himself, who could blame her?

"You'll call me as soon as you've spoken with him, right?" Byron said.

She nodded. "Promise me that you'll go easy on him. He's very fragile right now."

"As long as he tells me the truth."

"Will I see you on Sunday?"

"Sunday?"

"Katie's graduation party."

"I'm not sure yet. I'll try and make it."

Gently, Kay reached out and took hold of his hand. "It's good to see you, John."

"I'm glad you called," he said.

She gave him a wry grin. "Because it might help your case?"

"Of course. But I'm glad you called anyway."

"So am I."

They parted with another hug. This one far less awkward.

Chapter Seventeen

Saturday, 1:15 P.M., April 30, 2016

DIANE TALKED ONE of Sergeant Peterson's detectives into watching the monitor for her. Childress and his attorney were still in the middle of an animated conversation, and as much as she would have loved watching the contractor squirm in silence, she had a supplement to update.

Diane, having retreated to her desk, now sat staring at the flashing cursor on her computer monitor. Shirley's bombshell about who John was meeting left her unable to concentrate. Certainly not the amount of concentration needed to compose a document that might eventually be used to try a murderer.

Why would John lie about what he was doing? Was he really seeing Kay again? Or was Shirley making more of this than it was? But what if Shirley was right? What did that make her? The rebound girl? *Fuck that.*

Diane's desk phone rang, startling her out of her stupor. She answered it.

"CID. Joyner." Nothing. She waited. The line was definitely open. "Hello?"

"Hello," a feminine-sounding voice answered. "Are you one of the detectives who came by the Unicorn asking about Paul Ramsey?"

"I am. I'm Detective Joyner. To whom am I speaking?"

"Um. My name is Trixie."

"Trixie . . ."

"Just Trixie."

Diane flipped open her notepad and scrawled the name, date, and time. "Are you the person who left us the note?"

"Yes."

"Do you know something about the murder?" Diane could hear the woman breathing.

"Trixie, do you know something?"

"I don't know. Maybe."

Diane knew this dance all too well. A potential witness as nervous as a deer on the side of the highway and just as likely to bolt. She pressed forward as gently as she could. "If you do know something about this, it's important that we talk."

"I shouldn't have called you. If my boss knew I—"

"No one is going to tell your boss."

"I don't know."

"I can meet you somewhere? You name the place. I'll be there." More breathing as Trixie, or whoever she was, thought it over. "Trixie, your boss won't know you talked to me, you have my word."

"I'll be at Denny's on Congress Street."

"When?"

"One hour."

"How will I know you?"

"I'll sit near the door."

DURING HIS RETURN to 109, Byron called Haggerty. He tasked the squared-away veteran with locating Erwin Glantz.

"Why don't we just put out an ATL for him, Sarge?" Haggerty asked.

"I'd rather not spook him, Hags. The camp Gabe found in the woods might not even have been his."

"But you think it was?"

"Yes, and if it was, and if he saw anything, he's gonna try and hide. He won't want to get involved. I'm looking for the gentle approach on this one."

"Gotcha."

"See if you can get him to come see me."

"I'll put the word out, Sarge."

Byron thanked Haggerty and disconnected the call. He parked the car in front of 109 and trotted up the steps to the plaza. There were a number of things in need of his attention but most of his focus was on Kay's patient, whoever he was.

He tapped the elevator's up button and began the long wait. He often wondered how it was that a building only four stories tall, five if you counted the basement, equipped with two elevators, never seemed to have one at the ready. While waiting, he gazed absently at the various job postings pinned to a cork message board. The city was looking to fill several positions at the Barron Center, an assisted living facility, and a computer specialist in the M.I.S. lab. Each of the postings included a cover-your-ass caveat proclaiming that women and minorities were encouraged to apply as the city was an equal opportunity employer, a disclaimer he'd always found both amusing and mildly insulting, for all parties concerned.

One of the elevators was finally moving downward. He checked the display and saw that it had stopped on three. Impatiently, he went back to scanning the board. The promotional lists had been posted. The lists were supposed to be anonymous with each person assigned an identification number, followed by their test score, weighted to fifty percent of the total value, evaluation score weighted to forty percent, and seniority points straight up. The problem was, it didn't take a rocket scientist to figure out the candidates once you knew who had actually taken the test, how they normally fared, and seniority. Most years it only took a day or two for someone to scribble the names next to the numbers. A half point of seniority was earned for every year of service with a cap of ten points. The system had been implemented when the twenty-year retirement system was still active. Twenty-five was now the minimum. Byron wondered how it could be that five additional years of experience counted for nothing. Evidently the city must have assumed that officers with twenty years on knew all there was to know. *Hardly.*

He checked the names on the lieutenant's list first. Milliken had been inked in at the top followed by Sadler and Collins, two kiss-ass sergeants. Milliken was a good man, but Byron knew it was likely that he'd be passed over yet again in favor of one of the two yes men. A sad truth repeated time and again. Crosby's name was fourth. Byron couldn't help but smile. *Sorry, old chap, maybe next time.*

Next he perused the names written beside the anonymous list for sergeant. No surprises until he reached the fifth name. Joyner.

Diane had taken the test? He couldn't believe it. Surely someone must have penned her name in by mistake. She would have told him if she'd been planning to take the test. He double-checked the seniority, calculating in his head. The points matched. *She wouldn't leave the detective bureau. Would she?*

The doors to both elevators opened simultaneously. He grabbed the one on the right and punched four. Arriving at his destination, he walked into the entry vestibule of CID, stopping in front of Shirley's desk.

"Anything for me?"

She passed him another stack of pink phone message slips. "Your voicemail is full."

Of course it is, he thought as he scanned through the stack.

"The lieutenant's looking for you."

"Okay," he said absently. "Anything else?"

"Yeah. Diane said to tell you she and Mel are out following up on a new lead."

"I thought she was watching Childress," he said, now fully attentive.

"Nope. One of Sergeant Peterson's detectives is."

"She say what this new lead was?"

Shirley shook her head. "Nope."

He paused for a second, trying to read her face. She had the look of a cat who'd just finished gobbling the pet canary. "That it?" he asked.

She nodded but her expression remained unchanged.

He started toward the interview room and had nearly made the corner when Shirley blurted out, "How's Kay?"

DIANE HELD THE door for Stevens as they entered the restaurant. She made immediate eye contact with a young blonde woman sitting alone several booths in from the entrance, vaguely remembering her from the strip club.

"That her?" Stevens asked.

"I think so," Diane said. "She looked a little different the other night."

"Must be the clothes."

The woman, who couldn't have been much older than twenty-two, was attractive in spite of the artificial tan, heavy eyeliner, and hair stripped to the point that it was nearly white.

"Trixie?" Diane asked as she and Stevens stopped at the table.

"Thought you were coming alone," Trixie said defensively, hugging her purse close as if one of them might grab it.

"It's okay. This is my partner, Detective Melissa Stevens."

"Hello," Stevens said, extending a hand as they slid into the booth across from Trixie.

Trixie ignored the gesture, remaining focused on Diane. "I'm still not all that comfortable talking to you about this."

"Trixie, if it's about—"

"I know what you said. But I need this job, okay? I got a five-year-old daughter and I can't afford to go on welfare. And my name isn't Trixie. it's Abigail. Abigail Dees."

"Abby," Diane said, doing the math inside her head. "Is it okay if I call you Abby?"

Dees nodded, releasing her grip on the purse.

"Can I get you ladies anything?" a pimple-faced teenaged boy wearing a Denny's polo shirt and chinos asked.

"We're all set, thanks. Unless you'd like something else?" Diane said, addressing Dees.

Dees shook her head. "I'm fine."

"Okay," the waiter said. "Let me know if you change your minds."

Following his departure, Diane continued. "Abby, when Sergeant Byron and I stopped by the other night we asked if anyone was dating Paul Ramsey. Were you?"

She shook her head. "Not me. One of my coworkers at the club."

"Your note said, 'Talk to Joe.' Who's Joe?"

Dees looked away without answering.

"Why don't you want your employer to know you've spoken with us?" Stevens asked. "Are they involved in this?"

Dees's eyes widened. "I—I—I don't know. I never considered that. I hope not. I didn't want to say anything because they have a policy about not talking to the cops." She looked back at Diane. "You don't think they're involved, do you?"

"I don't know," Diane said. "We're just trying to piece this together. Let's not jump to any conclusions, okay?"

Dees closed her eyes and exhaled. "Okay."

"What about your coworker?" Diane asked. "The one with Ramsey."

"Candy. She had been seeing Ramsey on and off for a while."

"How long?"

"Months."

"Did he ever come by the club?"

"A few times when they first started dating, but not recently."

"Did your bosses know?"

"Yeah, that's why Ramsey stopped coming around. They told Candy that he was too well-known. He stuck out."

"Who's they?" Diane asked.

"Kakalegian."

"Do you know where they'd go on their dates?" Stevens asked.

"Sometimes her apartment, sometimes in his car."

"His car?" Diane asked.

"Yeah. Candy has a kid too. A daughter. She's divorced and only gets to have her at the apartment once in a while. When Candy wanted to meet up with Ramsey, she'd wait until her daughter went to sleep before going to meet him."

"Do you know if Candy met up with Ramsey Tuesday night?"

"You'd have to ask her."

"Do you know Candy's real name and address?" Stevens asked.

Abby sighed and looked away again. "Are you going to tell her I told you?"

Diane reached out, gently placing a hand on Dees's forearm. "We don't have to say it was you, but if you don't tell us how to find her we'll have no choice but to ask Kakalegian."

BYRON SAT OPPOSITE Childress and his attorney. He pulled the tollbooth photographs out of the folder and set them on the table again. "I understand you want to talk, is that right?"

Childress nodded.

"You understand that when you asked for your attorney, you invoked your Miranda rights. Are you now waiving those rights?"

Childress looked to his attorney. The attorney gave a nod of his own.

The big man kept glancing down at the black and white images in front of him, as if they might somehow change. "I wasn't at my brother-in-law's house that night."

No shit. "Which night?"

"Tuesday night."

"Where were you?"

"Somewhere else," Childress said as he looked sheepishly up at Byron. "Somewhere I shouldn't have been."

"Where?"

"At a motel. With my girlfriend."

"Which motel?"

Childress sighed deeply. "Riverside Inn, Westbrook. Right where you got my picture the next morning," he said, tapping on the second photo. "Used to be Exit 8. How did you find out? My dumb-ass brother-in-law tell ya?"

"Actually, you did."

"What?"

"Your E-ZPass," Byron said.

His shoulders sagged. "Shit. I forgot about that."

"What time did you arrive at the motel?"

"Guess it must have been around eight-thirty? That's what time I was supposed to meet her. She had already checked into the room by the time I got there."

"You know how she paid?"

"Cash. I reimbursed her."

"That the usual routine?" Byron asked.

Childress nodded silently.

"What is your girlfriend's name?"

Childress cocked his head to one side like a dog. "Fuck me. Do you really need that?"

"Right now, all I have is your word. Which, based on your previous bullshit alibi, isn't worth a damn. And I have digital pictures that show you were right here in Portland the same night a man you've been threatening for months was murdered. The attorney you blame for helping the guy responsible for your daughter's death go free. In case you haven't been keeping score, that means you had motive, opportunity, and the means to have killed Paul Ramsey." Byron waited a moment as Childress considered his options.

"We're going to need her name," Byron said.

"Please don't drag her into this," Childress pleaded.

"Too late. She's already in it."

Childress looked to his attorney for help, but all he got was a nod. Tilting his head back he stared at the ceiling, exhaling loudly. "My wife is going to fucking divorce me." He looked at Byron and shook his head, defeated. "It's Stacy. Stacy Adams."

Byron slid a blank sheet of paper and pen across the worn wooden the table. "Write down her phone number, work, and home address."

Childress scribbled Adams's contact information, including her place of employment, then handed the paper back to Byron. "Don't suppose I'm free to leave?"

Byron stood up and opened the door. "What do you think?"

He stared at Byron for a beat before lowering his forehead onto the table. "Fuck."

Byron left Childress to stew in the interview room, posting a uniform at the door. He sent Nugent and Tran to Westbrook to retrieve the records and any security video from Riverside Inn, while he headed off to find Ms. Adams.

BYRON WANDERED THE lobby of the Happy Days Child Care Center, checking out the various crayon drawings covering the walls as he waited for Stacy Adams. A high-school-aged girl with pigtails dyed an outrageous shade of purple manned the front desk. Byron caught her stealing glances at him, as if she'd never seen a cop before.

Adams looked nothing like Byron had pictured. Petite and wholesome-looking, not much makeup, if any. She was smartly dressed and polite. Certainly not the kind of woman he imagined

Childress stealing away to a cheap hotel room with. But as Byron knew too well, you couldn't judge a book by its cover.

After a brief introduction, Adams led him to a quiet area. The room, like the rest of the business, was painted in bright sunny tones, seemingly purposed as an employee lounge. It had a couch, several armless upholstered chairs, and a scattering of child development periodicals.

"So, Sergeant," Adams said after they were seated. "How can I help you?"

"Matthew Childress," Byron said matter-of-factly. "How do you know him?"

The color drained from Adams's youthful cheeks. "Is that why you're here?"

"Yes."

Adams looked down at her left hand and fidgeted nervously with the gold wedding band.

Byron continued. "I'm not here to cause you any trouble or embarrass you, Stacy. But you need to answer the question."

"Guess I knew this day might come," Adams said, lifting her chin in an obvious attempt to regain some dignity. Her eyes shifted back toward Byron. "Yes, I know Matt Childress. We attended high school together."

"Tell me about your relationship with him," Byron said. "And when you last saw him."

"SURE, YOU CAN check the videos," the motel manager said with a sardonic grin, revealing teeth in dire need of dentistry. "I just need to see a subpoena."

"Sure," Nugent said. "Why not? We've got nothing better to do than let you dick us around. I mean, it's only a murder case."

"Let me guess, no-tell motel?" Tran quipped.

"I assure you, we run a respectable business here for people who—"

"Want to do drugs, drink under age, and hide out from the law," Nugent said, finishing his sentence. "Yeah, we know. That's precisely why we might have to start checking your register every night to see who's in your rooms from now on." He turned to Tran. "What do you think, Dustin?"

"Sounds like a great idea. Might really impress the bosses to see just how many warrants we can clear."

"Ooh, maybe we start assigning the beat cars to check every registration in the lot for suspended drivers and warrants," Nugent said.

"Or have a black-and-white drive through the lot every hour," Tran added.

"Think all that police presence will have an effect on business?" Nugent asked the man behind the counter.

The two detectives waited as the manager mulled it over, his forehead beading up with nervous perspiration.

"Okay. I'll show you the video."

BYRON SPOKE IN soothing tones to Adams, gradually extracting the information he needed. As he listened to her spill her guts, two things became obvious. The first was that she now genuinely regretted her decision to chase the bad boy, straying from her own marriage for a bit of excitement. The second, and more important thing, was that Adams's Tuesday night rendezvous with "Bob the Builder" gave Childress an airtight alibi. Unless Nuge and Tran found something different. As if in response to his thoughts, his cellphone rang. He excused himself and stepped into the adjoining room to take the call.

"Byron."

"Hey boss, it's Nuge. We just finished looking at the videos."

"And?"

"Unless Childress crawled out through an air-conditioning vent to the back of the building, it looks like Mr. and Mrs. Smith stayed the entire night in room 135. The video shows her checking in just after seven-thirty Tuesday evening, about an hour before Childress. They left together the following morning at six-thirty."

"Even French-kissed in the parking lot," Tran hollered from the background.

BILLINGSLEA WAITED ANXIOUSLY as the newspaper's managing editor, Douglas Paxton, read over the column he'd just written. Billingslea's supervisor, Assistant Editor Will Draper, was off for the weekend, and Paxton had agreed to take a look at the piece. Paxton was a legend in the newspaper business, having been at it for close to fifty years. Legends are intimidating. Paxton answered only to the owners of the *Portland Herald*.

After several minutes, Paxton removed his reading glasses and set them atop his desk. He pinched the bridge of his nose between his index finger and thumb, massaging it. After he'd finished, Paxton fixed him with a look that Billingslea couldn't quite read.

"This isn't half-bad," Paxton said, his expression softening ever so slightly. "Adds a bit of spice to Ramsey's murder. Spice is good for readership."

"Thank you, sir."

Paxton held up the page. "It does, however, leave the mildest aftertaste of a gossip column."

Billingslea felt his heart sink.

"And we're not in that business, are we, Davis?"

"Mr. Paxton, I can assure you my story is not gossip. Byron and Ramsey have a past. I got the information from a reliable source inside the PD."

"And you confirmed everything with your own research, did you?"

"I did. Our own records confirmed it."

Paxton held up the printed page that Billingslea had given him. "I'm not signing off on this."

"Why not?" Billingslea asked, his voice sounding far more whiny than he had intended.

Paxton pulled out his top desk drawer, removing a pack of cigarettes and lighter. With an experienced hand, he tapped a single cigarette out of the pack and popped it between his lips. He paused a moment before lighting it, looking back at Billingslea. "You don't mind, do you?"

Billingslea knew that smoking inside the building was expressly prohibited but he also knew that Paxton occasionally violated the rule. Hell, truth be told, everyone knew about the editor's secret habit. He even kept one desk drawer empty, using it only as an ashtray. Billingslea watched as Paxton slid the drawer out, pulled a long drag off the lit cigarette, then exhaled slowly, eyes closed as if it were an orgasmic experience. Billingslea, who'd never picked up the habit, save for some recreational marijuana use in college, wondered if maybe it was. Paxton leaned back in his creaky leather chair and opened his eyes.

"Son, how long have you worked here now?" Paxton asked.

"Almost three years," he said, hating how much this felt like a dressing-down. *Why hadn't he just waited until Monday to run it by Will?*

"I remember when I was just starting out. Starry-eyed. Looking to break the biggest story of the century. Wanted to be the next Woodward or Bernstein, even before I, or anyone else, knew who they were."

"Mr. Paxton, I—"

Paxton held up the weathered hand holding the cigarette. "You'll want to hear me out, Davis."

"Yes, sir." Billingslea shifted nervously in his chair as Paxton stared over the desk at him, as if appraising him.

"You're a good writer. You have a way with words. And you're tenacious, a necessary attribute for any investigative reporter."

"Thank you."

"But you're the newspaper's police beat reporter, not an investigative journalist. You understand the difference?"

Billingslea waited to see if this was a rhetorical question. It was.

Paxton continued. "You seem to be at odds with Sergeant Byron quite frequently. Ever wonder why that is?"

Davis said nothing, knowing that anything he said wouldn't stop the lesson's progress.

"Well, I'll tell you. It's because he doesn't trust you."

"But I—"

Paxton raised his hand again. "I've been in this business a long time. Known a number of cops like Sergeant Byron. He's driven. Goal-oriented. Thorough. He's tough, but he's fair. I can work with someone who's fair. And so can you, Davis. But if you want Byron to trust you, you must stop trying to beat him to the punch." Paxton raised an eyebrow, as if checking to see that he was understood.

Billingslea nodded, resigning himself to the fact that this wasn't a discussion.

"Like you, Byron is tenacious. Unlike you, he has the experience to achieve his goal without getting in his own way. It's our job to report the news, not create it. Never lose sight of that."

Paxton sat upright and stubbed the remainder of his cigarette out in the ashtray that was in his top right drawer. He closed the drawer then handed the story back to Billingslea.

"My advice to you, son, try and reach an accord with Sergeant Byron. Perhaps extending an olive branch of some sort. The sooner he begins to trust you, the sooner you'll start to become an effective reporter."

BYRON WAS HEADED back to 109 to release Childress when his cell rang. It was Diane. "Byron."

"Hey," Diane said in a voice devoid of emotion.

"Shirley said you and Mel were following up on a lead?"

"Yeah, we just spoke with one of the dancers from the club. She says that Joanne Babbage, one of her coworkers, had been seeing Ramsey for a few months."

"As in Joe?"

"Exactly. Guess she didn't know how to spell the female variant of that nickname."

"You talk with Babbage yet?" he asked.

"Not yet. She gave us an address. Mel and I are headed over there now."

"Let me know."

"Childress still hiding behind his lawyer?"

"Actually, no. He's got an alibi. Turns out he was sneaking around with his girlfriend at a local hotel."

"Well, we can check him off." Diane paused for a beat. "Anything come out of your noontime meeting?"

"Yeah, I got a lead on someone who might have had a beef with

Ramsey. Some guy from his gym. A trainer. Oh yeah, and I also found out you tested for sergeant. When were you planning to mention that?"

It slipped out before he could stop himself. Challenging her wasn't what he'd intended. And doing it over the phone was plain stupid.

"Wasn't aware I needed your permission," she snapped.

"You don't." he said, backing down a bit. "Obviously. I'm just surprised you never said anything."

"Kind of like you failing to mention your mystery lunch date with Kay, huh?"

He was left momentarily speechless. *How the hell had she found out about Kay?* He thought for a moment. *Shirley. Of course.* "It wasn't a date," he said at last.

"Oh, really? Then why didn't you tell me about it?"

Realizing she had him on that one, he ignored the comment and moved on. "So, what are you going to do if they get to your name on the list?"

"I'm keeping my options open," she said.

"What does *that* mean?" he asked, unsure if she was still talking about the promotion.

"It means I haven't decided yet."

He opened his mouth to say something. *Watch it, John,* his inner voice cautioned. He closed it again.

"I'll call you back if we get something," Diane said before hanging up.

Byron held his phone up, staring at it. He wasn't sure he liked Diane's newfound habit of hanging up on him. He could feel the blood warming his cheeks.

He was about to slip the phone back into his jacket pocket when it rang again.

"Byron."

"Hey, John," LeRoyer said. "Just got off the horn with Crosby. They've got some good stuff on Tomlinson. Think they'll be able to grab him up tonight."

"Great," Byron said, sounding far less than enthusiastic.

"I thought you'd be happy about it. Everything okay?"

"Everything's peachy, Lieu. Just fucking peachy."

"By the way, heard you had lunch with Kay."

"THAT DIDN'T SOUND like it went very well," Stevens said.

Diane slipped the phone back into the pocket of her suit coat. "It didn't."

"Wanna talk about it?"

"Nope."

"Okay."

They rode in silence for a while. "He knows I'm on the list," Diane said at last.

"I'm guessing he didn't find out from you?"

"I hadn't told him yet."

Stevens stayed quiet.

Diane glanced over at her. "Yeah, I know. I should've listened to you."

Stevens held up her hands in surrender. "I didn't say a word."

"You didn't have to. Where the hell are we going anyway?"

"Babbage lives on State. Somewhere near Danforth. But I did tell you so."

They both laughed.

Chapter Eighteen

CID WAS A ghost town, same with the fourth-floor administration offices. The only people still working were his detectives. He'd even sent Shirley Grant home. Byron headed for the rear garage. He grabbed his unmarked, needing to gas up as the needle on the fuel gauge was tickling *E*. He was hoping the short trip down to the pumps at Public Works might just clear his head. Stopping for the red light at Pearl and Congress, he lowered both front windows, letting in some much needed fresh air.

Why are you such an asshole, John? He didn't know.

What he did know was that he needed to talk to this patient of Kay's. At the moment, that was far more important than Diane being pissed at him for having lunch with Kay. *Actually, that isn't why she's pissed, John. She's pissed about you not telling her.* The ever popular lie of omission.

"You think I don't know that?" he said aloud to an empty car.

A woman passing by on the sidewalk, with a dog about the size of a hamster, turned her head, eyeing him suspiciously. She looked away, quickening her pace.

"Yup, that's me," he called after her. "Batshit crazy. Just sitting here talking to myself."

It suddenly dawned on him that he wanted a drink. No, check that. *Needed* a drink. It had been several weeks since he'd felt his last craving. He tried to force the thought out of his head to no avail. *Was it this little spat with Diane? Was it the Ramsey murder? Was it Kay? Or was it just the same old John Byron trying to come out? The one who always looked for answers at the bottom of a glass?*

Mercifully, the traffic light changed from red to green and Byron accelerated through the intersection. Driving down Pearl Street toward Public Works, he pushed the thoughts, and the accompanying urge to wet his whistle, way down deep inside. Right where he hoped they would remain.

DIANE AND STEVENS stood in the vestibule of the State Street apartment building, their surprise visit thwarted by a glass security door. Abandoned junk mail and department store fliers were scattered about on the honeycomb tile floor. Most of the correspondence was addressed to "current resident," and none of it was for Joanne Babbage. Trixie hadn't known Babbage's apartment number, only the building address. There were eight buzzers on the directory panel but only four were labeled, meaning that the spaces were vacant, the tenants hadn't gotten around to it yet, or they didn't wish to be bothered. Diane, who'd spent years in the Big Apple tracking down people in multiunit buildings, pressed all eight.

They were preparing to leave when a disheveled-looking young man descended the stairs and opened the security door. He was wearing boxers and a cream-colored tee that Diane guessed had once been white.

"What?" he said.

Diane displayed her credentials. "Sorry to bother you. We're looking for Joanne Babbage."

He stared at her ID. "I don't know who that is."

"Do you know any of your neighbors, Mr. . . . ?" Stevens asked.

"No, I don't. Not by name anyway."

"What is your name?" Diane asked.

"Why?" he said, sounding indignant. "Have I done something wrong?"

"No," Diane said. "But we are trying to locate a possible witness on a murder case and it would be nice if you chose to help us."

He reached up and scratched his head through a greasy mop of hair as he considered it. "Sorry," he said, extending the same hand. "I'm Billy Wheeler."

Diane shook his hand. Resisting the urge to grimace, she thought about the brand-new bottle of hand sanitizer in her glove box.

"I live in apartment 7, top floor, but like I said, I don't really know anyone."

"The woman we're looking for might live alone," Stevens added.

"Besides me, there might be a couple like that," Wheeler said.

"She has a young daughter who might stay with her on occasion," Diane added.

Wheeler's eyes widened in recognition. "Ah, that's probably the woman in apartment 5. Babe."

BYRON WAS RETURNING the nozzle to the gas pump when his cell rang. It was Kay.

"Hey," he said. "Tell me you've got good news."

"I do. He's willing to speak with you."

"Great. When and where?"

"He'll meet you at eight-thirty tomorrow morning at the Miss Portland Diner."

His heart sank at the delay. "I was thinking more like now."

"Tomorrow is what we agreed on, John."

It wasn't what he'd hoped for. If this guy was legit and his boyfriend was responsible for Ramsey's murder, time was of the essence. "How will I recognize him?"

"He'll find you. He pulled your picture off the Internet."

Byron sighed. "Any chance we could dispense with the cloak and dagger stuff? I'm the detective, remember? It would be easier if you just told me who *he* is."

"Easier for you, you mean. Then you'll do what? Run his name through the system? Find out where he lives, or works? Nice try but I know you too well, John Byron. Besides, I'm bound by an oath to protect my patients."

"Except this one *wants* to talk with me."

"Yes, and *if* he decides to follow through, he will."

Byron could feel his anger rising. He knew Kay was doing all she could to help him, but he didn't like feeling helpless.

"John, this is something he has to do on his own. I've nudged him all I can. He's scared. Please go easy on him, okay?"

Byron ended the call and climbed back inside his car. *It would be easy,* he thought. *I'll just drive down to the package store on Portland Street and purchase a small bottle to set me straight. Something to give me a boost. Just a little edge.*

But he knew where it would lead. "A wee dram," his father would've said. One or two belts sounded good, after which he'd hide the bottle under the seat. Or under the spare in the trunk. Or under the wad of parking citations in the glove box. But the bottle wouldn't remain there and he knew it. Sure as shit, he'd wake up somewhere not remembering what had happened, drunk off his ass. Answering the sweet sirens' call would undo everything he'd done to this point. Months of sobriety down the drain. Alcohol didn't control him after all. That would make him no better than the drunks who roamed the streets looking for handouts. Drunks like Winn. And he *was* better than that, wasn't he? Truth was, he was afraid of finding out. If he caved in now he'd know the answer. And he was pretty sure he already knew what that answer was.

Leaning against the headrest, he closed his eyes. He needed to get his shit together. There was too much to do. Too much at stake. He was fucking things up with Diane. Confused about his feelings for Kay. And he had a case to work. A murder to solve. Ramsey's murder.

But the victim was an asshole, his inner voice reminded him. *Right, John? Or was he just good at his job? Could it be that the only reason you didn't like him was because he was an effective trial lawyer? Admit it. You've got more in common with him than you care to admit.*

"Fuck you," Byron said, slamming his fist onto the steering wheel.

His cell rang, startling him back to the here and now. Assistant Attorney General Ferguson.

"Hey, Jim," Byron said, quickly composing himself.

"Hey, yourself. See you're still hard at it."

"You know me."

"Figured I'd have heard from you by now if you were getting close."

Byron sighed. "*Yeah, close* isn't exactly the word I'd use to describe this mess."

"You getting pushback from the top?"

"Always. Ramsey's firm is playing politics too."

"You need me to make any calls for you? Rattle somebody's cage a bit?"

"Nah. Thanks. Nothing here I can't handle."

"Well, my offer stands. Listen, I also want to let you know that I'll be working from home this weekend. Trying to prep for a trial that starts next week. Picking a jury on Monday. Garcia homicide."

"The guy who killed his four-year-old stepson?" Byron remembered hearing the gory details from Lucinda Phillips, his state police CID counterpart. They were the kind of details that never made it into the papers.

"Yup. Alonzo Garcia, real piece of work. If I had my way, we'd skip the trial and string him up by his testicles."

"Ferguson's brand of justice, huh?"

"You disapprove?"

"Personally? No. But I swore an oath, remember?"

"Shit, that's right," Ferguson said. "Guess I did too. Well then, I guess we'll just have to try the son of a bitch."

As Byron laughed, something loosened in his chest. It felt good. Ferguson couldn't have called at a better time.

"Anyway, I wanted you to know I'll be around should you need anything on the Ramsey case. Oh, and the wife still wants me to pin you down on when you're coming to dinner?"

Byron laughed again. "Tell her very soon. I promise. And give her a big hug for me."

"Get your ass up here, John, and hug her yourself."

Chapter Nineteen

DARIUS TOMLINSON CRUISED slowly down Cumberland Avenue in the darkness. His body tensed slightly as the BMW's high-intensity headlights illuminated the reflective badge decal on the door of a black-and-white passing in the opposite direction. *Cops.* For a man who made his living selling illegal narcotics, the reflex was as natural as breathing. He monitored the police cruiser's progress in the rearview mirror, watching for brake lights or a change in speed. Nothing. No indication the cop had taken the least bit of interest in him. Darius relaxed, double-checking his own speed. Twenty-five, right on the button. No reason to worry.

Even if they did pull him over there'd be nothing to find. The rental had been returned an hour ago. The kilo already delivered. The money was secured in the trunk in a compartment hidden beneath the spare. He *was* strapped with his Glock 9 but they'd still need a reason to stop him. And a reason to search him. He rechecked the rearview. The cop had activated the cruiser's right turn signal. He watched as the brake lights illuminated and the cruiser turned down Boyd into Kennedy Park.

"Not this time, fucker," Darius said with a laugh. 2Pac was playing "Hit 'Em Up" on the Bluetooth. He moved his gaze from the darkened road long enough to crank up the stereo volume as he continued toward Munjoy Hill. His eyes returned to the road just in time to see the dark-colored sedan pull out directly in front of him. "Shit!" He stood on the pedal, causing the Beamer's anti-lock brakes to pulse violently. The car jerked to a stop then settled back as its weight redistributed to all four wheels.

"Motherfucker!" Tomlinson said as he slammed the transmission into Park and jumped out of the car without thinking. "Yo, what the fuck is your problem, you stupid fuck?"

A lone male sat behind the wheel of the Camaro. His face pale in the glare of the BMW's headlights.

Darius slammed his fist onto the hood of the Chevy. "You know who the fuck I am?" He was about to issue a challenge when he felt cold hard steel pressing against his skull, behind his right ear. He had a fleeting thought about going for the Glock.

"I know exactly who you are, asshole," a male voice said. "Twitch and you're dead. Hands behind your head, Darius."

Cops. Shit. Tomlinson did as he was told. Police cars seemed to come from every direction. The street was instantly awash with flashing strobes and flickering blues. Tires squealed, and lights blinded him.

"Get on the fucking ground!" another voice commanded. "Now!"

Again, he complied. He heard the sound of footsteps rapidly approaching. He felt a knee jammed roughly into his lower back, pressing him to the pavement. Both of his arms were grabbed and twisted behind him. The familiar pressure and clicks of cold metal cuffs.

"Easy, motherfucker," Tomlinson growled.

"He's secure," another voice said.

"Okay. Search him good."

Tomlinson knew the drill. He closed his eyes, remaining silent as hands roughly slid up and down his legs, torso, and arms.

"Gun!"

He felt the Glock being yanked from his shoulder holster. Then he was searched again, thoroughly from head to toe. The cop paid particular attention to his groin. Darius knew what he was looking for. Drugs. Hiding drugs in your pants was a rookie move. Darius was no rookie.

They stood him up and continued checking his clothes, even removing his shoes. The strobes from the police cars were blinding, making the officers look like nothing more than blurry armed silhouettes. After the cops finished searching him, they moved away. A single shape stepped into view. *Crosby.*

"Well, well, well. What do you know about this?" Crosby said, holding up Darius's Glock. "Hello, D."

IT WAS AFTER midnight when Byron walked into the bureau. Every light in CID was burning brightly, as if it were a weekday instead of the middle of the night. Several of Crosby's grungy-looking plainclothes detectives had commandeered desks next to the interview rooms. Were it not for the detective badges hanging from chains around their necks, Byron might've thought the bureau had been overrun by criminals. He had never worked the drug scene, but he still vaguely remembered LeRoyer back in the day. Bushy goatee, long hair dyed blond, diamond earring, not so much as a hint of the future CID commander in his appearance.

"Where's Crosby?" Byron asked the detective sporting a greasy ponytail.

"In with Darius," he said, pointing a disinterested thumb toward Interview Room Two.

Byron knocked on the blue door then stepped inside.

"Sergeant Byron, allow me to introduce Darius Tomlinson," Crosby said in his usual wiseass tone. "D, meet Sergeant Byron."

Tomlinson, sporting a diamond earring and handcuffs, was seated off to the left; Crosby, with one foot up on the table, to the right. The room reeked of cheap aftershave. Byron couldn't tell whose it was. Most likely an unpleasant mix of the two.

Tomlinson fixed Byron with a look of disinterest, which Byron assumed was a well-rehearsed front. He lifted his arms. "I'd shake your hand, yo, but I'm wearing charm bracelets."

Byron nodded and sat down beside Crosby.

"D was a bad boy tonight, Sergeant. Caught him carrying a loaded Glock and a big ol' bag o' money. He outsmarted us on the delivery but we still got the cash."

"I don't know what you're talkin' about," Tomlinson said. "Told ya, I won that at the casino."

"Really?" Crosby said excitedly, as if he might actually believe him. "Which one?"

Tomlinson hesitated a split second before answering. "Foxwoods."

Byron wondered if Tomlinson even knew in which state the tribal resort was located.

"Wow. Ten grand. You must be one lucky guy. I wonder if you'll be lucky enough to show up on their security video. And, in case you're wondering, we'll be requesting it."

"Whatever," Tomlinson said. "Just keep playing the game."

Byron looked over at Crosby. Crosby nodded.

Byron addressed Tomlinson. "D, is it?"

"Yeah," he said without looking at him.

"D, seems like we both could use a little help tonight. Maybe we could help each other."

Tomlinson looked over warily. "How?"

"I've got a murder to solve," Byron said. "And you've got a possession rap."

"I carry that 9 for protection, yo," Tomlinson blurted out.

"Yo?" Byron said. "What does that even mean?"

Crosby weighed in. "It means, he's looking at some serious time. Possession of a firearm by a convicted felon. Ain't that right, D."

"How am I supposed to protect myself? Ain't you guys ever heard of the Second Amendment?"

"You starting your own militia?" Crosby asked with a grin.

"What?" Tomlinson asked, looking confused.

"Never mind," Byron said, tired of the banter. He leaned in over the table. "D, I need information. You help me and I'll talk to the DA about probation on the gun charge."

"Guaranteed?"

"I can't guarantee anything. But I'll talk to them."

Tomlinson's eyes narrowed. "What about the cash?"

Byron looked at Crosby.

Crosby leaned back in his chair, smirking like he'd just hit every number on the Powerball jackpot. "Guess that depends on what you got for ol' Crosby."

Chapter Twenty

MANUFACTURED BY THE Worcester Lunch Car Company in 1949, the Miss Portland Diner had been feeding the residents of the Port City and its summer tourists for more than sixty years. Byron was seated at a booth overlooking Marginal Way, enjoying the heady aroma of bacon wafting in from the kitchen grill and listening to a Rolling Stones live cover of "Midnight Rambler" through the ceiling speakers. He glanced at the wall clock behind the counter. Kay's mystery patient was now fifteen minutes late.

"More coffee?" the tattooed waitress asked, holding out the carafe.

"Thanks," he said, sliding the azure colored mug toward her and wondering what significance, if any, the colorful tribal sleeve on her right forearm held.

She moved on to the next table before he could ask.

Byron passed the time listening to the silver-haired couple seated in the booth directly behind him. The man was speaking louder than normal. Byron figured it was probably due to hearing loss, though he didn't know which one of them might be afflicted.

"Ya know," the man said. "I was readin' an interesting article the other day about libido."

"That so," the woman responded.

"Yup."

"What did it say?" she asked.

"Said testosterone injections can help older women get their sex drive back."

"Well, ain't that something," the woman said, sounding mildly impressed. "What will they think of next, I wonder."

The man went on, explaining that testosterone was merely a derivative of estrogen.

Byron hid a smile behind his cup, unsure if the man's revelation was simply informative or if there was perhaps an ulterior motive. Then Byron noticed a husky, middle-aged man approaching. He was wearing faded blue jeans, dark glasses, and a teal windbreaker. The jacket could have been the man's attempt at combatting the early-morning chill but Byron figured it was more likely he was trying to hide an ever expanding midsection. He stopped next to Byron's table.

"Sergeant Byron?" the man asked.

Byron nodded. "That's right. You're Kay's patient?"

"I'm William Bagley," he said, extending a sweaty hand. "You look exactly as Dr. Byron described."

"Probably look like my Internet picture too."

Bagley's face flushed with color.

"I almost gave up on you, Mr. Bagley."

"I've been sitting in my car, outside in the parking lot, for the past fifteen minutes. I almost didn't come in."

Byron gestured to the other side of the table. "Have a seat."

Bagley was nothing like what Byron had pictured. Kay had never mentioned an age, but Byron had assumed she was talking about a younger man. Byron guessed Bagley was pushing sixty, and the decades were pushing back. His thinning white hair was parted on one side and the ruddy complexion suggested hypertension. Byron imagined Bagley would have looked much more at home in a suit and tie than his ridiculous attempt at a disguise.

"I have to tell you, I'm a little nervous," Bagley said. "I've never spoken to a detective before. How does this work?"

Byron wondered how many episodes of *Law and Order* Bagley had watched. "Have you eaten?" Byron asked, trying to put him at ease.

"I'm not particularly hungry. Maybe some coffee?"

Byron signaled the waitress. After she departed, Byron began the interview. "Kay tells me you might know something about the Ramsey murder."

Bagley looked down at the table, nodding almost imperceptibly.

"Does this have something to do with your boyfriend?"

Bagley nodded again and began playing with a sugar packet. "Roger."

"Tell me about Roger," Byron said, wondering if he would have to work this hard for every piece of information.

"He's a good person, really. But he's got a temper. Sometimes he can't control it."

Byron couldn't count the number of times he'd heard battered lovers say the exact same thing. He wondered how many times Bagley had been the target of Roger's ire. How many fat lips or black eyes had Kay's patient suffered at Roger's hands?

"What happened?" Byron asked.

Bagley sipped from his mug and continued. "The other night we, me and Roger, were out having drinks in the Old Port. Barhopping, I guess they call it. We were both feeling pretty good and decided to head back to my apartment. Roger agreed to spend the night. He keeps some personal stuff at my place. Toothbrush, clothes, things like that."

A creature of habit, Byron wanted to take notes but he was afraid to do anything that might prevent his fragile witness from continuing, so he held off.

"We'd just left the oyster bar on Commercial Street when Roger ran into this guy wearing a suit."

"Ran into?" Byron asked.

"Yeah, you know. They kinda bumped into each other as we were walking past."

"Did you get a good look at the guy your boyfriend ran into?"

Bagley shook his head. "No. I was more than a little drunk."

"You told Kay it was Paul Ramsey."

"I'm pretty sure it was. Roger said it was."

"Paul Ramsey?"

"Yes, the bigwig defense attorney. Always in the news."

"What happened?"

"Roger got pissed, started swearing at him. Told the guy, Ramsey, to watch where the hell he was going."

"What did Ramsey do?"

"He said something like, 'Fuck off.'"

Original, Byron thought. One might have expected something a little more from most prominent members of the bar, but not Paul Ramsey. "And then?"

"Roger punched him in the face."

"How many times?"

"Just once. Roger's really strong."

"Did Ramsey fight back?"

Bagley shook his head and began to fidget with his spoon. "He couldn't. Roger knocked him out."

"Where was this?"

"On Silver Street, I think. Between Commercial and Fore. Not too far from that hotel."

"Which hotel?"

"I always forget the name. Used to be an armory."

"The Old Port Regency?" Byron said.

"Yeah. Not far from there," Bagley said.

"What time?"

"I don't know exactly. It was getting late. I told you, I was tipsy."

"What happened next?"

"A woman ran toward us. I grabbed Roger and pulled him out of there."

"Did you get a look at the woman?"

Bagley shook his head. "I just wanted to get out of there."

"What was Ramsey doing when you last saw him?"

"Nothing. He was lying on his back."

"Was he breathing?"

"I don't know."

"I'm gonna need Roger's full name."

"You're not gonna tell him I said anything, are you?" Bagley asked with a worried look on his face. "I don't want him to get mad at me."

"Mr. Bagley, you're a possible witness to a murder. If your friend killed Ramsey, you'll be expected to testify."

"I shouldn't have said anything."

"What's Roger's last name?"

Byron waited a moment while Bagley mulled it over in his head.

"I need a name, Mr. Bagley," Byron said.

"It's Fowler," Bagley blurted out. "His name's Roger Fowler."

"Where can I find him?" Byron asked.

"He works at the gym on St. John Street. Fitness World. He's a personal trainer."

"We recovered Attorney Ramsey's body in the ocean. Any idea how he might have gotten there?"

Bagley shook his head again. "I don't know."

"Did either of you go back to check on him?"

Bagley was playing with the sugar packet again. "I did, about a half hour later."

"And?"

The packet ripped, spilling sugar across the tabletop. "He was gone."

"Where was Roger?"

"I don't know. We got into an argument on the way back to my place. Roger got pissed at me and took off."

"Where did he say he was going?"

"He said he went back to his apartment."

"You don't believe him?"

"I don't know. Now I'm worried he might have gone back and thrown Ramsey in the water, or . . ."

"Or what?"

"I don't know."

"Why would Roger do that?" Byron waited as Bagley mulled over his answer.

"He likes to have the last word. It's important to him."

Byron wondered if it was important enough to kill for.

"Have you ever known Roger to carry weapons?"

"Like knives? No, nothing like that."

"How about a gun?"

Bagley swallowed nervously. "I've heard him mention a gun before."

"How would a gun come up in conversation?" Byron asked.

Bagley absently began to play with another sugar packet. "A couple of months ago, he was telling me how some guy threatened him. When I asked how he got the guy to back off he said he threatened to shoot him."

"Has Roger ever shown you a gun?"

Bagley's eyes misted up and his hands began shaking.

"Has he?" Byron repeated.

"Yes." Bagley broke down, sobbing.

Byron spent the next ten minutes convincing the broken middle-aged man to give a formal statement, before driving him to 109.

AFTER OBTAINING A video recorded statement from Bagley, Byron gathered everyone in the conference room to bring them up to speed.

"You're telling me that two different people tuned Ramsey up that night?" LeRoyer asked.

"Told you he was popular," Byron said.

"So what? You think this Fowler guy might have gone back and shot him?"

Byron didn't know what to think. It was unusual for the same guy to be involved in two different physical altercations on the same night, but certainly not unheard of, especially in Portland's Old Port where excessive alcohol consumption was the norm and inhibitions were typically in short supply.

"It's possible," Byron said. "But still it wouldn't explain Ramsey's SUV ending up on Veranda Street."

"Or him in the ocean," Diane added.

"How could one guy have pissed off so many people?" LeRoyer asked.

"He had a gift," Nugent said.

"What about Darius?" Diane asked.

"Yeah, what'd he have to say?" LeRoyer said.

"Tomlinson said Ramsey used to be a regular," Byron said.

"Used to be?" Stevens asked.

"Said he stopped buying from him about six months ago. Thinks Ramsey was getting his Coke from a stripper named Candy."

"Jesus," Nugent said. "Trixie, Candy, it's Stripperfest 2016."

"That would be Joanne Babbage," Diane said. "She may have been dating Ramsey. Mel and I found her apartment yesterday but couldn't locate her."

"In Portland?" Byron asked.

"State Street," Diane said. "Near Danforth."

Byron recalled his conversation with Al Greene, parking control Nazi extraordinaire. Greene had said that Ramsey had outstanding parking violations from State Street. Byron wondered if they were overnight tags. He continued. "Tomlinson told us that Candy works out of the Unicorn for his competition, a guy by the name of Alonzo Gutierrez."

"I know Gutierrez," Stevens said. "He's a real shithead."

"We've gotta find Candy," LeRoyer said, once again stating the obvious.

"Did Darius mention whether Ramsey ever had trouble paying when he was still a customer?" Stevens asked.

Byron shook his head. "Said Ramsey always paid cash. Called him a good customer."

"How much was he using?" Diane asked.

"Five hundred a week."

"Damn," Nugent said. "You know what I could do with an extra five bills a week?"

"What about painkillers?" Diane asked. "Did he ever switch it up?"

"Not according to Darius. Strictly coke."

"So where did Ramsey get the fentanyl?" LeRoyer asked.

"Maybe he didn't get it anywhere," Byron said. "Maybe someone gave it to him without his knowledge."

"You're thinking they substituted fentanyl for his cocaine?" Diane said.

"Or laced it," Byron said. "Ramsey snorts it thinking it's pure coke. Or ingests it in a drink. Whatever. By the time he realizes what it really was, it's too late. It was already affecting him."

"Why would anyone do that?" Stevens said.

"My guess?" Byron said. "Slow him down. Make him easier to control. Easier to kill."

"Jesus," LeRoyer said.

"They probably knew he'd been drinking," Byron continued. "Adding a narcotic to a depressant would have been like slipping him Rohypnol."

"Mickey Finn strikes again," Nugent said.

"Did Darius mention if he knew anyone who'd want Ramsey dead?" Diane asked.

"Said he didn't."

"So what's our next move, Sarge?" Nugent asked.

Byron addressed Diane and Mel. "Why don't the two of you

locate Babbage. Let's lock her into something before she has a chance to come up with a story."

"On our way," Diane said.

Byron turned to Nugent. "Let's go find Bagley's boyfriend."

Chapter Twenty-One

Sunday, 10:15 A.M., May 1, 2016

BYRON AND NUGENT departed from 109 and radioed to meet Haggerty down the street from Fitness World. Haggerty's black-and-white was already parked nose-out in the lot of the St. John Street McDonald's when they arrived. Byron slid the Malibu up tight to the right side of the cruiser as he had a thousand times when he was still a beat cop. Some habits didn't change just because the uniform did.

"Hey, Sarge," Haggerty said after lowering the passenger window.

"Hags," Byron and Nugent said simultaneously.

"What are you guys up to?"

"We just joined the gym," Nugent said. "And we need a spotter."

"That'll be the day for you, Nuge. Maybe the sarge here, but not you, Stay Puft," Haggerty said, cocking his thumb in the direction of the burger joint. "You'd be better off hitting the drive-through here for a double quarter with cheese."

"Ouch. You hear what that big heartless oaf said to me, Sarge?"

Byron ignored the banter. "We're headed over to Fitness World to interview a guy named Roger Fowler. You know him?"

"Sure I do. He's one of their personal trainers. Used to lift competitively. He's a big dude."

"That's why I called you," Byron said.

"This have something to do with the Ramsey murder?" Haggerty asked.

"Yeah, Fowler's scared boyfriend coughed up some information. Said that big dude might've punched out Ramsey the night he was killed."

"Sounds like Fowler. He's got a temper. And he prefers men."

"You guys ever share a shower, Hags?" Nugent asked. "I mean, just between us."

"Actually, you'd be more his type," Haggerty said. "He likes 'em old and soft."

Nugent flipped him off.

"Ever known this guy to carry?" Byron asked.

Haggerty shook his head. "No, but there's always a first time."

Byron pulled out of the McDonald's lot and Haggerty followed in the black-and-white. They drove two blocks to the gym, parked in the lot, and walked inside.

A fit-looking brunette with pigtails, wearing a bright yellow Fitness World shirt and tight black spandex pants, was manning the front desk. "Welcome to Fitness World," she said, her hazel eyes immediately fixed on Haggerty. "Can I help you?"

"I hope so," Byron said, trying to pry her admiring gaze away from the well-built younger officer. "We're looking for Roger Fowler."

"Is he in some kind of trouble?" she asked, concern creasing her forehead.

"Nah," Nugent said. "We're thinking about signing up for a session."

Spandex looked confused.

"We just want to talk with him," Byron said, shooting Nugent a look of disapproval.

"Hang on a sec," she said. "I'll page him."

Byron stepped back from the desk, quickly scanning the room as Fowler's name came over the public announcement system. Byron spotted him on the opposite side of the room when Fowler's head snapped up upon hearing his name. Wearing a formfitting black tee, gray sweatpants, and red sneakers, Fowler had just finished spotting another man on the bench. He started walking toward Byron then stopped; like a squirrel attempting to cross the road, he did a quick about-face and headed in the other direction. Byron turned and looked at Haggerty's uniform. *Shit.*

"He made us," Byron said. "Come on."

"Here we go again," Nugent said.

Byron and Haggerty circled around to the right side of the gym while Nugent took the left in an attempt to head off Fowler's escape route.

Fowler quickened his pace.

Byron could see Fowler's intended destination was a staff office in the far left corner of the gym's main workout area. Byron glanced left and saw Nugent break into a jog as he raced to cut Fowler off.

Nugent arrived at the closed office door a split second before Fowler, and stood blocking his path. Byron and Haggerty hurried toward them. Both could see the bald detective flash his shield just before Fowler reached out and shoved him.

Big mistake, Byron thought.

Nugent's reaction was as quick as it was subtle. Anybody not watching intently would have missed it. A short jab to Fowler's solar plexus and the muscle-bound trainer was doubled over and gasping for breath.

"Roger Fowler," Byron said, coming up behind him. "We need to talk."

DIANE AND STEVENS came up empty at Joanne Babbage's State Street apartment once again.

"For a girl who works nights you'd think she might be home a little more during the day," Stevens said.

"Yeah, so you'd think," Diane agreed.

"Now what? The club?"

"Yeah. Let's swing out and see if her car's there."

"What about what Trixie said? The bosses at the Unicorn aren't going to like us tracking Babbage down there."

"She isn't leaving us any options," Diane said. "We can't wait any longer to talk to her. Unless you've got a better idea."

"What if we say we're doing follow-up on a burglary to her apartment or something? Her bosses can't be pissed at her for that, right?"

"The old 10–91 routine, huh? Okay. I'm game."

BYRON, NUGENT, AND Haggerty moved Fowler inside the private confines of the office, where they wouldn't be disturbed.

"I assume you know why we're here?" Byron said.

"You can't find a date?" Fowler shot back, still rubbing his stomach and trying to catch his breath.

Nugent, who was standing behind the seated Fowler, slapped him in the back of the head. "Don't be an asshole."

Fowler turned his head to the side, glaring back at Nugent. "Maybe we'll run into each other again, meatball."

"Anytime, Alice," Nugent said.

Byron saw Haggerty fighting back a grin.

"Wanna try again?" Byron said, pulling a chair over and sitting down directly in front of Fowler.

"I don't have any idea why you guys are fucking with me. I haven't done shit."

"Hmm. That's not exactly what William Bagley tells us."

Fowler's eyes widened. "Bagley's got a big mouth."

"Nice and soft too, I'll bet," Nugent said.

"Fuck you, meatball," Fowler snapped.

Nugent cuffed the back of the trainer's head again.

"Fuck," Fowler said.

"Watch your language, asshole," Nugent said.

"Tell me what happened in the Old Port the other night," Byron said.

"What did Will tell you happened?"

Byron shook his head. "Not how this works. You don't get to ask questions. I do. What happened?"

"Want another one?" Nugent asked as he drew back his hand.

"Okay, okay. Will and I were out having a couple of drinks."

"Where?" Byron asked.

"A few different places. We hit the oyster bar, then RiRa's, then we decided to head back to Will's apartment for a nightcap."

"And?"

"And some asshole in a suit staggered into me, near the alley on Silver Street."

Byron waited for him to finish.

"I yelled at him. It looked like he was gonna take a poke at me so I punched him first."

"He was going to assault you?" Byron asked.

"Looked like it to me. It was self-defense."

"How many times did you hit him, in self-defense?"

"Once. That's it."

Byron raised an eyebrow.

"I'm tellin' ya, one punch. Don't believe me? Ask Will."

"Then what happened?"

"We got into an argument about it, Will and me. He doesn't like me getting physical with people."

"And then?"

"Then I went home to my place and I assume Will went to his."

"You went directly home?"

"What I said."

"And you didn't go back out?"

"Nope."

"Anyone vouch for your whereabouts?"

"No. I went to bed *alone*."

"I'll bet that sucked," Nugent said. "Or on second thought, I guess it didn't."

Byron fixed Nugent with a dirty look. "You didn't go back to check on the guy you punched?"

"No. Why would I?"

"Did you know the man you punched?"

"No."

"*No?* Then why did you tell Bagley you did?"

"Is that what this is all about? Ramsey?" Fowler visibly relaxed in the chair.

"You tell us," Byron said.

"Look, I got into an argument with some asshole down in the Old Port the other night, okay? Just like I said. He was dressed like a big deal, wearing a nice suit."

"An argument?" Byron said. "I thought you just bumped into the guy. What was the argument about?"

"It was nothing. We had words inside the oyster bar while Will was in the bathroom. It was stupid."

"So stupid that you felt the need to level Ramsey?"

"Look, I told you, it wasn't Ramsey."

"Why did you tell your boyfriend it was?"

"I was just showing off. When I saw on the news that Ramsey was dead, I made a comment to Will about him. Something like, 'That will teach him to fuck with me.' But I was just fucking around."

"So you did tell Will that it was Ramsey you knocked out?"

"Who said I knocked anyone out?"

"Bagley did. Said he watched you do it after you bumped into the guy."

"Hey, that asshole bumped into me. Okay? Then he got all in my face. I could tell he was about to take a swing at me. You guys know how it is. You can just tell. It was self-defense. Anyway, he had it coming."

"So you did knock him out?" Byron said.

Fowler's eyes dropped to the floor as Byron awaited a response.

"You own a gun, Mr. Fowler?"

Fowler looked to Haggerty then back to Byron. "You're serious?"

"Well? Do you?"

"Look, I just said that stuff to scare Will. It wasn't even Ramsey I punched."

"Do you own a gun?" Byron shouted.

"No, man. I don't fuck around with guns. That ain't my thing."

"So, you've never shown a handgun to Will?"

Fowler swallowed nervously. "No."

"Then you won't mind if we check your apartment?"

Fowler sat back in the chair, defiantly, crossing his large arms over his equally expansive chest. "Of course not. Long as you don't mind getting a fucking warrant. And I want to file a complaint."

"What complaint?" Byron asked.

"This bald asshole assaulted me," he said, cocking his thumb in Nugent's direction.

Nugent's eyes widened. "Bald?"

"Actually," Byron said, "Officer Haggerty and I saw you shove Detective Nugent before he struck you. Isn't that right, Officer Haggerty?"

"Yup, that's what happened, Sarge."

"What about him smacking me in the head?" Fowler asked.

"Sarge, I did have to smack Mr. Fowler a couple of times," Nugent said.

"You did?" Byron said in mock surprise.

"Yeah, I thought he was gonna take a swing at me. You know how you can just tell sometimes?"

Byron nodded. "Sounds more like self-defense to me."

"So that's how it's gonna be?" Fowler said.

"That's how I saw it," Haggerty said.

Byron leaned in close to Fowler. "Ya know, for a guy who may well be the last person to have had contact with my murder victim, you're not taking this all that seriously."

"Why the fuck should I? I didn't do anything."

"No? Because you just admitted to knocking Ramsey out with

one punch and leaving him without checking to see if he was okay."

"I told you, it wasn't Ramsey."

Byron looked up at Nugent. "What's that sound like to you, Nuge."

"Sounds like negligence. Could be manslaughter."

"Hey, fuck that," Fowler protested as he started to get up from the chair.

Nugent grabbed on to his shoulders, shoving him back down. "Sit down, dickhead."

"It wasn't Ramsey and I didn't kill him. I just punched the guy. I swear."

"What about the gun?" Byron asked.

"What gun?"

"The one you told Bagley you threatened a guy with."

Fowler swallowed nervously again. Byron could almost picture the unused gears struggling to turn inside of the gym rat's head.

"Yeah, you know," Nugent said. "That gun you won't let us search for."

"We already have enough to get a warrant," Byron said. "You want to wait in jail while we get one?"

"*In jail?*" Fowler said, his voice rising two full octaves. "For what?"

"How about assaulting Detective Nugent for starters." Byron looked up at Nugent. "What do you think, Nuge? Feel like pressing charges?"

"Okay," Fowler said.

"Okay, what?" Byron asked.

"Okay, you guys can search my apartment."

"And your gym locker and car?"

"What the fuck? Why are you doing this to me?"

"Because somebody killed that attorney and tossed him in the ocean. Was it you, Roger?"

"No. I swear."

"It does sound like something he'd do, Sarge," Nugent said, mocking him.

"Fuck it," Fowler said, throwing his hands up in defeat. "Search whatever you want. I don't give a fuck. I didn't do anything to Paul Ramsey."

Byron turned to Haggerty. "Got a consent form in your car?"

"Back in a minute," Hags said.

DIANE AND STEVENS located Babbage's silver Hyundai parked behind the Unicorn. Standing beside it was Babbage herself, dressed in loose-fitting pink sweats and smoking a cigarette. She was talking animatedly on her cell and appeared upset. As soon as she noticed the detectives exit the car and start in her direction, she ended her call, tossed the butt away, and hurried toward the club's back door.

"Joanne?" Stevens asked.

"Nope, it's Candy," she called out from over her shoulder. "I gotta get back inside."

"Joanne, we're police detectives and we just want to talk with you a minute," Diane said. "I figured you'd rather talk out here than in front of your bosses."

Babbage stopped walking and turned to face them. "Look, I don't know what you want with me but I need this job. If my bosses see me talking to you, I'll get fired."

"We're here to follow up on the break-in to your apartment," Stevens said.

Babbage cocked her head, wearing a confused expression on her face. "My apartment wasn't broken into," she said.

"It was unless you want your bosses to know we're here about your relationship with Paul Ramsey," Diane said.

No sooner had Diane uttered those words than a short stocky man in a tight black T-shirt and tan slacks opened the door and stepped outside. He had dark short cropped hair with matching unibrow. "Everything okay out here, Candy?" he asked, casting a suspicious eye at the strangers.

Babbage looked back at Diane. "We're fine," she said. "I just gotta talk to these detectives about the break-in at my apartment."

"Oh, okay," Neanderthal said before stepping back inside and closing the door.

"See, that wasn't so hard, was it?" Diane said. "Why don't we chat in my car?"

Babbage followed them across the lot to Diane's unmarked. Stevens motioned Babbage to sit in the front passenger seat as she slid into the back.

Once they were all inside the car, Diane began. "How long were you and Paul Ramsey seeing each other?"

"Who?" she said.

"Joanne, you know we already know, or else we wouldn't be here," Stevens said.

"Who told you? It was Rachael, wasn't it? She can't keep her fucking mouth shut."

"Doesn't matter who," Diane said. "You were seeing him, weren't you?"

Babbage pulled out a pack of cigarettes and a green plastic lighter from the front pouch of her pullover.

"Uh-uh," Diane said. "Not in this car."

"You're kidding?"

"Nope," Diane said.

Babbage jammed the items back inside the pocket and sighed. "Yeah, I was seeing Paul."

"How long?"

"Awhile."

Stevens jumped into the conversation from the backseat. "You know, if you want us out of your hair you might consider being less vague."

Babbage made eye contact with Diane. "Guess it must have been about eight months or so. It was kinda on and off."

"Where did the two of you meet?" Diane asked.

"The Ritz. I always like to spend time at the high-class places."

Diane kept her expression neutral as she awaited a real answer.

"We met here," Babbage said. "Last fall. Paul came in with some work buddies, I guess. Bunch of suits, maybe someone's retirement party."

"And?" Diane said.

"And we just hit it off."

"So a couple of lap dances later, and he's in love, is that it?" Stevens asked.

Babbage shrugged the question off.

"Did you know he was married?" Diane asked.

Babbage rolled her eyes. "Yeah, and so are most of the guys who come here. I wasn't looking for a husband, just a good time."

"Where did you meet?" Diane asked.

"Here, there, wherever. We didn't have a schedule."

"Where, specifically?" Diane asked again.

"Sometimes we'd meet at a hotel room across the street, sometimes we'd hook up in a parking lot off of Riverside Street. One of the industrial parks. Couple of times on his boat."

"His boat?" Diane said. "Where was that?"

"It's at the marina, down on Commercial Street."

"Did he ever come to your apartment?" Diane asked, scribbling a note about the boat while trying not to make it look like too big a deal.

"Maybe."

"He either did or he didn't," Stevens said.

"He did. A couple of times."

"Did he ever buy drugs off of you?" Diane said, trying to catch Babbage off guard.

"No."

"No, you gave them to him? Or no, you never sold them to him?"

Babbage turned to look out the window.

"We've pulled your sheet, Joanne," Diane said. "We know you were busted for dealing."

"Yeah, well, that was the old me. Now I got a kid to look out for."

"Would that be the daughter who lives with her father?" Stevens said.

"Shared custody," Babbage snapped.

"When did you see him last?" Diane asked.

"Who? Paul?"

Diane nodded.

"I don't know. Couple of weeks, I guess."

"What about Tuesday night? Did you happen to see him then?"

"Nope."

"How can you be so sure?" Stevens said.

"'Cause my daughter was staying with me Tuesday night. You can ask her. I was home all night."

SEARCHES OF FOWLER'S gym locker and car turned up nothing. Byron called Tran to assist them in the search of Fowler's Brackett Street apartment, while Haggerty transported the trainer by black-and-white. Byron also requested Pelligrosso's presence in case they located something incriminating.

Fowler's second-floor abode looked less like an apartment and more like a gym. A weight bench, squat station, and dumbbell rack were featured prominently in the living room along with a large flat screen and leather couch. Where an area rug would normally have graced the center of the room's hardwood floor, Fowler had placed interlocking black foam workout mats. The walls in each of the rooms were decorated with framed pictures of Fowler competing at various weight-lifting events. Also hanging in each room was a large mirror.

"Jesus, Sarge," Nugent said. "And I thought the chief was bad. Could this guy be any more into himself?"

Byron continued his search of the dining room while Haggerty kept an eye on Fowler, who sat at the table pouting. Tran pawed through the kitchen and bathroom while Nugent went to work on the bedroom and den. Each of the detectives worked methodically, starting in one corner of the room and working clockwise floor to ceiling so as not to overlook anything. They were only twenty minutes into the search when Nugent and Tran walked into the dining room where Byron and Haggerty were speaking with Fowler.

"Look what I found," Nugent said, holding out a flat plastic container for the others to see. "It was hidden up in the suspended ceiling in the bedroom."

Byron looked inside. The box contained a baggie of what appeared to be a couple of ounces of marijuana, several glass vials containing a clear liquid, a large full pill bottle with no label, and a black semiauto handgun. A .380 handgun. "Thought you didn't own a gun," Byron said.

"Uh-oh," Nugent said. "Someone's a big fibber."

"That's not mine," Fowler said.

"It isn't?" Nugent asked. "Weird, 'cause it was above your bed."

"I've never seen it before."

"Get some photos and seize all of it," Byron said to Pelligrosso. He turned his attention to Fowler. "Just spitballing here but it looks like you've been supplementing your gym job."

"Whatever you think," Fowler said dismissively.

"What I think is, you lied to me about owning a gun and it looks like you're dealing weed, prescription drugs, and anabolic steroids."

"Think I'd like to talk with my attorney now. Oh, and I'm revoking my consent to search too."

"Not a problem. We'll just get a warrant. Hags, why don't you and Nuge give Mr. Fowler a ride to County?"

"It'd be our pleasure," Haggerty said as he placed cuffs on Fowler.

Following their departure, Byron turned to Pelligrosso. "How soon before you can tell me if that is the same .380 that killed Ramsey?"

"Should have something by tomorrow afternoon. I'll run the serial number through NCIC, check the gun, magazine, and casings for prints and fire a test round to see if it matches the round that Doc Ellis dug out of him."

ATTORNEY GERALD DEWITT was sitting in his car, waiting patiently out in front of the Cumberland County Jail, when he saw Darius Tomlinson strut through the front doors a free man. Tomlinson gave a halfhearted wave before walking in his direction.

DeWitt popped the door lock and Tomlinson got in.

"Yo, Gerry. Thanks for springing me. Gray bars cramp my style." Tomlinson held up his right hand in a fist bump gesture, which DeWitt did not return.

"You know what cramps my style, Darius? Having to put up fifty thousand for the likes of you."

"Yeah, well, cost of doing business, G. Ramsey never had a problem with it."

DeWitt reached down and shifted the car into Drive. "I'm not Paul Ramsey."

"Chill, Big G. We're cool."

Chapter Twenty-Two

Sunday, 2:00 P.M., May 1, 2016

BYRON WAS JUST pulling away from the curb in front of Fowler's apartment when his cell rang. Diane.

"How'd you two make out?" Byron asked.

"Babbage admits she's been seeing him since late last fall," Diane said.

"She see him Tuesday night?"

"Said she didn't. Said she was at her apartment all night with her daughter."

"You believe her?"

"If she was lying, she's good at it. Mel and I will head to Gorham to try and find the daughter right after we talk to Elwell. We're meeting him at Portland Transport on Warren Avenue."

"Okay, good."

"Did you know Ramsey owned a boat?"

"What?" he said, sounding as blindsided as he felt.

"Babbage said they occasionally hooked up on it."

"She know where the boat is?"

"She didn't know the name, but she described DiMillo's Marina to us."

"I'll put Dustin on it. What about drugs?"

"Said she's clean. Told us she'd seen Ramsey snort before but claimed to have no knowledge of where he got his drugs."

Byron filled Diane in on the search of Fowler's apartment and the discovery of the .380.

"Wow," Diane said. "That could be big."

"Maybe, but Fowler doesn't act much like a guy who just shot someone in the face."

"So, what are you thinking?"

"I've got Gabe on ballistics but I'm having Nugent run down a possible assault victim from the Old Port."

"From Tuesday night?"

"Yeah. It wasn't reported as an assault. Came in as a casualty. That's why we didn't see it. MedCu transported the guy to the hospital after he was found lying in the street. The paramedics just assumed he'd fallen."

"Think it could be the guy Fowler punched out?"

"Don't know. It's possible. Listen, I'm sorry I went off on you about the test. I had no right."

"Yup," she said. "I'll let you know what Elwell and Babbage's daughter have to say."

Byron looked down at the phone after Diane had hung up. *Yup? What the hell?* He'd been hoping his apology might prompt her to do the same, but it hadn't. He pocketed the cell and slid the car into a vacant spot on Middle Street directly across from 109.

BYRON DECIDED HIS need for food couldn't wait. After making a quick call to Tran, asking him to find out whether there were any boats registered to the Ramseys, he walked down to Calluzo's Bistro on Middle Street, hoping to grab a Boston Italian and soda. It would be the first thing besides coffee he'd had all day. He took the order to go and returned to 109. He was climbing the stairs to the fourth floor and stepping into the hallway when he nearly collided with LeRoyer.

"Didn't expect to see you still here," Byron said.

"I heard you made an arrest on Ramsey," LeRoyer said.

"Who told you that?"

"Did you?"

"No. We arrested some gym rat named Roger Fowler for trafficking."

"Who's he?"

"Long story, Marty."

After bringing the lieutenant up to speed, Byron walked down the back hallway to his own office, tossed the wrapped sub on his desk, and cracked open the soda, taking a long swig. It wasn't as good as a Guinness would have tasted, but it was carbonated and it was cold. It hit the spot. He looked down and found a new pink message slip from Tran. Stapled to it was the registration printout for the Ramseys' boat. It was in Mrs. Ramsey's name. Hopefully, she would continue to cooperate.

He picked up the phone and called AAG Jim Ferguson's cell.

"You think this Fowler guy might've killed him, John?" Ferguson asked after he was briefed.

"I don't know if he did or didn't but at this very moment Fowler's my most viable suspect."

"Who's working on the search warrant?"

"We handed it off to Crosby's guys. My people are running all over the place on Ramsey. Can't afford to tie them up on a drug case."

Anna Jacobson, one of Sergeant Peterson's weekend property crime detectives, poked her head in through the doorway.

"Hang on a second, Jim," Byron said. "What's up, Anna?"

"Sorry to interrupt you, Sarge, but I've got one of Sergeant Crosby's detectives on the line. They're just double-checking the information for the affidavit. It was Bagley who led you to Fowler, right?"

"Yes. He's the one who witnessed Fowler knock the guy out in the Old Port. Fowler also made the comment about having taken care of Ramsey as they were watching the news about Ramsey's death."

"Okay, they're also asking how we found out about Bagley in the first place."

"His psychologist approached me."

"They need his name for the affidavit," Jacobson said.

"Her name," he corrected. "Dr. Kay Byron."

Anna raised her eyebrows. "Kay?"

"Sorry about that," Byron said after Jacobson had departed.

"Sounds like you've got your hands full, John. How many balls are you trying to juggle anyway?"

"More than I'd like. Speaking of which, now I've got a boat to search."

"MR. ELWELL?" DIANE asked as she and Stevens approached the silver-haired man seated in the waiting area of Portland Transport.

The lanky Elwell stood up. "Detective Joyner?"

After the introductions were made, the three of them walked outside where they could talk without being overheard.

"I found out you were looking for me as soon as I got back from my run," Elwell said.

"When did you leave on this run, Mr. Elwell?" Diane asked.

Elwell dug around in his pants pocket, pulling out several folded pieces of paper, and handed them to Diane. "What's this?" she asked as she unfolded them.

"These are the run sheets. You can see the dates and times that I checked in. My boss said there was some question about where I was when our attorney, Paul Ramsey, was killed."

"Mr. Elwell, we're just trying to establish alibis for anyone who might have had a reason to want to kill Paul Ramsey," Stevens said as Diane flipped through the documents. "At the warehouse they told us you were supposed to be back earlier. Why were you delayed returning to Maine?"

Elwell pointed to the pages. "If you flip to the last page you'll see I photocopied the ticket I got for fudging my logbook so I could drive longer than I was supposed to. State police pulled me off the road for ten hours until I was eligible to drive again."

She examined the summons, confirming what he had told them.

Sighing, Elwell leaned back against the corrugated metal of the building's siding. He slid his hands deep into the front pockets of his pants and stared out toward Warren Avenue. "Detectives, I'd be lying if I told you that I wasn't pissed off at Attorney Ramsey. He told us not to take the settlement offer. We should never have listened to him."

Diane exchanged a glance with Stevens, but neither spoke.

"Our son is dead," Elwell continued. "Nothing's going to change that. Even if we'd won at trial. There are a lot of people I could blame for Robbie's death: the hospital, the surgeon, probably others as well. Truth is, I can't do this anymore. The grieving is killing my wife and me. Our marriage. Our lives. We've got to move on." He looked up, making direct eye contact with Diane. "You're both welcome to any information you need. I'll sign anything. Okay? I didn't have anything to do with murdering Paul Ramsey."

IT WAS AFTER four by the time Byron had obtained Mrs. Ramsey's signature on the consent to search. He met Diane in the DiMillo's parking lot and she brought him up to speed on Elwell.

"Literally hundreds of miles away when Ramsey was last seen leaving the Fox," Diane said.

"Guess we can cross Elwell off the list," Byron said. "What about Babbage's daughter?"

"We talked to her and the ex-husband. She did sleep over at Babbage's apartment Tuesday night."

"Of course, she still could've gone out to meet Ramsey after her daughter went to bed."

"True."

"Did her ex know about her hooking up with Ramsey?"

"Not Ramsey specifically but he told us Joanne had a habit of chasing the money."

They walked into the marina office building together. The space served multiple purposes: part slip rental, part general store, where the owners of million-dollar vessels could purchase necessary goods, and summer tourists and restaurant-goers could send postcards from the Maine coast to friends back home. The woman at the counter scanned the consent form then directed them to a dockhand named Evan.

Evan wore the long curly locks of a young man who either moonlighted as a musician or just thought the long hair made him look cool. He led them back outside to the parking lot and around to the steel security gate at the head of the docks.

"So, you guys wanna see the Ramsey boat," Evan said as he punched a code into the keypad on the gate.

"You familiar with it?" Byron asked.

"Sure, blue and white Sabre," Evan said. "I know all the boats out here."

"How long have you worked here?" Diane asked.

"This is my fourth year."

"Seasonal work?" Byron asked as they followed him down the ramp.

"My first year it was. Now I'm year-round. Summertime there's about eight employees. Winter we cut back to five."

"There's enough work to keep five of you busy?" Diane asked.

"You'd be surprised. Some people live on these boats."

"How many boats are kept here?" Byron asked.

"When we're up to full capacity in the summer it's about one hundred and forty. Right now, we're just shy of a hundred."

"When exactly does summer start for the rich folks?" Diane asked.

Evan grinned. "Depends. If you're from Texas, might not be till the beginning of July. Gotta be warm enough for those southern bones." Evan stopped walking. "Here she is."

Not Guilty was the name adorning the stern in large block letters. Prosaic until the end, Byron thought. He turned to Evan as Diane climbed aboard. "You said some of the people live on these boats. Did Ramsey?"

"No. The Ramseys pulled theirs out every fall. It actually just went back in the water. Couple of weeks ago."

Byron pulled out his notepad and jotted some of what Evan had said. "How often do the Ramseys use the boat?"

"Not too often. I've only ever seen Mrs. Ramsey twice, my first year on the docks." Evan looked around then leaned in toward Byron. "Between you and me . . ." he said quietly.

"Yeah," Byron said.

"Ramsey only rarely took the boat out. Think he was using it more as a fuck pad."

Byron looked up from his notes. "A fuck pad?"

"Yeah, you know. He'd bring women down here for a little somethin' somethin'."

"You ever see any of these women?"

"Sure. He never brought any dogs down here."

"You see any women down here lately? Like maybe last Tuesday night?"

Evan shook his head. "Didn't work last Tuesday night. But there's a video system."

EVAN TOLD THEM he didn't have authority to access the wharf security video, which was housed in the yacht sales office. He ran off to get the on-duty salesperson while Byron telephoned Pelligrosso to help with the search and to document anything they found.

Byron was just hanging up when a slick-looking character who looked about forty, dressed in chinos and a bright yellow polo shirt, sporting a tan that could only have come from a booth this early in the year, approached.

"Afternoon," the man said, flashing a fake smile. "Help you with something?"

Byron, who caught a Long Island or Jersey lilt in the man's speech, opened his wallet, displaying his badge and ID to Slick 40. "Detective Sergeant Byron," he said.

"Evan tells me you're looking for video stuff. Afraid I can't give you that without a court order. Privacy laws. I'm sure you under—"

"Dennis Merrill," Diane interrupted.

Slick looked at Diane. His smile faltered.

Byron didn't think he looked much like a Dennis. In fact, he'd already grown fond of the Slick 40 moniker.

"Sarge," Diane continued. "Allow me to introduce Dennis Merrill, formerly of New York City. Isn't that right, Dennis?"

Byron watched as Merrill squirmed like a kid needing to use the bathroom, shifting from one tan boat shoe to the other.

"I go by Richard now," he said.

"Dick. How fitting," Diane said.

It was obvious that Diane was enjoying every second of this.

"How do you two know each other?" Byron asked.

"Well," Diane began. "Dick and I met professionally. Back when I first started doing UC work in the fraud unit. Isn't that right, *Dick*?" she asked, accentuating the last word.

Merrill said nothing.

"Dick ran a local insurance office. They specialized in high-risk auto insurance policies. Guaranteed to get you back on the street, no matter your driving record. Right, Dick?" She turned her head toward Byron. "Only problem was, he never turned the money over to corporate. Charged people five hundred bucks for a temporary insurance card. He filled out the paperwork but never sent it in. The high-risk people who made it through the ninety-day policy without an accident never knew they weren't insured.

The ones that didn't, well, Dennis, now Dick, would backdate the records and send the forms in along with the money, claiming his office assistant misfiled it."

"Is this true, Dennis?" Byron said, playing along.

"I told you, it's Richard," Merrill said, sulking. "I changed my name. It's all legal."

"There's a first," Diane continued. "It was tens of thousands of dollars in fraud. Dick did a little time. But the real felony stuff was dropped down in a plea bargain to misdemeanor theft. The corporate people didn't want the negative publicity. It would probably suck for you if your current employer found out who you really are?" Diane said.

"What do you want?" Merrill asked.

"That's the spirit, Dick," Diane said.

"We're gonna need access to your security system," Byron said.

Byron looked around for security cameras atop the tallest of the pilings. None were visible.

"You have cameras monitoring this area?" Byron asked their reluctant tour guide.

"Not out here. The owners don't want them."

"Why not?"

"They like their privacy," Merrill said.

Byron could only imagine what kind of activities could be taking place on these boats that would put privacy above the millions of dollars in floating fiberglass surrounding them.

Merrill pointed back toward the parking lot. "The only camera is the one at the head of the ramp. It monitors the gate we just came through."

"We're gonna need to see those recordings," Diane said.

"Nothing's recorded."

"What?" she asked. "What good is that?"

"Not much, I suppose. The camera goes to a closed circuit monitor in my office but that's it."

"That's just great," Diane said.

"We're also gonna need a copy of the rental list for every occupied slip on these docks," Byron said.

Merrill opened his mouth to protest but Diane cleared her throat. "I'll get it for you," Merrill said.

"What about gate security?" Byron asked.

"What about it?"

"Evan punched in a code to get through the gate," Byron said. "Pardon the pun but how many of those are floating around?"

"There's only one key code. Each owner knows it."

"And anyone else they've told," Diane said.

"I guess," Merrill said.

With Pelligrosso's help, they searched Ramsey's boat from stem to stern. The boat was well-kept, but it was still obvious Ramsey had used the vessel as an occasional love pad, and not for much else. Merrill's fuel records confirmed Ramsey rarely took the boat out.

Mrs. Ramsey had told Byron that she'd purchased the boat for her husband as a gift but she had only been on it a few times. "I'm not really into boating," she'd said.

The only trace of blood Pelligrosso was able to find was in the stateroom lavatory where Ramsey had likely cut himself shaving. No doubt after sleeping one off, Byron thought. One more trait he'd shared with the dead attorney.

"What do you think?" Diane asked Pelligrosso.

"If he was killed on the boat, he wasn't on it long."

"Could they have shot him out here and not left even a trace of spatter?" Byron asked.

"Well, they'd be helped by the fact that the bullet never exited Ramsey's skull. Entry spatter only." Pelligrosso surveyed the deck. "The killer would have to have thought it through. Really planned it in advance. Plastic, maybe? Or something placed over Ramsey's face and fired through it. But yeah, it could be done. Maybe at the platform on the stern. Wouldn't matter then if he was conscious or not. Shoot him then roll him into the water."

"What if he was already in the water when he was shot?" Diane asked.

Byron and Pelligrosso turned to look over the stern.

"Yeah, he could have been shoved overboard and then shot," Pelligrosso said.

"He *was* pistol-whipped, right?" Diane asked. "Maybe they conked him on the head to knock him off the boat."

"You're right," Byron said. He'd wanted to lock the boat down as either definitely being the crime scene or not, but the search had accomplished neither. As with the rest of the case, every piece they turned up seemed ambiguous at best.

"We'll have to canvass all of the owners," Diane said. "I can have Mel help me."

"Good idea. Call the shift commander and have him send the beat officer down here to give you a hand."

Diane pulled out her phone. "You got it."

Pelligrosso's cell chimed. "Gabe here."

Byron watched as his evidence technician nodded and grinned, apparently pleased with whatever he was hearing.

Pelligrosso ended the call. "That was dispatch. Fowler's .380 was stolen out of New York about eighteen months ago."

IT WAS NEARLY six o'clock. Byron was sitting at his desk trying desperately to catch up on his ongoing investigative supplement when Nugent rapped on the metal doorframe.

"Hey, Sarge."

"Nuge. Any luck at the hospital?"

"No. The guy doesn't remember anything. Claiming amnesia."

"Was he wearing a suit when he was brought in?"

"Hospital tossed his clothes. Biohazard."

"*Nobody* remembers what he had on?"

"Apparently not. Some keen powers of observation, huh?"

"Check with the paramedics. Maybe they'll remember."

Stevens popped her head through the doorway. "Sorry to bug you, but I think you'll wanna see what's on the television, Sarge."

Byron shot her a quizzical look then followed her and Nugent to the conference room where Diane was already seated at the table.

"What's the big mystery?" Byron asked.

"Watch," Diane said, still sounding pissed. She pointed the remote at the wall-mounted television and increased the volume.

"Our top story tonight concerns an arrest made by the Portland Police Department. Police sources tell us that a local man has been arrested in connection with the murder of local attorney Paul Ramsey."

"What the fuck?" Byron said.

The pudgy newscaster with a bad comb-over continued. "We now go live to Jenny Kierstead at the Cumberland County Jail. Jenny, what's the latest?"

"Thanks, Tom," Jenny said, the entrance to the jail behind

her. "An hour ago I spoke on the phone with Lieutenant Martin LeRoyer, commander of the police department's detectives. Lieutenant LeRoyer told me that his detectives have arrested a person of interest in the Ramsey murder on an unrelated charge."

"You've got to be kidding me," Byron said.

Kierstead looked down at her notes and continued. "Lieutenant LeRoyer would not disclose the identity of the person, only that he is a local man. But sources inside the department have told me that the only man arrested by Portland detectives in the last forty-eight hours is this man. Roger Fowler."

Byron mouth dropped open as they displayed Fowler's mug shot. He could feel the anger welling within him like water coming to a boil.

"Fowler was booked this afternoon at the Cumberland County Jail on several different charges, including possession of controlled substances, and possession of a stolen firearm. Both serious charges. When I asked LeRoyer about the connection to the Ramsey murder, he would only say, 'No comment.'"

"Interesting development, Jenny," Pudgy opined. "Keep us posted."

Byron, who had ceased listening, marched back into his office and slammed the door. He grabbed the desk phone, forcefully punching in LeRoyer's number.

"What the fuck, Marty!" Byron said as soon as LeRoyer picked up.

"John, don't start. You have no idea how much pressure I've been getting from everywhere on this case."

"Pressure? You think I give a fuck about pressure?"

"Look, we made progress and I put it out there to shut some people up."

"We don't know for sure if this guy had anything to do with killing Ramsey."

"His boyfriend said he punched Ramsey out the same night he went missing, right?"

"He said he watched him punch out someone wearing a suit. We have no idea if it was even Ramsey."

"Regardless, you found the .380 at Fowler's apartment and Ramsey was killed with a .380."

"Yeah, we found a .380. Doesn't mean it's the same gun. Dammit, Marty, we haven't even checked ballistics yet!"

"Come on, John. What are the odds that this asshole would just happen to have the same caliber weapon?"

"Do you have any idea how many .380s there are in the world? And another thing, how in hell am I going to be able to show photo arrays of Fowler to any witnesses now that they've plastered his face all over the goddamned news?"

"Hey, I didn't give them his name."

"It wasn't that hard to figure out." Byron couldn't help but wonder if one of Crosby's guys had tipped his identity to the news. Payback for getting stuck with the search warrant. Either way, the damage was done. "What the fuck, Marty! This isn't like you. It's more like something Cross would've done," Byron said, referring to the late assistant chief. "Stanton didn't make *you* the new Ass Chief, did he?"

There was a brief pause at LeRoyer's end of the phone.

"Oh, that's just fucking great," Byron said. "So now *you've* gone over to the dark side too."

"Watch it, John," LeRoyer cautioned.

"Or what? You'll royally fuck up my case? Too late!"

Byron banged the phone down on its cradle then reached

instinctually for the bottom right desk drawer. The drawer where he used to hide a bottle. He pulled his hand back, realizing the Irish no longer resided there.

"Fuck." Byron rolled his head back then side to side, cracking his neck in an attempt to relieve the stress. He was getting out of his chair when the desk phone rang.

"Byron," he snapped as he answered it.

"Sarge, it's Johnson. I'm working down at the IO desk. There's someone here to see you."

"I'm little busy right now, Officer. Who is it?"

"Some guy named Bagley."

"You arrested him?" Bagley said, loud enough to draw looks from several people sitting on the lobby benches. "How could you?"

"Mr. Bagley, I can appreciate how upsetting this whole thing must be for you, but Roger may have killed Paul Ramsey. Isn't that why you came to me in the first place?"

"I came because Dr. Byron said I could trust you. I didn't think you'd charge out and arrest Roger without investigating it first."

Bagley looked mad enough to take a swing at him.

"Mr. Bagley, I assure you we didn't just run out and arrest him. But we still have charges pending against Roger, whether he's responsible for Ramsey's murder or not."

Bagley's feelings betrayed him. Tears ran down his cheeks. "I care about him, Sergeant. Very much. I only told you about the assault because I was worried. Now you've gone and arrested him. He'll probably never speak to me again."

Byron tried consoling him. "You did the right thing coming forward. I know it doesn't seem like it right now but—"

"Just save it. I don't want to hear it."

He watched as Bagley marched out through the vestibule double doors and down the steps to Middle Street. Then he turned and signaled the desk officer to buzz him in.

"Sorry, Sarge," Johnson said.

Byron ignored him, proceeded directly to the elevator, and punched the up button with the side of his fist. As he waited, the promotional list caught his eye again. He tore it from the bulletin board, crumpled it up, and flung it toward a nearby trash can. He missed.

God, I need a drink.

Chapter Twenty-Three

Sunday, 10:30 P.M., May 1, 2016

BYRON SAT ON the darkened hillside, staring out at the cityscape below. Lit windows twinkled like stars. The air was still warm and the grass dewy. Nearby crickets harmonized in soprano. Highway traffic pulsed around Back Cove like an artery supplying Portland with a vital flow. A siren wailed in the distance. He came here to reflect, as his father had before him. As Ray Humphrey had. Byron missed his old friend, missed their conversations about life. The cop's life. He sighed. *How had things gotten so fucked up?*

He wished he could go back in time. Back to the Portland of his youth. It was a different city then, a different time, when his father and Ray had shared this view. The waterfront had been a tougher place. People still dressed up and attended church every Sunday. Families still ate together at the dinner table. And later, when he and Ray had frequented this spot, Portland had changed yet again.

Byron wondered how many of the city's seventy thousand ever

stopped to smell the roses. How many ever came to this spot, or any spot, to pause and reflect? Take a brief respite from the working and living and dying on the coast of Maine. It was mostly the dying upon which he focused. After all, it was how he earned his money.

His gaze shifted to the paper bag lying on the ground beside him. Inside the bag was his old pal, his confident, Officer Jameson, ready for duty. Still sealed. He'd purchased the bottle at the variety store after leaving 109. He knew how dangerously close he was coming to ending nearly nine months of sobriety. But he also knew there was a big difference between buying a bottle and drinking one. This wasn't the first time he'd found himself tested. There had been others. On each of the other occasions he'd managed to talk himself out of it, opting instead to smash the bottle on a rock or toss it out the window, unopened, on his way home. Though something about this time felt different. Maybe it was the way the clerk had eyed him as he wandered the store, like he was a shoplifter, wrestling with his conscience. Perhaps it was the tension between him and Diane, the first real problem they'd had since becoming involved. Or maybe it was seeing Kay again, and realizing that he still loved her. Byron didn't know what it was but he could feel himself weakening by the moment. Slipping. And that's the way it was, wasn't it? The way it always was. Incremental. He tore his eyes away from the bag and forced his mind back to the case.

If Ramsey was killed at the SUV, why had the murderer bothered to dump him in the ocean? Why not just shoot him in the SUV and leave him? If they shot him on the boat, why drive his SUV to Veranda Street? It made no sense. But neither did the idea of three different people assaulting this guy independent of each other on the same night. Ramsey was a son of a bitch but it was still a hard explanation to swallow. Byron could understand McVail following Ramsey out of the bar to administer some street justice; he'd considered doing that himself on occasion. He could even believe that Fowler had come along and punched Ramsey as he staggered about on his feet. But the idea that Fowler would walk all the way to his apartment then return to shoot Ramsey was a stretch. And if it wasn't Fowler, then a third person had to have driven him out to Veranda Street and shot him.

This third person would have to have been watching Ramsey, Byron thought. Maybe even following him.

His concentration was momentarily broken by the sound of a pair of slamming car doors from behind, back at CB Circle, at the intersection of North Street and the Eastern Prom where he had parked. Following the slamming doors came the unmistakable giggling of a young male and female. He'd forgotten about the other things, besides reflection, that the younger residents of Portland came here for. The giggling gradually faded as they moved away from him. Byron's thoughts turned to Diane. *Why had she taken the exam in the first place? Was she seriously considering leaving CID? Or was this some ill-contrived plan to get him to commit?* He didn't know. It seemed out of character. Either way, one of them would be forced out of the detective bureau. He was far too set in his ways to even consider lieutenant's bars and the unit couldn't afford to lose a detective as good as Diane. Truth be told, he couldn't afford to lose Diane.

He glanced down at the bag, hearing the siren song of the bottle contained therein. It had solved so many problems. *Hadn't it? Or had it caused more than it ever solved?* He closed his eyes tightly, trying to focus on his breathing.

"Thinking about throwing it all away?" the voice of his dead mentor, Ray Humphrey, said as clearly as if he were right beside him. "You really think the answer's in that bottle, Sarge?"

"No. Not really," Byron said aloud.

"Then why are you even considering it?"

"I don't know. Habit, maybe. It's familiar."

"So's hell."

Byron opened his eyes and looked around. He was alone. Humphrey wasn't there, of course. Only the grassy hill and the city lights beyond. Humphrey was only a memory, a ghost, like so many others. An imaginary voice in Byron's head.

His cellphone vibrated. He pulled it from his pocket. It was a text from his niece.

"Missed U 2day, Uncle John:("

Fuck. He'd missed her graduation party. It was official. He was now the world's worst uncle. How could he have forgotten about her party? What in hell was he thinking?

He was rereading Katie's text through watery eyes when the cell began to ring and the screen changed. He expected it to be Katie but the ID identified the caller as Pelligrosso. Byron cleared his throat then answered.

"Hey, Gabe."

"Sarge. Just finished comparing the bullet from Fowler's gun to the one taken from Ramsey's head."

Byron closed his eyes, hoping, praying. "And?"

"They don't match."

Byron powered the phone off and reached for the bag.

WITH THE LIVE band's bass notes booming in her ear, Diane sat alone at the far right end of the bar. She was upset for allowing herself to get into this position in the first place. Why had she taken that damn test? For that matter, why had she started sleeping with John? *Because he's sexy as hell.* She knew how stupid bedding her supervisor was, but she'd done it anyway. Certainly there is no such thing as casual sex between coworkers. Sooner or later someone gets hurt, no two ways about it. Either it becomes serious, in which case the job is fucked, or it ends badly, in which case the job is also fucked. Maybe she'd be better off accepting the city manager's offer. Take the bullshit PR sergeant's position, ride it out for six months, and see what happens. At least then, *if* she and John kept seeing each other, nobody would care.

She finished her Boston lager and was about to signal the bartender for another when a young man slid onto the stool to her left.

"Can I buy you a drink?" he said, raising his voice to be heard above the music.

"Save your lame pickup line for someone who's—Davis?" She'd expected to see some hard luck loser, looking to get lucky with a stranger. She hadn't been expecting the *Portland Herald*'s most dogged crime beat reporter. "What the fuck do you want?"

"I just want to talk."

"So you can print some more BS in that rag of a paper? Take something else out of context?" She furrowed her brow, appraising him suspiciously. "Are you following me again, you little dweeb?"

"Relax, Detective. You're not that hard to find."

"Yeah, well, you found me, now you can just go find your way out of here."

"I need to talk to you. It's important."

"What could we possibly have to talk about?"

"The Ramsey murder."

She glared at him. "You're not gonna get me to say anything about the case."

"I'm not here to *get* info."

She cocked her head to one side. "What's that supposed to mean?"

"Just hear me out," Billingslea said. "Let me buy you a drink."

"You've got to be kidding."

He held up both hands in mock surrender. "Please."

"One drink. After that, if you're still annoying me, I'll have you thrown out of here. Or, better yet, I'll throw you out myself."

Billingslea turned as the bartender approached.

"What can I getcha?" the bartender asked.

"I'll have a glass of Pinot and a refill for my friend."

"Don't push it, Davis. We aren't friends."

The bartender shot Diane a worried look.

"It's okay," she said. "He's buying."

The bartender wandered off to get their drinks.

"The clock's already started," Diane said. "You got something to say, I suggest you say it."

"I know we've had our differences, Diane, but I'd like to try and fix that."

"It's 'Detective.' You're a long way from 'Diane.' How can *you* fix it?"

"I think I can help you guys with the Ramsey case."

Again, Diane eyed him suspiciously.

"I'm serious."

"Why the hell would you want to help us?"

"Let's just say my bosses haven't exactly been supportive on this case. I've been getting good information but they won't let me print any of it."

She cupped her hand behind her ear. "Hear that, Davis? That's me not giving a fuck. If this intel of yours is so great, why haven't you approached Sergeant Byron? Why come to me?"

"Truthfully? Because I'm afraid he'd kick my ass."

Diane hid a faint smile. "And you think I won't?"

The bartender returned, placing the drinks on the bar in front of them.

Diane watched Davis as he sat on the stool, sulking and sipping his wine.

"Okay," Diane said finally. "I'll play along. Where are you getting this bullshit information you think is important enough to share with the police?"

"I have an inside source."

"At the firm?"

Billingslea nodded.

"Does your source know you're approaching me?"

"Yes."

"How do you know that this isn't just some employee with an axe to grind, Davis?"

"I don't think she is."

Diane's eyes widened. "A woman?"

He nodded again.

"Let me guess, someone Ramsey slept with?"

"No. She's not like that."

Diane took another drink from her pint glass.

"Getting this from you, whatever it is, won't help me much, even if it's true. I'm gonna need to speak with your source."

Billingslea's expression brightened. "I was hoping you'd say that. She's here."

Diane pivoted on the stool, scanning the tables until she spotted an attractive young woman seated alone. She looked back at Billingslea. "That her?"

"Yes."

Diane grabbed her drink and accompanied the reporter over to the table.

Billingslea made the introductions. "Detective Joyner, I'd like you to meet Amy Brennan."

Brennan stood up and the two women shook hands.

"Ms. Brennan," Diane said.

"Amy, please."

All three of them sat down.

"Davis says that you work at Newman, Branch & DeWitt."

"I'm a paralegal."

"How long?"

"Three years."

"Ask her about—"

"If you don't mind, Davis, I usually do my own interviews."

"Sorry."

Diane continued. "You know I'm one of the investigators working on Ramsey's murder, right?"

Brennan nodded.

"Do your bosses know that you're talking to a reporter, and now the police?"

She shook her head. "No. I'd be fired if she found out."

"She?"

"I'm Attorney Lorraine Davies's assistant."

"So why are you talking out of school?"

Brennan looked down at the table. "I don't know."

"You're pissed at your boss? Is that why you're here?"

Brennan reestablished eye contact. "No. She's very good to me."

"Why, then?"

Brennan looked to Billingslea for help.

He nodded. "Go ahead. Tell her."

Brennan looked back at Diane. "Paul Ramsey was having an affair with Branch's wife."

Chapter Twenty-Four

Sunday, 11:00 P.M., May 1, 2016

BYRON DROVE DIRECTLY to 109. Once again he'd bested his demons, smashing the bottle on a rock before returning to his car. Katie's text had pushed him back. He'd let her down and he knew it. It made him feel like shit. He was letting his weakness control his life. It was time to take back control. He would refocus on catching the killer. Start over. Go back to the beginning. That's what Humphrey had always pounded into his head. When you find yourself lost, unable to find a way forward, go back to the beginning. Figure out what you missed.

He sat in the conference room staring at the whiteboard. A maze of names, times, and dates written in red and black marker. At the center was Paul Ramsey, attorney, stepfather, husband, drug addict, asshole. But now only a dead asshole. Murdered by someone even more loathsome than himself. Someone who wanted Ramsey out of the way. Removed from the equation, permanently. But who? Certainly not Darius Tomlinson. Oh, Tomlinson might have killed Ramsey, but if he had it was at someone else's behest. Maybe someone used Tomlinson to get to Ramsey. Was it blackmail gone bad? Had Ramsey decided not to play ball?

And there were other names circled, with arrows pointing to and away from them. Devon Branch, Lorraine Davies, Gerry DeWitt, Donny McVail. Just pieces of a puzzle that didn't quite fit together. They were still missing something. But what? Something they hadn't found yet. Or maybe they had found it but were overlooking its importance.

So many people could have wanted Ramsey dead. He had enemies. Too many to count. Byron couldn't really bring himself to care that Ramsey was dead. Had it happened in another jurisdiction he wouldn't have been involved. But it hadn't. It happened right in Byron's backyard. Right smack in the middle of his city. And that made it his problem. His murder to solve. He would never grieve for the deceased attorney, but until Ramsey's killer was brought to justice, Byron would never rest.

His cellphone began vibrating across the table. He picked up and checked the ID. Diane. "Byron," he answered.

"Where are you?" Diane asked.

"109. CID conference room. Making my eyes cross looking for a piece that joins this puzzle. You?"

"On my way in. And I may have found a great big piece."

BYRON AND DIANE sat across from Brennan at the worn wooden interview room table. Billingslea waited outside in the CID waiting room.

"Thank you for coming forward, Amy," Byron said.

"I don't know if it has anything to do with Mr. Ramsey's murder but I thought you should know," Brennan said.

"Why did you go to Davis Billingslea in the first place?" Diane asked. "Why not come directly to us?"

"I didn't dare come to you with this. I already knew Davis. He actually contacted me. I'd met him during the civil trial. Davis had come by the office several times to try and get information for his trial coverage."

"Are the two of you seeing each other?" Byron asked.

Brennan flushed at the question. "Not really. We've been out a couple times."

"Tell me about the affair between Branch's wife and Ramsey," Byron said.

"I think it started around the time of the firm's Christmas party, last year."

"You think?" Byron asked.

"Devon Branch and Lorraine Davies host an annual Christmas party at their house in Topsham. Last year's was the second one I've been invited to. Anyway, I was feeling a little tipsy and needed to use the bathroom but someone was already using it. So I wandered up to the second floor to try and find another bathroom. I accidentally walked in on them."

"Ramsey and Davies?" Diane asked.

Brennan nodded. "Yes."

"What happened?" Byron asked.

"I opened a door thinking it might have been a bathroom but it led to a spare bedroom. It was dark but I could tell what they were doing."

"What were they doing?" Diane asked.

"Ms. Davies's shirt was off and Ramsey's pants were down and they were making out next to the bed."

"What did you do?" Diane asked.

"Got the hell out of there. I was afraid I'd get in trouble for seeing that."

"Did either of them ever approach you about what you'd seen?" Byron asked.

"Mr. Ramsey didn't but Lorraine did. A couple of days after the party. She said that she was sorry that it happened. Told me it was a one-time thing and asked for my discretion. I said I hadn't really seen anything."

"That was it?" Byron asked.

"Yes. She thanked me and we never spoke of it again."

"Amy, did Branch know?" Diane asked.

"I think he may have found out, later."

"About the Christmas party?" Diane asked.

Brennan shook her head. "About the affair."

"So, it wasn't just a one-time thing," Byron said.

"No. It kept happening. It was one of those things that everyone in the office knew about but pretended wasn't happening."

Byron made eye contact with Diane. He knew exactly what Brennan was talking about. They both did.

JOANNE BABBAGE PACED about the hotel room nervously waiting. She checked the alarm clock on the bedside table—11:20. He was late. *Had something happened? Had he changed his mind?* She walked to the window and looked outside. Nothing. She went back to pacing.

She'd done her part. Told the police exactly what she was supposed to. Those acting classes had paid off. Wasn't really all that different than the acting she did each night. Pretending to want the attention of the customers while she danced half-naked around the stage. Then, every so often, pretending to be in love with one of the well-to-do patrons, like Paul Ramsey. Picking up a little more on the side as she pushed for Darius. It was all make-believe. Acting out the roles she was paid to play. And she had just nailed a new role, a top-notch performance with the police. Now she expected to be paid the rest of what she was owed.

She sat down on the edge of the bed and crossed her arms, tapping her foot nervously on the stained Berber carpeting. She glanced back at the plastic clock on the nightstand. The red LED display read twenty-two past. *Where the hell was he?*

A sharp knock at the door startled her. She stood, went to the door, and opened it.

"Well, it's about fucking t—"

"Hello, Candy."

"You did the right thing, you know," Billingslea said as he steered the car onto the Washington Avenue off-ramp.

"Why don't I feel better knowing that?" Brennan asked.

The truth was Billingslea was conflicted about it himself. He realized this was his first time actually helping the police instead of trying to beat them to the punch. It wasn't sitting well with the reporter inside him, but he remembered what Paxton had said about gaining Byron's trust. He was a long way from that yet, but perhaps this olive branch to Detective Joyner was a start.

"You don't think Devon would ever do anything to Lorraine, do you?" Billingslea asked.

Brennan looked at him wide-eyed. "I'd never considered it."

Several minutes later, Billingslea pulled up in front of Brennan's apartment and stopped.

"Thank you for talking me into that, Davis."

"You sure?"

"Yeah, I mean, at least I got it off my chest. Just because Ramsey was having an affair with Lorraine doesn't mean that Branch killed him, right?"

"Of course it doesn't." But even as he said it, Billingslea realized how hollow it sounded. It absolutely made Devon Branch a suspect. And they both knew it.

"Well, good night, Davis," she said as she reached for the door handle.

Billingslea had been thinking about this moment all evening. He finally got the courage up and leaned over to kiss her. She pulled back slightly.

"I'm s-s-sorry," he stammered. "I thought—"

Brennan smiled. "Don't be sorry," she said. She kissed him on the cheek then got out of the car. "Good night, Davis."

"Good night."

IT WAS JUST after two Monday morning. Tomlinson stood beside the Beamer, at the rear of the deserted parking lot, waiting for his payday. He lit another cigarette, then pocketed the lighter. He didn't like waiting for anyone, but with Crosby's guys on him, he had to be more careful. This wasn't like one of his drug deals. Normally, he'd have one of his couriers be the go-between. That way he wouldn't get caught holding. The only time he ever got personally involved was with high-end customers, when the payment was made face-to-face. Cash only. Kept the bigwigs honest. Facing him on his turf outside of their ivory towers discouraged delinquency. A couple of former customers had made the mistake of taking delivery without paying. It was a mistake they only made once. This payment was different, however. It wasn't for product. This payment was for services rendered. He'd need a new mule, but that wasn't a big deal. Girls like Candy were a dime a dozen.

Tomlinson looked up as a vehicle rounded the corner at the far end of the lot. He studied its profile. The car definitely wasn't an unmarked, not with the low-profile high-intensity headlights. He knew a luxury when he saw it. He checked his watch. Eleven minutes late. He dropped the cigarette butt to the pavement, twisting it under a black Salvatore Ferragamo high-top. They'd be having a chat about price increases if this shit continued.

Tomlinson watched as the car slowed and turned in next to him. The driver lowered the tinted power window.

"Yo, you're late," Tomlinson said as he started toward the car. "If you're gonna keep the D Man waiting, prices are goin' up. You feel me?"

Four gunshots rang out in rapid succession. He saw the muzzle flashes and felt burning lead ripping through his torso. There was a strange disconnect, no feeling from below his waist. His legs gave out beneath him and he collapsed to the asphalt. He struggled to reach the gun in his ankle holster but the pain was too intense. Each breath brought white-hot agony. Powerless, all he could do was watch as the car door opened and the driver stepped out.

"Please," he croaked, holding a hand up in a futile attempt to try and shield himself. The semiauto was pointed directly at him. The opening at the business end of its barrel looked as big around as that of a cannon. He could see the look of determination on his assailant's face. There would be no mercy. He saw but did not hear the final flash from the gun.

BYRON AWOKE GRADUALLY to an annoying buzzing sound. He lifted his head from the pillow and saw the illuminated screen of his cellphone as it danced across the nightstand, the only light in the darkened room. He grabbed it and checked the time and incoming ID. Four-thirty. LeRoyer. He threw the covers back and forced himself to sit up on the edge of the bed. Unsure of the day, his mind was still wrapped in the gauzy fabric of slumber.

"Morning, Marty," he croaked. "What's up?"

"Rise and shine, John," LeRoyer said. "Got another body. Get dressed."

It was nearly five by the time Byron and Diane pulled into the lot. Three black-and-whites formed a half circle around the crime scene. Sergeant Bobby Perry approached as they exited the unmarked.

"Hey, guys," Perry said. "Sorry to get you out of bed this early."

"No you're not," Byron said.

"Bobby," Diane greeted.

"Why the wagon train?" Byron asked.

Perry looked back at the cars surrounding the BMW. "Figured it was better than nothing. Couldn't find anything to wrap the crime scene tape around."

"What've we got?" Byron said.

"Black male, thirties. Multiple gunshot wounds to the body and face. Shell casings on the ground."

Byron nodded his understanding. "Who found him?"

"Gibson. Slow night. He was checking businesses when he saw the car parked out here. Thought it was unusual. Drove up to take a look. Found this."

"He touch anything?"

"Nah. Kid's new but he's bright."

"Refreshing," Diane said.

Perry grinned. "You guys even sound alike."

"No one called about the gunshots?" Byron asked.

"Nope."

Byron wondered what it said about a city when someone could empty a gun into a person, in the middle of a parking lot, and nobody called the police. "E.T.?" Byron asked.

"Gabe's on his way. Just left 109."

"Any idea who this is?" Diane asked as they surveyed the scene.

"Like I said, we didn't touch anything." Perry referred to his notebook. "Ran the plate on the Beamer, it's registered to one Darius Tomlinson."

"Oh, fuck," Diane said.

Perry looked up from his notebook. "Know him?"

"We were just getting acquainted," Byron said.

BYRON WAS HOLDING the flashlight for Pelligrosso as the evidence tech focused the camera on a spent shell casing lying on the pavement next to Tomlinson, when he heard the sound of rapid acceleration. They both turned to look as LeRoyer's Crown Vic sped across the empty lot toward them.

"He's up early," Pelligrosso said.

"You got this?" Byron asked as he passed the light back to Pelligrosso.

"Yeah, I'll get one of the rookies to help me. They should be out here anyway."

Byron walked over to meet the lieutenant.

Byron noted LeRoyer's disheveled appearance. "You didn't have to come out for this, Marty," Byron said.

"Evidently Chief Stanton disagrees with you."

"Ah. Checking up on me?"

"Don't start, John. It's too goddamned early for jousting," LeRoyer said. Dressed in a light sweatshirt and jeans, he shivered and rubbed his upper arms. "Fuck, it's cold. Thought it was supposed to be summer."

"Not for another month or so," Byron said. "Besides, this is what it's like when the sun goes down. You must not remember working the street at night?"

"Funny." LeRoyer pointed to the body. "So, who's the stiff?"

"Ramsey's supplier, Darius Tomlinson."

LeRoyer's eyes grew wide. "The guy we just brought in?"

"Yeah, Crosby grabbed him up for us."

"Thought he was still in jail."

"So did I. Evidently it's easier to make bail than it used to be."

"He give us anything?"

"Didn't think what he told us was all that valuable." Byron turned to look back at Tomlinson's body. "I'm rethinking that."

As they watched Pelligrosso working with one of the uniformed officers, Byron ran down what little information they had.

"My guess, he was probably waiting here to meet someone when he was shot," Byron said in summation.

"Drug rip?" LeRoyer asked.

"Maybe. Too soon to say."

"Any indication someone was waiting with him?"

"No sign of anyone. We checked for shell casings and blood trails leading from the area but it all seems compartmentalized around Darius. Either way, if there was someone else, they beat feet."

"Witnesses?"

Byron shook his head. "No one even called in the shots. Beat cop found him."

"Have you called Crosby yet?"

Byron frowned. "This is a homicide, Marty. Last I checked, Crosby's a drug guy. I don't see any trafficking going on here. Do you?"

"Where's Diane?" LeRoyer asked, looking around for Byron's partner and ignoring the comment.

"I sent her and Mel to pull the security tapes from every business facing this lot."

"It's not even five-thirty in the morning, John. Nobody's gonna be up at this hour."

"They are now. I had Dispatch call every one of their emergency numbers."

LeRoyer ran his hand through his hair. "Great."

"Hey, Sarge," Pelligrosso hollered over. "Got a sec?"

"What's up?" Byron asked.

The evidence tech held up a pen. A brass shell casing hung atop it. "I just started collecting the casings. Thought you'd be interested in the caliber. They're .380s."

BYRON, DIANE, AND Nugent hovered over Tran's desk. Byron had called in the department's computer specialist as soon as they realized they might have something on one of the security cameras.

"I thought this desperado was in jail," Tran said.

"He *was*," Byron growled.

"Okay, got a couple of things for you," Tran said. "Here goes. The time stamp in the upper right of the screen is slow by sixty-two minutes. Figure they missed daylight savings. The date is obviously right."

"Is this black and white?" Nugent asked.

"No, but it might as well be," Tran said. "Low light kills all the color."

"Anything happen before Tomlinson arrived?" Byron asked.

"No. And I went back an hour just to make sure. Here's his BMW coming in."

"Looks like he's alone," Diane said as they watched Tomlinson park and exit the car.

"It's a little grainy," Byron said. "Can you clean that up?"

"I'd love to, Sarge, but this camera is crap. They've got a state of the art recorder but never bothered to upgrade the camera."

"Typical," Nugent said.

"Some of the reason it's so pixelated is because I've zoomed in as far as I can. If I hadn't, you wouldn't be able to see it very well."

"Can you print out stills?" Byron asked.

"Sure can. I'll go back and print some after I show you." Tran used the mouse to skip ahead in time. "Okay, Tomlinson stands there doing something for about fifteen minutes before the other car shows up."

"He was smoking," Byron said. "We recovered three cigarette butts."

"And there's your mystery guest," Tran said, pointing.

On the screen a dark sedan drove toward Tomlinson, slowly.

"I can't tell what kind of car it is," Nugent said.

"Might be a Lexus," Diane said.

"That's what I was thinking," Tran said. "Either that or a Jag. It's tough to tell."

Byron leaned in closer to the monitor for a better look. It didn't help.

"Does the shooter get out?" Nugent asked.

"Wait for it," Tran said. "There. See the muzzle flashes?"

"Yeah," Byron said.

They watched as Tomlinson fell to the ground and the driver's door on the second vehicle opened. A shadowy figure emerged and approached Tomlinson.

"And there's the final shot," Tran said, freezing the image at the point of the flash.

Diane turned toward Byron. "So, Tomlinson doesn't react to the threat."

"Must have known who it was," Nugent said.

"He was waiting for them," Byron said.

"Easy way to ambush someone," Tran said.

"Does the shooter go into Tomlinson's car?" Byron asked.

"Nope. Just gets back into their own car and drives away," Tran said.

"There goes the drug rip theory," Diane said. "So he was executed by someone he knew?"

"Sure looks that way," Byron said. "And we've got a grainy video that doesn't help us at all. What about when the car leaves?" he asked Tran. "Any chance we get a look at the driver? Or the plate?"

"I'll play it for you," Tran said. "But the short answer is no. Plate's not visible and the sodium arc lights in the parking lot actually reflect off the windshield. Nothing but a glare."

Byron stood upright, staring at the still image, hoping something would materialize that they could use. Nothing did. "You said you had two things for us."

"Indeed I do, kemosabe," Tran said. "Gabe found something interesting while searching through Tomlinson's clothing." He held up two small rectangular pieces of plastic.

"SIM cards," Diane said.

"Yup," Tran said. "And he still had one inside the phone tray. Our drug lord had three different SIM cards."

"Why didn't Crosby's guys find them?" Nugent asked Byron.

"Don't know. Maybe he didn't have them on him when he was busted." Byron looked back at Tran.

"How long will it take you to process whatever's on those?"

Tran shrugged. "Depends on how much activity and contacts there are on each. Guy is—excuse me—*was* a dealer. Could be a lot."

"Then don't waste any more time on the video," Byron said.

"Nice work, geek boy," Nugent said.

"Good work, Dustin," Diane agreed.

"Thanks, Soon to Be Striped One."

Byron said nothing as he walked out of the lab.

Chapter Twenty-Five

Monday, 11:18 A.M., May 2, 2016

JUANITA RODRIGUEZ STRUGGLED to push the heavily loaded cart along the cracked gray asphalt of the hotel's front walkway. The Vacationland Inn on Riverside Street in Portland owned several of the molded plastic cleaning supply carts and she always seemed to get the only one with the bum wheel, causing it to pull to the left. She had to fight to keep it from slipping off the curb.

Rodriguez had been cleaning rooms for as long as she could remember. She'd begun working full-time after dropping out of high school in Plano, Texas. Four years ago she'd come to Maine to live with her aunt, hoping for a better life than the one her drugged-out parents had provided. She had taken a job as a housekeeper at the inn. Some of her friends worked in town at high-class hotels. The Vacationland was not one of those, and never would be.

During her time at the inn, Rodriguez had seen it all: high school kids passed out in their own vomit, love juice on the pillowcases and walls, even feces smeared all over a bathroom mirror. She pushed the cart up the sidewalk, stopping at room 121. She removed the brightly colored Do Not Disturb sign from the knob and knocked on the door.

"Housekeeping," she said.

The room's shades were drawn. She waited and checked her watch. It was 11:20. The rental board located in the office had listed this room as a one-night rental and whoever had rented it was supposed to have checked out at ten-thirty. She knocked once more, for good measure, then inserted her passkey and opened the door.

The window shades made the room as dark as a tomb. "Hello," she said with a thick Venezuelan accent. "Housekeeping." There was no response.

She stepped inside, pulling her cart in with her, using it as a makeshift doorstop. She reached out with her left hand and flipped the wall switch on, illuminating the room.

Her eyes widened in fear. On the unmade bed was the nude body of a woman. She was covered in blood. Her eyes were wide open and her throat had been cut from ear to ear.

Rodriguez's legs became wobbly then finally gave out. She dropped abruptly to the carpet like a rag doll and began to scream.

BYRON WAS STUCK in traffic, listening to his stomach's demanding growl and thinking he needed to take care of that basic human need when his cell rang. It was PPD dispatch.

"Byron," he said, answering it and hoping the call might provide answers.

"Sarge, it's Jeff in Dispatch. Sorry to bother you at lunchtime."

Byron grinned. Jeff in Dispatch was obviously new to the department and had no idea how rare a normal schedule was for him. Mealtime, nights, even weekends, meant nothing to the detective sergeant supervising CID's Crimes Against Persons Unit. Lunchtime was just another time of day when people could do bad shit to one another. Murder being the ultimate bad shit. "What's up, Jeff?"

"The dispatcher didn't want to put it out over the air, Sarge."

"Put what out?"

"Patrol just confirmed another body."

FORTY-FIVE MINUTES LATER, Byron was standing on the sidewalk of the Vacationland Inn, outside the crime scene, formerly a hotel room, speaking with Dr. Ellis. "So, what do you think?" Byron asked Ellis as he watched LeRoyer's car turn into the parking lot.

"Another one, Sergeant? What are we running, a two for one? Hey, come to think of it, that's not a bad idea. We could have a weekday special."

Byron continued. "Normally, I wouldn't ask but—"

"Ha! Sure you would, my boy. And I'd be disappointed if you didn't. I'm still at the Maine Med morgue. I'll grab my bag of tricks and be right over."

"Thanks, Doc."

Byron ended the call as LeRoyer was approaching on foot.

"What the hell is going on in this godforsaken town, John?" LeRoyer said, looking just as disheveled but somewhat warmer than he had during their meeting several hours prior. "Tell me this isn't related to the Ramsey case."

Byron shook his head. "I can't. Candy the stripper, AKA Joanne Babbage, checked into this hotel last night. She won't be checking out." He waited while the lieutenant processed the news and began to pace in front of him.

LeRoyer's hands went right to his hair, combing it back, his trademark nervous tic. "We sure it's a murder?" LeRoyer asked with a mildly hopeful tone.

"Pretty sure, Marty. Unless you think Candy slashed her own throat."

"Stanton is gonna lose his shit," LeRoyer said, as much to himself as to Byron. The lieutenant stopped pacing and took a deep breath. He turned to face Byron. "Okay, run it down for me."

"She checked in late last night. Paid cash. I sent Mel and Nuge out to grab up the night desk clerk at home. Dustin's on video recovery. Diane is canvassing the nearby rooms with a couple of beat officers. And I've got Gabe processing his second murder scene of the morning."

LeRoyer's cell rang. "Shit. It's the chief." He looked at Byron. "What the fuck am I supposed to tell him?"

Byron wanted to tell the lieutenant that life as the Ass Chief under Stanton wasn't likely to get any easier, but he resisted the urge. "Tell him we're making progress."

STEVENS AND NUGENT were just climbing the front stairs of the dated Deering split-level when a middle-aged woman appeared on the other side of the ripped screen door.

"Yes?" the woman said. "May I help you?"

Stevens took the lead. "Good afternoon, ma'am. I'm Detective Stevens and this is Detective Nugent." They both displayed their IDs. "Does Chris Miller live here?"

The woman's pleasant expression turned to worry. "He does. He's my son. Is he in some kind of trouble?"

"No, ma'am," Stevens said. "There's been an incident at the hotel where he works. We need to speak with him."

"An incident?"

"Yes, ma'am."

"Well, he works nights and he's still sleeping. Can't it wait?"

"It's important that we speak with him now, Mrs. Miller," Nugent said.

"May we come in?" Stevens asked.

Miller hesitated a moment before unlocking the door, and pushed it open. "Come inside. I'll go and get him."

JOHN BYRON STOOD in the corner of the room, trying to stay out of the way while watching Dr. Ellis work. Byron saw the glint in Ellis's eye. The doctor always got excited about anything gruesome. What made a man like Ellis? Byron couldn't imagine doing what the doctor did for work every day. Years ago he'd asked him how he could dissect human bodies all day then go home and be able to take any physical pleasure in his wife. After careful consideration, Ellis had said, "My boy, there's work and then there's play. I try not to confuse the two." Somehow he'd known the doc's answer wouldn't leave him feeling any more comfortable.

Byron knew in his gut the three murders were connected, about that there was little doubt. What he didn't know was how. Had Darius and Candy both been complicit in Ramsey's murder? Were they both eliminated simply to keep the police from working their way back to the attorney's killer? Or was something else entirely happening here?

Fowler the gym rat was still in custody on the drug charges, ironic after Tomlinson, a major drug dealer, had gotten out so easily. Still, Fowler being in custody when the last two murders occurred combined with the ballistic evidence pretty much negated his involvement in any of it. Fowler had said he was just trying to impress his boyfriend by claiming he'd shut Ramsey up. Perhaps he had been telling the truth after all.

Diane had told him that Candy was very convincing in that she had broken off her relationship with Ramsey. But had she? Tomlinson said Candy worked for the competition, selling drugs at the club for Alonzo Gutierrez, but when the drug guys picked him up to question him Gutierrez seemed shocked about the intel. According to Gutierrez, Tomlinson had been the club's only supplier. The Unicorn was Tomlinson's territory and unlike the Fox he wasn't sharing that one. Was this about drugs? Was Ramsey's involvement more than just as a customer? And if so, who else was involved? Someone from the firm perhaps. Branch or DeWitt?

"Hey, Sarge," a uniformed officer said, standing just outside the door to the room. "The K-9 is here."

Byron stepped outside to meet the dog's handler. There was no mistaking the sounds of an excited German shepherd coming from a nearby black-and-white. Ginny Tozier's K-9, Rico, was known as one of the best tracking dogs around. Tozier's shepherd had once successfully tracked a robbery suspect for two miles in a wooded area of Windham. The suspect, who was tired and lost, finally gave up and waited for the officers to find him. About the only way a suspect could lose Rico was to get in a car and drive away.

"Hey, Sarge," Tozier said. "We're ready when you are. I imagine I can't enter the room."

"Not for a while, I'm afraid. You think you can track using the victim's blood as a scent trigger?"

"We can try it. You have anything you can bring out to Rico?"

Five minutes later, the vocal and excited Rico was tugging his partner hard toward the Pine Tree Shopping Center. Byron watched them until they were out of sight before reentering the room.

"Well, I'd say there's no mystery here," Ellis said as he peeled off his latex gloves and absently rubbed his stubbled chin. "Her assailant overpowered her then sliced her throat."

"Any chance the victim inflicted injury on the killer?" Byron asked.

"Nothing under the nails. No defensive wounds on her hands. Looks like she was clobbered with something on the right side of her head. Most likely she either didn't see it coming or didn't have time to react. She probably collapsed on the bed, either dazed or unconscious, then the killer sliced her open, causing her to bleed out. That any help?"

"It might have been," Byron said. "If the security cameras functioned."

Byron stared at the body. Struck in the head as Ramsey had been. Only this time the killer used a knife instead of a gun.

"She's naked," Byron said. "Any sign of sexual assault?"

Ellis shook his head. "No sign that she'd engaged in any sexual activity, forced or otherwise. How bad do you need me to post?"

"On Tomlinson? Badly. This one, not so much. I need the bullets from Tomlinson's body for comparison."

Ellis looked over at Pelligrosso. "You got enough gas in the tank, my boy?"

Before the evidence tech could answer, Byron was summoned back to the door by the beat officer.

"Sarge, I think the K-9 found something."

STEVENS AND NUGENT sat across from Chris Miller, waiting for an answer to the question she had just posed. Miller appeared to be giving his answer careful consideration before verbalizing it. Miller's mother pretended to be doing something housework-related in the next room, but Stevens knew she was listening closely.

"Did you not understand the question, Mr. Miller?" Stevens asked.

"You're asking if I knew the woman who paid for the hotel room," Miller said, squirming in his chair and glancing toward the room occupied by his mother. "No. I didn't know her."

Nugent raised an eyebrow. "So you'd *never* seen her before?"

Miller swallowed nervously. "I didn't say that."

"Why are you being coy with us, Mr. Miller?" Stevens asked.

"I'm not. It's just—I don't want to get in trouble with my boss."

"How would admitting that you'd seen Ms. Babbage before get you into trouble with your boss?" Stevens asked. "Was she a regular?"

Miller nodded.

"Was she usually with a different man every time?"

Miller nodded again.

"Did you know what she was doing?"

Before he could nod a third time, Nugent jumped in. "Speak up, young man. Did you know she was taking these men to the hotel to have sex for money?"

"Yes," Miller said weakly, casting another glance toward the next room.

Stevens's cell buzzed with an incoming text. It was from Tran. "Only one camera off-line. The one covering the vic's room." She frowned and held it up for Nugent to read.

"Figures," Nugent said.

Stevens clipped the cell to her belt and returned her attention to Miller. "Did you see the person she was with last night?"

"No. She came in alone."

"Tell us about your security cameras," Nugent said.

Miller's pale face turned a shade whiter. "What about them?"

"It looks as though only one of them is broken," Stevens said. "Is it a coincidence that you gave Ms. Babbage a passkey to one of the rooms with no surveillance?"

Stalling, Miller toyed with something atop the table that looked like a bread crumb. He shook his head.

Nugent cleared his throat.

"No," Miller said.

"How long has that camera been broken?" Stevens asked.

"It's not broken. It's unplugged."

"By whom?" Stevens asked.

"Was it you?" Nugent said, intentionally making his tone accusatory.

"No. I swear I didn't—"

"Then who?" Nugent said.

"I don't know. It was like that when I started working there."

"How many people know that those rooms aren't videotaped?" Stevens said.

"I don't know. But all the girls from the Unicorn know. They ask for those rooms when they come in."

BYRON HELD THE padlock while Pelligrosso screwed the hasp onto the doorframe with a small electric driver. The decision had been made to delay the autopsies after bloody clothes, believed to belong to Babbage's killer, were located in a nearby dumpster. Byron handed him the lock as his cell rang. It was Stevens.

"How'd you make out with Miller?" Byron asked.

"It was tough getting him to admit anything with Mommy

sharking about but he finally came clean. The girls from the Unicorn, including our vic, have been using the rooms for extra money."

"Did he see who Babbage was with?" Byron asked hopefully.

"No. Said she checked in alone."

Byron wasn't at all surprised. If the owners of the hotel could count on filling the rooms regularly, it wouldn't matter to them if they were being rented by prostitutes or partying teenagers. A dollar was still a dollar. But none of that was important. What was important was the fact that the girls all knew about the lack of video coverage, and if the girls all knew, it was likely that others did too. Like maybe the murderer. "Will he give us a signed statement?"

"On our way to 109 with him now."

"Thanks, Mel." Byron was pocketing his phone when Diane returned.

"Any luck?"

"On the canvass? Nada. But I just got a call from one of the supervisors at County. Darius was bailed out by an attorney."

"Who?"

"Gerald DeWitt."

BYRON SENT DIANE and Tran to the Unicorn in hopes of finding out who Babbage might have met up with before checking into the no-tell motel. But Byron had a phone call to make. It was time to rattle some cages, he thought. And no better cage to start with than the one belonging to the person responsible for Tomlinson's bail. Gerald DeWitt.

DeWitt had readily agreed to meet. He told Byron he was at the office getting caught up on some pressing business and would meet him there. Byron, who had some pressing business of his own, sat across from DeWitt in the attorney's corner office, on the eighth floor of the Emerson Building, waiting for an answer to his question.

"Sergeant, if you're asking me if I bailed Mr. Tomlinson from jail, the answer is yes. You already know that."

"The question is why?" Byron said. "Why would one of the senior partners in one of the biggest law firms north of Boston go personally to the county jail and bail out a piece of shit like Darius Tomlinson?"

"That piece of shit, as you so eloquently put it, Sergeant, was a client of Paul Ramsey."

"So you took him on as your personal client after Ramsey died?"

"He was a client of Paul's, but our firm still represents Mr. Tomlinson. I was merely posting his bail. Innocent until proven guilty, remember?"

"Did he telephone you directly?"

"No. I received a call from a third party asking me to help facilitate his release."

"Who called you?" Byron asked, pen poised at the ready above his notepad.

DeWitt's lips spread into a grin. "Sergeant Byron, we both know I'm under no obligation to answer that question."

"Because I know the number Darius called from the jail. It's a TracFone. Untraceable. You're telling me it's not your phone?"

"I'm telling you that I'm not obligated to answer that. Besides, last I knew, it isn't a crime to provide a person charged with bail money. Has there been some change in the statutes of which I'm unaware?"

"No, bailing someone out isn't a crime. As long as the provider of that bail isn't also facilitating the suspect's demise."

"Are you accusing me of murdering Mr. Tomlinson?"

"I'm saying it's quite a coincidence that you'd post bail for Darius, someone you've never been in contact with, and that he'd end up murdered less than twenty-four hours later. Doesn't that strike you as a bit odd, Gerry?"

DeWitt shrugged his shoulders indifferently. "Mr. Tomlinson was suspected of drug dealing, isn't that right?"

"He was."

"Well, I have no information to support your suspicion, but let's assume for a moment that he was involved in drug trafficking—as I understand it, that is a very dangerous line of work to be in."

"You're speculating that Darius was killed by a rival dealer?"

"I am merely offering up a possibility for your consideration."

"I can see you're all torn up about it."

"All I can tell you for certain is that I had nothing to do with the murder of Darius Tomlinson. In fact, I was home with my wife when he was killed."

Byron studied him for a beat. "All that means is that you didn't pull the trigger."

"Think whatever you like, Sergeant. But we're finished here."

BYRON DROVE BACK to 109 pissed off. He knew DeWitt would continue to dance around any attempt the police made at uncovering the facts surrounding Tomlinson's death. Guys like DeWitt always used legal loopholes to avoid doing anything that might actually assist the police in finding a killer, even if the victim was a client, then publicly criticize them when they couldn't solve the case.

Byron was normally very astute at reading people, but he

hadn't been able to get a good read on DeWitt, and it was bothering him. Was DeWitt hiding something? Or was he just doing
what came natural to a guy who made his living getting bad guys
out of trouble?

He parked the unmarked in front of 109, in one of the police-
business-only spaces, behind a rust-colored minivan displaying
Tennessee plates, a plethora of bumper stickers, and a broken
passenger window. He was already playing a familiar scene inside
his head. The angry owner complaining to a desk officer about
the break-in and missing items. As if it was good sense to leave
valuables in an unattended vehicle in Tennessee. Maine wasn't the
only state with a drug problem. Crossing the lobby, he listened
to the middle-aged husband and wife at the counter berate the
officer, who likely wasn't even on the clock when the break-in
occurred, for their shortsightedness. Byron wondered if the irate
couple had any idea that there were bigger problems in the world
than their missing property. Problems like the unsolved murder
of Paul Ramsey. As the complaints of the Tennessee tourists faded
into background noise, Byron punched in the passcode to the
security door and stepped inside.

BYRON FOUND DIANE typing her supplement in the CID conference room.

"How'd it go with DeWitt?" she asked.

"How do you think?" Byron said as he fell back into a chair and
closed his eyes.

"That good, huh?"

"How about you? Any leads from the club?"

"Babbage didn't work last night. She called in sick."

"Great. Any of the girls willing to talk?"

"I rattled a few cages but they're as well trained as politicians, talking without saying a damned thing. Tran is back working on the SIM cards. There's a lot of data."

"Figured as much."

"You look like crap, John. I know you haven't slept. Why don't you go home? Get some sleep."

"I'd love nothing more but I'm not sure I can shut my brain off."

"Have you eaten?"

He shook his head. "I forgot. You?"

"Nothing worth mentioning. Let's take a ride. We both need real food."

Byron opened one eye. "You still pissed at me?"

"Who could possibly stay mad at you, John Byron?"

"Lots of people, I imagine."

She stood. "Come on, let's get out of here."

Chapter Twenty-Six

Tuesday, 8:00 A.M., May 3, 2016

"I'm having a difficult time following all this, John," LeRoyer said. "So, who do you think killed Ramsey? DeWitt?"

"It's possible," Byron said. "But if he is responsible, he was doing it for someone else. I'm thinking Branch had the best motive. Ramsey was shagging his wife."

"And that's Lorraine Davies?"

"Correct."

"Jesus," LeRoyer said, running his fingers back through his hair.

Byron frequently wondered how it was that the lieutenant's nervous tic hadn't caused him to go completely bald.

"So you think Branch might have killed Ramsey," LeRoyer said.

"Or had him killed," Diane added.

"Okay," LeRoyer said. "Or had him killed. Then what? He killed the stripper and the drug dealer to shut them up?"

"Could be that simple," Byron said. "He had motive, but did he have the opportunity? We need to establish timelines for Branch, DeWitt, and Davies on the day Ramsey went missing."

"What about the other two murders?" LeRoyer asked.

"If we can prove who it was that killed Ramsey, the other two might just fall into place," Diane said.

LeRoyer shook his head in disbelief. His face had taken on a deeply troubled expression. "Branch?"

"Makes the most sense," Byron said. Diane nodded her agreement.

"Stanton is gonna lose his mind when he finds out you're looking into Branch," LeRoyer said.

"Why does he need to know?" Byron said.

LeRoyer looked Byron up and down.

"Because he's the goddamned police chief, for one," LeRoyer said.

"Yeah, and he also seems to have a direct line to Branch," Diane said.

"I don't give two shits how much money Branch has donated to the department's K-9 program," Byron said.

"Maybe you don't, Sergeant, but Chief Stanton does."

"Can I add my two cents to this?" Diane asked.

"No," LeRoyer barked. "I don't need the two of you ganging up on me. I get it." He gave his hair several more passes for good measure.

"It's pretty simple, Marty," Byron said. "You have to decide what kind of lieutenant you're going to be." LeRoyer shot him a "watch yourself" look. "Either you want to be the kind that goes to bat when his people really need him or the kind that has to point to the bars on his collar to remind people he's in charge."

The lieutenant's eyes narrowed but his smirk betrayed his

feigned ire. "Oh, you want me to show you who's in charge, huh? Okay, both of you get the *fuck* out of my office."

Byron and Diane were headed for the door when LeRoyer stopped them.

"I'll keep it quiet as long as I can, although I'm not sure what good it will do. As soon as you start questioning people at the firm, Branch is gonna know. Fuck. Just tread lightly, okay?"

"Thanks, Marty," Byron said.

"It's 'Lieutenant,'" LeRoyer said, pointing to his collar. "Now get the hell outta here!"

DIANE WAS UPDATING the board in the conference CID room with the most current information while Byron sat at the end of the long table updating the others. Pelligrosso, who had already headed to Augusta for the post, was the only member of the team not present.

"I watched the video of Amy Brennan's interview," Stevens said. "I don't know her, but I've seen her hanging out at one of my favorite bars."

"Looking for Mr. Gay Bar," Nugent said.

Stevens reached over and punched him in the arm.

"Your point?" Byron asked.

"Does Brennan think that any of the people at the firm will talk to us?"

"She doesn't know," Byron said. "But I don't want to burn her as the source if we can help it. I'm thinking we say that we have several different people telling us about this affair and we interview Brennan right along with everyone else in the office if we have to." He looked at Stevens. "If we end up doing that, you want to interview her?"

"Sure," Stevens said. She fixed Nugent with a menacing stare. "Want another one?"

"Hey, I didn't say anything," Nugent said, grinning.

"Hopefully it doesn't come to that," Diane said.

"No," Byron said. "Hopefully they'll admit it to keep it from involving the entire firm."

"So how do you want to do this?" Nugent asked.

"I was thinking Mel and I could talk with Davies," Diane said. "She might be more open to confiding in us."

"Good idea," Byron said. "Branch is less likely to be embarrassed if it's just us guys."

"What about me, Boss Man?" Tran asked.

"Sorry, Pencil Neck," Nugent said. "He said guys."

Tran flipped Nugent off without looking at him.

"Dustin, I want you to dig up everything you can on everyone at that firm," Byron said. "Especially on Branch, DeWitt, Davies, and Brennan."

"Why Brennan?" Tran asked.

"Because, my young Jedi," Nugent said. "Wouldn't be the first time someone pretended to be helpful just so they could fuck up an investigation."

"No, it wouldn't," Byron agreed.

As soon as the meeting in CID ended, Diane phoned Attorney Davies, requesting to speak with her in person.

It was nearly eleven as Amy Brennan led Diane and Detective Stevens down the hall to Davies's office.

"Detectives," Davies said as she stood to greet them. "Won't you both have a seat?"

"Thank you," Diane said.

Diane was surprised to see Brennan sit down beside Davies.

"Thank you for agreeing to meet with us, Attorney Davies," Diane said.

"Please, call me Lorraine. You indicated over the phone that you wanted to discuss something with me."

"We do," Diane said, glancing at Brennan. "However, it's actually rather personal. It's about Paul Ramsey."

Davies turned to Brennan. "Would you excuse us, Amy?"

"Certainly," Brennan said.

They waited until Brennan had departed before speaking further.

"We are all still in shock, I think," Davies said. "It's just so tragic. Do you have any information about what may have happened to him?"

"We're still working on that," Diane said. "There's no easy way to ask this, Lorraine, so I'm just going to come out with it. Were you having an affair with Paul Ramsey?"

Davies's eyes widened as she looked from Diane to Stevens then back to Diane. "Why would you ask such a thing?"

"We have reason to believe that the two of you were involved when he was murdered," Stevens said.

"Who told you that?"

"I'm afraid we can't divulge that," Diane said.

Lorraine looked down, folding her hands together and placing them on her desk. "Paul and I were involved, but I broke it off."

"Did your husband know?" Stevens asked.

"Yes. Devon came to me in March and asked if I was having an affair."

"Did he know it was Paul?" Stevens asked.

Davies nodded.

"What happened?" Diane asked.

"How do these things ever happen? Last year Devon and I hosted the firm's Christmas party at our home in Topsham and it just happened. I guess I could blame it on the wine. But it was more than that. Mutual attraction, maybe. Paul was very attractive, and charming, when he wanted to be. Somehow we ended up upstairs in a spare room and it just happened." Davies dabbed at the corners of her eyes with her fingertips.

"But your husband didn't find out till later?" Diane asked.

"No. Not until March. He never knew about the party."

"How did he react?" Diane asked.

"Ha," she said, giving a short mock laugh. "Not very well."

"Did he ever threaten either of you?"

"Devon?"

The detectives nodded.

"Of course not. If you knew my husband you'd know that he's not capable of violence. Or, for that matter, any other emotion."

"Meaning?" Diane asked.

"Meaning that's probably why I got mixed up with Paul. He is—*was* a very passionate man. He never hid his emotions. Guess maybe I needed that in my life."

"When did you break it off with Ramsey?" Stevens asked.

Davies shook her head. "I don't know the exact date. The end of March, I think. May I ask what any of this has to do with Paul's murder?"

Diane paused a moment for effect. "Lorraine, do you own a gun?"

Byron and Nugent sat across from Devon Branch in his office. Unlike the last meeting, when the attorney had established his power by keeping his desk between them, the only thing separating them now was a coffee table and three mugs.

"I can't imagine where you heard such a thing," Branch said, absently rubbing his fingers over his chin then checking his hand as if he expected to see something there.

"Are you saying it isn't true?" Byron asked.

Branch looked up from his hand, staring directly at Byron. "Am I now suspected of having brought about Paul's demise?"

"This is a homicide investigation, Mr. Branch," Byron said. "Everyone is a possible suspect until we rule them out."

"I suppose you wouldn't be very good detectives if you didn't think that way."

"No, sir, we wouldn't," Nugent chimed in.

"You still haven't answered my question, Mr. Branch," Byron said. "Was your wife having an affair with Paul Ramsey?"

"Kind of a no-win for me, isn't it?"

"How do you figure?" Byron said.

"I tell you she wasn't and you'll merely run roughshod over my entire firm asking everyone if she was, causing Lorraine and me a great deal of embarrassment. If I say she was, you and your entire department will know my personal business."

"Contrary to what you obviously think, Detective Nugent and I take no satisfaction in asking you about your marital troubles, but we do need to know the truth."

The detectives waited while Branch thought it over. Byron maintained eye contact. The room was noticeably and uncomfortably silent.

"Yes, Sergeant Byron," Branch said at last. "She was. But it was over."

"How do you know?" Byron asked.

"I know because Lorraine told me she was ending it," Branch said, his tone full of indignation. As if his unfaithful wife would never lie about such a thing.

"When was that?"

"Several weeks ago."

"And you believe her?"

"Of course I do. She is my wife. Are you married?"

Byron knew he'd hit a nerve. The well-versed defense attorney was used to going on the offensive. Turn the tables if you're losing. It was right out of the trial lawyers' handbook.

"My personal life has nothing to do with your marital problems," Byron countered.

"I disagree, Sergeant. You asked me if I believed Lorraine when she told me the affair had ended. I love my wife, Sergeant Byron. In spite of what happened between her and that fu—" Branch took a second to compose himself. "Between her and Paul, I still love her and respect her. If she says it was over, then it was. Would you believe your wife?"

Byron ignored the question and pressed on. "When did you find out about the affair?"

"Near the middle of March. I suspected something was wrong because, well, because I did. We'd been having problems. This job requires a monstrous commitment. Lorraine and I both work close to eighty hours a week, a schedule that makes meaningful communication difficult." Branch glanced over at Nugent. "Given your line of work, I'm sure you both can understand."

Nugent nodded.

Byron remained silent.

Branch paused to pick up his mug before resuming. "I confronted her about Paul and she admitted it."

"What did you do?" Byron asked.

"What could I do? We separated for a while. Told me she needed some time to figure it out. She already had the apartment in town, so she stayed there. It would've been embarrassing, both to me and the firm, if it got out."

"Embarrassing to Lorraine as well," Byron said.

"Obviously," Branch snapped.

"Evidently it did get out, or we wouldn't be here," Byron said.

"Evidently," Branch said.

"Did you ever confront Ramsey?" Nugent asked.

"No," Branch said. "Paul was an arrogant son of a bitch. I wasn't about to give him the satisfaction."

"Were you afraid of him?" Byron asked.

"I certainly was not," Branch said, emphasizing each word. "This is *my* firm. Paul Ramsey worked for me."

"If you hated the guy so much, why keep him around?" Nugent asked.

"Because he was a good trial lawyer. He won cases. Period. This firm is a business, gentlemen. Unlike the cushy taxpayer jobs that you have, I have to stay in the black. In spite of all those cutesy commercials our advertising arm puts out about getting results and being in your corner, we are in business to make money. It's that simple. We don't take cases we can't win. We settle when the money is right or we go to trial and take a third off the top, plus expenses."

"Too bad you don't include that in your commercials," Byron said, pushing him harder for a reaction. "Imagine how illuminating that would be."

For a moment, Byron saw a flicker of rage in Branch's eyes, then it was gone, just as quickly as if he'd extinguished it with water. Control returned.

"Must have really pissed you off when Ramsey lost the case against the Medical Center. I'm no lawyer but I would assume that ten percent of ten million is much better than nothing. Plus, can't imagine how many hours went into that suit. Billable hours matter in this business, right?"

Branch awkwardly set his mug back on the table. His hands were visibly shaking. Byron could see that he was struggling to maintain composure.

"You came in here and asked me if my wife was having an affair, and I've answered your questions, for a second time. If there is nothing else, Detectives, I'm afraid I must get back to *my* job."

"Actually," Byron said. "There is. Where were *you* the night Ramsey was killed?"

"When was that?"

"Last Tuesday," Nugent said.

"Let me think. I left here about six-thirty, drove to Brunswick, had dinner at Giovanni's, then went directly home."

"Who were you with?" Byron asked.

"No one."

"Where was your wife?" Byron asked.

"You'll have to ask her. I'm somewhat surprised you don't know already, seeing as how you know so much about her."

"Did your wife come home last Tuesday night?"

"I don't know. I don't remember. As I said, you'll have to speak with her."

"Because?" Byron said.

"What?" Branch asked.

"You said earlier that you suspected that your wife was having an affair *because*, but you didn't tell us why."

"You know what, Sergeant? I think I'm done, with both of you. You can show yourselves out."

"Thanks for your time," Byron said.

The detectives had almost reached the door when Byron stopped and turned toward Branch. "One more thing. Do either of you own a gun?"

Branch appeared momentarily taken aback by the question.

Byron waited for him to respond.

"We did, but it was stolen."

AFTER LEARNING THAT Branch had reported a break-in, in which a handgun was stolen, Byron telephoned the Topsham Police Department then dropped Nugent off at 109. He knew that Branch would be on the horn to Stanton in short order, if he hadn't called already. He didn't want LeRoyer trying to interfere with his next step, meeting with the detective who'd followed up on the burglary report.

"You sure you don't want me to come with you?" Nugent asked as he opened the passenger door.

"Someone has to stay here and run interference with the LT, Nuge."

"You got it." He leaned into the car before shutting the door. "If LeRoyer asks, do I know where you went?"

"Why, I didn't tell you," Byron said, grinning.

A light rain had begun to fall as Byron drove north on the interstate. His eyes were on the road but his thoughts were elsewhere. Driving on autopilot was par for the course when working a murder. He stared straight ahead, nearly oblivious of the cars he was passing. The wipers had a hypnotic effect on him.

Why hadn't Branch mentioned the stolen gun before? he wondered. What else was he hiding? So many questions still unanswered and unresolved. But not only questions about the case. There were other questions eating at him. Distracting him.

Why hadn't he told Diane about his lunch with Kay? It was only work-related after all. Right? Then why did he hold that back? Because he still had feelings. Of course he did. Kay had been his wife for two decades. He had loved her even during their separation and subsequent divorce. He'd never stopped loving her. The problem was that he'd loved the job more. And Kay knew it. She knew what he was and what he always would be. He hadn't consciously put her second, but it happened just the same. But now he had feelings for Diane. He cared for her. Did he love her? He didn't know. He thought he might, but he wasn't sure if he was ready to commit again. It had ended so badly the last time. Byron slid back into the passing lane, shaking off the hypnosis long enough to check the side and rearview mirrors before passing the tractor trailer.

His head ached dully and his stomach grumbled.

His wipers began bouncing across the dry windshield. He realized that he'd passed through the rain shower. The sky was clearing once again. He flicked the wipers off.

His relationship with Diane was totally different from the one he'd had with Kay. She was a cop, for one. Like him. She understood the demands of the job. The cost of obtaining justice for the dead. The long hours, the frustration, the politics, the thrill of the hunt—Diane got it. All of it. It was something that he and Kay never had in common. Never would. Why then was he afraid of committing? Why were he and Diane keeping secrets from each other? She with the sergeant's exam and he with Kay. Was this about trust? They had trusted each other as cops, as partners, with their lives. So why was this different? He didn't know and he didn't need the distraction. He needed to focus on Ramsey's murder. And Branch's stolen .380.

Chapter Twenty-Seven

Tuesday, 10:45 A.M., May 3, 2016

"WHAT PART OF 'tread lightly' didn't you understand?" LeRoyer barked. He was hot. All three detectives knew enough not to provoke him.

"Guess Stanton knows, huh?" Nugent said.

"Yeah, he fucking knows. Devon Branch called his office right after you and John left." LeRoyer picked up the receiver on his desk phone and punched in the number for Byron's cell. As he waited, LeRoyer turned his attention to Diane and Stevens. "What about you two? Am I gonna get my ass chewed out for something *you* did?"

Diane spoke up. "Mel and I spoke with Lorraine Davies, but she seemed fine about it. I'd be surprised if she made any trouble."

"Well, Branch did. Wish I shared in your optimism, Detective. Why can't you guys ever go easy, huh? Just one fuckin' time." LeRoyer turned his attention to the phone. "John, where the hell are you? Stanton is wild and so am I. Get your ass back here."

He slammed the receiver down and looked back at the three detectives standing in front of his desk. "And what's this about a gun?"

Diane, Nugent, and Stevens filled the lieutenant in on each aspect of their interviews. Including what they knew about the burglary of Branch and Davies's home.

"What was the caliber of the gun taken?" LeRoyer asked.

"A .380," Stevens said.

"Same caliber as the hole in Ramsey's head," Nugent said.

"Goddammit," LeRoyer said, combing the fingers of his right hand through his hair. "So what do you think? That one of them *staged* the break-in?"

"It is possible," Diane said. "But, of course, we don't have the gun, so there's no way to match it to the round Ellis pulled out of Ramsey."

LeRoyer glared at the three of them. "Why the hell am I hearing this from you and not your sergeant? Where the fuck is Byron!"

BYRON TURNED INTO the paved lot at 100 Main Street. At its entrance stood a blue and white painted sign declaring it to be the Town of Topsham Municipal Complex. He parked next to a handsome two-story brick building. White block letters, attached to the building's façade above the entryway, identified the structure as the Public Safety Building.

He displayed his credentials to the bored-looking dispatcher seated on the opposite side of the bulletproof glass. "Sergeant Byron, Portland PD. I'm here to see Detective Shaw."

"Have a seat, Sergeant, and I'll see if he's in the building."

Byron had barely gotten settled on one of the uncomfortable lobby benches when a security door to the inner offices swung open, revealing a short balding man with bushy eyebrows and an infectious smile, instantly reminding Byron of Dickens's lovable Fezziwig. "Sergeant Byron, Gene Shaw."

"Gene. Thanks for seeing me on such short notice."

"Not at all. Come on in."

As they made small talk, Byron followed the fireplug of a man up a flight of worn carpeted stairs to the second floor and down a long corridor to a small office. The room was overflowing with metal cabinets, file boxes, and a single desk.

Shaw lifted a box from one of the visitor's chairs and set it atop a file cabinet. "Here. Have a seat. Sorry about the mess. I don't get many visitors up here."

"Thank you. Not a problem."

Detective Shaw sat down behind the metal desk with a dingy Formica top. Byron noted with some amusement that the desk was littered with the same pink message slips as his own.

"I took the liberty of pulling the file after you called. Not a lot to go on with this one, I'm afraid. Entry through the rear. Perp broke a window. Went through the house, grabbed some jewelry and a handgun. A .380 semiauto."

"Mind if I have a look?"

"By all means. Here," he said, handing the folder to Byron.

Byron leafed through the anorexic case file. "What can you tell me about the victims?"

"Devon Branch? I can tell you that he's a big supporter of this department. Does a lot for the town as well."

Byron felt a sense of déjà vu as Shaw ran down Branch's bona fides as if this were an employment screening instead of a criminal investigation in which the victim, in Topsham's case, might well become a suspect in Portland's.

"Have you had much contact with either Devon Branch or his wife?" Byron asked.

Shaw blushed. "Lorraine Davies? Why, she's just the most charming woman. She and her husband actually helped us to fund this new municipal complex. They're *big* supporters."

"So you said." Byron continued scanning the file, only half listening as Shaw prattled on about what great benefactors Branch and his wife were. "Nice neighborhood?" Byron said, interrupting the detective in midprattle.

"How's that?"

"Branch's home. Is it located in a nice neighborhood?"

"Yes. Well, it's not really a traditional neighborhood. More like a dozen or so executive-style estates on the edge of town. It's pretty nice. Lots of woods, close to the highway, but away from the shopping malls and such. They've got tennis courts and a spa," Shaw said, obviously enamored.

"Had much of a problem with burglaries in that area?"

Byron noted that Shaw's smile had vanished. The detective was evidently not liking the direction in which the conversation was headed. "Sergeant, if there's some question as to the character of either Mr. Branch or Ms. Davies—"

Realizing his mistake, Byron quickly softened his approach. "No, not at all, Gene. I'm just trying to establish if they may have been victimized by someone they knew or if this was some random thing. Maybe a transient high on drugs?"

Shaw's brow unfurled. His former cheery self returned. "See, that's what I was thinking too. The drug problem is getting pretty bad down your way," Shaw said, as if to suggest that Topsham was pure as the driven snow and entirely unlike the City of Portland with all of its evils. "Lot of those crazies come through here on their way to the 'big city,'" he said, making air quotations. "Can't keep track of 'em all."

"Nope, I guess you can't," Byron agreed. "Any of the jewelry turn up? Maybe in one of the local pawn shops?"

"I checked the one at the Topsham Fair Mall a couple of times. No luck, though."

"How about any of the surrounding towns?"

Shaw's smile vanished again and his eyes narrowed. "This isn't Portland, Sergeant Byron. I work alone, investigating every single crime that happens here. I don't have the luxury of running down every possible lead. I entered the gun into NCIC, serial number and all, and I checked the pawn shop for the jewelry. Sorry if my methods don't measure up to your standards. We're a small department here. We do the best we can."

"I wasn't criticizing your investigation, Gene. I'm just trying to get a feel about whether or not this incident could be connected to our homicide."

"Well, I just get a little defensive whenever some big city detective shows up and starts telling me what's what."

Byron, resisting the urge to climb over the desk and pummel Shaw, gave him his most disarming smile. "Can I get a copy of this for my files, Gene?"

"Sure thing," Shaw said sarcastically, reaching for the folder.

Ten minutes later Byron, finally free of Shaw, drove west toward Pine Bluff Estates. The myopic detective had halfheartedly offered to give Byron a guided tour of Branch's neighborhood but Byron turned him down. He didn't want Shaw reporting his every move back to Branch.

Pine Bluff was located exactly where Shaw had described, at the edge of town, in the middle of nowhere. A dozen or so grand homes were nestled back into the wooded foothills, reminding Byron of Maine's many ski resorts, like Sugarloaf and Sunday River. The only thing missing was an actual mountain.

The road through Pine Bluff was a winding paved drive that circled up the hill through the subdivision and back to the entry road off Route 24 near Bowdoinham. Two things were immediately apparent to Byron as he drove slowly up the hill. The neighborhood wasn't close enough to the highway to afford a quick B and E for some Portland-bound drifter. The burglar would need to be familiar with the area to even find this place. Secondly, if someone had cased out the home shared by Branch and Davies, they wouldn't have stopped at one break-in. Each of the homes screamed money. The fact that the only things taken were jewelry and a gun was also troubling. Either this was a spoiled rich kid from Pine Bluff or something else entirely was happening here. Byron suspected the latter.

He pulled off to the side of the road, stopping near the entrance to Branch's driveway, marked by a six-foot-high granite post into which had been carved the number seventeen. The home, blocked by trees, was invisible from the road. A red and white American Security Systems sign graced the bushes at the end of the drive. Byron pulled out the folder and checked for mention of an alarm. The report had been filed by Branch one night after coming home from work late. He'd found a basement window to the rear of the home broken. The report stated that the alarm hadn't been set. According to Shaw's supplement, Branch told him that Davies often left the residence forgetting to set the alarm. *Convenient*, Byron thought.

His cell rang. Pelligrosso.

"Hey, Gabe," Byron said. "Tell me you've got something."

"Ellis just dug three comparable rounds out of Tomlinson's body."

"And?"

"They match, Sarge. The bullet that killed Paul Ramsey was fired from the same gun used to kill Darius Tomlinson."

Finally, something was going their way. Now all they needed was the gun. "Thanks, Gabe."

He disconnected the call, slid the shifter back into gear, and headed up the drive.

The Branch-Davies home was a massive Tudor-style mansion. Byron guessed it to be close to five thousand square feet of stucco and darkly stained trim. The house was situated in the center of an acre-sized clearing in the woods. Lush green lawn graced both sides of the drive leading to an attached three-car garage. Opposite the garage sat a two-story carriage house. Byron parked between the two buildings and got out of the Chevrolet.

Both the residence and its landscaping were impeccably maintained. Not so much as a loose shutter or a single blade of grass out of place. Byron walked over to the carriage house and peeked in through the darkened windows. In the gloom he could only make out the shapes of two covered vehicles. He couldn't distinguish a make or model but assumed them to be valuable. He turned and strolled toward the main house.

A brick walkway, set in a basket weave pattern, led past several tarnished brass lanterns atop granite posts up to the front entryway and its granite steps. He pressed the doorbell and waited, half expecting to see a butler, dressed in a black coat with tails, answer the door. After several minutes with no answer, he resumed his inspection of the home's exterior.

The back of the property was as well landscaped as the front.

A finished daylight basement made the rear of the home appear as three stories. There were two windows on either side of the entryway, each affixed with stickers bearing the American Security logo. *And yet, according to the report, the burglar had thought it prudent to smash through one of them.*

Byron was leaning in to look through the window when a voice startled him from behind.

"Find what you're looking for?"

He whirled around, instinctually reaching for his gun, and found himself face-to-face with a uniformed Topsham police officer.

"Whoa. Easy there, Sarge."

"Fuck. You scared me."

"Name's Jim Mason," the officer said, extending a hand toward Byron.

"John Byron," he said, shaking it.

"Detective Shaw told me you were headed out here to check out Attorney Branch's place. Figured I'd say hello."

"This your area?"

"Part of it. Topsham is over thirty-four square miles."

"How many other officers work patrol with you?"

Mason laughed. "There's only eight full-time patrolmen. Sometimes it's just me out here."

As he listened to Mason talk, Byron realized that the odds of catching a burglar in the act out here were a million to one.

"Shaw says you're working a homicide. Think this burglary is connected?"

"Too early for me to think anything," Byron said, wondering if Mason was as taken with Branch and Davies as Shaw seemed to be. "I'm still running down leads. Don't want to overlook something."

Mason nodded. "Don't s'pose you would."

"A lot of reported burglaries out here?" Byron asked.

"Not really. In town mostly. Not so many out this way. All these homes are alarmed."

"You must have some trouble spots, though."

"Oh yeah. Like any small town, there's pockets of trouble. The majority of our homegrown idiots would be too lazy to come all the way out here. Easier to bust out a store window and pry open the register. Not too many escape routes out of here either. It's either east or west on 24. Easier to get busted."

Byron resumed walking the home's exterior with Mason. "How long have you been on the job here, Jim?"

"Oh, I've been a cop for ten years, but only here for the last six. Started in Oakland."

"You know much about the people who live here?"

"Branch? Only that he's some bigwig attorney down in Portland. Think the wife is too."

"Shaw seems pretty enamored with him."

Mason laughed again. "Shaw's pretty enamored by anyone with money. Branch donates a shitload of money to the town."

"You ever deal with him?"

"Me? I'm just a lowly patrolman."

They completed the circle, arriving back at the driveway where Mason's cruiser was parked in front of Byron's unmarked.

"You ever get sent out here for any domestic type calls?" Byron asked.

Mason grinned and shook his head. "This is a small town, Sarge. None of these rich folks are from here originally. They tend to keep to themselves. If there were some trouble on the home front, likely we'd be the last to hear about it."

Byron nodded in agreement then reached out and shook Mason's hand again. "Nice meeting you, Jim. Thanks for the info."

"Good to meet you, Sarge. Best of luck with your investigation."

BYRON JUMPED BACK on the interstate southbound toward Portland. He pulled out his cell and punched Diane's number on speed dial.

"Hey, lover," she said. "How'd you make out?"

"I hope you're alone," he said.

"Actually, you caught me in the middle of a three-way with Stanton and the city manager. You want to speak to either of them?"

"I'll pass, thanks."

"Jealous?"

"Nauseous."

Diane gave a hearty laugh. It was good to hear. Maybe the tension between them really was beginning to loosen.

"By the way, LeRoyer is looking for you."

"I heard. He won't have to wait much longer. I'm heading back now."

"So, are you gonna share what you found out?" she said.

"This whole burglary thing stinks. I'm not buying it. Branch has his tentacles into this town too."

"Seriously?"

"According to this Gene Shaw, the detective I spoke with, Branch donated money to help them build their new public safety facility. Police, fire, town hall, the works."

"Spreading cheer and buying goodwill wherever he goes."

"Or control freak. I imagine Topsham's chief is just as starstruck as our own. I wonder how many favors he's owed?"

"Shaw give you anything useful?"

"I imagine the words *Shaw* and *useful* don't often coincide. He's so far up his own ass he could use it as a hat."

Diane laughed again.

"I managed to get a copy of the report and the follow-up investigation, if you can call it that. Looks like Shaw did the absolute minimum on this one."

"Anything recovered?"

"Nothing. Only jewelry and the gun were taken. The report confirms the gun was a .380. Branch's statement says he kept it in a box in a bureau drawer."

"Prints?"

"Doesn't look like Shaw even tried."

"No alarm?"

"They have one. Apparently, Lorraine Davies routinely forgets to set it."

"Convenient."

"My thoughts exactly."

LEROYER INTERCEPTED BYRON as soon as he exited the stairwell into the hallway of the fourth floor. Byron figured he had been lying in wait.

"Why is it that you're the only sergeant who won't return my calls?" LeRoyer said.

"Shitty reception?" Byron said, stepping around the lieutenant and heading for his office.

LeRoyer followed on his heels. "Goddammit, John. Are you trying to get both of us kicked out of CID?"

"I thought you were leaving anyway. Aren't you about to become the next Ass Chief?"

LeRoyer followed him into the office and slammed the door. "I know you went poking around in someone else's jurisdiction. Your detectives told me that Branch's house was burglarized."

"It was. And a firearm was stolen. A .380."

"Aren't you the one who told me that there's a million of those out there?"

"Yes. I did. But there's only one stolen .380 that belonged to the guy whose wife Ramsey was fucking."

"Did I stutter when I said to go fucking easy on this? You know Branch already called Stanton. You're creating a shit storm for me!"

Byron settled into his chair and looked at LeRoyer. "I go where the case takes me, period." He waited a moment before speaking again, hoping to bring his hot lieutenant back to earth. "How's Sam like Sacred Heart?" he asked, referring to LeRoyer's daughter.

LeRoyer blinked at the unexpected question. "What?"

"Samantha. How's she like college?"

"Dammit, John, you always do that to me. How the fuck am I supposed to stay pissed off at you if you won't let me?"

Byron shrugged. "Beats me."

"Aw, hell." LeRoyer dropped into one of the chairs across from Byron. "She likes it. I guess. Homesick, though. Calls her mother every night. Can't believe what that school costs. You know?"

After LeRoyer finished, Byron brought him up to speed on what he'd learned in Topsham.

"You think the break-in was staged?" LeRoyer asked, now fully calm.

"Yeah. I do."

"So who do you think set it up?"

"I don't know, but Branch was the one who found it and made the report."

"Shit. And the gun just happened to be a .380?"

"Yup."

LeRoyer exhaled loudly. "Why can't anything ever be easy?"

Chapter Twenty-Eight

Tuesday, 5:30 p.m., May 3, 2016

BYRON PACED SLOWLY around the SUV inside the evidence cage in the basement of 109. Aside from him and Diane, the garage was empty.

"What are you hoping to find, John?" Diane asked. "Gabe went over every inch of this vehicle."

"I know he did. I'm not questioning his evidence collection skills. I just feel like there has to be something else."

"Back to the beginning?" she asked, referring to Byron's learned habit of starting the investigation over when things stalled.

Back when Byron was first learning the ropes as a detective, his mentor, Ray Humphrey, was fond of pointing out that often the best way to move an investigation forward is to go back to the beginning. The advice had served him well.

"Works for me," he said.

He knew she was right about Gabe. When it came to processing a scene, Pelligrosso was second to none. But sometimes the obvious things were the easiest to miss. The mind plays tricks, tending to skip right past those items that are expected to be at a scene. Cops look for evidence brought into a crime scene and left behind. Fingerprints, DNA, hairs, fibers, blood. All of the usual suspects were searched for. What did they have? A partial print that was smudged. Two blond hairs from a wig, probably from one of the countless women Ramsey had slept with.

He walked over and opened the driver's door. The overhead dome light came on along with an audible chime, signifying the keys were still in the ignition. *What had they overlooked?*

Byron signaled Diane to open the passenger door. She did. Both of them stood next to the open doors staring inside the empty SUV.

"What do we know?" Byron asked.

"Well, if Ramsey wasn't killed on the boat we know he was probably killed by whoever met him down on Veranda Street," she said.

"Good. Where?"

"Maybe on the shore or standing in the water."

"How?"

"One shot to the face. The killer may have softened him up a bit by mixing fentanyl into his usual cocaine. After the coke wore off, the effect of the narcotic combined with his high blood alcohol would have significantly impaired his ability to mount any defense."

"That and not having a gun," Byron said. "Swap sides with me."

"Okay," Diane said as she walked to the opposite side of the vehicle. She looked across at him. "Now what?"

"Now get in. You'll be the driver, presumably Ramsey, and I'll be the killer."

"Why do I feel like I drew the short straw on that deal?" she said.

They both climbed in and sat there looking around but not touching anything.

"What are we looking for?" Diane said.

Byron looked her up and down. "Comfortable?"

"Not really. The seat's up a little too far."

Byron grinned. "How tall is Ramsey?"

"I don't know, a little over six foot, I think."

"Meaning?"

Her eyes widened in understanding. "Meaning he couldn't have driven this to the dump site. The seat's too far forward for me and I'm five-ten."

"Okay, so our driver and probable killer must be shorter than you."

"Brilliant deduction, Watson," Diane said.

"What does that make you?"

She grinned. "Holmes, of course."

"You don't look much like a Sherlock," he said.

"Thanks, I think."

"How tall is Branch?" Byron asked.

BYRON SAT IN the dark on the steps to his condo. It was a perfect early June night. The sun had long since set but the air temperature remained mild, foreshadowing the summer warmth still to come. He'd have given anything for an icy brew, but he knew better than most where that would lead. He hated the distance that had grown between him and Diane. Although things had gotten much better at work, the distance remained. She hadn't even been to his condo since Thursday. If she were here now he wouldn't be thinking of beer. She possessed an innate ability to keep his mind occupied on other things. He closed his eyes and imagined the smell of her skin, her playful laughter, bright smile, and soft touch. But she wasn't here. She was at home, in Westbrook. Partly because of his stubbornness. He should have told her about his meeting with Kay. It was stupid and childish. That same stubbornness was probably also why she hadn't told him about taking the sergeant's exam. He was pushing Diane away, like he had pushed Kay.

He opened his eyes and stared up at the sky. The stars were out and, in spite of the city lights, they were brilliant. He remembered sneaking out of his parents' house and riding his bike down to the Eastern Prom in the dark, where he'd lie on the grassy hill and stare up at these same stars. They made him feel so small, so insignificant. But at the same time they seemed to confirm a belief that anything was possible. His cell vibrated, whisking him back to the here-and-now. Pulling it off his belt, he checked the phone's illuminated screen, hoping that it might be Diane. The caller ID read "Dispatch."

"Byron," he answered.

"Sarge, it's Will in Dispatch."

"What's up, Will?"

"Shift commander wanted us to call you. We've got units out at a DV assault involving Lorraine Davies. He thought you'd want to know."

"Where?"

"Eastern Prom."

Davies's apartment. Could this be the break they'd been hoping for? Had the information about Davies's affair with Ramsey precipitated this? There was only one way to find out.

"On my way," he said.

BYRON WORDLESSLY BADGED the night security guard seated in the lobby of Davies's building. Not knowing that Byron had previously visited, the guard pointed him toward the elevators. Byron stood waiting in the hallway for someone to answer his knock on the locked door to Davies's condo. Officer Haggerty opened the door.

"Hey, Sarge."

"Hags," Byron said. "Give me a rundown."

"Officer Richardson is taking Davies's statement in the living room. Looks like her husband, Devon Branch, punched her in the face. She's got a pretty good shiner."

"Who called it in?"

"She did."

"Where's Branch?"

"He was GOA. She says he threatened to kill her if she called the police."

Byron pulled out his cell and dialed Dispatch.

"Dispatch, Mary speaking."

"Mary, it's Byron. I need you to put out an ATL."

"Sure. Go ahead with it."

"I'm out at the DV on the Eastern Prom. Devon Branch just assaulted his wife. I want him picked up for assault and criminal threatening."

"You're talking about the Portland attorney Devon Branch?"

"Yes. He lives in Topsham." Byron checked his watch: nine-thirty. "And given the hour, he may be en route there. Let the state police know, then have a couple of our officers swing by his office on Union Street."

"You know what he drives?"

"It's a silver Lexus. I don't have the plate number."

"Okay, I'll run him through BMV and put it out. You want it over the air?"

"Yes. And let me know the minute he's located."

Byron pocketed the phone and addressed Haggerty. "Let's go talk with Davies."

Lorraine Davies was sitting on the couch. Richardson sat on the coffee table facing her, balancing his clipboard awkwardly as he attempted to get her statement down on paper. Mascara had run onto Davies's cheeks, giving her a clown-like appearance. Byron noted that the left sleeve of her blouse was torn at the seam. He scanned the room quickly. Aside from Davies, nothing appeared disturbed. No broken or overturned furniture. No smashed glasses.

"I can't believe this happened," Davies said, visibly shaken.

"Has he ever done anything like this before?" Byron asked.

She shook her head. "No. He's never hit me. I've seen his temper but he's never done more than break things."

Byron had glimpsed it too. Recently, in fact. When he'd tried to goad the high-priced attorney into unleashing it.

"He threatened you?" Byron said.

She gave a tearful nod. "He told me if I called the police, he'd kill me."

"Mind if I ask what the argument was about?"

Davies lowered her eyes. "About my affair with Paul."

"How long has he known?"

"He found out a few months ago. Before Paul was ... murdered."

"What set him off tonight?"

"I don't know."

Byron turned as someone rushed into the room. It was Amy Brennan.

"Oh my God," Brennan said, rushing over to Davies.

"It's okay, Amy," Davies said.

"I shouldn't have left you alone with him," Brennan said, sitting down next to Davies and placing an arm around her.

Byron, using the interruption to allow Richardson to finish taking Davies's statement, signaled Haggerty to follow him. They retreated to the hallway out of earshot.

"Have we interviewed the security guard downstairs?" Byron asked.

"Not yet."

"Let's see what he has to say about Branch's arrival and, more importantly, his departure."

"You got it, Sarge."

Byron's cell vibrated. He grabbed it without looking. "Byron."

"Sarge, it's Mary. S.P. found Devon Branch. They've got him stopped on the interstate, near Brunswick."

BYRON SLID THE Chevy up next to the curb, directly in front of 109. Diane hurried down the steps to the Middle Street sidewalk and jumped in.

"Sorry I couldn't get here sooner," she said.

"Wasn't much to do at the scene anyway," Byron said. He executed a quick U-turn in front of the station, just managing to catch the yellow light before turning left onto Franklin. He gunned the accelerator and sped up the hill past Congress Street toward I-295.

"Did Topsham find Branch?" she asked.

"Nope, state police. Stopped him about three miles from the Brunswick exit."

"Think he'll talk to us?"

"Doubt it. They just found a loaded firearm in the car."

"You're kidding."

"Nope."

"Son of a bitch. Caliber?"

Byron turned his head to look directly at her. "A .380."

BYRON PULLED IN behind the two marked S.P. units parked in the breakdown lane just south of the Brunswick exit. A dizzying array of blue strobes blocked their view of Branch's car. Byron activated his own emergency lights as he and Diane stepped out onto the pavement. As they approached the second cruiser, Branch's silhouette could clearly be seen through the rear windshield.

A tall trooper, wearing a light blue campaign hat tilted to the front and partially obscuring his eyes, approached them. "Sergeant Byron?"

"That's me. Thanks for the assist," Byron said as they shook hands. "This is Detective Diane Joyner."

"Detective."

"Is he talking?" Diane asked.

"Hasn't said a word since I asked him to step out of the car. But he's been cooperative other than that."

"Where was the gun found?" Byron asked.

"Under the driver's seat."

"Was he alone?"

"Yup. Just him. Acted like he had no idea why we were stopping him. Your dispatcher said he beat up his wife?"

"And threatened to kill her if she called us," Diane said.

"Nice guy. What do you want done with the car?"

"Can you get a flatbed out here?" Byron asked.

The trooper nodded. "Probably take close to an hour."

"I want it towed to the basement of our headquarters. I'll have one of my evidence techs waiting for you."

"I'll see to it personally. What about him?" the trooper asked, cocking his head toward Branch.

"Give me a minute with him," Byron said.

Byron opened the rear door of the state police cruiser. "Evening, Mr. Branch."

"Sergeant Byron. May I ask what all of this is about?"

Byron was surprised to find Branch so calm. Maybe even disappointed. He'd expected the attorney to be a bit more frazzled after assaulting his wife.

"I'd be more than happy to explain it to you if you'd care to accompany us back to the police station."

Branch looked back and forth between Diane and Byron. "Can I safely assume this has something to do with your continued harassment of me regarding Paul Ramsey's murder?"

"Actually, Devon, this is about you assaulting your wife," Diane said. "Would you be willing to come to 109 and help us clear this matter up?"

Branch's eyes widened ever so slightly, but enough that Byron picked up on it.

"Think I'd rather speak with my attorney first," Branch said.

"Figured you'd say that," Byron said before closing the car door. He turned to the trooper. "Go ahead and take him to the Cumberland County Jail. Charges are DV assault and criminal threatening."

"You got it. What about the gun?"

"We'll take possession of that."

AFTER SIGNING THE chain of custody form for the firearm, Byron and Diane headed back to Portland. Byron placed a call to LeRoyer while Diane woke Pelligrosso.

"You what?" LeRoyer asked, his voice rising a full octave.

"You heard me right," Byron said. "We just arrested Branch for assaulting his wife. Well, actually, it was the state police who arrested him."

"You're shitting me."

Byron could visualize his high-strung lieutenant pacing the floor in his bathrobe while combing his hair back with the fingers of his free hand until he resembled the Lieutenant Einstein moniker they'd playfully stuck him with.

"No, Marty. I'm not *shitting* you."

In the middle of her own call, Diane glanced over at Byron and grinned.

"Are you sure we're on solid ground here, John?"

"For the DV? Absolutely. Lorraine called in the assault herself. Building security said Branch arrived all in a huff then left in a hurry ten minutes later."

"Jesus."

"And that's not all. They found a loaded .380 under the driver's seat."

"Tell me the search was good?"

"Textbook. Searched incident to arrest. I've got 'em towing Branch's car to 109."

"You're gonna get a search warrant, right?"

"Yes, Mother. Making the call now."

BYRON AND DIANE had been waiting at 109 for close to an hour. He'd left several messages on Jim Ferguson's voicemail but the assistant attorney general had yet to call him back. Byron was growing impatient. Branch's car was secure in the basement cage, ironically sitting right beside Ramsey's. They'd need to find other accommodations if any other vehicles were seized, as the space was only big enough for two. Pelligrosso was in the lab just waiting for the green light from Byron to dust for prints and compare ballistics from Branch's gun. The car could wait until tomorrow, but the gun might tie Branch to at least one murder if anything matched. Diane had long since finished writing the search warrant and accompanying affidavit. All they needed now was Ferguson's okay and they'd be on their way to a judge.

Diane stuck her head through the doorway of Byron's office. "Any word from Ferguson?"

"Nah. Fuck. I don't know where he is. This isn't like him."

"You wanna keep waiting or should we go back to the list and reach out to another attorney?"

Byron would've preferred it be Ferguson, primarily because he already knew the case, but he also knew they couldn't wait forever. The clock was ticking. "I'll call Presby."

"Okay. I'll email you the affidavit."

"Thanks, Di."

Byron was perusing the documents that Diane had prepared when AAG Presby picked up in mid-ring. He was groggy and obviously pissed off at having been awoken. He reminded Byron that he wasn't the on-call attorney, not until next week, then reluctantly agreed to check the documents. Byron, who didn't need reminding, forwarded Diane's email.

THE GREEN LIGHT, which would've taken less than ten minutes with Ferguson, took thirty-five with Presby. Following that, it took Byron and Diane fifteen minutes to drive to Judge Millar's house in Scarborough and another thirty before His Honor finally scribbled his illegible John Millar Hancock on the documents.

Byron phoned Pelligrosso from Millar's driveway, giving

him the go-ahead. The detectives were on their way back to 109, signed warrant in hand, when Byron got a call from one of the jail deputies telling him that Branch had been bailed on personal recognizance over an hour ago. The deputy apologized for not having called sooner.

BYRON SAT NEXT to Diane in the CID conference room. He felt like an expectant father awaiting news from the delivery room. And he was hoping Pelligrosso would announce the arrival of identical twins. In the ballistic sense.

Byron studied the updated and ever-expanding whiteboard while Diane read over a stack of incoming case supplements. He'd lost track of how many large coffees he'd consumed, but figured it was too many, based on the way his left leg was jumping.

At some point, Byron realized that he'd nodded off in the chair. He looked up at the clock. It was nearly 5:00 A.M. Through the window the sky was beginning to brighten. Diane was snoozing at the table, head resting on her arms like a schoolgirl. Byron got up, stretched and headed for the CID printer. He grabbed the overnight stack and returned to the conference room. He was trying hard to focus on Haggerty's DV report, still warm from the printer, when Pelligrosso walked in.

"I have news, Sarge," Pelligrosso said.

Diane awoke with a groan. Sitting upright, she rubbed her eyes.

"Go with it," Byron said, yawning.

"The serial number on the gun matches the number on the burglary report filed by Branch," Pelligrosso said.

"Prints?" Diane asked.

Pelligrosso shook his head. "Nothing on the gun. Wiped clean."

Odd, Byron thought.

"What about the partials on the shell casings?" Diane asked.

"They belong to Branch."

Byron could feel the noose closing on Branch's neck. "What about ballistics? Do they match or not?" Byron asked.

The young evidence tech grinned. "They match."

BYRON'S FIRST CALL was to LeRoyer. He had to relay the story twice before the sleepy lieutenant understood the implication.

"You're shitting me!"

He really needs a new catchphrase, Byron thought. "I am not."

"Branch killed Ramsey?" LeRoyer said, sounding flabbergasted.

"And apparently Tomlinson," Byron reminded him. "Not only do the bullets that came out of Darius match, so do the extractor marks on the shell casings. Same gun Branch reported stolen from his house."

"What about the hooker?"

"Stripper. We don't have anything tying Branch to her murder. But hey, two out of three ain't bad."

"Fuck me," LeRoyer said. "Stanton's gonna shit a brick."

Looks like the chief may have backed the wrong guy, Byron thought. He wondered how Portland's top cop would try to spin it.

BYRON DIDN'T HAVE to wait long for the spin. Stanton, afraid of the political fallout that always came with betting on the wrong horse, decided to get out in front of it by holding an impromptu press conference announcing that they had made an arrest in the Ramsey murder. Byron hadn't been present for the 8:00 A.M. meeting of the command staff. Likewise he hadn't been privy to the phone call between the chief and the state's attorney general. He learned of both developments after the fact, from LeRoyer.

"I don't see the problem, John," LeRoyer said, sounding exasperated as he plopped down behind his desk and logged on to his computer. "I thought you of all people would be happy."

Byron, who'd followed him into the office, remained standing. "And I don't understand the goddamned rush, Marty."

"You've got more than enough to charge Branch with both murders. You told me so."

"We do, but I still feel like we're missing something."

"What?"

"I'm not sure. But I'd like to do more legwork on this before we charge anyone."

"Well, that's not an option," LeRoyer said, checking his watch. "It's 9:05 now. Stanton plans to roll it out for the media live during the noon broadcast, so you've got almost three hours to pick Branch up and book him."

"Why is Stanton so hot on rushing this? If memory serves he was in love with this fucking guy last week. Hell, even yesterday. Devon Branch, benefactor of the new and improved K-9 program. Remember?"

Byron watched as LeRoyer turned away from the computer screen, studying him. The lieutenant's eyes narrowed suspiciously. "Why are you stalling, John? This isn't like you. Don't tell me you actually think he's innocent?"

He shook his head. "It just feels too easy. Like we're missing something. Branch isn't stupid. Why in hell wouldn't he have ditched the gun after killing Ramsey? Doesn't make sense."

"Well, after you pick him up you can ask him."

BYRON AND DIANE were bringing the other detectives up to speed in the conference room when his cell rang. He recognized the Augusta area code but not the number.

"Byron."

"Sergeant Byron, it's Tammy Dufresne. I'm the receptionist in the AG's office."

Byron felt a sickening feeling in the pit of his stomach as he stepped from the room. "Yes, Tammy," he said, struggling to keep his composure. "What can I do for you?"

"I'm sorry for calling you like this but I thought you'd want to know. Jim Ferguson is in the hospital. He's had a heart attack."

Chapter Twenty-Nine

Wednesday, 9:10 A.M., May 4, 2016

DIANE FINISHED ADJUSTING the Velcro straps on her ballistic vest. She buttoned her blouse as she walked around the women's locker room, even checking the shower stalls to be sure she was alone. Empty. She pulled out her cell and quickly dialed the number.

"Newsroom," the bored male voice at the other end of the line answered.

"Davis Billingslea, please," she said.

"Hang on."

Diane glanced nervously at the door to the hallway as she counted the rings. She was about to hang up before the call could go to voicemail when the breathless reporter answered.

"Billingslea."

"Davis, it's Detective Joyner. You'll want to be out in front of the Emerson Building in ten minutes."

"Why? What do you—"

"Just be there."

Diane ended the call just as two uniformed officers entered the locker room.

"YOU CAN'T JUST barge in on him," the receptionist called after the detectives as they headed down the hall to Branch's office.

Diane, who was followed by Nugent, Stevens, and two uniformed officers, ignored the warning, never breaking stride. She opened the doors to the attorney's office and stepped inside. Branch was seated in front of his desk in one of the visitor chairs, across from Gerald DeWitt.

"May I help you with something, Detectives?" Branch said through gritted teeth.

"Devon Branch," Diane said. "You're under arrest for murder."

"You must be joking."

"No joke," Stevens said. "Stand up and put your hands behind your back."

Branch glanced at DeWitt, then did as he was instructed.

"May I ask whom he is alleged to have murdered?" DeWitt said as Diane and Stevens placed Branch in cuffs.

"Paul Ramsey and Darius Tomlinson," Nugent chimed in. "Sorry we didn't have a chance to make an appointment."

BYRON STEPPED OUT of the elevator and into the hall of the cardiac unit of Central Maine Medical Center in Lewiston. The floor was slick, still damp from having recently been mopped, and he nearly slipped. He slowed his pace and shortened the length of his strides so as not to repeat his acrobatic feat.

He breezed past the nursing station and headed down the hall directly to Ferguson's room. The assistant attorney general was dozing lightly as Byron walked in and sat down beside the bed.

Clear plastic tubes protruded from each nostril and down to a stainless steel oxygen tank. Byron watched his friend's chest rise and fall with each breath. A computerized monitor displayed the vitals, emitting a dull beep in synchronicity with Ferguson's heartbeat. It never ceased to amaze Byron how frail people looked while lying in a hospital bed. As if the mere act of lying down added a decade to a patient's age. He noticed Ferguson's gold wire-rimmed glasses folded atop the bedside table beside a plastic cup of water. Byron couldn't recall ever having seen his friend without his glasses. The bedridden man's eye sockets had taken on a dark and hollow look. Byron wondered if they had always looked like that and he'd just failed to notice.

Ferguson's eyelids fluttered then gradually opened. His rheumy eyes looked directly at Byron until the recognition showed on his face.

"You could have just said you wanted a day off," Byron said.

Ferguson gave a chuckle that was half cough.

"You need the nurse?" Byron asked, concern evident in his tone.

Ferguson waved his hand. "Water," he croaked.

Byron retrieved the cup, carefully handing it to Ferguson.

The AAG struggled to line up the straw with his mouth then sipped.

After a moment, Byron took the cup and set it back on the table. "Better?"

Ferguson nodded. "Damn oxygen dries me out. Like I got a mouth full of sand."

"How are you feeling?"

"Top notch, for a guy who's just had a heart attack."

"I see your sense of humor's still intact," Byron said.

Ferguson lifted both arms, displaying the IVs. "About the only thing."

"What's the doc telling you?"

"Same thing they all say. Gotta change my diet."

"Blocked arteries?"

"Big-time."

"How bad?"

"Bad enough. He's talking about a six bypass surgery. Guess that's worse than a quadruple bypass. What the hell do they call a six bypass surgery anyway?"

"I think the technical term is six bypass surgery," Byron said, grinning.

"I knew you'd know. You missed Mrs. Assistant Attorney General by a couple of hours."

"How is Betty?"

"She's fine. Worried. Gave me the 'I told you so' speech about my heart. Threatened to put me on some fad low-fat, high-fiber, gluten-free diet. What the hell is a gluten?"

"She cares about you, Jim."

"Yeah, yeah. She's pissed at *you* though."

"Pissed at *me*?" Byron said. "What'd I do?"

"It's what you haven't done. How many times has she asked you to come to the house for dinner?"

"I know. It's just, you know. I've got a crazy job. Don't have as much time as I used to."

"Ha. Look at me. Guess I could say the same."

"You've got plenty of time. Done much painting?" he asked, referring to Ferguson's oil painting hobby.

"Painting, shmainting. What I do is push colors around on the canvas. But no, I haven't. Too many trials as of late. Guess maybe I'll have some time to work at it, what with my convalescing."

"Don't count on it," Byron said. "The doc will likely have you running in circles with rehab."

"Oh great. Just what I need. Exercise."

"Don't knock it."

"Exercise and Betty's new dietary cooking. That will be the crap that kills me, you know. You shoulda come to the house for dinner before my heart attack. Now you'll have to eat that healthy shit too."

Byron laughed. It felt good to laugh. Loosened him up.

"When are *you* gonna take up a hobby?" Ferguson asked.

"Already got one. I catch killers."

"That's no hobby. That's a calling. Speaking of which, how's my case coming? Boss was in a short time ago. Told me you've officially charged Branch. We gonna fry this guy at trial or what?"

Byron frowned. "Yeah, Diane locked him up while I was driving up here."

"You don't sound too excited about it."

"I'm not. I don't like it."

"What's not to like? Heard you recovered the murder weapon—in his possession, I might add." Ferguson held up his hand, folding his fingers down one at a time as he listed out the points of the case against Branch. "You've got motive, opportunity, even a history of domestic violence. Jesus, John, what else do you want? A big red bow? I've gotten convictions with a helluva lot less."

Byron shrugged.

"Say, you never tried returning a gift to Santa when you were a kid, did you?" Ferguson asked. "What's bugging you, John?"

"The whole damn thing. It was way too easy? Branch is smarter than that."

"Why? Because he's an accomplished trial attorney? That doesn't make him smart. Look at me. I'm an accomplished attorney and I still eat shit that's gonna kill me," Ferguson said with a wink. "One would think I'd be smarter than that too. Wouldn't one?"

"I guess."

"Look, John. Devon Branch went to law school, not murder academy. Maybe he just slipped up."

But Byron didn't believe it. He stood up and walked over to the window and looked outside at the parking lot. "Nice view."

"Hey, nothing but the best for me. Your bosses must be happy."

"Fucking giddy."

"You share your apprehension with them?"

"Of course. Think it made one bit of difference?"

"Based on today's update, I'd say no. So then, keep working it. Figure out whatever's bothering you. Either you'll prove to yourself that Branch is guilty or you'll prove he isn't."

Byron turned around and leaned on the sill. "But we've already charged him with the murder."

"Yeah, and you've still got probable cause."

"You sound like my lieutenant."

"Big difference between probable cause and beyond a reasonable doubt, my friend. You can arrest a ham sandwich."

"I think that's indict a ham sandwich."

"That too." Ferguson struggled to take another sip of water.

"What if he *was* set up, though?"

"They all say that, John. Did Branch tell you he was set up?"

"Lawyered up. He's not saying anything."

"This is really bugging you, isn't it?"

Byron nodded. "Yeah, Jim. It is. Can't help thinking I may have arrested the wrong guy."

"Well, as the prosecutorial authority on this case, I hereby grant you permission to continue digging." Ferguson lifted his right hand and made the sign of a cross, mimicking a priest. "Way I figure it, you've got a year until the trial, eighteen months if I croak during surgery and my boss has to reassign the case to a lesser assistant AG."

"Don't even joke about that."

Byron could feel Ferguson's eyes on him. Sizing him up.

"You're a good detective, John. One of the most thorough I've ever worked with. The fact that this bothers you is exactly why I've always fought to try your cases. Most guys would be out toasting their great success on having made a murder arrest and yukking it up with their chief, but not you. No, here you are trying to convince yourself that the number one suspect is innocent."

"I'm off the booze. And I don't like my chief."

"Listen, if you believe in your heart that Branch was set up, prove it."

"What if I'm wrong? What if all I manage to do is fuck up the case we have?"

"You know I'll back you up, John."

Byron checked his watch.

"You got somewhere to be?"

"I gotta get back," Byron said. "I'm meeting Stanton for drinks at three."

BYRON HANDED MONEY to the toll attendant, waited for his receipt, then accelerated out of the booth toward Portland.

He tapped the power window switch, pulled out his cell, and

punched in Diane's number on the speed dial. She answered on the first ring.

"How's Jim Ferguson?" she asked.

"Looks old and tired," Byron said. "Think he's more worried about the bypass than he let on. "How'd it go with Branch?"

"Uneventful. We just finished booking him down at County."

"Did he have anything to say?"

"Wasn't in the talkative mood, I guess. DeWitt asked about our evidence."

"What'd you tell him?"

"I said ballistic evidence doesn't lie."

Byron knew that was true. Devon Branch had been found in possession of a smoking gun. Damn near literally. In any normal case he'd consider that a slam dunk. But this wasn't any normal case. Ramsey was a son of a bitch who had a multitude of enemies. Motive wasn't exactly in short supply either. Even Ramsey's fellow employees at the firm held great disdain for him. But still, Branch getting caught with his pants down was far too easy. It would have been foolhardy to hang on to the gun after killing Ramsey, but to still have it in his possession after assaulting his wife was simply idiotic. Byron knew Branch might have been a lot of things, but an idiot wasn't one of them.

"Will you be back in time for Stanton's dog and pony?" Diane asked.

Byron checked the time on the dashboard clock. "Unfortunately, I will."

BYRON NUDGED HIS way through the throngs of media folk and police department employees blocking the double doors to the auditorium on the second floor of 109. The cavernous space was two stories tall with corrugated wooden strips running vertically up all four walls. The wood was supposed to help with the room's acoustics. It didn't. With the exception of a few rows of chairs near the podium, Stanton's presser was standing room only. Flanking the chief were LeRoyer, Diane, and Captain Simons. Simons, who always looked to Byron like he had a rather large stick up his ass, was all spit and polish. Byron couldn't help but wonder if he was looking at the chief's promotional pool.

Byron slid in against the back wall, intentionally taking up a position behind and well out of view of the television cameras. Stanton was waxing poetic about teamwork, CID, and the number of man-hours that went into solving the Ramsey murder. Byron wondered if the chief knew or even cared how many woman-hours had gone into the investigation. Stanton singled out LeRoyer and Diane for their efforts in solving the case. For Diane's sake, Byron hoped the chief was right about Branch.

"It's always a shock when a distinguished member of our own community is alleged to have committed murder," Stanton said. "Devon Branch has been a friend and benefactor to many in this community, including the police department. But no amount of benevolence can outweigh taking the life of another."

Byron didn't know how much more of Stanton's scripture he could stand. Mercifully, he didn't have to. Stanton completed his oratory and opened it up to questions.

"Chief, Chief," several reporters shouted in unison.

Stanton pointed out a petite blonde reporter from WGME, the local CBS affiliate. Byron thought he caught a mischievous twinkle in the chief's eyes. He wondered what Mrs. Chief would think.

"Chief Stanton, can you tell us the motive behind the Ramsey murder? Why would Attorney Branch kill one of his own lawyers?"

Stanton stepped away from the microphones as LeRoyer leaned over and whispered in his ear. The chief reapproached the podium and cleared his throat. "I believe we know the motive, but as the investigation is still ongoing, I'd rather not share certain aspects of the case at this time."

Byron was glad he didn't have a chair as he would've been tempted to hurl it at the chief.

"Chief," a dark-haired reporter called out.

The young man's shabby clothing and acne-scarred face betrayed his origin as either radio or one of the local papers. No self-respecting television news channel would've stuck him in front of a camera, Byron thought. Professionally speaking, he had a face for radio.

Radio Face continued. "We know that your agency is currently investigating several other suspicious deaths. Can you tell us if the murder of Paul Ramsey is related? Do you expect that Branch will be charged with additional crimes?"

Stanton paused a moment before answering. "As I said, we are still investigating, but at this time we have no reason to believe that any of the deaths are connected."

Byron, who believed they were, and had heard enough, made his exit.

BYRON TOOK THE back stairwell out to the PD's rear garage. He grabbed his car and headed for Deering, Portland's version of the suburbs. He jumped on the interstate heading north and took the Veranda Street off-ramp. He turned into 331 Veranda Street and drove through the lot, up the hill, and around to the rear of the old school administration building. From his vantage point he could see straight through the Martin's Point

Bridge across the channel and into Falmouth. He exited the car and stood leaning against the fender.

Ramsey's SUV had been abandoned right below where he now stood, but why? He couldn't see why Branch would even go to the trouble of bringing the vehicle to this location. There were plenty of other places where he could have driven Ramsey if he wanted to shoot him and dump him in the ocean. Why here? And why would Branch go to all this trouble just to leave the .380 in his car? It didn't make sense. Branch was much smarter than that. This felt like a setup, like someone had framed Branch for the murder. But who? Who would have something to gain from Ramsey's death and Branch going to prison? The obvious choice was Davies. She'd had an affair with Ramsey, which meant she didn't care enough about her husband to stay monogamous. She said she'd broken it off with Ramsey, which meant she no longer cared about him. But she had an airtight alibi. She was in her condo when Ramsey was killed. The security video showed her car entering the garage while Ramsey was still at the Fox. She never left the building. The only one who didn't have an alibi was Branch. Davies could have hired someone to do her bidding. But then why go through the trouble of staging the break-in?

Byron looked around. The spot was certainly remote. Too remote. Whether it was Branch or not, someone could have driven Ramsey out to this spot, killed him, dumped the body in the ocean, and abandoned the SUV. But then what? How had the accomplice left the scene? They'd have needed transportation. Did they call for a ride? It wouldn't have made sense for the killer to use a cell, unless it was a TracFone, because there would be a record of the call and possible location history. And they wouldn't have risked calling someone to the murder scene for fear of getting caught. He walked around to the front of the building and looked back down the length of Veranda toward Portland. Quattrucci's Variety was only a quarter mile away. A variety store with a public pay phone out in front. If Byron had needed a ride away from this spot and didn't want to chance connecting himself with the SUV location, Quattrucci's is the phone he would have used.

As he was walking back to the car his cell rang. The caller ID wasn't a number he recognized. "Byron."

"Sergeant Byron, this is Attorney Gerry DeWitt calling."

"What can I do for you, Mr. DeWitt?"

"We need to talk."

"Okay. Are you at your office? I can be there in—"

"I'm not in the office. Can you meet me?"

"Where?"

"South Portland. Bug Light Park."

Chapter Thirty

Wednesday, 12:55 P.M., May 4, 2016

BYRON STOPPED AT Quattrucci's pay phone long enough to make sure it worked and record the number. The phonebook was missing but the phone was in working order. He copied the number into his notebook then drove to South Portland.

DeWitt was seated on a concrete bench overlooking the Portland Breakwater Lighthouse, nicknamed Bug Light due to its diminutive size.

"Didn't take you for a smoker, Mr. DeWitt," Byron said as he approached the attorney.

DeWitt looked up. "I quit once before."

"When was that?"

"Fifteen years ago."

"The job that stressful?" Byron asked, sitting down beside him.

"Not the job. The stakes."

"What did you want to see me about?"

"Devon didn't kill Paul Ramsey."

"How do you know that?"

"I know what I know." He tapped out a fresh cigarette from the pack and offered one to Byron. "Smoke?"

"No thanks. One habit I never took up."

"That's good. These things will kill you," DeWitt said as he lit another. "How long have you been a cop?"

"Long time. Over twenty."

"Probably worked closely with some of those other cops a long time as well, huh?"

"Some of them."

"Ever surprised by what they're capable of?"

Byron thought for a moment before answering. "Not anymore."

"I've worked with Devon a long time, Sergeant Byron. And it's like that. I know him better than I know myself some days. He didn't kill Paul."

"What if I told you that Lorraine was having an affair with Ramsey?"

DeWitt turned his head toward Byron. "Paul wasn't the only one she was fucking."

"You say that like it's a fact? How do you know?"

He looked away. "Because I was one of them."

Byron hadn't known why Devon had wanted to see him. He'd expected the attorney to make some revelation, but sleeping with Davies wasn't one of them. "You had an affair with her too?"

"I was drunk the first time. She came on to me. It just happened. It only lasted a couple of months. But she's been fucking me ever since."

"I'm not following."

"Fucking me. Using the affair to blackmail me into doing whatever she wanted."

"She threatened to tell Branch?"

DeWitt shook his head. "No, not Devon. My wife. Devon already knew what she was like. Lorraine enjoys sex, Sergeant. But not just the sex, the power that comes with it. She uses it like a weapon. She's a very resourceful woman."

"Is that why you were backing her for full partnership?"

"I had to. She threatened to go to my wife and tell her that we'd been having sex regularly. I've been married for twenty-five years. I have three children. Lorraine threatened to take all of that away from me if I didn't back her play."

"Why not deny it?"

"She said she kept a soiled item of clothing that would prove we'd been together." DeWitt inhaled deeply. Byron watched as the cigarette burned away like some trick of time lapse photography.

"What does any of this have to do with Ramsey?" Byron asked. "She was sleeping with him, too. You think she was also blackmailing him?"

"I don't know if she was or she wasn't, but I do know that she wouldn't have been with him if there wasn't something in it for her. Lorraine doesn't do anything without a reason."

"Are you telling me that you think she killed Ramsey?"

"If she didn't, she had someone else do it."

"Why?"

"Maybe to get Devon out of the way."

"Of her partnership?"

"Of everything. There's a prenup in place between Devon and Lorraine. Devon had me put it together. If she divorces him, she gets nothing. But if he dies—"

"She's the sole beneficiary," Byron said, completing his thought.

DeWitt nodded.

"How much is he worth?" Byron asked.

"Plenty."

"Who called and told you to bail out Darius Tomlinson?"

DeWitt exhaled a plume of smoke through his nose before answering. "Who do you think?"

BYRON DROVE AWAY from the meeting with DeWitt, armed with something he'd previously been missing, a solid motive for setting Branch up. He still didn't have a solid motive for why Davies would want to kill Ramsey. Although given what DeWitt had said and knowing what kind of creep Ramsey had been, blackmail wasn't out of the question. He was trying to decide his next move when his cell rang. It was Dispatch.

"Byron," he answered.

"Sarge, it's Lisa from Dispatch."

"Hey, Lisa. What's up?"

"We just had a shift change and I found a note saying that there was someone to see you at the IO desk."

"How old is the note?"

"A half hour."

"Does it say who or want they want?"

"Nope, just somebody asking to see you."

"Be right in."

BYRON STEPPED OUT of the first-floor stairwell into the hall. He passed the IO desk, where a young officer was talking on the phone, and opened the door to the lobby. Empty. Whoever had wanted to speak with him had evidently left. He returned to the information desk and waited.

"Hey, Sarge," the officer said, replacing the phone to its cradle.

Byron glanced at the name tag. Timmons. "Where's the person who was looking for me, Officer Timmons?" Byron asked.

"Got rid of him, Sarge. He was just a homeless bum, stinking up the lobby."

Glantz. Byron could feel himself getting hot. "What did this homeless *bum* look like?"

"Ratty, forties, long gray hair."

"Shopping cart?"

"Yeah, he parked it down on the Middle Street sidewalk."

Byron was struggling to maintain control. "I don't suppose you asked him what it was he wanted to talk to me about?"

"Nah, he's just a stew bum. Figured you had more important stuff to do."

Byron contacted the watch commander, got a replacement for Timmons, then ordered Officer Impetuous to bring a cruiser around to the front of the station.

"Where are we going?" Timmons asked as Byron climbed in on the passenger's side of the black-and-white.

Byron glared at him. "To find a bum."

TIMMONS HAD BEEN cruising the Old Port looking for either the bum or the bum's carriage for the better part of ten minutes when Byron yelled stop.

"What? I didn't see anything," Timmons said.

Byron wondered if the kid was really cut out to be a beat cop. "Back there. In the alley," he said, motioning with his thumb over his right shoulder.

Timmons pulled to the curb and parked. He sat there looking at Byron as if he thought Byron was going to go look for the guy himself.

"Come on, Officer. Time for your lesson in real policing."

Byron and his new uniformed and uninformed partner cut through the pungent alley running between Exchange and the Fore Street Parking Garage. They found Timmons's bum rummaging through a Dumpster at the rear of 10 Exchange Street.

"Winn," Byron said, startling the homeless man.

"Sarge!" Glantz said, his excitement obvious. He climbed down from the pallet he'd propped up against the trash container.

"Officer Timmons, I'd like you to meet Erwin Glantz."

Glantz eyed Timmons with suspicion. "You're not gonna bust me for collecting cans, are ya?"

Timmons looked at Byron. "You can't be serious, Sarge."

Byron leaned in close to the young beat cop. "Either you shake this man's hand or I'll see to it that you work the IO desk for the next year."

Timmons begrudgingly complied. "Officer Timmons."

Byron fixed Timmons with a scowl as he watched the officer wipe his hand on his uniform pants.

Timmons continued. "Sorry about giving you the bum's—ah, about throwing you out of the station."

Glantz looked to Byron.

Byron nodded.

"No problem, Officer," Glantz said, addressing Timmons. "Water under the bridge."

"Have you eaten?" Byron asked Glantz.

"Not since yesterday. I hate waitin' in line at the soup kitchen."

"Come on," Byron said.

"What about my stuff?" Glantz asked, looking back at his shopping cart.

Byron grinned. "Pretty sure that cart doesn't belong to you. I'm guessing Hannaford or Shaw's."

Glantz gave him a sheepish look. "The stuff inside's mine."

Byron looked at Timmons. "Give him a hand with his bags. You can put 'em in the trunk."

Timmons stood there without moving, like a puppy testing his master's will.

Byron walked closer to him. "An entire year, Officer. With extra days added on for every vacation or sick day you take."

The three men walked back through the alley. Timmons and Glantz struggled with the trash bags of refuse. The bags were stuffed into the trunk, then all three men got into the car. Byron caught a glimpse of the grimace on Timmons's face as Glantz climbed into the back seat.

"Might wanna put the windows down," Glantz said. "I'm a little ripe."

"Where to?" Timmons asked Byron.

"Commercial and India. The food cart."

Glantz dug into the sausage sub like it was the first real food he'd had in weeks. Maybe it was. Byron handed a large Styrofoam cup of coffee to Glantz, popped the lid on his own coffee, then turned to the sound of Timmons clearing his throat. "Pay the man, Officer Timmons. Lessons like this aren't free."

Byron waited until Glantz had polished off the first sandwich before asking where he'd been. "I've been looking for you, Winn. Beginning to think maybe you were dodging me."

Glantz looked down as if he'd been punished. He toyed with the plastic tab on his coffee lid.

"Have you been avoiding me?"

"Yup."

"Why?"

Glantz shrugged his burly shoulders. "Scared, I guess."

Byron caught Glantz's nervous look at Timmons. It was time for kid gloves. First rule of a good interview: remove all obstacles.

"Officer Timmons, why don't you give us a minute," Byron said.

Timmons shuffled back toward the cruiser, sulking.

"What are you scared of, Winn?"

Glantz looked up at Byron. The fear in his bloodshot eyes was unmistakable. "Somethin' I saw."

"What did you see?"

Glantz looked over nervously to see if Timmons was coming back. He wasn't.

Byron reached out and gently placed his hand on Glantz's shoulder. "What did you see, Winn?"

"I saw someone dump that dead lawyer's truck."

Byron waited. Not saying a word. He'd gotten Glantz this far but the rest was up to Glantz himself.

"Can I ask you a question, Sarge?" Glantz said finally.

"Of course."

"How did you know to look for me?"

"Your hat," Byron said. "You left it behind when you broke camp."

Glantz nodded. "Didn't want to get involved. I was camping there in the bushes near the water. It was late. Dark and foggy. I saw a truck pull up. One of those fancy utility jobs."

"Did you see who was driving?" Byron asked.

Glantz nodded again. "A light-haired lady."

"Was she alone?"

"Yeah."

"You get a good look at her?"

Glantz shook his head. "Couldn't see much, just the shape of a woman and blond hair."

"You said she dumped the vehicle. Did you see how she left the area?"

"No. I assume she just walked away. I listened for a while thinking someone might come pick her up but no one else came."

"You see anything else?"

"Nope. She drove it down there and left it."

"You remember about what time this happened?"

"Don't own a watch, Sarge. Late. After eleven. Midnight, maybe." He paused a minute, then looked at Byron. The fear had returned to his eyes. "Someone murdered the guy who owned that SUV, the lawyer."

"Ramsey? Yes. How did you know it was his SUV?"

"Big story about him found dead in the paper. I've been checking every day since. That's how I found out it was his SUV I saw the woman dump near my camp. Newspaper had a picture of it and you were there."

"You got a subscription?" Byron asked, kidding.

"Don't need one. Just grab 'em out of the Dumpsters. I like the puzzles."

TIMMONS TRANSPORTED THEM back to 109. Byron turned Glantz over to Nugent for a recorded interview. Timmons was still pouting. Byron pulled him aside.

"Still don't get it, do you?" Byron asked the rookie.

"He's a bum who happened to see something. What's the big deal?"

"First off, Officer Timmons, that bum did two tours overseas during the first Gulf War. He actually served his country. Winn's seen more death than you'll ever know."

"I didn't know."

"Of course you didn't."

"Sorry."

"It's not me you should be apologizing to. I've solved more crimes over the years than you could imagine talking to guys just like him. Nobody even notices people like Winn. They hide in plain sight and they see everything. If you're ever gonna make it on this job, you'd do well to remember that."

BYRON FOUND DIANE in the conference room with Stevens, watching Nugent's interview on the monitor.

"Ramsey wasn't shot on Veranda Street," Byron said.

"How do you know?" Diane asked.

"That guy in there with Nuge is an old snitch of mine, Erwin Glantz. He saw a woman drive Ramsey's SUV to the place it was dumped. A blonde woman. She was alone."

"Fuck," Stevens said. "So Ramsey may have been killed on the boat?"

"Did we find anyone at the marina who remembered hearing Ramsey's boat leave the dock the night he was killed?" Byron asked.

Diane shook her head. "No, and we spoke with all of them."

"But I got the distinct impression that some of them wouldn't have told us either way," Stevens said.

Byron looked at Diane. "Let's take a ride. I need something to eat."

Chapter Thirty-One

Wednesday, 3:25 P.M., May 4, 2016

DAVIS BILLINGSLEA SAT in his cubicle banging away on the keyboard like a madman. He was putting the finishing touches on the Ramsey update. Prominent Local Attorney Charged in Ramsey Homicide. Billingslea was on top of the world. Half of it was due to the Ramsey story. Thanks to Detective Joyner, he'd finally been the first to break a major story. After Diane's call, he'd been the first to tweet the arrest. He'd even posted the teaser update to the *Herald*'s webpage along with a cellphone pic of the powerful attorney being led out of his building in cuffs. A picture *he* had snapped. His bosses were elated. This was his fifteen minutes. And, Warhol be damned, he was going to do his best to make it thirty. But his newfound celebrity wasn't the only thing making him feel this way. Amy Brennan was infecting his every thought. She was absolutely stunning, by far the most attractive girl he'd even been out with. Hell, if he was being honest, she was the prettiest girl who'd ever shown any interest in him. He'd had to blow off their date the night before because of the Branch story, but he'd promised to make it up to her. He glanced at his desk clock—3:25. She'd asked that he not phone her while she was at work, but he had to. He was bursting. He rolled out of his cubicle and checked the work spaces on either side. *Empty.* He hit the speed dial for her cell then waited anxiously as it rang.

"Hello?"

Just the sound of her voice made his heart race.

"Amy. It's Davis."

"Oh, hey."

She sounded funny. Was she pissed at him about last night? She hadn't let on that it bothered her.

"I'm sorry for calling you at work but I've got some unbelievable news. Besides, I felt bad about canceling our date. I want to make it up to you. Take you someplace really nice tonight."

"Um, Davis, I've been thinking. I don't think it's a good idea for us to keep seeing each other."

"Wh-what?" The words caught in his throat. "Why not?"

"The police just arrested my boss and, because of you, I helped them do it."

He was stunned. "But your boss killed Paul Ramsey. He needed to be locked up, Amy. This doesn't have anything to do with you. Or us."

"I'm sorry, Davis. You're sweet. But I just can't."

He was speechless.

"Take care of yourself," she said before hanging up.

Billingslea stared down at his cellphone. The picture of Amy that he'd added to his contacts disappeared as the call was disconnected, replaced by a Beyoncé screensaver. *What had just happened?* It had never occurred to him that involving Amy in the story would be a problem. But in a matter of minutes he'd fallen off his newfound life high to a depth he'd never imagined.

"Davis!" Draper hollered from somewhere across the newsroom. "How much longer before that story's done?"

"I—I'm almost finished," he lied. The truth was, he didn't feel like finishing the story. He'd been looking forward to a festive evening with Amy. Hoping for more than just a dismissive kiss on the cheek. Maybe even a sleepover. Now he was doomed to spend another evening eating leftover pizza snuggled up with Simba. And his Siamese roommate was a poor substitute for Amy.

"Four o'clock, Davis," Draper called over. "On my desk."

"Got it," he said, projecting zero enthusiasm. He placed the cellphone on his desk and resumed typing. Slowly.

BYRON AND DIANE grabbed takeout at the Burger King on Forest Avenue. While they ate, he filled her in on the latest information from DeWitt.

"You think he's telling the truth?" Diane asked.

"I think he is. Of course the information he's providing still doesn't get Branch off the hook. We're gonna need more."

Byron's cell rang. "Byron," he answered.

"Hey, Sarge," Tran said. "You in the building?"

"No. But I can be. You got something?"

"I think so, Number One."

"I'll be right in."

Byron and Diane drove back to 109 then ascended the stairs to the third floor. Tran, dressed in an outrageously loud pink and gold Hawaiian shirt, was waiting for them.

"What's up?" Byron asked.

"Well, I've been working some of my tech magic on the list of employees from the law firm of Newman, Branch & DeWitt that you gave me and I think I may have found something."

"This more of that stuff we don't want to know about?" Diane asked.

Tran fixed her with a sideways grin. "Kind of hard to answer if you don't want to know."

"These are lawyers we're fucking with, Dustin," Byron said. "We don't want to get caught with our pants down."

"Fear not, Striped One. My data mining friend leaves zero trace. This can't be used—it's just to give you guys an edge."

"Go ahead."

"Okay. So I took the phone numbers from each of the firm's employees looking for patterns. Who's calling who and how often."

"Not the landlines, I hope."

"No way. I'm not totally crazy."

"Good to hear."

"Using the cellphone numbers provided, I looked at time of day, frequency of calls, both to and from, that kind of thing."

"Using numbers from every single employee at the firm? That's a lot of data."

"Yeah, I quickly discovered that. Diane helped me compile a short list of principals. The senior partners, Ramsey, Davies, and a few others along with their assistants."

"And?"

"Well, I found something kinda weird when I looked at Davies's number and the number for her assistant, Amy Brennan. They call each other quite a bit. With the majority of the calls coming after five o'clock at night."

"How frequently?" Diane asked.

"They average about thirty calls a week."

"That a lot?" Byron asked.

Tran shrugged his shoulders. "Beats me. I'm just glad my boss doesn't call me that much during my time off."

"Point taken. So they work a lot of hours—not sure that's big news, Dustin."

Tran shook his head. "That's not the news. About a month before Ramsey's murder some weird stuff started happening. First, the calls between Davies's and Brennan's cells dropped by seventy-five percent."

"Maybe they weren't as busy," Byron said. "Or maybe one of them was on vacation."

"Maybe. But I don't think so. I found that Brennan's cell was in contact with a new number not on the list." Tran pointed at the number on the screen.

"Do you know whose number it is?" Byron asked.

"Nothing listed. My tech buddy says it's a TracFone. Untraceable."

"Like the drug dealers use," Diane said.

"Yup, and terrorists and anyone else who wants anonymity. Activated at the same time Davies's and Brennan's call volume dropped off."

"How many times was Brennan's cell in contact with the Trac-Fone?" Byron asked.

"Just a couple of times."

Byron took a moment to process what Tran was telling him. "Do any of the other employees of the firm call the new number or receive calls from it?"

"Nope."

"So you think Davies may have purchased a throwaway?" Diane asked.

"That'd be my guess."

"Interesting."

"Know what else is interesting?"

"What?" Byron asked.

"The calls between Davies and Ramsey stopped at about the same time."

"Nice work," Byron said, putting a hand on Tran's shoulder.

Tran's face lit up with pride. "Thanks, Striped Dude."

They were turning to leave when Tran stopped them.

"One more thing. I found another number, one you might recognize, in repeated contact with Brennan's phone. And vice versa."

"Someone else from the firm?"

"Nope. Ran the number through HTE. It belongs to Billingslea. Looks like Ms. Brennan's been talking out of school with Davis Billingslea, reporter extraordinaire for the *Portland Herald*."

Byron paused in the doorway, thinking it through. *Was Amy Brennan playing both sides? Talking to the press while feeding info to the investigators?*

"When did those calls start, Dustin?" Diane asked.

"About three weeks ago."

"Speaking of phones," Byron said, pulling out his notebook. "I've got another one I need you to check out for me." He copied the number onto a piece of scrap paper and handed it to Tran. "I need a printout of all incoming and outgoing calls for this number on the night Ramsey was killed. As soon as possible."

"Is this someone's cell?"

"No, it's a public pay phone."

"I'm on it."

BYRON PACED THE length of the conference room while Diane and the other detectives sat at the table analyzing the board and slinging around ideas. He'd called the meeting to discuss the direction the investigation needed to go while he connected the dots swirling in his own head.

"But ballistics confirm it was the gun we took off Branch," Nugent said. "So, what else are we looking for?"

"His accomplice," Stevens said. "A woman dumped Ramsey's car on Veranda, then walked away."

"He's still the shooter though, right?" Nugent asked. "I mean, Ramsey was putting the boots to his wife. Makes sense that Branch would be the one to shoot him."

"He's too smart to shoot two people, then keep the gun," Byron said.

"I don't know, Sarge," Nugent said. "Jealousy can make even smart guys dumb. Maybe he was so pissed about Ramsey shagging his wife that he just lost his shit. Wasn't thinking straight."

"One problem with your theory, Nuge," Diane said. "If Branch *was* acting impulsively, why would he report the gun stolen from his house a month before killing Ramsey?"

Amazingly, Nugent had nothing witty to say.

"Diane's right," Stevens said. "Staging a break-in to make it look like someone else had the gun took a lot of thought. It would mean that Branch preplanned this whole thing. Nothing impulsive about that."

"And why didn't we find prints on the gun?" Byron asked.

"That is kind of fucked up," Pelligrosso said. "There were no gloves found in his car. Why wipe your prints off a murder weapon if you're just gonna hang on to it? Doesn't make sense."

"No," Byron said. "It doesn't."

"Maybe he didn't plan on getting pulled over and arrested," Stevens said.

"Normally, I'd say you were right," Diane said. "Problem is, he had to know the police would be looking for him. He'd just punched out his wife."

"Unless he didn't," Byron said, stopping abruptly in mid-pace.

"I'm not following," Diane said. "We have a witness."

"Yeah," Nugent said. "Amy Brennan. She was there when Branch showed up all pissed off, remember?"

"It's in her statement, Sarge," Stevens said, flipping open one of the file folders and removing a piece of paper. "It's right here. Says she was in the condo when Devon Branch arrived."

"Did Brennan tell us Branch was expected?" Byron asked.

Stevens scanned quickly through the document while they waited. "Doesn't say. Why?"

Byron turned to Diane. "What did Lorraine Davies say about that? Did she know her husband was stopping by?"

Diane shook her head. "No. Said he came by unannounced."

Byron looked at Stevens. "Mel, check through Branch's cell records. I want to know if he received or made any calls just prior to going to see Davies."

"I got the printout right here," Stevens said. "Hang on a sec."

"What are you getting at, John?" Diane asked.

"The security guard at Davies's building said Davies got regular visits from Brennan and for a couple of months she also had visits from Ramsey."

Nugent grinned. "The Ramsey visits were what kids nowadays refer to as a booty call."

"And?" Diane said, ignoring Nugent.

"And," Byron said, "he *never* saw Branch stop by. Not once."

"Here it is," Stevens said, sounding excited. "About twenty minutes before Davies said she was assaulted by Branch, the cell records show an incoming call to Branch from Davies's cell."

"So?" Diane said.

"So, why didn't she mention it?" Byron said. "She told the officers that he showed up unannounced. Why didn't she mention calling him?"

"Probably didn't think it mattered," Nugent said.

"Or she didn't want us to know that she'd asked him to come," Byron said.

"Why?" Nugent said.

"Maybe to set him up for the assault," Stevens said.

"You're thinking what, Sarge?" Nugent said. "That she intentionally said something to set him off so he'd drive over and assault her?"

"Or, maybe, he *never* touched her," Byron said, leaning against the wall and crossing his arms across his chest. "What if the call was just a ruse to get him to her condo?"

"She had a bruised eye, John," Diane said, pulling out a plastic viewing sheet of the photos Pelligrosso had taken.

"Doesn't mean it was Branch who hit her," Byron said.

Byron waited as the group thought it through.

Diane spoke up first. "You're suggesting Davies did that to herself?"

"Or she had Brennan do it," Stevens said.

"Brennan?" Diane said. "Why Brennan?"

"What if Amy Brennan is more than Davies's personal assistant?" Stevens said.

"You think Brennan's visits were booty calls, too?" Nugent said, smirking.

"Why not?" Byron said. "Mel said she got that vibe off Brennan."

"My gay-dar," Stevens said. "That, and I'm pretty sure I've seen her before at one of the local clubs. More than once."

"Okay," Diane said. "So what are you suggesting? That Brennan and Davies set Branch up for the domestic assault charge?"

"Why not the murder too?" Byron said. "Plant the gun in his car where the police will find it?"

"Holy shit," Nugent said, his eyes widening.

"But the gun was just stuffed under the front seat," Pelligrosso said. "Wouldn't they be taking a big chance that he might find it? What if it slid out while he was driving?"

"Not if they planted it at the same time he stopped over to see Davies," Byron said. "It would only be there until he got home or until the police stopped him."

"That would mean Brennan would have to have planted it while he was upstairs," Diane said.

"She could have," Stevens added. "Brennan said she left the condo right after Branch showed up," Stevens added.

"But Branch had the car keys," Nugent said.

"I'd be willing to bet Davies has a spare set to every car they own," Byron said.

"So if we think there's a possibility that Branch was set up, who do we think killed Ramsey?" Stevens asked.

"The only person we know who might possibly benefit by both men being out of the picture is Davies," Diane said. "But we already know she didn't leave the condo after seven-thirty that night. We've got video."

Byron tapped the marker on the metal whiteboard eraser tray. "Unless she knows a way out of that building undetected or has an accomplice. Winn said a woman drove Ramsey's SUV to Veranda

Street," Byron said. He looked at Pelligrosso, waiting for it to register. "A blonde woman."

"The two long blond hairs I pulled out of Ramsey's SUV," Pelligrosso said.

"Artificial blond hairs," Byron corrected.

Nugent chimed in with something helpful. "The stripper's a ginger."

"*Was* a redhead," Stevens said.

"She could have been wearing a wig," Nugent continued. "Maybe she slipped Ramsey the fentanyl-laced coke on the boat, then drove his SUV out to Veranda to dump it. Take our attention away from the marina. Maybe that's why she was killed."

"What about Ramsey's wife?" Stevens asked.

Diane shook her head. "Short brown hair, no motive, and she'd never wear a wig."

"So that just leaves Davies and Brennan, right?" Nugent asked.

"Right," Byron said. "Only one of them isn't a blond." He looked at Stevens. "Mel, I want you and Nuge to dig up everything and anything you can find on Brennan and Davies."

"You got it," Stevens said.

Byron's cell rang. It was Tran.

"That was quick. Tell me you got something."

"I've got something," Tran said.

"Be right there."

Chapter Thirty-Two

Wednesday, 3:30 P.M., May 4, 2016

BYRON AND DIANE took the stairs down to the third-floor computer lab.

"Well?" Byron said.

Tran pulled up the list on his monitor. "From six o'clock the night Ramsey was murdered until 6:00 A.M. the following morning there were twenty-four outgoing calls and three incoming on the pay phone you gave me." He turned the screen toward them. "Have a look."

"What are we looking for, John?" Diane asked.

"That," Byron said, pointing to the screen. "Someone called that TracFone number, the one we think might belong to Davies, at 11:37 P.M."

"Holy shit," Diane said.

"That's not the best part," Tran said.

"What's the best part?" Byron asked, knowing how much his tech-savvy detective was enjoying the drama.

"Remember I told you that the calls between Davies and Brennan dropped substantially after the new number showed up?"

"Seventy-five percent, you said."

"Well, I wondered if maybe Davies wasn't the only one with a second cell. Look at this."

Byron studied the new screen.

"Cellphone A, the one I believe might belong to Davies, has been in contact with another TracFone, which I dubbed cellphone B, repeatedly, including the evening Ramsey was killed."

"You think cellphone B might well be Brennan?"

Tran nodded. "My educated guess."

"Can you go back to the pay phone screen?"

"Sure." Train clicked the mouse and the previous screen reappeared.

Byron pointed out the number dialed after the TracFone. "Google this one, Dustin."

"You recognize that number, too?" Diane asked.

"No," Byron said. "But I've got a hunch."

"Portside Taxi," Tran said.

"That's it," Byron said. "The way out. We need to find the driver who picked up that fare."

"YES, I REMEMBER her," the Somali taxi driver said with a heavy accent. "She was standing in front of the store on Veranda Street."

"What did she look like, Mr. Ahmed?" Diane asked.

"She was blonde, very pretty, but not real."

"Not real?" Byron asked.

"Dark eyebrows."

"Bleached hair?" Byron asked.

"Not bleached. Fake. Like—what do you call it?"

"A wig?" Diane asked.

"Yes, yes. A wig."

Byron could feel the excitement building as another piece clicked into place. "Was she alone?" Byron asked.

"Yes."

"Did you ask her how she got there?" Diane asked.

Ahmed nodded. "Yes. She told me she had car trouble."

"Did she say anything else?" Byron asked.

"No. Just car trouble."

"Where did she ask to be taken?"

"Washington Avenue and Ocean Avenue."

"Did she give you an actual address?" Diane asked.

Ahmed looked confused. "No. She just said Washington and Ocean. At the gas station."

"Cumberland Farms?" Byron asked.

"Yes, yes. The Cumberland Farms. I dropped her off on the sidewalk and she walked to the parking lot."

"What time was that, Mr. Ahmed?" Byron asked.

"I am not sure, but I know it was after midnight."

"Would you recognize her if you saw her again?" Diane asked.

"Perhaps."

BYRON AND DIANE drove directly to the Cumberland Farms and waited the twenty minutes it took the grumbling store manager to retrieve the video.

"Think we'll be lucky enough to have caught her on this?" Diane asked as they drove back to 109.

"I hope. We were so focused on Davies's alibi that we missed Brennan," Byron said.

"You sure it's Brennan?"

"Aren't you?"

"It's hard to imagine, but it could be. If you're right and it is Brennan, the only question remaining is, did she do it on her own or did Davies put her up to it?"

"And how do we get either of them to admit it?" Byron said.

"YOU ARE KIDDING, right?" LeRoyer said, running his hands through his hair. "You're telling me we arrested an innocent man?"

"I'm telling you it's possible Branch was framed," Byron said.

Diane and Byron sat on either side of Tran, studying the security video from Davies's apartment as the lieutenant nervously paced the floor in Tran's cramped office.

"Jesus," LeRoyer said. "Stanton's gonna go ballistic."

"We had probable cause," Byron countered.

"Yeah, but Jesus. And if he didn't kill anyone why did he lawyer up?"

"Did you seriously just ask that question, Marty? He's a goddamned attorney—he'll always try and get a look at the prosecution's hand before he makes a play. Guilty or not. Besides, if he's not the killer, he knows there is still someone on the outside setting him up as a patsy in all of this."

Tran wisely remained silent as he advanced the video.

"Right there," Diane said. "Back that up a little."

"What?" LeRoyer said, sounding anxious. "You got something?"

"There," Diane said, pointing at the screen. The outside camera had captured the front end of a vehicle stopping on Washington Avenue at the left edge of the frame.

"Can't tell if that's a taxi or not," Tran said.

"We'll be able to when it pulls away," Byron said.

"The inside light just came on," LeRoyer said, stating the obvious.

They watched as the dark vehicle pulled away from the curb and continued outbound on Washington, the taxi light now illuminated and clearly visible atop its roof.

"Print a still of that," Byron said.

"You got it," Tran said.

"What's the time?" Diane asked Tran.

"Let's see, the clock is off twenty-three minutes, so that makes it . . . 12:18 in the morning."

Byron recorded the time in his notebook.

Still beyond reach of the building's exterior lights, a dark figure approached the lighted plaza cutting through the gas pumps. The four detectives waited with bated breath as the figure moved closer to the building.

"Freeze that," Byron said.

"Who is it?" LeRoyer asked.

"*That* is Davies's personal assistant," Diane said. "Amy Brennan."

"Wearing a blond wig," Byron said. He looked at Diane. "Let's get eyes on Brennan. I wanna know everything there is to know about her. Do we have an address?"

Tran spoke up. "The only thing the firm supplied for Brennan was a P.O. box."

"What about her registration or license?"

"Same," Tran said.

"I thought the state of Maine required a physical address now?" LeRoyer asked.

"Apparently not," Byron said.

"Why don't we just get it from the firm?" Tran asked.

"If we did, we'd risk tipping Brennan," Diane said.

"You're right," Tran said.

"What about the postal service investigator you're friends with?" Byron asked Tran. "Can't we get him to fast-track that for us?"

"Already tried. He's on vacation. His office told me at least a week to process my request."

"Fuck," Byron said. He was way beyond tired of the bureaucratic hoops they were constantly forced to jump through.

Diane spoke up. "I may know a way to get her address."

DIANE KNEW BYRON wouldn't be happy when he found out how Brennan's information had come to light. She didn't trust Davis Billingslea any more than John did. But the information about Davies's marital infidelity was important and, at the time, it had seemed legitimate. But if John was right, if Branch had been set up to be a patsy in Ramsey's murder, and now Tomlinson's, Brennan may have used Billingslea to get what she wanted. Fed him information for a purpose. If that was true, she'd most likely be finished with him.

Billingslea picked up on the second ring.

"Newsroom. Billingslea."

"Davis, it's Diane Joyner."

"Hey," he said, sounding anything but chipper.

"I need a favor."

"You and everyone else," he snapped. "What am I, a fucking rug? Everyone thinks they can just walk all over me?"

"Davis, what's wrong?" Diane asked.

"Nothing. It's nothing. What's the favor?"

"I need to know where Amy Brennan lives."

"Ha! That's great. Why do you think I'd know that?"

"I just assumed you were seeing each other."

"Yeah, so did I."

"What do you mean?"

"She just dumped me."

Brennan *was* done with him, Diane thought. She *had* cut him loose, realizing she no longer needed him. "I'm sorry," she said, trying her best to sound sympathetic.

"She said helping me was the reason Devon Branch got arrested. Can you believe that?"

"Davis, I really am sorry, but I need your help. Where does Amy live?"

"WHERE ARE WE headed, John?" Diane asked as Byron pulled out onto Middle Street and headed up Franklin.

"The overnight security guard from Davies's building lives out in North Deering. I want to ask him about visitors to Davies's apartment."

"Didn't we already talk with him?"

"No. The video was from the day security supervisor. We never talked to this guy."

MAX KELLER WORE his hair high and tight. His neatly pressed security uniform hung from a wooden wall hanger, above a pair of gleaming black Corcoran leather boots, in the spotless kitchen of his tiny Auburn Terrace apartment.

"I just took the test again for Portland," Keller said proudly.

"Well, we wish you the best of luck, Mr. Keller," Diane said.

"Thank you, ma'am. I'm really hoping to get on the force this time."

"Yeah, good luck," Byron said.

He knew the type. Keller had most likely purchased every study guide he could get his hands on, worked out every day, kept his gear spotless, dying for his law enforcement break to come. Provided he had the intelligence to score high on the test, he'd probably make it, as long as there were no historical skeletons in his closet. Four years of high school and two to four years of college allowed plenty of time for the youthful indiscretions and missteps made by many police candidates. Hopefully, Keller had been smarter than some.

Byron also knew that Keller likely took his security job very seriously, wanting to make a good impression. Byron assumed that when it came to the routines of the building's tenants, Keller probably missed very little.

"Are you familiar with Lorraine Davies, Mr. Keller?" Byron asked.

"Yes, sir. Fourteenth floor, apartment D, overlooks the ocean." His instincts had been right about Keller.

"Does she get many visitors?" Diane asked.

"Yes, ma'am. A few."

"Male? Female?"

"Both."

"Any regulars?" Byron asked.

"Yes, sir. The most frequent visitor is a pretty brunette named Amy. Amy Brennan."

"You know her last name?" Diane asked with a raised brow.

"As I said, she's very pretty."

And possibly very deadly, Byron thought.

"And they have to show ID to get into the building," Keller said.

"Any other regulars?" Byron asked.

"For a few months she got the occasional nighttime visit from that attorney who was murdered. Mr. Ramsey."

"Nighttime visit?" Diane asked.

"Yes, ma'am. He'd show up late, like ten or eleven, then leave around midnight."

"Ramsey come by lately?" Byron asked.

"No, he stopped coming to see Ms. Davies a few weeks before he died. Maybe even a month."

"You ever see her husband, Devon Branch, pay her a visit?" Byron asked.

Keller thought for a moment, then shook his head. "No, sir. I don't believe I've ever met him."

"How long have you worked security at the tower?" Diane asked.

"Eighteen and a half months, ma'am."

Byron noted the exactness of his tenure, as if every day counted. Like a child saying four and a half when referring to their age.

"How long has Brennan been stopping by to see Davies?" Diane asked.

"For as long as I've been working there."

"Were Brennan's visits like Ramsey's?" Byron asked.

"Sir?" Keller said, obviously not understanding the question.

"You described Ramsey's visits as arriving late and leaving around midnight. Are Brennan's like that?"

"No, sir. When she visits it's usually for the night."

"Anything unusual about her recent visits?" Diane asked.

"Not that I can recall."

"And Brennan parks in the rear visitor's lot, correct?" Byron asked.

"Yes. Only the tenants can park in the underground garage," Keller said. "There's an automatic computerized record whenever a tenant enters or exits using their opener."

A thought popped into Byron's head. "Can we obtain a print-out of the tenants and their corresponding garage IDs?"

"Sure. My boss can get that for you."

"When was the last time you spoke with Davies?" Byron asked.

"A few days ago. She called down by phone about a visitor."

"That visitor was me, right?" Byron asked.

"Yes, sir. That was the evening you stopped by to see her."

"Can you remember the last time you saw her in person?"

"Yeah, it was the Tuesday before last. She called down to the desk and asked me to take a look at the door to her apartment. She said she thought it had been tampered with. Swore she heard someone in the hallway."

"What time was this?"

"Around midnight, I think. I'd have to check the logbook. She was dressed in a nightgown," Keller said, blushing.

"Did you find anything?" Diane asked.

"No, ma'am. I told her that I'd keep an extra eye out. Make a few extra rounds of the building."

"Was this the first time she'd ever complained of anything like this?" Byron asked.

"No. She called a few weeks ago about her sliding glass doors. They wouldn't lock."

"What did you do?" Diane asked.

"Nothing I could do. I logged it in a report but I wasn't really too concerned about it. The doors only open onto her balcony. She's fourteen stories up. No way to get to it from outside the building.

"WELL, MR. WANNABE certainly is taken with Amy Brennan," Diane said as Byron started the car and pulled away from Keller's apartment.

"Interesting that she spends the night with Davies," Byron said.

"As opposed to Ramsey's hit and run sessions, you mean."

"Odd having a personal assistant for sleepovers."

"Oh, I don't know, John. Look at us," she said with a wink. "So, what are you thinking?"

"Maybe they're lovers and Ramsey got in between them?"

"Okay, so let's say Davies does swing from both sides of the plate, *and* she's married. If you're saying that Brennan killed Ramsey out of jealousy, wouldn't she also be jealous of Branch?"

Byron looked over at her, waiting for her own question to sink in.

"You think Davies orchestrated the whole thing?"

"The thought had occurred to me. Makes a lot more sense than Branch killing Ramsey without an alibi, and being dumb enough to hide the murder weapon in his car."

"But why would Brennan risk using a public pay phone to call for a taxi?" Diane asked.

"I don't know. Maybe her cell died. Maybe she forgot to charge it. She might not have had a choice."

They drove in silence. Each thinking it through. Looking for holes in the theory.

At last Diane spoke up. "Let's say you're right. Why wouldn't Davies just pick her up after Brennan dumped Ramsey's SUV?"

"She couldn't," Byron said. "Davies had to go back to the high-rise to establish her alibi with Max. Someone tampering with her locks? And she just happens to report it at midnight?"

"I've gotta say, this theory of yours is pretty sound. But as good as it is, it's still just a theory. How do we prove it?"

Byron turned to her and grinned. "How fast can you write an affidavit?"

"You have got to be kidding!" LeRoyer said as he jumped up from behind his desk.

Byron remained stoic, waiting until the lieutenant finished his brass tantrum.

"Do you realize what the fuck is going to happen if you were wrong in charging Branch?" LeRoyer continued.

Byron couldn't help but notice how quickly LeRoyer shifted his use of pronoun from *we* to *you* at the thought of a fucked-up arrest. "Yeah," Byron said. "Think I've got a pretty good idea."

Byron waited as LeRoyer paced the room, furiously combing his fingers back through his hair. He'd seen the lieutenant react like this to bad news too many times to count.

"We've gotta let someone know," LeRoyer said. "We gotta let Branch out of jail. Drop the charges."

"I've already talked to AAG Ferguson," Byron said. "Branch is staying put for the time being. We're not just gonna go off half-cocked. We still have PC for the arrest."

"Yeah, but the video, John. Jesus."

"Circumstantial. All we've got is Brennan taking a late-night cab ride."

"From the crime scene."

"From a variety store close to where we recovered Ramsey's SUV," Byron countered. "We can't even put the gun in her hand."

"Goddammit, John," LeRoyer said, continuing to pace and glaring at Byron. "Why can't it ever be simple with you? I wonder if my uniform still fits. 'Cause I'll be wearing it when they bust me back to Patrol."

"Think it through, Marty," Byron said. "Davies would have access to her husband's car, so she could have planted the gun later on. And if Davies had access then so would Brennan. Davies could have used her to plant the evidence."

Gradually, LeRoyer began to calm down and think rationally. He closed the door to his office, returned to his desk, and sat down across from Byron. "I know you must have a plan or you wouldn't be sitting here telling me this. Right?"

Byron nodded.

"Am I gonna like it?"

Byron shrugged his shoulders. "Not after your approval."

LeRoyer shook his head. "God, you're a dick sometimes, John. Okay, go on, then. Tell me."

Byron filled him in on everything he and Diane had discovered. Including the revelation by the night security guard working in Davies's building.

LeRoyer sat back in his chair, rubbing his palm over the side of his face. Byron wondered if this was the start of a new tic. "So, you think Davies was sleeping with Brennan and Ramsey?"

"Not at the same time, but yeah."

"How does that lead to a conspiracy?" LeRoyer asked.

"I think Davies may have put Brennan up to it. Davies sees how smitten the younger woman is with her and uses that adoration to manipulate her into removing the two biggest impediments in her professional life—Ramsey and her husband, Branch. Brennan kills Ramsey, then frames Branch."

"Jesus. How the hell are we ever gonna prove any of this?"

"We need a confession," Byron said. "There are only two possibilities—if Brennan is the killer, either she did it on her own or at the behest of Davies."

"Why would she murder Ramsey and set up Branch if she was acting on her own?" LeRoyer asked.

"Could be some kind of a fatal attraction thing."

"So, how do we go about getting either of them to confess?" LeRoyer asked.

"Oldest trick in the book," Byron said.

"I must not have that book," LeRoyer said. "What are you saying?"

"Turn them against each other."

Someone knocked on the door to LeRoyer's office. Both men turned to look.

"Got it," Diane said, waving a stack of papers at them. "Oh, and Nugent found something rather interesting in Davies's past."

Chapter Thirty-Three

Wednesday, 6:00 P.M., May 4, 2016

DIANE, PELLIGROSSO, AND Nugent were parked in an unmarked just down the street from Brennan's Morse Street apartment, waiting for her to depart. Parked directly across from them in a second unmarked was Tran. Inside Diane's jacket pocket was the affidavit and a signed warrant to search. In her left hand she toyed with the key that Brennan's landlord had provided to them. They watched as Brennan, alone, exited her building and entered her car.

Diane picked up her portable radio. "You got her?" she asked.

"Got her," Tran said.

Brennan drove down the street, past them, toward Washington Avenue. Tran followed. The three detectives moved quickly, jumping out of the car as soon as Brennan turned the corner.

As they approached the apartment on foot, Diane picked up the radio again. "Seven twenty-one to 720."

The static crackled loudly from the radio. "Seven twenty, go," Byron's voice said.

"Target has departed our location," she said. "Dustin has eyes on."

"Ten-four. Seven twenty copies."

They hurried up the steps to Brennan's empty apartment. For their plan to work, timing was everything. Timing and finding that TracFone. They only hoped she still had it.

AMY BRENNAN HAD taken her time dressing for her rendezvous. She'd purchased new black shoes and a skirt. Completing the outfit was a tight-fitting white blouse that enhanced her best attributes. It never failed to get a response from some of the male employees at the firm. But tonight she was only interested in Lorraine's reaction.

Anxiously, she made the short drive across town, the anticipation nearly killing her. She wasn't expected for another hour but she couldn't wait. She and Lorraine had accomplished so much and soon it would be over. Soon nobody would ever come between them again. It was time to celebrate. Time for them to be together. Forever.

She turned into the driveway of the Eastern Promenade highrise, drove past the entryway and into the rear lot. Soon she'd be able to give up her apartment permanently. Likewise she'd no longer have to park in this visitor's lot. She and Lorraine would share a space. They'd finally be able to share everything. The thought made her happy.

Brennan parked then paused to check her makeup in the mirror one last time. She smiled, secretly hoping that the young security guard, Max, was on duty. Max was never quite able to hide his lust for her. It made her feel sexy, even if men weren't her thing. But Max wasn't seated in the lobby as she strode along the entry hall toward the front desk. It was the day supervisor, Miller, and someone was standing beside him. Someone she recognized. It was that detective, Byron.

"Excuse me, Ms. Brennan," a female voice said, startling her from behind. "You need to come with us."

THEY'D BEEN INSIDE Brennan's apartment less than five minutes when Diane found a TracFone. It was plugged in, unlocked, and fully charged, half-hidden behind a Longaberger basket on the kitchen counter. Diane quickly checked the history log. It was the phone they were after.

"Got it," Diane called to the others. "Come on, Nuge. We gotta go."

Pelligrosso turned the corner from the adjoining room, almost colliding with her. "Look what I found." He was grinning as he held up a blond wig.

BYRON KNOCKED AGAIN on the door to Davies's apartment.

She opened the door dressed as if she was expecting a visit from one of her lovers and not a police detective. The surprise that registered on her face disappeared as quickly as it came. Chameleonlike, her features shifted to warm and inviting. "Good evening, Sergeant," she said in an overtly sultry tone. "Won't you come in."

He wondered how many things Davies had obtained in her life simply by using her sexual charms.

"Can I interest you in something to drink?" she asked, once again leading him into the living room.

"No, thank you."

"Oh, that's right, I forgot. You're on the wagon. Perhaps a soda, then?"

"I don't want to put you to any trouble."

"It's no trouble." He watched her stroll over to the bar and begin fixing his drink. "Diet Pepsi with lime okay?"

"Fine," he said.

He heard the muted chime of a cellphone text message, then watched as she picked it up from the bar and responded.

"Am I interrupting anything?" he asked.

"Not at all. Just work stuff. It'll keep."

A cool breeze tinged with the brine of seawater blew in through the open slider door, causing the sheer curtains on either side to dance.

"What about you, Sergeant Byron? Working, are we, or is this a social call?"

"Working, I'm afraid."

"Don't you ever let your hair down?" she asked as she picked up their drinks and walked over to him.

"After the job is done."

"Oh? I thought you'd already charged Devon with Paul Ramsey's murder?"

"We have. I'm just tying up some loose ends."

"I'm intrigued," she said, handing him his glass. "What else is there?"

"Well, I'm still not clear on Devon's motive."

Davies walked away and took a seat in the center of the sofa. "I'm not a detective, but it would seem that jealousy would be the most likely."

"Jealous about your affair with Paul Ramsey?"

"Of course. You saw what he did to me," she said touching her eye gingerly.

Byron sat across from her on the love seat.

"That's the thing I'm having trouble with. Why would he go

off on you for sleeping with Ramsey? It's not like he was your only conquest."

"Sounds like someone's been spreading rumors about me."

"Oh, I'd say more than rumors."

"Who have you been talking to?"

"Why didn't you tell the officer that you called Devon the night he assaulted you?"

"I didn't think it mattered."

"You said he just showed up in a rage and assaulted you. What did you call him about beforehand?"

"I can't remember."

"You don't seem too broken up by any of this," Byron said.

"Should I be?"

"Your lover is killed, then your husband is charged with his murder. I would think that might be upsetting."

"It's a tough world—I do what I have to to survive. You know, you don't have to sit way over there." She gave him a coquettish grin, and patted the cushion next to her. "I won't bite, Sergeant."

"I think it'd be better if we kept our relationship professional."

Davies stuck her bottom lip out in a mock pout. "You won't sit with me, you won't drink with me. Don't you find me attractive?"

"On the contrary, I find you very attractive. That's just the problem."

"And why is that a problem?"

"It isn't. At least, not until you use those charms to manipulate others into doing your bidding."

Davies frowned. "Not sure I understand the implication, Sergeant Byron."

"Actually, I'm not implying anything. I'm telling you, I know what you did."

Davies took another sip from her glass. Her eyes appraised Byron above the rim. "And what is it you think you know? Why don't you enlighten me?"

"Lorraine Davies, thirty-six years old, attractive, intelligent, top of her class in law school. Takes a position with Newman, Branch & DeWitt and marries one of the firm's senior partners. She continues to climb the corporate ladder until, in the short span of five years, she's suddenly in position to become the youngest full partner in the history of the firm. Only two things stand in the way of that goal: a husband who thinks she's too impetuous and immature and a boyfriend who believes that it should be *his* name added to the sign."

"Not a very flattering picture you're painting, but so far it's not an altogether inaccurate description. I assume there's more?"

"There is. Davies, being a bit of a manipulator, uses her ravenous sexual appetite to get whatever she wants. Blackmailing the other two married senior partners by sleeping with them. Intentionally bedding Ramsey, her only real competition for the partnership, coincidentally her husband's choice."

"I'm not sure what my sex life has to do with anything? Especially since you seem so determined not to be a part of it."

"Doesn't it? Sleeping with Ramsey, then creating the impression that your husband would be jealous about the relationship. Jealous enough to kill."

"I never implied any such thing."

"No, *you* didn't. You had your other lover take care of that."

"My other lover?"

"Amy Brennan, your personal assistant. You had her approach a newspaper reporter and pretend to have inside information about a love triangle gone wrong. You knew that the paper would never print anything like that for fear of being slapped with a multimillion-dollar slander suit. But you also knew that Billingslea wouldn't let it go. You knew Brennan could convince him to feed that story to the detectives investigating Ramsey's murder."

Davies laughed. "You have a very vivid imagination, Sergeant Byron. If I wanted Ramsey dead, why wouldn't I just have done it myself?"

"You didn't want to get your hands dirty. Better to coerce someone else to help you with your plan to frame Devon for the murder of Paul Ramsey. Someone who looked up to you. Someone who would do anything you asked because she believed that you really loved her."

"Amy?" Davies laughed again. "Is that what she told you? She means nothing to me. She's nothing more than a sexy toy to me. Something fun to pass the time. If she has done anything like you're suggesting, it was because she was upset when I broke it off."

"You broke it off with her?"

"Of course. You don't think for a second that I really care for that little tramp, do you?"

"She told me that the two of you were in love."

"In love," she scoffed. "It should be obvious that I am way out of her league. If you're trying to tell me little Miss Fatal Attraction has accused me of something, I will fire her first thing in the morning. I have an alibi for the night Ramsey was killed. Where was Amy? If she did something to Paul, she did it all on her own."

Davies looked up to the sound of the apartment door opening. "Excuse me. You can't just waltz in here!"

Byron didn't bother turning around. He knew that Diane and Nugent were escorting Amy Brennan into the apartment.

"How dare you break into my apartment?" Davies shouted. "I'll have your badges."

"It's not a break-in, Lorraine," Diane said. "Amy gave us permission. We used her key."

Davies looked at Byron. Her rage was obvious. "Now what, you're going to try and turn us against each other with lies?"

"I thought the two of you were quits?" Byron said, pulling out a digital transmitter from the breast pocket of his suit coat. "Ms. Brennan has been listening to everything we've said."

Davies's eyes widened. She turned and faced Brennan.

Tears streamed down the young woman's face, leaving a trail of mascara behind.

"We told her that you'd probably make sure that she never talked about this to anyone," Byron said. "Sooner or later she'd have to have an accident. Maybe an overdose, like your roommate in college. The student who was actually tops in the class until her best friend found her dead from too many Xanax."

Davies followed Byron's gaze toward the other bottle of wine on the table.

"I noticed you're drinking cabernet," Byron said. "Guessing the merlot is Amy's brand. I wonder, would you have added a little something to it? Something along the lines of what you had the stripper give to Ramsey. Something that might make it look like Amy died of an accidental overdose, effectively putting an end to your accomplice."

"Aim, please, don't listen to any of this," Davies said. "You don't have to say anything."

"It was all her idea," Brennan said in a barely audible voice.

"Shut up, Aim," Davies warned.

"No! I won't! You told me you loved me. You said we could be together if I helped you get Paul and Devon out of the way."

"This girl is delusional. Look at her. You can't honestly believe this story."

"Actually, I do," Byron said. "That text message you just responded to, thinking it was Amy, was actually Detective Joyner."

Diane held up Brennan's TracFone for Davies to see.

"Interesting how those phones were used leading up to Ramsey's murder," Byron continued. "Even now. Interesting, too, that yours was in direct contact with Darius Tomlinson the night he was killed."

"I was right here when you said that murder happened."

"Your car was here, but you weren't," Diane said. "It took us a while to figure out how you could be here and at the murder scenes simultaneously."

"Until we found out that your elderly neighbor from down the hall lives in Florida," Byron said. "You've been using her door opener and vehicle for the kills."

"This is crazy," Davies said. "You can't prove a thing you're saying."

Brennan spoke up again. "Lorraine told me that both men were abusive to her and controlling. She said Devon wouldn't give her a divorce. She told me that he threatened to fire her if she filed."

"What about Ramsey?" Byron asked.

Brennan looked back at Davies. "She said if she slept with him we could convince everyone that Devon was jealous and that he killed Ramsey."

Byron watched as Davies's expression changed from controlled and calculating to one of pure rage. He'd been hoping for a reaction, that Davies might let her guard down when she realized her plan was exposed. And now it was happening.

Davies hurled her glass at Brennan but missed. The glass shattered against the wall, staining it crimson and sending shards in all directions. "Shut the fuck up, you bitch," she hissed.

"How did the gun get into Branch's car?" Diane asked.

"I put it there," Brennan said. "Lorraine gave me the key and I stuck it under the seat. She told me say that I witnessed Devon attack her."

"How did she get the black eye?" Byron asked.

"She did it to herself," Brennan said.

"I will kill you for this!" Davies yelled as she glared at Brennan.

Byron pulled out a pair of handcuffs. "Actually, Lorraine, I think your days of killing anyone are over."

Lorraine stepped back behind the couch as Byron approached. "So now what? You're just going to believe everything she says. Send me to prison for a few years. Ruin my life."

"You've killed at least two people and set another up for murder, Lorraine. I'd say it's more likely you've ruined your own life. And you'll be spending the rest of it in jail."

"So this is it, then, Aim?" Davies said, addressing Brennan. "This is how it all ends?"

"This is it," Byron said, answering for her. "Now turn around and put your hands behind your back. You're under arrest for murder."

Davies turned and eyed the knife lying on the bar.

Byron caught her glance but wasn't in position to prevent her from reaching it. She rushed toward the bar and grabbed the weapon.

"Knife," he shouted as he drew his Glock and stepped in front of the couch, putting it between them.

Nugent also drew his sidearm.

"Put the knife down, Lorraine," Byron ordered.

Davies pointed the knife at Byron and took a step back. "Don't come any closer."

He signaled Nugent to head around the other side of the couch toward Davies.

Davies backed away from Byron while looking directly at Brennan. "Is this what you wanted?"

"Drop it, Lorraine," Byron repeated.

"You betrayed me," Davies said, addressing Brennan again.

Byron and Nugent closed in.

"Now you can live with it," Davies said. She looked back at Byron.

"Last time, Lorraine," Byron said.

Davies dropped the knife and whirled around, heading toward the slider doors.

"Stop her, Nuge," Byron yelled, realizing what she was about to do.

Taking the most direct route toward Davies, Byron leaped over the couch. He lunged at her but missed, only managing to tear off a piece of her blouse as he landed hard on the floor. He looked up just as she reached the balcony, mere steps ahead of Nugent.

"Stop!" Nugent yelled.

Horrified, they all watched as Davies grabbed onto the steel railing, and vaulted headfirst over the side.

Byron slowly regained his feet. He walked through the open slider onto the balcony and stood next to Nugent, looking down.

"Holy shit," Nugent said.

Lorraine Davies lay in a crumpled heap, motionless on the hillside far below.

From behind them, Byron heard the anguished wail of Amy Brennan. It was over.

Epilogue

A POLICE BASE radio squawked as Diane and a uniformed officer escorted a handcuffed and emotionally subdued Amy Brennan across the parking lot, carefully placing her into the back of a black-and-white. Byron and Nugent followed.

"Watch your head," Diane said, gently guiding Brennan's head past the roofline and into the car's interior.

Byron watched as Diane secured Brennan's seat belt. He knew there was never any telling what was in a man's heart, or a woman's, for that matter. The best you could hope for was to judge people by their actions. Anyway, the damage was done. Lives had been taken. Both women were responsible, but only one of them would pay the legal price for those lives. The other, answering to a higher power, had already paid.

The three detectives stood in the lot, watching as the marked unit pulled away.

"Hell hath no fury, huh, Sarge?" Nugent said.

Byron turned to face him. "Something like that." He turned back toward Diane. "You ready?"

She nodded.

"Where are you guys going?" Nugent asked. "Aren't you gonna stick around and watch Mel and me bag what's left of Davies?"

"As inviting as that sounds, Nuge, we've got an innocent attorney who needs to be released from custody," Diane said.

"Aw, can't we let him stew a little longer?" Nugent asked. "When my mom used to smack me for something I hadn't done and I told her it was my brother, she'd say, 'That's for the times I didn't catch you.'"

"I think Branch has stewed long enough," Byron said.

"Besides," Diane said, winking at Byron. "We've got to get him out so he can start working on the lawsuit against us."

"Gotta love lawyers," Nugent said as he walked toward the other side of the building.

THE FOLLOWING DAY Byron, Diane, and LeRoyer met in the lieutenant's office.

"I don't understand," LeRoyer said. "Wouldn't Davies still be taking a big chance that Branch might not be convicted?"

"Maybe she never intended on having the matter go to trial," Byron said.

"She may have planned to have someone kill him after he made bail," Diane said.

"What if he didn't get bail?" LeRoyer asked.

Byron shrugged his shoulders. "How hard is it to believe that an attorney stuck in general population might fall prey to one of the violent offenders?"

"Jesus," LeRoyer said. "Davies sounds like pure evil. I guess it's true about beauty only being skin-deep."

"It's what's beneath the depths that matters most," Byron said.

"So now Branch will likely sue the city, the department, and each of us," LeRoyer said, giving his hand a quick pass through his hair.

"Don't be so sure about that," Byron said. "We've got a lot of dirt on Branch and his partners. Tran has been busy unlocking digital files on Davies's personal computer. She actually kept files on each of them, including blackmail pictures of the trysts she had with Newman and DeWitt."

"Doubt they'd wanna take the chance on that juicy information coming up during a trial," Diane said.

"Well, I hope you're right," LeRoyer said. "Diane, would you give us a minute, and close the door behind you?"

"Sure," she said, casting a glance at Byron as she rose and headed for the door.

"What gives?" Byron asked after they were alone.

"I know about you and Diane."

He looked back at LeRoyer, sizing him up. *Was this the end of the line? Was the lieutenant about to throw him out of the bureau?*

"How long have you known?" Byron asked.

"Quite a while now," LeRoyer said.

"Does Stanton know?"

LeRoyer shook his head. "No."

"You never said anything. Why?"

"What? You two think you were the only partners to ever hook up?"

"You?"

LeRoyer sighed. "You remember Rachel DeGrinney?"

"Sure I do. Worked Patrol for a few years. Kind of a babe if I remember right. She left the force and went back to college or something, didn't she?"

"Law school."

"You and Rachel?"

LeRoyer nodded. "Jenny and I had been married for about six years at that point. She was traveling a lot for work. Our days off, when we got them, never seemed to match up. We barely spoke to each other. And then, only in passing. Rachel and I, we worked neighboring beats in town. Spent a lot of time together. It just sorta happened."

"Jenny ever find out?"

"I told her."

"Fuck, Marty."

"Yeah, I know. Stupid, right? Anyhow, we went to counseling, righted the ship, put the train back on the tracks, and all that."

"Kids, even," Byron said.

LeRoyer grinned. "Yeah."

"Good for you. Glad you guys worked it out."

"My point is, sometimes the job eats you up. Can't take it home. You don't share that shit with your spouse. Believe me, I know. But you gotta share it with someone. You and Diane work great together. I assumed it was only a matter of time before you both figured out how great you were together. And I wasn't about to fuck that up for either of you."

Were they great together? Byron wondered. A lot had happened during the previous week. "Well, it might be coming to an end anyway."

"What makes you say that?" LeRoyer asked, cocking his head to one side like a German shepherd.

"City hall. They offered her some new sergeant's position."

"Yeah, I know. And hopefully she's smart enough to accept it."

"Why would you want her to leave the bureau?" Byron asked.

"Because unlike you, my stubborn friend, her career still has a chance. I think she's destined for things greater than CID."

"What's wrong with CID?"

LeRoyer grinned. "My point exactly. Besides, your next boss isn't likely to allow this fraternization between a sergeant and a detective. He'll probably be a real prick."

"Next boss?" Byron said.

"Yeah. You were right. Stanton tapped me to be the next assistant chief."

"Ass Chief LeRoyer. It has a nice ring. Kinda suits you."

"Watch it."

"Congratulations, Marty."

"Thanks, but it isn't gonna happen. Not now, anyway."

Byron raised an eyebrow. "Why not?"

"Stanton is leaving the PD. It's not public yet but he just accepted a job in Tampa."

"Can't say that breaks my heart. But what's that got to do with you becoming the Ass Chief?"

"He told me he's decided to leave a big promotion like that to the next chief."

"What a dick. Didn't he promise you the job?"

"Guess I shoulda asked for it in writing, huh?" LeRoyer said, giving Byron a weak smile.

"Well, at least you'll be the acting until the city finds a replacement," Byron said hopefully.

LeRoyer shook his head. "Nope. He's making Danny Rumsfeld the acting."

"Captain Rumpswab?" Byron said with a grimace. "You're not serious."

"'Fraid so."

"Guess it's true what they say."

"What's that?"

"Nice guys *do* finish last."

"Yeah, I guess so. Think I should become more of a prick?"

"Couldn't hurt."

"Okay, then, try this." LeRoyer pointed at the door. "Get the fuck out of my office, Sergeant!"

Byron stood up. Grinning, he gave the lieutenant a mock salute. "Good to have you back, Marty."

BYRON LOOKED ACROSS the table at Diane. She was silently pushing a small pile of pad Thai noodles around on her plate, studying them but not eating.

"Penny for your thoughts," he said.

She looked up absently. "Sorry, just thinking."

"About?"

"Everything. How that crazy bitch used everybody around her. How she almost got away with it."

"But she didn't."

"Yeah. Thanks to you."

"Thanks to all of us," he said.

"Don't give me that shit, John. You know I'm right."

Byron shrugged.

"You fought the powers that be, again. Stood up to Stanton and LeRoyer."

"Ah, Marty's not such a bad guy. You just haven't known him long enough."

"Maybe, but I'm not sure I could have done that. Besides, you have a history with LeRoyer that I don't have."

"Give it time. He respects you."

The wine steward stopped beside their table. "More?" he said, gesturing with the open bottle of cab.

"Please," Diane said, holding up her glass. "Top it off."

She thanked the steward, who nodded politely then wandered off.

"Did you ever connect up with your niece?" Diane asked.

"Yeah, we talked on the phone."

"And?"

"And I'm taking her out to dinner next week. Kind of a late celebration."

Diane set the chopsticks on her plate and leaned back in her chair.

"John, I have something to tell you."

He wondered when she'd finally broach the topic of the sergeant's position again. It had been the elephant in the room for days.

"I'm all ears," he said.

She picked up her glass and gulped the red wine.

Byron knew she was stalling but he waited patiently.

She placed the glass back on the table then looked directly into his eyes. "I've made a decision about the promotion."

Acknowledgments

I RETIRED IN 2012, following nearly three decades in the field of law enforcement, to pursue my lifelong dream of becoming a writer, more specifically a novelist. I remain eternally grateful to a number of people instrumental in helping me to successfully make the transition from cop to published author, a list now long enough to fill the pages of another book, which I promise not to do. I must, however, give a well-deserved shout-out to a few special people: My agent, Paula Munier, and the good folks at Talcott Notch Literary for believing in me and my stories; my editor, Nick Amphlett, and everyone at HarperCollins/Witness Impulse; David and Teresa Cote for the introduction; Kate "Doc" Flora for your continued friendship, sage advice, and counsel; Gayle Lynds for everything; Chris "Anthony" Holm for your encouragement; Dick Cass and our friends at the Esposito; Brenda Buchanan, Paul Doiron, Al Lamanda, and all of my fellow bloggers at Maine Crime Writers; the former Level Best Books editorial team of Mark Ammons, Kat Fast, Barbara Ross, and Leslie Wheeler for giving me my first big break; Otto Penzler and Elizabeth George for giving me my second; and fellow retired cop and novelist Brian Thiem for drawing a clear *Red Line* for me to follow.

My newest proofreaders—although I suppose technically, if I'm to use the correct vernacular, you're now all beta-readers—Mike Flannery, Judith Green, David Arenstam, Nancy Tancredi, Peggy Greenwald, Jim Minott, and Shirley Wilson.

My fact-checkers, Marc Montminy, Kevin MacDonald, Andy Hutchings, Rob Nichols, and Mike Mercer. Any mistakes were mine.

My immediate family and friends, some of whom are beta-readers, for their invaluable encouragement, advice, and support along the way.

Special thanks to the DiMillo family and their staff for helping me to get the details right.

The multitude of men and women in the field of criminal justice, true professionals, I was fortunate to have served with, as well as those who continue to serve. These are their stories.

Lastly, and most importantly, my wife, Karen, for her love, inspiration, and infinite patience. Without her in my life, there would be no story.

About the Author

BRUCE ROBERT COFFIN retired from the Portland, Maine, police department in 2012, after more than twenty-seven years in law enforcement. As a detective sergeant, he supervised all homicide and violent crime investigations for Maine's largest city. Following the terrorist attacks of September 11, he spent four years with the FBI, earning the Director's Award (the highest honor a non-agent can receive) for his work in counterterrorism.

Bruce's short fiction has been featured in several anthologies, including *Best American Mystery Stories 2016*.

He lives and writes in Maine.

Discover great authors, exclusive offers, and more at hc.com.